THIS IS
HOW IT
ALWAYS
IS

By Laurie Frankel

This Is How It Always Is
Goodbye For Now
The Atlas Of Love

LAURIE FRANKEL

THIS IS
HOW IT
ALWAYS
IS

REVIEW

First published in the United States by Flatiron Books in 2017

First published in Great Britain in 2017
by HEADLINE REVIEW
An imprint of HEADLINE PUBLISHING GROUP

2

Cataloguing in Publication Data is available from the British Library

ISBN 978 1 4722 4158 0 (Hardback)
ISBN 978 1 4722 4159 7 (Trade Paperback)

The paper this book is printed on is certified against the
Forest Stewardship Council® Standards. McPherson's Printing Group
holds FSC® chain of custody certification SA-COC-005379. FSC®
promotes environmentally responsible, socially beneficial
and economically viable management of the world's forests

HEADLINE PUBLISHING GROUP
An Hachette UK Company
Carmelite House
50 Victoria Embankment
London EC4Y 0DZ

www.headline.co.uk
www.hachette.co.uk

For
D.R.M.H.M.F.
my someone

Do I contradict myself?
Very well then I contradict myself,
(I am large, I contain multitudes.)

Walt Whitman, 'Song of Myself'

PART
I

Once Upon a Time, Claude Was Born

B ut first, Roo was born. Roosevelt Walsh-Adams. They had decided to hyphenate because – and in spite – of all the usual reasons
but mostly so their firstborn could have his grandfather's name
without sounding too presidential, which seemed to his parents like a lot
of pressure for a six-pound, two-ounce, brand-new tiny human. First Roo
was born, all pink and sticky and loud and miraculous. Then Ben was
born. Then they debated and deliberated and decided just one more and
therefore got twins – Rigel and Orion – who were no doubt going to
voice hostility about their names when they became older than four, especially when Rigel found out he was named after the constellation's toe,
but who for the moment were too little and too loud to care. The leap
from two to four felt astronomical, so their parents had turned to the
heavens.

All of which was why, despite being a woman of considerable science,
a disciple of logic and reason, a person grounded firmly in the right
half of her right mind, and besides all that a doctor who knew better,
Rosie Walsh was spending the fifteen minutes immediately preceding
the kickoff of Claude dragging her bed from its spot on the wall into the
middle of the room so that it faced east-west rather than north-south.
The Talmud, her mother reported, was very clear that many sons were
born to a man whose bed was facing north, and though Rosie doubted it
sincerely, along with most of what the Talmud offered, she couldn't take
the chance. She'd also quietly served salmon to her husband for lunch
and, though of course they were adults, chocolate-chip cookies, German

folklore prescribing red meat and salty snacks for men in need of heirs and afternoon delight for those desirous of daughters. The same website also suggested putting a wooden spoon under the bed to conceive a girl, and she did, then felt like an idiot and threw it on the dresser then thought Penn would mock her – and rightly – if he saw it there so stashed it the only place close at hand: under the bed. Couldn't hurt.

The sources, dubious and dubiouser, also recommended missionary position, and she was happy to oblige. Missionary position was, as far as she could tell, like vanilla ice cream: purported to be boring and chosen only by passionless, unimaginative, exhausted people but really the best one. She liked to look at Penn's face so close that it split into pieces like a modernist painting. She liked the length of his front pressed against the length of hers. She felt that people who needed to do it upside down and backward from behind – or who added candied bacon or smoked sea salt or pieces of raw cookies to their ice cream – were probably compensating for a product that was inferior to begin with.

The dubious sources also recommended that the woman refrain from orgasm. But you could only take these things so far.

Once upon a time, Dr Rosalind Walsh and her husband had had sex that started spontaneously and uncontrollably, sex that demanded itself, sex they had for any number of reasons but also because they really had no choice. Now, with four sons and two jobs, the sex was better but less inevitable. More evitable? Preceded, in any case, by light planning and a conversation rather than the tearing off of clothing and slamming into walls. Rosie was working the night shift at the hospital that week. Penn worked from home. They ate lunch, and then he did some research for his book while she worked out, and then she got a spoon, pulled the bed into the center of the room, and took off all her clothes.

Penn sat on the edge of the bed, still wearing his reading glasses, still holding a highlighter in one hand and an article on World War II food shortages in the other. 'The last thing I want to do is dissuade you from what's about to go down.' He put away his article, took off his glasses and then his clothes, and climbed in next to her. 'But you realize this is how we got into this mess in the first place.'

'Trying for a girl?' It was true. A surely-this-time girl was how they'd talked themselves into more after Ben.

'Getting naked in the middle of the day,' said Penn.

'What mess?' She smiled.

'Have you seen the rec room this week?'

'I never go in the rec room.'

'Mess would be a generous term. Mess conveys the level of disaster but not the degree of danger. If the rec room were an airport, its security level would be red.'

'Always,' she said, kissing his mouth and then his neck and then his mouth some more.

'Always,' he agreed, from around her tongue.

A short time later, but not too short, Claude happened, in the way these things do, though none of the three of them knew it at the time. It always struck Rosie that it would be a useful human evolution if the female could feel the sperm enter the egg. That way she could stop drinking and eating sushi and the good kind of cheese a whole month or more before she generally actually got around to doing so. Such an important part of life, conception, and you missed it altogether. Also once upon a time, sex was followed by napping in a heap together, tangled legs still tingling, or by deep, meaningful philosophizing late into the night, or sometimes by more sex. Now Penn fetched back his food shortages article and gave himself seven minutes to read it nakedly against the headboard before going down to start dinner for thirty-five minutes before driving to preschool to fetch Rigel and Orion. Rosie got dressed and then ready for work and then went to the bus stop to meet Roo and Ben. All the while, Claude worked quietly at becoming, first arriving together and then, in the days and weeks and months to come, dividing and dividing and dividing.

What people always said to Rosie was, 'What are you, Catholic?' though without raising their voices at the end like you do when you're really asking a question. Or they said, pretending to be joking, 'You know there are ways to prevent this sort of thing.' Or they said, 'Better you than me,' which they needn't, since this was obviously true, or they said, 'Are they all yours?' They all were. A mom at a PTA meeting the year before had taken Rosie aside to advise her not to tack condoms to a bulletin board next to the bed, no matter how convenient a storage solution that seemed, a lesson she confessed, nodding at a first-grader in the corner licking paste off his fingers, she had learned the hard way. Making a family seemed just as intimate to Rosie as the usual kickoff to that

process and just as impolite to discuss – never mind openly judge – in polite conversation with acquaintances. But that's what happened to her,
usually several times a week. And that's what was happening at the bus
stop while she waited for Roo and Ben and one half of almost-Claude
raced frantically for the other half.

'I don't know how you do it.' Heather. Her neighbor. This was another thing people always said, criticism disguised as compliment.

Rosie laughed. Fake laughed. 'Well. You know.'

'No, I mean seriously.' But she did not mean seriously. 'I mean, I
guess Penn doesn't have a job. But you do.'

'Penn works from home,' Rosie said. Again. This was not their first
time through this particular conversation. They had it every time the
bus was late. Which was every time it snowed. Which was every day
some months. She thought Madison Wisconsin's Public Schools should
specially train their bus drivers for snowy conditions – was this not just
common sense? – but apparently she was all alone with this idea. Now it
was September and hot and smelled like a late-afternoon thunderstorm,
so who knew why the bus was late.

'I mean, I know he works.' Heather started almost every sentence
with 'I mean', which Rosie felt was implied. 'But it's not a job.'

'Writing's a job.' Penn's work in progress – he called it DN for Damn
Novel – was not yet feeding them, but he wrote diligently, every day. 'It's
just not a nine-to-five sort of job.'

'Does that really count?'

'My job isn't nine to five.' She looked at her watch. In fact, she had to
be at the hospital in just more than an hour. Night shifts were brutal but
easier to schedule around. Sometimes, it was just less painful to forgo
sleep than to try to find child care for all the early dismissals and vaca-
tions and holidays and staff developments and parent-teacher conference
days. It was also true that nights in the ER were often more peaceful
than nights at home with her family. Sometimes they even involved less
blood.

'Yeah, but I mean, you're a doctor,' Heather was saying.

'So?'

'So doctor's a real job.'

'So is writer.'

'I don't know how you do it,' Heather said again, shaking her head.
And then added, giggling, 'Or why.'

In fact, how was an easier question than why. How was the same answer as it is for all impossible things you do anyway. One day at a time. One foot in front of the other. All for one and one for all. Anyway, some cliché with the word 'one' in it, ironic since it had been so long since she was just a one. She herded the boys – some of the boys – toward the car. If she was going to have to have this conversation with Heather at the bus stop every day, she might just start picking the kids up from school. Driving to and from the bus stop seemed absurd to her. Wasn't the point of the bus to bring kids from their home to the school? She loved their sprawling old farmhouse, their fifteen acres of rangy, overgrown land, going ceaselessly to seed. There was a barn that was only the memory of a barn, a stream that was mysterious and wet enough to be fun, but not deep or fast enough to worry about. The house was designed for a family of farmers, a family with lots of children who rose before dawn to help milk cows or slop livestock or whatever it was farm children did. Rosie and Penn had nothing to milk nor any animals beyond the puppy (Jupiter, a present for the twins' fourth birthday), but they did, more frequently than not, have children up before dawn. Those children needed lots of bedrooms, and the farmhouse had plenty, plus a perfect nursery off the master which smelled perpetually of talcum powder and was painted yellow, just in case the baby was a girl one of these days. The floors were not even. The walls were not soundproof. The water took a long time to be hot. But Rosie loved the rough-and-tumbleness of the house, which matched the rough-and-tumbleness of her family. Among other things, when the molding got nicked – and it did – no one cared. Some days though, plain old suburbia and a cul-de-sac at the top of which a bus stopped seemed easier. Some days, she just didn't have the energy. This day she felt tired. She didn't know why. But she needed to shake it off anyway. Her workday had not yet begun.

At home, she proceeded with the business of one foot, one day, one for all. Penn kissed the boys hello, kissed her goodbye, went off to fetch Rigel and Orion. She took over dinner prep – sautéing the vegetables Penn had chopped, seasoning the rice Penn had boiled, grilling the shrimp Penn had marinated. (She did not yet know that the racing-together Claude halves precluded any chance that avoiding red meat would beget a girl.) While the beans simmered, she emptied lunch boxes, checked folders, sorted forms. While the sauce reduced, she finished washing dishes from the night before. While she dried them, she interrupted the roller-skating contest Roo and Ben were holding in the living room three times. (It wasn't that she finally succeeded in getting them to stop. It was that she finally succeeded in not caring anymore.)

Then Roo set the table. Then Ben poured water into water glasses. Then Penn, Rigel, and Orion came back in, all three of them wet and emotional, Penn from the traffic, which he reported was a mess because of the thunderstorm, Rigel and Orion from something having to do with a sand table that Rosie couldn't make out but made sympathetic noises toward anyway. If traffic was bad, she needed to leave early for work. If she needed to leave early for work, she needed to leave now. Penn pulled the shrimp from the grill and the rice from the pot, threw both in with the vegetables in the wok, combined sauce and beans, and dumped some of all of the above into a giant to-go container, added a spoon, and shoved it into Rosie's hands as she checked to see how many of the many things she absolutely must not forget had actually made it into her bag. Some. She gave quick kisses all around and headed for the car. If traffic was as bad as Penn said, she'd be able to eat dinner on the way to the hospital.

That was how. One day at a time. One foot in front of the other. All for one. It wasn't so much that she and Penn had set out to practice Zen marriage equality and perfect-balance parenting. It was just that there was way more to do than two could manage, but by their both filling every spare moment, some of what needed to got done.

One good turn deserves another. Two heads are better than one.

Why was a harder question. Rosie thought about it all the way to the hospital, not that day, but 257 days later on the one when Claude was born. Labor had begun in earnest during dinner, though she'd known it was coming all morning and afternoon. Her feet itched peculiarly just before contractions started. She knew that sensation from long experience and had figured the baby would come the next day or even the one after that, so even though the contractions came closer and harder, she made dinner. But between passing the salad around and actually finishing the pasta, contractions had gone from every seven minutes to every three. Penn said, 'So, how about dessert?' Rosie said, 'Instead, maybe the hospital.'

How they were going to get home was an open question, but for the moment, they all still fit in one car. Rosie installed herself in the front seat, calmly but with no little effort. Penn grabbed the bags. They weren't for Rosie, who needed so little. She had never been the type to prepare a soundtrack or a collage or a special pillow for the delivery room, but by now she realized that even the handful of things she'd brought the first few times were unnecessary. No, the bags were for her mother. They contained provisions to spend hours and perhaps days on end in a waiting room with four small, giddy boys – books, trains, LEGOs, glue sticks, juice boxes, granola bars, stuffies, blankies, and particular pillows. Rosie did not need a special pillow for the hospital. This was the difference between her and her sons.

One boy's trash is another boy's treasure. Back to square one.

All the way to the hospital while the kids sang *Peter Pan* in their car seats and boosters – their babysitter was starring in her high school musical – and Penn squeezed her hand and pretended, unsuccessfully, to be nonchalant by obeying all posted speed limits, and she resisted the temptation to tell him to hurry the hell up, Rosie was thinking one word over and over: *Poppy*. If the baby was a girl – and surely, *surely* it had to be: she had eaten fish and cookies; she had had sex in the afternoon facing east; she had done the thing with the spoon, and besides, it was her turn – she would name her Poppy.

They had had the name picked out from the first pregnancy. Rosie had had it for even longer, since one dark day sitting on her little sister's hospital bed while their parents were in the cafeteria taking a break. Rosie was braiding Poppy's wig hair and Poppy was braiding Poppy's doll's hair when she said, out of nowhere, 'I'll never have a little girl whose hair I get to braid.' Her voice was raspy. Rosie knew now it was from the chemotherapy, but at the time it seemed like something inside her little sister was fighting to get out – and winning – a goblin or a witch or a demon, something that was already breaking through in snatches here and there: a croaking voice, red rolling eyes, bruises that raised slowly then seemed to spread and multiply as if peeling back from a sea of purple skin roiling just beneath her ever more delicate surface. Rather than being frightened, Rosie found this idea comforting. She welcomed the demon on its way out of her sister because it was becoming increasingly clear that Poppy could not survive this terrible, unspeakable, unthinkable disease, but maybe the demon could. Demon Poppy seemed much stronger. Demon Poppy had more fight in her.

'Will you take care of Clover for me?' Poppy croaked. Like all the children in the Walsh home, Poppy's doll was named for a flower.

Rosie nodded. It was all she could manage. But then Poppy's regular voice came back: 'Where should we go on vacation?'

'When?'

'When I get out of here.'

'I dunno.' The only place they'd ever been on vacation so far was their grandparents' house, which smelled like basement. 'Where do you want to go?'

'Siam,' Poppy said immediately.

'Siam?'

'Like *The King and I.*' The hospital had a poorly stocked video library of which that was the highlight. And Poppy had a lot of lying-around time.

'We'll go everywhere,' Rosie promised. 'As soon as you're out. Well, we probably have to wait four years till I get my license. Is Siam in driving distance?'

'I dunno. Probably.' Poppy smiled happily. 'You're such a good hair braider.' It was the best thing about cancer it turned out. Poppy's wig hair was much longer and less tangled than her real hair. 'Your daughter's going to be so lucky.'

At that very moment, Rosalind Walsh, aged twelve, decided two things: her daughter would have long hair, like really long, like long enough to sit on, and she would name her Poppy. Eventually, Rosie discovered Siam was now called Thailand, but it was several lifetimes later before she got there, and then it was not for vacation. This was the last time she was ever alone with her sister.

All the way to the hospital, while Penn murmured, 'Breathe, breathe,' and Roo sang about how he just had to crow and Ben and Rigel and Orion cawed back at the tops of their little boy voices, Rosie whispered, 'Poppy. Poppy. Poppy. Poppy.'

Twenty minutes after they pulled up at the front door, the baby was ready.

'Push,' said the doctor.

'Breathe,' said Penn.

'Poppy,' said Rosie. 'Poppy. Poppy. Poppy.'

Was that why? Was she just trying endlessly to make a daughter to fulfill an ancient dream of her sister's, a ten-year-old's dream at that? Did she believe this daughter would grow up and be, at ten, the little girl she'd lost, Poppy herself, picking up where Poppy had left off, fulfilling all the promise of that stymied, hacked-off, stubbed-out little life? As long as she kept her womb full, might Poppy, some version of Poppy – some waiting, watchful, wandering Poppy demon – gather up all her errant atoms and come home again? Was it creepy to imagine your dead sister taking up residence in your uterus? Wasn't it purported to be a sign of insanity to do the same thing over and over expecting different results?

One card short of a deck. One waffle short of a stack. One horse short of a . . . group of horses.

Or was it some long-bred, deep-sown conviction that the more children the better because you never knew when you might lose one? They had all been so broken when Poppy died, Rosie and her mom and dad. One was not enough. One was always out of balance. It was no longer two against two. There was no longer anyone to play with, to run to, to spare. Her mother, she knew, saw double, saw Poppy always at the edges, in Rosie's shadow, at Rosie's side during school plays and dances and graduation ceremonies, Poppy just behind Rosie and Penn at the wedding, Poppy panting quietly at Rosie's side while her babies were all being born. Even when Rosie's father left the world just before Roo came into it, her mother saw Poppy's ghostly outline alongside Rosie's swollen belly at graveside, quietly weeping for all that was lost, and it wasn't just their father. At least then, it was one against one again. Balance restored.

One is the loneliest number. Never put all your eggs in one basket.

So maybe that was why. Or maybe Rosie and Penn just liked babies, their promise and chaos and mess, the way babies all started the same and almost instantly became entirely different. Rosie loved the high-pitched pandemonium of her big, sprawling family, muddled love filling up their farmhouse-clubhouse, a cacophony only she could make out, a whirling storm with her and Penn, grinning together, spinning together, at the center.

'Push,' said the doctor.

'Breathe,' said Penn.

'Poppy,' said Rosie.

And then, soon, 'It's a boy! A healthy, beautiful, perfect, impatient baby boy,' the doctor said. 'Fast little guy. Good thing you didn't hit traffic.'

One fell swoop, Rosie thought. Once upon a time.

Takes one to know one. A baby brother. At least the boys would know what to do.

One Date

Penn was an only child. On their first date when Rosie said, 'So, do you have brothers or sisters?' and Penn said, 'Nope. Only child,' Rosie had replied, 'Oh, I'm so sorry,' as if he'd said he had only three months to live or had been raised above an artisan deli by vegans.

'Oh, thanks. It's okay,' he'd said, and realized only a few beats later that that response was entirely wrong. He was having trouble concentrating. He was having trouble doing anything because blood was coursing through him twice as fast and hard as usual owing to the fact that he could not slow his heart, which had been in a state since several hours before he'd driven over to pick her up. Before he'd done so, he couldn't imagine why. Rosie was a friend of a friend of a friend, an arrangement someone he'd not even known had hit upon at a party one night, drunk and silly. He was in grad school at the time, getting an MFA and waking each morning to wonder why he was getting an MFA. A woman from his medieval lit class (what this class had to do with writing a novel he could not even begin to guess) had dragged before him a woman he did not recognize, who had looked him over appraisingly for a bit before finally asking, 'So. Want to date a doctor?'

'I'm sorry?'

'I know a single doctor who's into poets.'

'I'm not a poet.'

'You know what I mean.'

'I don't.'

'She's real cute. I think you might really hit it off.'

'You don't know my name.'

'She's not into names.'

'That wasn't my point.'

'Still.'

How could he argue with that logic? Still. There was nothing to say in response to still. He shrugged. He had a policy at the time never to say no to new and potentially peculiar experiences in case he needed things to write about later. Dating a doctor who liked poets because someone he'd never met before thought they'd hit it off seemed like it fell into this category.

And that's all it was. Writing fodder. Writing fodder and a change of pace and a new life philosophy that was not to say no. He wasn't dreading it, but he wasn't looking forward to it either. He felt entirely neutral toward the date, like a quick trip to the grocery store for milk. But then, about an hour before he was going to take a shower and get dressed, sitting in his studio apartment on his sofa reading Dante's *Inferno,* his heart started racing. He felt his cheeks flush, and he felt his lips go dry and his palms go wet, and he felt this absurd need to try on a few shirts to see which one looked best, and he felt, all of a sudden, nervous, and for the life of him, he could not imagine why. He thought it might be the flu. He actually thought about calling her to cancel in case he was contagious, but the woman worked at a hospital so probably had a germ-avoidance strategy of some sort.

He pulled up in front of her apartment and sat in his car trying to slow his breathing, waiting for his knees to stop shaking, but when it became clear that wasn't going to happen, he gave up and rang her bell. When she opened the door and he saw her, Penn said, 'Oh.'

It wasn't that Rosie was so beautiful, though she was, that is, he thought she was, that is, he felt she was. He had to rely on this vague sense of what she looked like because he couldn't see her. It was as if she were back-lit, bright sun behind her preventing his eyes from adjusting so he could see her properly. Or it was as if he were fainting, the black bits at the sides folding his vision into smaller and smaller origami boxes. But it was none of those things. It was like when your car spins out on an icy road, and your senses turn up so high that time seems to slow because you notice every-thing, and you just sit in your spinning car waiting, waiting, to see if you're going to die. He couldn't look at her because every sense and every fraction of a moment and every atom of his body was being in love with her. It was weird.

Penn was getting an MFA, yes, but he was a fiction writer, not a poet, and he did not believe in love at first sight. He had also congratulated himself in the past for loving women for their minds and not their bodies. This woman had not yet spoken a word to him (though he assumed since she was a doctor that she was probably pretty smart), and he couldn't get himself to concentrate on what she looked like, but he seemed to love her anyway. She was wearing – already – a hat, a scarf, and a four-inch-thick down parka that came all the way down to her boots. There was no way to fall in love with a woman just for her body in Wisconsin in January. He reminded himself though, still standing dumb in her doorway, that it wasn't love at first sight. It seemed to have happened quite a bit before that. He seemed to have fallen in love about an hour and a half earlier on his sofa in the middle of 'Canto V' before ever laying eyes on Rosie. How his body had known this, foreknown this, he never did figure out, but it was right – it was quite right – and very quickly, he stopped caring.

So at the restaurant, he was a little off his game. For one, he was distracted. For another, he knew. He had already decided. He was in – they could dispense with the small talk. So when Rosie, glowing, luminous, unpeeled from all her layers, lovely underneath, smiling shyly at him Rosie, said she was sorry he was an only child, that's what he said first: it's okay. Then a few seconds later, when his brain caught up, he added, 'Wait. No. What? Why are you sorry I'm an only child?'

She blushed. He would have too, but his blood flow must already have been at capacity. 'Sorry,' she said. 'I always think . . . My sister, um . . . Weren't you lonely?'

'Not really.'

'Because you were really close with your parents?'

'Not really that either.'

'Because you're a writer? You like to be alone in the dark brooding by yourself deeply?'

'No!' He laughed. 'Well, maybe. I don't know. I don't think I was brooding alone in the dark. But I don't think I was lonely either. How about you? I take it you had brothers and sisters?'

Rosie's glow clouded over, and Penn was immediately sorry all the way down to his toes. 'I had one sister. She died when I was twelve and she was ten.'

'Oh Rosie, *I'm* sorry.' Penn knew he'd said the right thing that time.

She nodded at her roll. 'Cancer. It sucks.'

He tried to think what to add, came up with nothing, reached for her hand instead. She grasped him like someone falling off something high. He gasped at the sudden sharp pain of it, but when she tried to ease off, embarrassed, he squeezed back harder. 'What was her name?' he asked gently.

'Poppy.' Then she laughed, a little bit embarrassed. 'Rosie. Poppy. Get it? My parents were into gardening. She's lucky they didn't name her Gladiola. Gladiola was totally on the table.'

'Is that why you think only-childhood is so sad?' He was glad to see her laughing again, but no one he'd ever met had treated the fact that he lacked siblings as a tragedy. 'Because it was for you?'

'I guess.' She shrugged. 'Maybe that's why I like you already. We're both only children.'

He tried to stay with her, but all he heard was she liked him already.

Later, much later, she said the same, that it was love *pre* first sight, that she'd walked around that whole morning and afternoon somehow knowing that this would be the last first date of her life. Whereas this had made him nervous as hell, it had made her calm. Whereas he'd felt impatient with the small talk, she knew they had all the time in the world. To the extent that time was guaranteed in the world. Which it was not.

Later, less later, Penn lay in his own bed, grinning at the ceiling in the dark. He tried to stop himself, he did, and he made fun of himself for doing it, but he couldn't help it. He could not keep down, keep away, keep at bay what felt like a tiny seed of secret, certain knowledge, stable as a noble gas, glowing as gold: Poppy. My daughter will be named Poppy. Not a decision. A realization. Something that had long been true – since Rosie was twelve, half his lifetime ago – except he hadn't known it yet.

Residency

Penn could never remember the name of the friend of the friend who knew a doctor who was interested in dating a poet. Maybe he never knew it. He could never remember the friend either, though he clearly owed her. Rosie was only just barely a doctor, as it turned out. She was in year one of an emergency medicine residency. She did not have the time to have a boyfriend. She did not have the brain space to have a boyfriend. Penn had not been aware that having a boyfriend took up brain space, but he could see how there were a great many facts, terms, drugs, treatments, protocols, and patient scenarios to memorize, none of them remotely familiar, all of them life-and-death important, and it was clear that this would be stressful.

'Then why did you want to date a poet?' he asked her when she explained that it wasn't personal, she just didn't have time for any boyfriend. If she were going to have a boyfriend, it would be him. But she wasn't.

'I didn't say I wanted to date a poet. I said one *should* date a poet. A theoretical one. A theoretical poet. Everyone in my program is hooking up with everyone else in my program, and then you're dating some over-caffeinated, overextended, exhausted egomaniac who finally gets a day off and uses it to study. My point was date someone who sleeps instead, someone who thinks slowly and deeply and talks in words that don't need to be memorized from flash cards. A poet. But I didn't mean it. I don't have the energy or the time. That's why residents are always sleeping with each other. They're the only ones who fit into each other's schedules.'

'Then why did you say yes?' Penn asked.

'You sounded nice when you called.' Rosie shrugged. 'And I was bored of doing patient charts.'

Penn was going to be irritated by this except that he recalled he only went out with her for writing material. Besides, this meant she was going to need wooing after all. He was delighted. Penn was a student of narrative and knew that lovers should be wooed, relationships fought for, that anything too easily won was soon lost or else not worth winning. He suspected she was worth winning. He was up for the challenge. It would – he'd been right all along – make for good writing fodder. She may have been studying the human heart. But so was he.

It seemed like getting a degree in creative writing would mostly involve writing, but it didn't. It mostly involved reading and not reading what he wanted to read and not reading what he wanted to write. It was mostly literary theory – incomprehensible, jargon-filled, irrelevant to his own projects. It wasn't as hard as chemistry and anatomy and human physiology, but it was a bigger waste of time. And it took a lot of it. Fortunately, it could be done anywhere. Where Penn did his was in Rosie's ER waiting room.

The summer after his sophomore year of high school, when everyone else he knew had a summer job or an internship or was attending some kind of enrichment program disguised as camp, Penn had gotten up every morning to take the commuter train out to Newark International Airport. This was back in the days when anyone could go through the metal detectors and hang out at the gates, and you didn't need a boarding pass, and the fact that you were there every day by yourself with no luggage and no ticket and no intention of going anywhere, dressed in a black hoodie and scribbling ceaselessly in a notebook, bothered no one. He'd pick a departure gate and sit watching and listening for a while and make up stories about the passengers, the businessmen with their briefcases and paunches and nose bridges that needed constant squeezing, the old people with their hideous shoes and piles of presents, and especially the people traveling alone, always, in his stories, headed off to some kind of illicit, romantic rendezvous. When he got tired of departures, he'd head off to baggage claim and watch tearful reunions, the hugging that looked like people trying to stuff themselves inside each other. Or he sat on a bench just inside the front doors and watched the other kind of crying, the departures and letting-gos, the loved ones torn from each other only to find themselves sniffling in a long line to get their boarding passes, check their bags. The transition seemed profound to fifteen-year-old Penn, that someone could be weeping in her boyfriend's arms one moment, desperate to squeeze out every last second with him, and the next could be waiting on line, impatiently checking her watch, and shifting from foot to foot, scowling at the elderly couple at the front who were holding up everyone else.

Studies in Airports was Penn's first manuscript. He'd taken the stories to the copy place on a disk and had them printed then bound with a black, plastic spiral, but his guidance counselor refused to consider hanging around an airport making stuff up a real internship anyway. Still, he'd learned a lot more than he did proofing ad copy for the *Rockaway Gazette,* which is what he'd done the following summer. And he'd gotten a lot more writing done.

So reading and writing in Rosie's hospital waiting room was something he was long practiced for: lots of crying people, lots of pathos, the heights of tragedy, the heights of relief, which looked a lot like the heights of tragedy, and lots of that odd paradox he'd observed at Newark International that lay at the heart of waiting – that even when what people were waiting for was the worst news of their life or the best, even when the waiting was heavy with implication and consequence, waiting people still transformed into cranky toddlers, impatient and frowning and red-faced infuriated with vending machines that dispensed the wrong thing, and kids who did not use their inside voice. You'd think people in a hospital waiting room would be kindred spirits, compatriots, like soldiers who'd served together, fellow citizens of a hollowed, harrowed world, but no, mostly they avoided one another's eyes and heaved great passive-aggressive sighs in one another's direction whenever someone had the audacity to get attention from the nurses first.

Penn wooed and studied, watched and listened and made notes for stories. He read. He wrote. Rosie would emerge every few hours, sometimes blood-spattered, sometimes vomit-splashed, always frazzled, always exhausted and red-eyed. Always rosy. And always glad to see him in spite of her protestations. And these were many: Aren't you uncomfortable out here? The chairs are gross, and the food is awful. Do you know how many germs are in hospital waiting rooms? Do you know how weird a place this is to read literary theory? Didn't I tell you I don't have time for a boyfriend? Wouldn't you like to go home and get some sleep? One of us should. Wouldn't your living room be preferable? The risk there is so low of someone coming in with a gunshot wound.

At first Penn wouldn't write about the sick kids and their sick parents, the kids struck with cancers and heart diseases and accidents and violence in their homes, the parents struck with sick kids. Sick kids defied all narrative theory he'd ever known. There was nothing redemptive about a dying child. There was nothing that could be learned from a kid coming in shot or beaten that made it worth a kid getting shot or beaten. This had always pissed him off about *Romeo and Juliet,* its ending platitude that at least the feud was laid to rest and the fighting families had come together as if this somehow made it worth losing their teenagers. As if Romeo and Juliet would have been willing to die just so their parents would get along.

When Rosie came out just after two one morning and collapsed into the seat next to him, too exhausted to feel surprised, never mind grateful, to find him still there, Penn took her hand gently. 'Romeo and Juliet didn't give a crap whether their parents got along.'

'Sure.' Eyes closed. Probably not even listening.

'In fact, Romeo and Juliet thought it was kind of sexy that their parents hated each other.'

'Who wouldn't?'

'They weren't willing to die to put an end to the feud. They were willing to do anything to live. Juliet died so they could live. Romeo killed so they could live.'

Rosie nodded. 'What's your point?'

'There's nothing good that can come out of a child being sick.'

'No.'

'There's nothing that makes that fair or worth it.'

'No, there isn't.'

'It's narratively insupportable,' Penn explained.

'It's weird how little narrative theory there is in hospitals,' said Rosie. 'Yours might be all there is.'

'Then it's a good thing I'm here,' said Penn.

The waiting room stories weren't the ones that stuck though. Some nights later, Rosie arrived for her shift to find Penn already installed in the waiting room. He was typing furiously on his laptop and didn't even look up as she scooted through on her way to rounds.

'Figured out a new narrative theory?' she asked on her way past.

'New genre.' He barely looked up. 'Fairy tales.'

'Sure,' said Rosie. 'Because nothing bad ever happens to kids in fairy tales.'

Her shift was twenty-eight hours. Penn sat and wrote for every one of them. They took a coffee and breakfast break together toward dawn. Penn tried every flavor of corn chip in the vending machine. When she emerged the following night, changed back into street clothes but with something alarmingly viscous tacking her bangs, Penn had closed the laptop and was writing marginalia about the progress being made in *Pilgrim's Progress*.

'Come on,' said Rosie.

Penn looked up, a little bleary-eyed himself. He might have been napping between words.

'Where?'

'Dinner,' said Rosie. 'Then bed.'

He was awake.

They went to the Eggs 'n' Dregs Diner, despite its coffee being about as good as advertised, because they served the best late-night waffles in town. Rosie talked about her patients. She talked about her program, her fellow residents, the attendings, the nurses. She talked about the difference between medical school and medical practice, between what she'd thought being a doctor would be like and what it in fact was, between anatomy textbooks and actual anatomy.

'What did you do?' she asked.

'Same.' Penn tried to say as little as possible. He liked to hear her talk. And he was too tired to make conversation.

'Same?' Rosie tried to say as much as she could. It kept her from falling asleep at the table. 'It's true you've spent a lot of time at the hospital lately, but I'm not sure that qualifies you to treat patients.'

'Not treating patients. Thinking about the difference between school and practice, books and life. What you think things are going to be like and how they actually are.'

'Is everything in your life a metaphor?'

'As many things as possible,' Penn admitted. 'So what now?'

'Bed.'

It was important to keep his face exactly neutral. He froze his eyes and eyebrows and lips and mouth and cheeks. He tried hard to go into a coma.

'Don't look so excited,' she said. 'I'm too tired to do anything but sleep. So are you.'

'What makes you say that?'

'You've been awake for thirty-seven hours. Your eyes are glassy and bloodshot. You're losing brain tissue as we speak. I know the signs. I'm a doctor.'

'Barely.'

'You took a nap while they made your eggs. That's the first sign of exhaustion. They covered that our first year of med school.'

'I can rally,' said Penn. 'I can get a second wind.'

'You need to sleep,' Rosie insisted. 'First we sleep. Then we'll see.'

Penn thought 'we'll see' sounded like a good start. He agreed to these terms. He couldn't remember another time when his first foray into the bed of a woman he was wooing was for sleep, but he was willing to give it a shot. Her sheets had pictures of basset hounds and that softness you get not from thread count but from washing again and again and again. They were well-loved sheets. Among those basset hounds, just as his eyes were closing, she said, 'Tell me your story.'

'What story?'

'The waiting room story.'

'You just lived that one.'

'I wasn't waiting,' she said. 'I was on the other side.'

He couldn't keep his eyes open, but he didn't think he'd need to. 'How about a bedtime story?'

'A bedtime story would be perfect,' she said.

'Once upon a time . . .'

'Not a very original opening.'

'There was a prince.'

'Aren't you supposed to start with a princess?'

'Named Grumwald.'

'Grumwald?'

'Who lived in a far-off land where being a prince was, well, just not that fulfilling. Or impressive. He hadn't been elected to it. He hadn't earned it with good deeds or quick thinking, clever problem solving or hard labor. He was the prince for the same reason princes are always princes. Because their fathers are kings and their mothers are queens. And yes, he had his own wing in a castle with that funny roofline that looks like bad teeth.'

'Crenelated.'

'And yes, he had robes and crowns and those sticks with balls on the end.'

'Scepters. God, Penn, I thought you were a word guy.'

'I'm tired.'

'What are those things even for anyway?'

'That was Grumwald's question too. What was the point of any of it? It's true there was an actual suit of armor in the hall right outside his bedroom. But otherwise, he was a fairly ordinary guy. He cleaned his own bathroom. He saw no use for sticks with balls on the end. The crown gave him a headache.'

'Cranial neuralgia due to continuous stimulation of cutaneous nerves.'

'And it seemed that his friends, with their ordinary lives, who had summer jobs, whose rooflines were flat or at least roof-shaped, were a lot happier than he was.'

'How did he meet these friends with ordinary lives and roofs?'

'High school,' said Penn.

'He went to public school?'

'His parents –'

'The king and queen.'

'– were progressives who believed neither money nor class nor royal status meant that one child deserved a good education while another child did not. They realized the world would be a better place if all children had knowledge, intelligence, problem-solving and critical-thinking skills, and a fair shot at a good career which supported them financially as well as spiritually.'

'Enlightened.'

'Yes. But hard for Grumwald, who had no career to prepare for, who would not be going off to college, who thought it unlikely his parents, no matter how liberal, were going to be wild about his dating a peasant, no matter how impressive her bootstraps. He was allowed to play sports but couldn't because no one would throw a pitch inside to the prince or try to sack him or block his shots. The school dances that so thrilled his friends with their opportunities for fancy dress and limousines and expensive meals were just an ordinary Tuesday night for poor Grum. He skipped graduation altogether because he couldn't stomach one more moment of pomp and circumstance in a life made up of little but. His world, though beautiful, shrouded in layers of purple mist, warmed by a sun that seemed to shine just for him, smelling of forest and the promise of adventure and the possibility of magic, proved, however, very small indeed. Education served only to show him what was out there, not to offer it as an actual possibility.'

'But the birds were his friends?' Rosie asked hopefully, sleepily. 'He had long, deep, middle-of-the-night chats with the mice who were his bosom companions?'

'This is a fairy tale, Rosie. A real one, not a Disney one. The mice can't talk. The birds seemed to mock him by being so much more free than he was. He had friends from school, sure – he was SGA president, of course, and met a lot of kids that way. Plus Mathletes – but no one who really understood him. Until he looked in the suit of armor.'

'What suit of armor?'

'The one in the hall outside his room.'

'Did you tell me about that before?'

'I did. Pay attention.'

'I was paying attention. I was falling asleep because you said it was a bedtime story. If I'd known it was a fairy tale with hidden information, I'd have tried harder to keep my eyes open.'

'It wasn't hidden information. I told you: roofline like teeth, sticks with balls on the end, suit of armor in the hall, cleans his own bathroom. The whole story's right there. That's all you need to know.'

'What was in the suit of armor?' She had her hands pressed together underneath her cheek like a little girl going to sleep on a greeting card, smiling at him sleepily and trying, failing, to keep her eyes open.

Penn reached out and smoothed her hair, her forehead. 'I'll tell you the rest of the story in the morning.'

'Is this just a ploy to keep me here?'

'You live here.'

'Like Scheherazade?'

'Scheherazade lives here?'

'Don't forget where you are in the story,' Rosie said just as she was falling finally asleep. 'When we wake up, I want to pick up right where we left off.'

When they woke up, however, they picked up somewhere else.

'Last we discussed the matter,' Penn reminded her helpfully, 'you said "we'll see".'

'Well, let's see then,' she said.

It was one of the enduring ironies of their relationship how well the residency schedule worked for Penn. Even once she was wooed, Penn remained camped out in the waiting room, reading, writing, telling her stories in installments during her breaks between patients. He was happy to sleep when she did and to stay up when she had to. She'd have traded anything toward the ends of those thirty-hour shifts – her place in the program, her career prospects, her eyeballs, say, and even Penn – for eight hours of sleep, and she knew in her heart that had their roles been reversed, she'd have been comfortably in her bed at home while he worked inhumane stretches of days and nights and days on end.

It was good preparation for parenting, though of course that didn't occur to her until years later. At some point midway through Roo's sleepless, staccato first month, she thought what an effective screening process a waiting-room residency had been. Here was a husband she knew would get up every two hours with the baby through the dark middles of the nights. Here was a partner who would wake for predawn breakfast with the first and second children, never mind having been up with the third and fourth well past midnight the night before. It wasn't why she chose him. But it wasn't a terrible reason either.

Now, all these years later, she found herself in the hospital's wee hours all alone with no one to tell her stories. It had been years since her residency – the hideous carpet and uncomfortable furniture had turned over and turned over again since then – but she still emerged from the swinging doors into the waiting area expecting for a beat to see Penn's face. It was one of the strange things about having stayed where she'd trained. The folks who had been there for decades still thought of her as a resident no matter her title or accomplishments. What was the same always outweighed what rotated and rostered and changed. And Penn's absence from a chair in the corner of the waiting room, never mind his sheer presence in her home, her family, her bed, her life, never failed to stop her for a moment.

Staying had been another thing she was wooed to do. An Arizona girl, she was not remotely prepared for Wisconsin in February. Her car freezing during her second semester had seemed a clear sign that as a human she should probably have stayed inside. She nearly failed endocrinology because she missed so many lectures, not because she wanted to cut class per se but because she could not bring herself to go out of doors. She was a visual learner who closed her eyes in order to picture nerve charts and skeletal layouts and muscle patterns. One morning, on her way from the parking lot to an exam, she kept her eyes closed too long and they froze shut. She vowed to get out of Wisconsin the moment she graduated.

But the program was too good. Her teachers wanting her to stay, wanting to work *with* her, had been too flattering to say no to. And Penn liked the waiting room. She'd been wooed to stay so she stayed. Just for a fellowship year, she told herself. Just a small stint as an attending. After that, she'd be unwooable. After that, she'd have to go elsewhere anyway for breadth of experience, a different part of the world where she'd develop expertise in more than frostbite and lost toes and idiots frozen to their fishing poles.

But Roo followed by Ben followed by Rigel and Orion had put a stop to that plan too, children being the enemies of plans and also the enemies of anything new besides themselves. UW knew her work ethic and track record, never mind her taking yet another maternity leave, never mind the final months when she couldn't even fit bedside, or the months before that when she couldn't lift patients or much of anything else, never mind the mornings she was too nauseated to work and the nights she called in sick because the only place more germ laden than a hospital is an elementary school. She was worth it. But no one outside UW Hospital knew it. And so she stayed.

And she was worth it. On the night that Claude became, she caught a pulmonary embolism masquerading as a sore back, a teenage pregnancy – or, if you prefer, severe denial and extreme delusion – masquerading as irritable bowel syndrome, a stroke masquerading as 'probably nothing but my tongue feels kind of weird,' and a first-year resident masquerading as a knowledgeable surgical consult. This was another thing parenting boys had prepared her for: ferreting out. She also, that night, waited with a little girl who'd fallen down the stairs at a sleepover party. Her leg hurt and her arm hurt, but that wasn't, Rosie knew, why she was crying. She was crying because she was alone and scared. Her parents had taken the opportunity to go away for a night, so they were a couple hours getting back, and the party hosts who brought her in had a house full of six-year-old girls they needed to return to. Crying little girls, even ones who were going to be fine and whose parents were on their way, broke Rosie in a way none of her other cases did. The terminal ones, the ones in pain she could not control, the ones she could do nothing for, the ones she had to let go, none of these felled her quite the way the little girls did. So when an hour after she'd called Transport, no one from Transport had come, she took the girl to X-ray herself. The tech let her stay with the patient so the child had a hand to hold, and though the wrist was just sprained, the tibia had a greenstick fracture. Once Rosie knew that, she knew what else to do for the girl, and she gave her pain meds and three oatmeal cookies and made her laugh. Those were the people Rosie was the night of Claude's becoming: mom, wife, emergency-room doctor, mystery ferreter. But also little-girl comforter. And also X-ray tech.

She knew that wasn't why. But she always wondered anyway if that was why.

Bedtime Story

That night that Claude became, while he and Rosie were being X-rayed, Penn was home putting children to bed. Bedtime was a study in chaos theory. Roo liked to soak, but a bath just riled up Orion, who thought all Ben's stuffed animals might like to snorkel in the tub. Ben was mollified by a warm milk, but it came out Rigel's nose when Roo ran through the kitchen wearing only a towel (and only around his shoulders), singing, 'Penis Maaaaan! *Able to leap tall buildings . . . owing mostly to his profound motivation not to get snagged on a lightning rod.'*

Penn closed his eyes and took deep breaths, removed Rigel's snot-milked pajamas, drained Orion's bath with Orion still in it, dug clothes-pins out of the junk drawer and used them to set Ben's stuffies to drip dry in the Proving Ground (the laundry room – Rosie felt it wanted a name more in keeping with its usual state). Three of his four children were naked, which, while one step closer to pajamas, was still a long way off from bed. Ben was wearing PJs, admittedly, but also rain boots, rain hat, raincoat, and an umbrella, singing à la Gene Kelly in the raindrops of his stuffed-animal storm.

For variety, Penn lined them up tallest to smallest and made a PJ bucket brigade, tops, bottoms, blankies, and sippy cups passed one boy to the next until each found a home. Yes, Orion ended up in Roo's pajama top, which came down to the floor like a Victorian nightgown, and so Roo himself was topless, and so Rigel refused to wear pajama bottoms and therefore needed socks so that his underpants would not feel lonely. And yes, Roo snagged Ben's blankie for a cape and ran up and down the stairs three times singing, '*Penis Maaaaan! Able to slide down banisters . . . but not especially likely to do so all things considered.*' But Penn thought it close enough and declared it a bedtime victory.

'Which room tonight?'

'Shark Cave!' four boys chorused. Roo, aged eight on the night Claude became, had named his room himself. Rigel and Orion, aged four and a half, were just next door in a room everyone called POH but which only Penn and Rosie knew to stand for Pit of Hell. Again, her christening. Ben, aged seven, lived in Ben's Room. Ben was a literalist.

It was beyond imagining, even when Rosie wasn't working and they were both home in the evenings, even when Rosie's mom was staying with them to help out as she did for a couple months after each child was born, to consider reading to each son separately. Bedtime stories were a group activity. And because showing the pictures all around to everyone involved a great deal of squirming and shoving and pinching and pushing and get-outta-my-ways and he-farted-on-mes and you-got-to-look-longer-than-I-dids, Penn often resorted to telling stories rather than reading them. He had a magic book he read from. It was an empty spiral notebook. He showed the boys it was blank so that there was no clamoring to see. And then he read it to them. Like magic.

When he'd told it to Rosie, the suit of armor outside the prince's bedroom had been full of roses. The prince had been stunned to find it brimming over with blooms, but Penn knew it was narratively inevitable when you woke up in bed next to an ER resident named Rosie who insisted she had no time for a boyfriend. Not just the first time but every time the prince peeked under the visor, ardent red and pink and yellow petals burst forth, and his hallways filled with their rosy perfume. But for the boys, the suit of armor was filled with something even better.

'So the prince lifted up the visor and looked inside, and there he saw . . . absolutely nothing.'

'Nothing?' shrieked Roo.

'Nothing,' Penn reported soberly.

'No fair,' said Rigel.

'"No fair," said Grumwald. "I just realized this stupid hunk of metal has been outside my bedroom my whole life, and I expected there'd be a charmed knight inside or a mummy or at least a magic rodent of some kind."'

'Or a talking spider.' Ben was reading *Charlotte's Web*.

'"Or a talking spider," Grumwald thought. "Or some roses."'

'Roses?' said Roo. 'Why would there be roses in a suit of armor?'

'Yeah,' said Rigel.

'Yeah,' said Orion.

'You'll understand in a few years. In any case, there was nothing in there, and Grumwald was about to close the visor and climb down from the stool he'd needed to reach it when he heard something.'

'A ghost?' said Ben.

'A zombie?' said Roo.

'It was a voice,' said Penn. 'And the voice said . . .'

'Boo!' yelled Rigel.

'Roo!' yelled Roo.

'"Once upon a time,"' said Penn.

'Once upon a time?' said Ben.

'The armor wasn't empty. The armor was full. What was inside the armor was a story, a story wanting to get out.'

'Why did it want to get out?'

'That's what all stories want. They want to get out, get told, get heard. Otherwise, what's the point of stories? They want to help little boys go to sleep. They want to help stubborn mamas fall in love with dads. They want to teach people things and make them laugh and cry.'

'Why would a story want to make someone cry?' Ben was so much more serious than his brothers.

'Same reason you cry anyway,' said Penn. 'You cry and then you feel better. Your owie stops stinging. Your feelings get less hurt. Sometimes you feel sad or scared, and you hear a sad or scary story, and then you feel less sad and less scared.'

'That doesn't make sense,' said Ben.

'Nonetheless,' Penn explained.

'Was that all the story said?' Orion got back to the point. 'Once upon a time?'

'Nope, the story was a magic story. It was endless. It had no end. It was unlimited. Every time it seemed like it was going to come to some kind of conclusion or moral or denouement, it went in a different direction and began again.'

'What did it say on the last page' – sometimes Ben's literalism strained Penn's creative talents – 'where it's supposed to say "The End"?'

'There was no last page. It was magic.' He showed them his blank spiral notebook again, how you could keep turning and turning the pages and never lack for another page to turn.

'Like a circle?' said Ben.

'Exactly like a circle.'

'Stories aren't circles,' said Roo.

'Stories are all circles,' said Penn.

'I don't understand, Daddy,' Rigel and Orion said together.

'No one understands,' said Penn. 'Stories are very mysterious. That's their other point. To tell themselves. And to be mysterious.'

'What happened next?' said Roo. 'In the story?'

'Which one?'

'Which one what?'

'Which story? The story about Grumwald? Or the story coming out of his suit of armor?'

'Both.'

'Lots. Lots happened next. In both.'

'Tell us! Tell us!'

Penn considered how clever it was of him to have birthed a Greek Chorus to hear his tales. 'Tomorrow. More tomorrow. Tonight, we sleep.'

Bedtime took a further forty-five minutes and was followed by Penn's scraping toothpaste off the downstairs bathroom ceiling, gathering up a whole load of discarded laundry from the floor in the hallway, and accidentally crushing a LEGO jungle dinosaur castle for which he knew he'd pay dearly the next morning. In all, a successful bedtime and an accomplishment on par with finishing a particularly difficult chapter or a tax return. It wasn't diagnosing a pulmonary embolism, but it was not unimpressive, and it allowed a pulmonary embolism to be diagnosed. It could not, unfortunately, be followed up by work or by house cleaning, dish doing, lunchbox packing, exercising, or any of the other things that needed doing. Bedtime could only be followed by TV. Or drinking. On the night Claude became – the fruition of which, of course, would only make bedtime worse – Penn thought both at once sounded best and gave it a good try but was asleep on the couch before he was very far into either one.

Things They Told Doctors

C laude's first word, when he was only nine months, one week, and three days old, was 'bologna'. There was no mistaking that one. Maybe the cooing mas and das and bas were words, and maybe they weren't, and maybe when he sat in the bath slapping the water and saying wa-wa-wa he was talking, or maybe it was just a coincidence, but he said 'bologna' clear as a PA announcer. When had Claude started talking was one of the many questions on the many forms, one of the random facts medical professionals counted as clues. The doctors always looked at Rosie with condescending amusement when she got to the speaking-at-nine-months part. Then she was forced to have this conversation again:

'Babies do start babbling around six months or even earlier, Mom,' the doctors would say. Only a few of them called Penn Dad, but she was always Mom. This must have been covered in the fellowship year if you did peds because no one in all her years of training had ever suggested to her that she call a patient's parent Mom. If anyone had, she would have explained that its subtext – you know less about your child than I do, for I am a trained professional and also because, as a woman, you are slightly hysterical – was offensive, untrue, and frankly embarrassing for the physician.

The doctors would always continue, 'The babbling is an important first step, of course, but it's not what we mean when we say "speech". "Ma" and "da" don't count.'

'Bologna,' said Rosie.

'No, I'm afraid it's true,' said the doctors.

In Claude's linguistically formative weeks, meat had been a source of great discord in their household. Rigel was refusing to eat anything but deli. He demanded bologna for breakfast and lunch, roast beef for dinner and dessert, salami for snack. He came home from kindergarten with pictures of corned-beef rainbows. His dump trucks and spaceships all delivered ham. To balance this out, Orion ate nothing but carrots and carrot-shaped foods, and though his parents were grateful for the nutritional options thus available in the form of veggie dogs and granola bars with the ends chewed to a taper, this arrangement was not sustainable. The upshot, Penn explained to the doctors, was that a nine-month-old saying 'bologna' was remarkable, yes, but sometimes even the remarkable got lost in the fray. Rosie's point was more this: the normal state of children is nothing remotely resembling normal. Which makes it hard to identify the aberrations when they come.

Claude said 'bologna' at nine months, was talking in full sentences before his first birthday.

'Does he have an older sibling?' said the doctors.

'Oh yeah,' said Penn.

And they seemed satisfied.

But Claude was precocious in other ways too. He crawled at six months. Walked at nine. During the year he was three, Claude wrote and illustrated a series of mysteries in which a puppy and a panda teamed up to solve crimes. He made a birthday cake – three-tiered – for Rigel and Orion with no help from anyone except with the oven. He said he wanted to be a chef when he grew up. He also said he wanted to be a cat when he grew up. When he grew up, he said, he wanted to be a chef, a cat, a vet, a dinosaur, a train, a farmer, a recorder player, a scientist, an ice-cream cone, a first baseman, or maybe the inventor of a new kind of food that tasted like chocolate ice cream but nourished like something his mother would say yes to for breakfast. When he grew up, he said, he wanted to be a girl.

'Okay,' Penn said the first time as he had to everything else, including the ice-cream cone. 'Sounds great.'

And Rosie said, 'You can be anything you want when you grow up, baby. Anything at all.'

She meant this to be encouraging, of course. She meant it as an assertion of faith in her baby boy, that his future was limitless because he was smart, talented, thoughtful, and a hard worker, that he would, in short, be able to do anything he came to want to do. She figured by the time he got there, he'd no longer want to be a cat or a train or an ice-cream cone, so his inability to achieve these goals wouldn't be upsetting. That's what she meant.

Remarkable though he was, however, Claude was still only three. 'Mama?'

'Yeah, sweetie?'

'When I grow up and become a girl, will I start over?'

'Start over from where?'

'Start over from being a baby.'

'What do you mean, sweetie?'

'Will I have to start being a girl from the beginning and grow up all over again? Or will I be a girl who's the age that I am when I'm growed-up and can become one?'

'You lost me,' said Rosie.

'I want to be a little girl when I grow up, but when I'm grown-up, I won't be little anymore.'

'Ahh, I see.' She didn't. 'I don't think you'll probably want to be a little girl anymore when you grow up. I don't think you'll want to be a train or a cat or an ice-cream cone either.'

'Because that's silly,' said Claude.

'Instead, you'll probably want a job. Maybe it will be farmer or scientist. Or maybe it will be something you haven't even thought of yet. It's okay. You have a long time to decide.'

'Are there girl farmers and girl scientists?' said Claude.

'Of course,' said Rosie. 'I'm a girl scientist.'

'That's what I want to be then,' said Claude decisively. 'A girl scientist. Can I have a Popsicle?'

'Sure,' said Rosie.

Later – was it later that day or that week or that month? Neither Penn nor Rosie could remember when asked, again and again over the many years, how persistent, how consistent, he'd been, how sure – Rosie opened her eyes in the middle of the night to find Claude standing next to her bed.

'Hi, Mama.'

'Sweetie. You scared me.'

'When I'm a girl scientist, can I wear a dress to work?'

She willed her eyes to focus on the clock then wished she hadn't. 'It's 3:04, Claude.'

'Yes.'

'A.M.'

'Obviously.'

'I guess you'll wear a lab coat.'

'Like my raincoat?'

'Yeah, but white usually. And not waterproof. And no hood.'

'Okay. Good night.'

'Good night.'

Rosie slept in. When she came down for breakfast, Penn reported, 'Claude wants to know if he can wear a dress under his lab coat when he's a girl scientist.'

'It's okay with me.' Rosie was pre-coffeed, still bleary-eyed, catching up with being awake.

'I asked why he wanted to be a girl scientist instead of just a scientist.'

'What did he say?'

'So he could wear a dress under his lab coat.'

In November, it was Ben's birthday. Later, when it turned out Penn and Rosie were going to have to catalog for doctors in a focused, specifics-filled way a life they were living by more of a skin-of-their-teeth/seat-of-their-pants/bundle-of-their-nerves approach, they were glad for the formative moments that coincided with birthdays or holidays so they could remember when they happened. Claude wanted to make another cake for Ben's birthday, but Ben wanted the pecan and pumpkin pies he saw all over the Thanksgiving displays at the grocery stores, and Claude's culinary skills did not yet extend to pies. Instead, Claude wrote him a musical with a cast of brothers. If the specifics of the plot were a bit muddled – it involved a princess, a farmer, and, for some reason Penn and Rosie could never fathom, two clouds carrying toilet plungers – the sentiment was sweet and the recorder music quite moving.

'Claude made the princess's dress himself,' said Rosie. 'It was one of my old dresses – we have a bag of dress-up clothes the kids like to play with – but he added ribbons, sequins, a cape off the shoulders.'

'We only have boys,' Penn always added. 'Someone has to play the girl in the skits and the games. It was no big deal.'

'Until the next morning,' said Rosie. 'He wore the dress all weekend getting ready for the play. He said he was in dress rehearsals. After the play, he didn't take it off, but Orion wouldn't relinquish his cloud costume either. Dress-up is fun. Claude even wore the dress to bed. The next morning I made him take it off to go to preschool, and he really didn't want to.'

Rosie was underplaying this. He more than didn't want to. That was the one thing that was predictable about that morning: it had to fit exactly within the time allotted in order to work, and therefore it did not even come close. When Rosie woke at six, Claude was already up, had made himself cereal, was watching *Sesame Street* in his very rumpled princess dress. 'Change into school clothes,' she said, kissing him on the head. Penn made breakfasts. She made lunches. 'Claude,' she called over to the sofa as she sealed her fifth bag of mini pretzels, 'get changed for school, please.' Penn made coffee, thank God, and Rosie unloaded the dishwasher. 'Claude sweetie,' she called, unfolding the stool she needed to reach the shelf where the jelly jars lived, 'school clothes.' She went upstairs to wake everyone else. Roo showered. Ben showered. Rigel and Orion threw fits about not wanting to take showers until Rosie decided she preferred hot water to clean children and let the twins go to school dirty. 'Claude. Now,' she said. Penn took clothes out of the dryer. Rosie assembled after-school appurtenances then went upstairs again to get showered and dressed herself. 'Claude,' she called down, 'we're walking out the door the minute I get back.' At 7:59, she was downstairs, dressed, packed up, and quite pleased with herself, ready to drop Roo through Orion at the bus stop and Claude at preschool and be on time for work by not a moment later than 8:29 a.m.

Claude was still sitting on the sofa in his dress.

'Claude!' she shrieked. 'Why are you not dressed for school?'

'I am dressed for school.'

'You're still wearing your dress!'

'I'm wearing it to school.'

'Claude, honey, we don't have time for this this morning. The boys are going to miss their bus. Go change.'

'No.'

'I said go change.'

'No.'

'Claude,' said Penn, 'Mommy told you to go get ready for school.'

'Several times,' said Rosie.

'You can't tell her no.'

'No,' said Claude.

'Claude. I am not going to ask you again. Go take off that dress and. Get. Ready. For. School.'

Claude stood up on the couch, clenched his fists straight out behind him like booster rockets, and yelled at the top of his tiny voice, 'I am ready for school!' Then he threw himself onto the carpet and cried.

Rosie and Penn had a brief conversation with their eyeballs. Penn went up to change out of his robe and drive the boys to the bus stop. Rosie sat on the floor next to weeping Claude and rubbed his back.

'Claude. Honey. It's time for school. Do you feel okay? Don't you want to go see Ms Danielle and Ms Terese? Don't you want to see Josie and Taya and Pia and Annlee?'

'I have to wear my dress.'

'Sweetheart, you cannot wear that dress to preschool.'

'Why not? Josie wears a dress to preschool. Taya and Pia and Annlee wear dresses to preschool.'

'Is that why you want to wear a dress? Because all your friends wear dresses?'

'I guess,' Claude guessed. 'And tights.'

'Well. Usually boys don't wear dresses to preschool,' Rosie admitted carefully. 'Or tights.'

'I'm not usually,' said Claude. This, Rosie reflected, even at the time, was true.

'I think this dress is a little long for preschool,' Rosie tried. 'Tea length is a bit formal for the occasion.'

'What's tea length?'

'It means the dress comes down to your ankles. That would make it hard to run around on the playground. Aren't your friends' dresses pretty short so they can play?'

'But it's my only one,' Claude whispered. 'I didn't know it was too formal.'

'And you've been wearing this dress all weekend. It's dirty.'

'No it's not.' Claude was still sniffling, still looking at the floor.

'Ladies don't wear rumpled, dirty dresses.'

'They don't?'

'No, they wear clean, pressed ones.'

'All ladies?'

'Well, real ladies,' said Rosie. She'd been tongue and cheeky – and exhausted already with a long day ahead – but this one came back to haunt her.

'Oh,' said Claude. 'Okay.' And he toddled off to his room to change into a sweatshirt and jeans.

But in the car, his little voice piped up from the backseat. 'Mama?'

'Yeah, baby.'

'I need another dress. A short, informal one for school.'

'Okay, love. We can talk about it when you get home.'

'Thank you, Mama.'

'Sure, honey.'

'And Mama?'

'Yeah, baby?'

'Will you to teach me how to do the washer and dryer and iron?'

'That's Daddy's job,' said Rosie.

'No, it's mine,' said Claude. 'For my new dress. Real ladies wear clean, pressed dresses.'

Didn't you know then, the doctors said later? Weren't you listening?

Losers

That night at bedtime, Claude was worried. 'Daddy, is this too formal for bed?'

Penn looked up from cajoling Orion to brush the backs of his teeth too. Claude was wearing Rosie's nightshirt, lavender with lace around the collar and hem. On Rosie, it came down just to the bottom of her underwear, which meant that every time she reached for something or moved too quickly or rolled over in bed, the nightshirt gave up the goods, at least a peek at the goods. On Claude, it came down to just above his ankles.

'It's tea length,' Claude added, looking worried.

'I don't think there's a dress code for bed,' said Penn. 'I wouldn't worry about it. Orion, molars are teeth too, my friend.' Orion was wearing a-size-too-small green footy pajamas with the footies cut off so as to resemble as much as possible the Incredible Hulk. Rigel streaked by the bathroom in nothing at all.

'Boys,' Penn called. 'It's Monday. Roo's room,' and from every corner of the house, seemingly from every corner of the Earth, naked, half-naked, and oddly dressed boys tumbled longways onto Roo's bed, backs against the wall, shoulders pressed together, knees and elbows where knees and elbows aren't meant to go, layered like lasagna.

'Get your bare ass off my pillow,' Roo shrieked at Rigel.

'Don't say "ass", Roo.'

'But it's on my pillow,' said Roo. 'Where my head goes.'

'Get your bare ass off his pillow, Rigel,' said Penn. Rigel scooted his ass down the bed like Jupiter did along the carpet, which in fact seemed worse, but Roo was mollified.

'Your hair smells like bananas,' Ben complained to Claude.

'It's no tears,' Claude explained.

'Just close your eyes,' said Ben. 'Then you can use big-boy shampoo and not smell like bananas.'

'I don't want to be a big boy,' said Claude.

'I don't want to smell bananas during stories,' said Ben.

'Banana Boy Hulk smash!' Orion jumped up from his spot in the middle and began smashing his brothers indiscriminately in the face with Roo's pillow.

'Ew, it smells like Rigel's ass,' said Roo.

'My ass is awesome,' said Rigel.

'Don't say "ass",' said Penn.

'Banana Ass Hulk smash!' said Orion.

'Enough!' Penn shouted, which was the signal to plug mouths with thumbs, pull blankies out from underneath brothers, and settle in. Penn was continually amazed, night after night, year after year, that everyone was still up for storytelling, now Ben was eleven and Roo was twelve, practically a teenager, now every one of them could read himself. Still, they were all of them happy to put their own books away to listen to the continuing – really continuing – adventures of Grumwald and his own indefatigable storyteller in shining armor instead. Not just happy. Expectant. Which was, Penn thought, after all the point of storytelling. 'Where was I?'

'Grumwald was using fern leaves to capture the night fairies who came to his window every night—'

'And lit up green and blue and pink like the neon sign at that pizza place where Rigel puked that time—'

'Because he needed neon night-fairy hair to make a potion for the witch—'

'Who was all like, "Grumwald! I need that hair! If you can't get me that hair, I'm going to place a spell on you!"'

'But the fern leaves kept ripping open, and the night fairies kept escaping, even though he promised he wasn't going to hurt them and just needed to give them a little trim—'

'Which they could use anyway because they were kind of scruffy fairies, but they wouldn't listen—'

'And Grum was wary of how to make a night fairy tarry—'

'And other things that rhymed.'

'Yeah, and other things.'

His Greek Chorus of sons. No wonder this was the best part of his day. Except . . .

'Can we have a girl tonight instead?' Claude interrupted.

'Instead of night fairies?' said Penn.

'Instead of Grumwald,' said Claude. 'I'm bored of a prince. I want a princess.'

'Grumwaldia?' said Penn.

'Yeah! Grumwaldia!' said Claude.

'Grumwaldia sounds like a lake in Vermont.' Roo had never been to one but was right about that anyway.

'Princesses are boring,' Rigel whined.

'Girls in fairy tales are losers,' said Roo.

'No they aren't,' said Claude.

'Yes they are. Not like losers. Losers. Girls in fairy tales are always losing stuff.'

'Nuh-uh,' said Claude.

'Yuh-huh. They lose their way in the woods or their shoe on the step or their hair even though they're in a tower with no door and their hair is like literally attached to their head.'

'Or their voice,' Ben put in. 'Or their freedom or their family or their name. Or their identity. Like she can't be a mermaid anymore.'

'Or they lose being awake,' said Roo. 'And then they just sleep and sleep and sleep. Boooring.'

Claude started crying. 'A princess could do cool stuff. A princess could be better than Grumwald. She wouldn't have to sleep or lose her shoe.'

The boys' emotions looked divided between worried they'd get in trouble for making their baby brother cry and antsy about how much story-time had passed and how much was left and how no story was yet being told. Worried about getting in trouble and antsy were in fact the boys' predominant emotions. Well, maybe not worried. More like chagrined after they'd already gotten in trouble and antsy to get in more trouble.

'It's no fair,' Claude whined. 'We never get a princess.'

'It's no fair,' Rigel and Orion whined. 'We'll never find out what happened with the night fairies.'

THIS IS HOW IT ALWAYS IS   41

'It's no fair,' Claude added. 'They always get their way because there's two of them.'

'Enough!' Penn said again. 'We can do both at once.'

'We can?' Ben was unconvinced.

'Yes, because those night fairies the witch was making Grumwald capture? They had a night fairy leader named Princess Grumwaldia.'

'Stephanie,' Claude corrected.

'Princess Grumwaldia Stephanie,' Penn amended.

'What was she wearing?' said Claude.

'She was wearing a lavender nightgown but short, not tea length, so as to leave her legs free for fleeter flight. And she thought Grumwald was a big baby because he was so whiny about having to rule over his little kingdom and at the same time study for Algebra II, which he thought was really hard. He also had a lot of extra student government work to do since the secretary dropped out after the treasurer took the social coordinator to homecoming. Princess Stephanie, as a night fairy, didn't go to high school, obviously, but her kingdom was much, much vaster than Grumwald's. His stretched from the north fork of the forest to the horizon of the east sea. Hers . . . well, Stephanie was in charge of the night sky.'

'All of it?' Claude was impressed.

'Not all of it—'

'See?' Rigel and Orion: Captains, Team Grumwald.

'Just the stars.'

'Wow.' Claude snugged up against Penn, a kind of thank-you.

'It was Princess Stephanie's job to oversee the night fairies, and it was the night fairies' job to manage the stars.'

'This is starting to sound like reality TV,' said Roo.

'You didn't think the heavens just managed themselves, did you? You didn't think all the night fairies did their whole lives was tease poor Grumwald? They had to see that the stars came out on time, sparkled as appropriate, dimmed so the moon didn't get pissed off when it was full, fell just when wishers were watching. This was a stressful job – way more stressful than SGA president or even prince – because there are a lot of stars out there, and Stephanie was in charge not just of making sure they were behaving properly but also that they were happy.'

'How do you keep stars happy?' Claude whispered.

'Well, exactly,' said Penn. 'It was a big job. A big, big job. Stephanie and the other night fairies started every evening at dusk, and it often took until nearly dawn to get everything set. "Look alive there, Sirius. A little more light, please, Centauri. How do you feel, Ross 248? Anything we can do to make you more comfortable?" So by the time dawn came, Princess Grumwaldia Stephanie was exhausted and ready for bed. Just like all of you.'

Ben and Roo went off to finish homework, but the little ones were ready, and Claude was already mostly asleep. He stirred when Penn transferred him to his own bed to ask, 'Can I stay up till dawn too, Daddy? To help with the stars?'

'Sure, sweetie.' In the few seconds that passed while Penn fumbled with the nightlight, Claude was already fast asleep, lavender nightgown bunched up around his waist, not so tea length after all.

Absent her usual nightshirt, Rosie came to bed that night in a button-down of Penn's which, like Princess Stephanie's, was short enough to leave her legs free for fleeter flight. And like two-fifths of her sons, she had nothing on underneath.

Through that whole winter and spring, Claude came home every day from preschool, shed his clothes, and put the princess dress back on. And there at the beginning, after the first afternoon or two, no one – not Claude, not his brothers, not his parents – gave much thought to his dress, for he was still and always just Claude, and was it any stranger, really, than Roo performing a séance in the downstairs bathroom or than Rigel licking the spine of every book in the house to prove he could taste the difference between fiction and nonfiction? It was not.

Then summer arrived and with it the boys' grandmother, and everything got even better. Improbably, Rosie's mother's name was Carmelo.

'Like the candy bar?' Penn had asked the first time.

'Not Caramello. Carmelo,' said Rosie, as if the former were ridiculous but the latter as reasonable as Anne or Barbara.

Roo, because he was the eldest, had an opportunity to intervene and rechristen her something normal. Instead, he'd gone with Carmy, some combo of Carmelo and Grammy, which truly sounded like something chocolate-covered. But she was not a chocolate-covered sort of grandma. She did not bake. She did not inveterately hand out sweets. She loved from a different place than that, better for the teeth. She was always threatening to move to be nearer to Rosie and the boys, but Wisconsin was – obviously, nonnegotiably, self-evidently – too cold. So she stayed in Phoenix and held the weather to her heart as a talisman, clutched to her breast against all counteroffers.

But she came up for the summers. Phoenix's weather need not be clutched to the breast for June through September. Every year, she rented the same rundown lake cottage from a colleague of Rosie's who couldn't be bothered to fix it up enough to rent to tourists. She stood on its front porch and watched the sun rise over the lake every morning and smoked Camels. She was the only grandmother any of the boys' friends knew who would have been willing – never mind able – to take out six or seven of them at a time in the ancient green rowboat that came with, and perhaps predated, the house. She swam every day out to the glacial rock in the middle of the lake that felt like it had very lately been glacier itself, hauled herself onto the mammoth slab, sunned the chill out of her bones, and then swam back. She was the most glamorous thing the boys had ever seen.

It was one of those hot, humid, buggy Wisconsin summers where it went from snow to sauna in a week and a half and stayed there. The boys spent it perpetually wet from the lake, the sprinkler, a surprisingly durable water slide Roo built out of trash bags on his grandmother's front lawn. Carmelo taught Rigel to knit. At first, she thought it was the resemblance of the needles to something a ninja might own that appealed to him, and maybe it was, but he fixed on it like sand to sunscreen and spent the summer trailing training scarves everywhere, dropped stitches unraveling like plot threads. Ben used practice tassels as bookmarks. Jupiter used abandoned projects as bedding. Orion employed them as bandanas, sweatbands, do-rags, tube tops, cummerbunds, and toga tails, coming down to lazy summer breakfasts as Bruce Springsteen and Julius Caesar (equally ancient in his mind), 50 Cent and Fred Astaire. But Claude wore them as long, flowing hair – tresses that cascaded down his back or could be attached via headband then rubber-banded up like a real ponytail. Roo began a practice he would hone to an art in the years to come: pretending he wasn't related to any of them.

Carmy let Claude try on her dresses and jewelry and shoes. When Claude made tea to go with his tea-length dress, she pulled out cookies or cheese and crackers to go with it and changed out of her T-shirt and shorts so that Claude didn't have to be fancy alone.

Only once, early on, did Claude wonder, 'Carmy?'

'Yes, dear?'

'Will you love me even if I keep wearing a dress?'

'I will love you even if you wear a dress made out of puppies.' Carmelo nuzzled his neck, and he giggled. 'I will love you even if you wear a hat made out of toe cheese.'

Claude wrinkled his nose. 'You will?'

'Of course.'

'How come?'

''Cause I'm your grandma. That's what grandmas are for.'

'Loving you no matter what you wear?'

'Loving you no matter what.'

Claude considered that distinction. 'Is that why you still like Orion?' who was at that moment wandering through the kitchen wearing an unspooling umber pot holder as a loincloth.

Carmelo squeezed her eyes shut. 'No matter what.'

Carmelo was also the one who took Claude to buy a bathing suit as a preschool graduation present. She let him pick it out himself, which is how Rosie arrived home from work one day to find her youngest son running through the sprinkler in a pink bikini with white and yellow daisies.

'Where did that come from?' She bent from the waist to kiss him way out in front of her so she would stay dry.

'Isn't it great?' Claude looked lit up. At first she'd taken him to be sunburned, but in fact he was glowing. 'Carmy got it for me for graduation.'

'Graduation?'

''Cause next year I'm going to kindergarten.'

'I see.'

'I picked it out myself.'

'I can tell.'

'Isn't it beautiful?'

At the least, he was beautiful in it, his body lean and flat as the piano, which hadn't been tuned since Roo switched to flute, and covered in the little nicks and bruises that showed he was doing a good job of being almost five.

'Sorry.' Carmelo shrugged when Claude had run off again. 'Once I told him he was old enough to pick out his own suit, there was no going back.'

'Empowering children.' Rosie sighed. 'Always a mistake.'

'Are you worried?' Was Carmelo asking because her daughter looked worried? Or because she thought she should be?

'No?' It came out as a question. It was a sweltering almost-evening, no clouds, no wind. Rosie squinted against late-afternoon sun glinting off the water genuflecting from the sprinkler. Was it time to worry? Was the dress one thing but the bikini another somehow? Gnats danced lines and crosses just above her eyes, but she was too tired suddenly to wave them away. 'Maybe a little worried,' she admitted to her mother.

'Fiddlesnicks.' Carmelo dragged hard on a cigarette Rosie hoped might induce the gnats to dance elsewhere.

'Fiddle *snicks?*'

'Poppyrock.'

'I think the word you're looking for is "poppycock".'

'Bullshit then.' Carmelo was not a woman bogged down by semantics. 'He's fine. Look at him! He's ecstatic. He's euphoric.'

'For the moment.'

Carmelo looked at her daughter. 'For the moment's all there is, my darling.'

'Spoken like an indulgent grandmother,' said Rosie. But deep down she knew that wasn't it. It was spoken like someone whose baby didn't get to grow up.

'He's happy,' said Carmelo as if that settled it, as if it were just that simple. 'Happy, healthy, and fabulous. What more could you ask?'

'Other kids will make fun of him.'

'What kids?' said Carmelo.

'I don't know. Kids.'

'Kids don't care about stuff like that anymore.'

'They don't?'

'No. And why do you?'

'You do realize,' Rosie turned to her mother, 'that *I'm* supposed to be calming *you* down about all of this, not the other way around? I'm the one who's supposed to be talking you off the ledge. You're supposed to be panicking and dragging him off to church or something.'

'So few Jews at church these days,' said Carmelo.

'You're too old to be open-minded and tolerant,' said Rosie.

'I'm too old not to be.' She sucked coolly on her cigarette again, then waved it at Rosie to punctuate her point. Not for the first time, Rosie envied smokers their rhetorical device. 'I've lived life. I know what's important. I've seen it all by now. You think he's the first boy I ever saw in a bikini? He's not. You think your generation invented kids who are different?'

'There are different kinds of different.' Rosie chewed on the side of her thumbnail.

'Fiddlecock,' said her mother.

It wasn't Claude who most worried them that summer anyway – which was, in some ways, his last – but Ben, who had always been quiet but was quieter than usual, who had always been bookish but spent that summer he was eleven reading Shakespeare while his brothers swam. They'd decided he didn't need sixth grade and should skip right to seventh, where he'd be a year younger but only a year or two ahead of everyone else as opposed, in sixth grade, to being so far ahead there was no point in his being there at all. Penn thought the fewer years in the hellscape that was middle school the better. Rosie thought being in class with Roo would make up for any of the social stuff he might miss. They'd broken it to the two oldest boys gently, worried Roo would feel his world cramped and horned in on, worried Ben might rather be smarter than everyone around him by four or five times rather than just two or three. Roo had been delighted and immediately started scheming for them to secretly switch places so Ben could take his tests for him, as if promoting Ben to seventh grade would also render them identical twins. But Ben had clammed up, worried about neither Rosie nor Penn knew what, worried in a way that the sun and the summer and even Shakespeare could not touch.

The Sunday afternoon before school started up again, there was a picnic at the pool: crockpot-boiled hot dogs, American cheese slices, limp pickles, watermelons hacked to pieces by someone who evidently had bad blood with the fruit going back generations. Because they'd spent all summer in the lake, it was their first – and last – foray of the season to the public pool. Orion wore orange flippers, a rainbow snorkel, and a fake fin. Ben wore khaki shorts and a button-down shirt, just to make sure no one thought there was any chance he was going swimming. Claude wore his bikini because Penn found he could not say to his son, 'The suit you love is okay at home but not in public,' because Rosie would not say, 'We're proud of you in private but ashamed of you at the pool.'

They staked out chairs, a table, a corner of grass on which to pile towels and goggles and flip-flops. Every flat surface seemed sticky with melted ice cream. Late-summer bees, not easily deterred, nosed their bottles of sunscreen. The dark parts of the sidewalk were too hot to walk on bare-foot for more than a few steps. The whole world smelled of chlorine and sugar. A few kids shaded their eyes to stare at Claude. A few pointed and laughed. A few – maybe more than a few – adults raised hands to their mouths and whispered behind them to one another as if, Penn thought as they stared at his family, this masked what they were talking about. A classmate of Rigel and Orion's ran over to them.

'Cool fin,' he said to Orion.

'Thanks.'

'Why is your brother wearing a bikini?'

'I dunno,' said Rigel, for he did not, and what other answer was there really?

'Weird.'

'Yeah.'

'Bet I can do a bigger belly flop off the diving board than you two.'

'Cannot.'

'Can too.'

And they all ran off to prove it.

The adults were less easily diverted but didn't have much more to add, and for the same reason: what was there to say really? Rosie's bus-stop nemesis, Heather, galloped over without preamble to demand, 'Where did Claude even get that suit? I mean, you guys only have boys.'

'He got it from his grandmother,' Rosie answered truthfully then added, also truthfully, 'She's a girl.'

Several fathers approached Penn with some variation of 'Nice pink bikini', as if he were wearing it himself, so Penn thanked them, and they seemed not to know what to say to that.

The lifeguard manager opened with 'Wow, that's quite the getup your son has there.'

'It's true,' Penn agreed. 'I told Orion fake fins were only funny in an ocean, but we're in Wisconsin, so what are you going to do?'

Someone dumped a package of plastic cups and a mess of goldfish in the pool, and the kids dove in en masse, like a wave, to catch the ones with the other and take them home. It seemed like every child for twenty miles was in the pool swimming like goldfish, after goldfish. Even Claude,

who had not yet learned to swim underwater, was in doggy-paddling
pursuit of a fish. But Ben had tepee'd a lounger, bringing the head part
and the feet part overhead like wings, and crawled inside his own private
triangle of plastic straps. Penn crawled in beside him, best he could,
curled up like a pill bug with giant hairy feet that had to stay outside.

'You okay, sweetie?'

'Fine.'

'How come you're not swimming?'

'Don't feel like it.'

'Are you worried about school?'

Ben shrugged. Said nothing.

'Are you worried about going to middle school? Skipping a grade? Not
knowing everyone? Being younger than everybody else? Going to class
with Roo?'

Nothing.

'Am I warm?'

'Yes.'

'Yes, I'm warm?'

'Yes, that's what I'm worried about.'

'Which one?'

'All of them. And everything else too.'

'Everything else too?'

'I'm worried about middle school, skipping a grade, not knowing
everyone, being too young, and being so much smarter than Roo that the
teachers won't believe him when he says I'm his brother. I'm worried my
friends will think I think I'm too smart for them, even though I don't,
even though I am. I'm worried about taking a shower with a whole bunch
of other kids after gym. I'm worried about art class because art is required, and I suck at art. I'm worried about Claude because other kids
are going to make fun of him and be mean to him and maybe try to hurt
him, and he doesn't even care. And you and Mom don't even care.'

'We care,' Penn said softly.

'Why are you letting him wear that bathing suit?'

'He loves it.'

'He can love it at Carmy's where it's just us, but here . . . everybody's
whispering stuff about him. Everyone's staring. It's weird.'

'I don't think he's actually noticed.' Penn watched Claude on the
other side of the pool singing to his rescued goldfish and rocking its cup

in his crooked arms like a baby. 'Isn't not noticing even nicer – and better preparation for kindergarten – than not being whispered about in the first place?'

'I don't know,' Ben said.

'Me neither,' his father admitted. And then, 'Is that all?'

'All what?'

'All you're worried about?'

'I'm worried about those fish.' Ben squinted against late-summer, late-day sun in the direction of the pool where goldfish swam like foxes from neighbor-kid hounds. 'I don't think goldfish are built to handle that much chlorine and stress.'

'You neither,' said Penn.

'Chlorine and stress?'

'Well, the former would come off in the shower, but I think you have too much of the latter maybe.'

'I can't help it,' said Ben.

'Pick one.'

'One what?'

'One thing on your list to worry about. Put all your worry into that one thing. Worry about it as much as you like, as much as you need to. But only that one thing. Anytime any of the other things flits across your mind, take that concern and channel it into your one thing.'

'That's the same amount of worry, just less spread out,' said Ben.

'Consolidation is good,' his father promised. 'If you give all your worry to one thing, soon you'll realize that's way too much and worry about it less, and you'll feel more in control of it for keeping it at the front of your mind, and that will help you worry less too. So what's it going to be? That was a long list. What on it concerns you very most of all?' Penn expected the showers or Roo being weird at school or the whole smartest-youngest-smallest-kid thing.

But Ben didn't even hesitate. 'Claude. By far. I am most worried about what's going to happen to Claude when he goes to school this year.'

Penn was increasingly, creepingly worried too, but he took his own advice. The kids who stared at Claude, the parents who gossiped, the classmates who laughed, the neighbors who sniped, the acquaintances who made brazen comments about what wasn't remotely their business, the strangers who scowled, the brother who fretted, Penn boiled all those worries into a fine reduction he could put in a jelly jar in the back of the refrigerator and forget about, at least for the moment. It was easy to believe, as summer waned and school began once more, that all things would be new again, that old worries would turn and dry and float away like autumn leaves. Easy to believe but not necessarily warranted.

The next morning Claude came downstairs for his first day of kindergarten. He was wearing his tea-length dress – clean, pressed, and, his mother could not deny, appropriate for such an auspicious occasion – and he was in tears, holding a plastic cup of water with a very still upside-down goldfish.

Air Currents and Other Winds

While Rosie was puzzling how to talk him out of his dress, Claude accidentally, in his grief, spilled dead fish down his front. Through fonts of tears and snot and disappointment, he had to change out of the dress and settle for an old red patent-leather purse of Carmelo's, which Rosie consented to as a compromise position in the hopes he could pass it off successfully as an ill-suited lunch box. She put his peanut butter and jelly, banana, pretzels, and, as a first-day treat, chocolate-chip cookies – plus a note – in the purse to give it lunchbox cachet. Claude's kindergarten was full-day, six whole hours of sitting quietly and following rules and being away from home where someone – everyone – loved him best of all. Ben and Roo were off to their first day of middle school. Orion came down for breakfast wearing an eyeball sticker between his brows, and when she started to question him about it, he winked one of his other ones at her. So Claude's lunch purse was only seventh or eighth on Rosie's list of concerns that morning.

But when she arrived back at school at the end of the day, Claude was nowhere to be seen, and Orion and Rigel rushed out with the bell singing, '*Claude got in trouble. Claude got in trouble.*' Then the kindergarten door opened, spilling tiny children into their parents' eager arms, all except Claude, who was being held to his new teacher's side by what seemed a very firm hand on the top of his head.

'Mrs Adams?' The kindergarten teacher's name was Becky Appleton. At orientation, she'd told the parents to call her Becky, but Rosie just couldn't. First of all, Becky was the name of a child, not a person in whose charge she put the care and education of her baby boy, and though the teacher did look to be about fourteen years old, Rosie still thought she should have the decency to go by Rebecca already. But mostly, kindergarten classrooms always made Rosie feel more like a child herself than the parent of five of them. She remembered her own first day of kindergarten with a clarity that really should have been foggy all these years later. She had been through this four times now, and it never got any less weird. The tiny desks and chairs, the bins of still-pointy crayons and pencils, the smell of new eraser, these made Rosie want to sit down and learn the alphabet rather than be on a first-name basis with the teacher. 'You're Mrs Adams? Claude's mother?'

'It's Walsh, actually.' Rosie decided to let go, for the moment, the fact that it was Ms not Mrs, and Dr not Ms.

'Claude had a great first day, Mrs Walsh.' Becky's tone was belied by the look on Claude's face. 'But he had some trouble at lunch. The school does not allow peanut butter, so Claude had to sit and eat by himself at his desk in the classroom.'

'I read the kindergarten materials cover to cover,' said Rosie. 'There's nothing in there about not sending peanuts to school.'

'Oh, we just assume people know that. I guess we forget that not everyone is as aware as we are about skyrocketing peanut allergies among children today. No peanuts is implied.'

'Claude is my fifth child to go through this school. The one I made him today was perhaps the eight or nine hundredth peanut butter and jelly sandwich I've sent here. Is this a new rule?'

'We don't check their sandwiches,' explained Miss Appleton. 'It's about good faith and respect. Doing unto others. The Golden Rule.'

'It's a no-peanut honor system?'

'Exactly. We'd never have known Claude had a forbidden sandwich except he was bragging to his new friends about how ladies who lunch, lunch on finger sandwiches, cucumber usually, but in his case peanut butter because cucumbers make the bread soggy unless eaten right away.'

'That's true.' Rosie wondered, vaguely at the time, more pointedly later on, whether the issue here was the peanut butter or the patent-leather purse it had come out of. Or the lesson about ladies who lunch. 'Is anyone in Claude's class allergic to peanuts?'

'It's a precautionary rule.'

'Does his eating his sandwich in the classroom protect precautionary peanut-allergy sufferers better than in the cafeteria?'

'Well' – Miss Appleton pretended to hesitate to share the next part – 'I skipped my own free period to supervise Claude in the class-room while he ate. I was able to make sure he didn't touch anything.'

'Let's go home, baby,' Rosie said to Claude.

'Bye-bye, Claude,' said Miss Appleton. 'It was nice to meet you today. I am so excited for our year ahead.'

Claude did not raise his gaze from the ground.

'Oh, one more thing Mrs AdamsImeanWalsh. We generally discour-age accessories at school, especially at this age.'

'Accessories?'

'Jewelry, headgear, shiny shirts. Purses.'

'Shiny shirts?'

'Anything distracting. We like students to be able to concentrate during class.'

'Sure, but—'

'If they're fiddling, it's hard for them to learn.'

'Was Claude fiddling?'

'No. He was not. But other children found his purse distracting.'

'Was he doing anything distracting with it?'

'Just the presence of the purse was distracting.'

'Like the peanuts?'

'How do you mean?'

'You are prophylactically ruling out purses and peanuts,' said Rosie.

Miss Appleton blushed from head to toe. 'Prophylactically? Like,' she whispered the next word, 'condoms?'

'Prophylactically like preventatively and defensively. Anticipatorially, if you will.'

'Um, sure.'

'It means you are banning peanuts and purses just in case they might cause problems even though they've caused none yet and despite the fact that doing so may infringe on the rights and well-being of your stu-dent citizens.'

'We-ell, I guess we hope you'll just make something else for lunch? And we don't really think boys, uh, children, um, need purses. For school.'

'It's not a purse,' Claude interrupted. Rosie was relieved to hear his voice. 'It's a lunch tote.'

'Come on, sweetie,' Rosie said. 'It's been a long day. Let's go home.'

Rigel and Orion were waiting for them on the playground, Orion hanging upside down from the little-kid monkey bars so that his hair brushed the ground and his face looked like a (three-eyed) strawberry, Rigel climbing up the sliding board then sliding down the stairs on his butt. They headed toward the car and home to see whether Roo and Ben had fared any better at middle school. Orion put his ten-year-old arm around his baby brother. 'Kindergarten's tough, kid. But we still love you.'

'Yeah, we love you,' Rigel echoed, '*and* your purse.'

'It's a lunch tote.'

'And your lunch tote.'

The next day Rosie made cheese sandwiches all around. As Penn was packing them into a variety of lunch bags, boxes, and the patent-leather tote, Claude came downstairs and slid into his breakfast seat without a word. His already short hair was clipped back anyway with four rainbow barrettes, and he was wearing a dress made by pulling his own T-shirt – light-blue with a silk-screened unicorn eating a hot dog on a bicycle – over a longer shirt of Penn's so that it flared into a skirt just below his waist.

'Nice dress, dude.' Roo's mouth was full of Cheerios, so it was hard to guess his tone.

'Thanks.' Claude gave a small smile to his own cereal bowl.

Rigel looked up from the webbed foot he was knitting. 'You're not wearing that to school, are you?' and Rosie held her breath, waiting for the answer.

'Some of it,' said Claude.

'You'll get your butt kicked,' said Rigel.

'*Butt, butt, butt.*' Orion giggled, wiggling his toes into the done-already other webbed foot.

'It's not that it's not a nice outfit,' Ben tried gently. 'It's just not very manly, is it?'

'He's not a man,' said Penn. 'He's five. He's a little boy.'

'He may not even be that,' said Roo.

'Roo!' Rosie's voice sounded like warning, but was what he said unfair? Untrue? Unkind? She had no idea. Of course Claude was a little boy because if he wasn't a little boy, what was he? This seemed like such a simple question, but it was one she'd never encountered before as a parent, and that was saying something. It seemed like such a simple question, but somehow it was terrifying. What you were if you weren't a little boy ranked as maybe Rosie's fourth concern of the morning. She tabled it. 'No one's kicking Claude's anything. If anyone tries to kick Claude's anything, I'll kick *their* anything.'

Penn knew in his heart that Claude should be who he was. But he also knew that Claude would be happier if neither his clothes nor his sandwich nor the bag it came out of attracted anyone's attention because another thing his heart knew was this: it was more complicated than that. Five years of Orion wearing all manner of weird stuff to school had occasioned not so much as a raised third eyebrow from anyone. 'What an imaginative boy Orion is,' his teachers said. 'His spirit brightens everyone's day.' If an eyeball sticker was creative self-expression, surely Claude should wear what he wanted to school. How could you say yes to webbed feet but no to a dress, yes to being who you were but no to dressing like him? How did you teach your small human that it's what's inside that counts when the truth was everyone was pretty preoccupied with what you put on over the outside too?

These were Penn's second through twenty-ninth concerns. He felt bees buzzing behind his rib cage. But before Penn could settle on a parenting path, Claude slipped out of his chair, padded upstairs, and emerged again wordlessly, defrocked and de-barretted, Penn's skirt-shirt gone, only his own remaining over a pair of navy shorts. Claude shouldered his peanut-free purse, and everyone went off to school. When he got home at the end of a much smoother day, he went straight to his room and pulled Penn's shirt back on under his own, stuck the barrettes back in his hair, added a pair of Carmelo's clip-on earrings, and sat down at the dining-room table to homework with everyone else. Penn bit his bottom lip. The outfit itself didn't much worry him – it ranked in the high thirties, maybe – but its persistence was starting to creep into the top ten. Instead, he turned to homeworking.

Penn was in charge of homework, and he had rules. Homeworking never commenced – even complaining about homeworking never commenced – until after snack. And it had to be a good snack. Penn recognized peanut butter on a celery stick for the bullshit it was. Blueberry pancakes. Chocolate banana pops. Zucchini mini pizzas. These were snacks. Then the dining-room table was cleared, wiped down, and requisitioned for work. All boys – Penn included – sat down and got to it, homeworking quietly, asking questions or for additional help as necessary, calming so that others could concentrate. Homeworking en masse made it more fun. Penn recalled hours in his room as a child, slogging through math problems or write-ups of science experiments or memorizing the words for things in French. Downstairs, his parents would be watching TV or laughing together about their day while upstairs he suffered the isolating boredom and nagging insecurity of *passé composé*. At his dining-room table with his cadre of boys, however, he could approach homework, aptly, like dinner – everything shared, the trials and triumphs, each according to his abilities, everyone pitching in to help. Roo might say, 'Can anyone think of another way to say "society"?' or Ben might say, 'Is there even a word for "soufflé" in Spanish?' or Rigel and Orion might be building a rocket together while their father hoped it was for a science project and not just for the sake of blowing stuff up.

Over the years, kindergarten homework had gotten more . . . Rosie said 'intense'; Penn said 'asinine with an emphasis on the ass'. When Roo was in kindergarten, there was playing with blocks and in the sandbox. There was learning to sit quietly on the rug and listen to a story. Now Claude had kindergarten homework of his very own. On this second night of school, it was to draw a picture of himself and write a sentence about what he hoped to learn this year. Claude's sentence was 'I hope to learn about science including stars, what kind of frogs live in Wisconsin, why oceans are salty, air currents and other winds, and why peanut butter is not allowed at school'. Penn marveled at his youngest son. So many children seemed somehow to age the littler ones more quickly, like some kind of obscure Einsteinian law of physics. Claude's picture was of the whole family, and Penn could not decide if it was wonderful or alarming that, assigned to draw himself, Claude drew them all. Penn and Rosie and Carmelo stood with lanky arms around one another's lanky shoulders, heads grazing the clouds just above them, the blue of the sky creeping occasionally over the outline of their faces so that their cheeks were smeared with the firmament. In front of them, sitting crisscross-applesauce all in a row in the grass, were five brothers: Roo's hair curling out wider than his body; Ben's glasses owling huge, dark eyes straight off the page; Rigel and Orion with ears unfairly cocked at right angles from pointy, parallel heads. And small in the corner – because he'd run out of room? because he got lost in his overlarge family? because he felt insignificant in the face of the vastness of the universe? – Claude had drawn himself in his tea-length dress with ruby slippers and wavy brown hair down to the ground, held back off his face with a dozen barrettes that snaked colored ribbons in all directions, cascading over his brothers, over his parents, over the clouds and the trees and the grass and the sky, a small, windblown child in his own personal tempest, puzzling over air currents and other winds and his place in the world, which, it struck Penn, was right about there, right where he'd imagined it. Penn's concern over the drawing subsided into the high teens.

The picture went without comment by Miss Appleton except for a hastily penned and not very convincing 'Nice work!' plus a sticker of a grinning check mark (because, Penn wondered, actually making a check mark was too much effort?). So did the lunch purse as long as it didn't contain peanut butter. And Claude, for his part, merely changed clothes four times a day: PJs to a dress when he woke, then into school clothes after breakfast, then back into a dress and heels and jewelry when he got home, then back into PJs before bed.

Saying good night one night, smoothing the hair back off Claude's forehead, listening to him tell them sweetly, sleepily, about his day, Rosie squeezed Penn's hand for support and took a deep breath. 'Does it make you tired, all that changing of clothes?' she asked gently.

Claude's forehead wrinkled. His tiny shoulders shrugged. 'It's okay.'

'You know,' Penn said carefully, so carefully, 'you could wear a dress or a skirt to school if you wanted. It would be okay.'

'No it wouldn't,' said Claude.

Rosie felt her eyes produce actual tears of relief that Claude didn't leap at this chance immediately. But she persisted anyway. 'Sure it would.'

'The other kids would make fun of me.' Claude's eyes were full too.

'That's true,' Penn admitted. 'They would. But that would be okay. They wouldn't mean it. They would make fun of you for a day or two then forget all about you and make fun of something else.'

'They would never forget. They would make fun of me every day forever.'

'We would help you,' said Rosie. 'We could think of things to say back. We could think of ways to ignore them.'

'We could not.'

'We could talk to Miss Appleton.'

'Miss Appleton doesn't like me.'

'Of course she does!'

'No, she thinks I'm weird. And if I wear a dress to school, she'll think I'm really weird.'

'You wouldn't be weird. You would be you in a dress. Smart, sweet, kind, funny you in a dress. It would be okay.'

'No,' said Claude, 'this is okay. Real clothes at home, school clothes at school. I can just change.'

That 'real' reverberated around in Penn's brain until it was deafening. 'Well that's okay too, of course. But you should be able to be who you are, wear what you like. The other kids, your teacher, your friends, everyone would be fine. Everyone loves you for who you are.'

'No one but you,' said Claude. 'No one but us. We are the only ones.'

We are the only ones. This was the part that haunted Rosie, hunted her. It supplanted quite a few other concerns to leapfrog up to number three or four. Rosie was gratified that Claude felt so supported at home. Rosie was horrified that Claude felt so precarious outside of it. But Rosie was also used to conflicting emotions, for she was a mother and knew every moment of every day that no one out in the world could ever love or value or nurture her children as well as she could and yet that it was necessary nonetheless to send them out into that world anyway.

Rosie's number-one concern was: what would make Claude happy?

Penn's number-one concern was: what would make Claude happy?

But happy is harder than it sounds.

Halloween

So Claude changed clothes, his parents worried and did a lot of laundry, and a couple months of kindergarten passed without further incident. With five kids in school, Rosie took more day shifts at the hospital, worked fewer nights. Penn put more DN words on pages. They weren't always good ones, but they occurred, and that was something. The weather turned cold. The air smelled of snow, the house of fires in the fireplace and soups on the stove. There was a lull as everything froze over, froze in place.

For Halloween, Roo wanted to be a pirate which was easy enough, and Ben wanted to be Roo which was easier still, and Rigel and Orion wanted to be conjoined twins which they practically were anyway. Everyone waited for Claude to say he wanted to be a princess or a mermaid or Miss Piggy. But Claude could not decide what he wanted to be. It was breakfast conversation for many chilly weeks running.

'Everyone else was a pumpkin in kindergarten,' Rosie offered. For a few years there, they'd gotten away with passing costumes – or at least costume ideas; often the costumes themselves did not survive the day – to the next brother down. 'You would be the cutest pumpkin.'

'I could knit you a stem,' Rigel offered, 'or a leaf, but the orange part would take forever.'

'I could make you a policeman,' said Orion. 'Or a fireman. Or a fisherman. I have supplies for all of those.'

'Police officer,' Rosie corrected. 'Firefighter. Fisher . . . person? Mariner? What do you call that?'

'Girls don't fish,' said Roo.

'Sure they do,' said his father.

'Not for a living,' said Roo. 'And Claude is a man. So if he were a po-lice officer, he would be a policeman.'

'Claude is a boy, not a man.'

'Policeboy,' said Orion. 'Fireboy. FISHBOY!'

'Why doesn't he just dress up as a girl?' said Roo, as if his brother weren't at the table with him. 'That would be easy. He does it every day anyway.'

'Do you want to be a girl for Halloween, Claude?' Rosie was careful to keep her voice exactly neutral. If he were going to wear a dress to school, Halloween was the day to do it. Maybe this wasn't a bad idea. Maybe he'd get it out of his system.

'Girl's not a costume,' Claude said reasonably. And then, 'I want to be Grumwald.'

'Grumwald?' said Penn.

'Yeah. Grumwald.'

'You can't be Grumwald.'

'Why not?'

'Grumwald doesn't look like anything. Grumwald's only a story we made up. Grumwald doesn't exist corporeally.'

'Core what really?' Claude was still precocious, but he was only five.

'Grumwald doesn't exist except in our heads,' Penn revised.

'That's good,' said Orion. 'Easy costume.'

'I don't need help,' said Claude. 'I'll make it myself. What does he look like, Daddy? In your head?'

'He looks like you,' Penn said.

'Why him?' said Roo.

'Well, he used to look like you,' Penn told Roo. 'He looked like each of you. He looks like all of you really.'

The morning of Halloween was the first one in months Claude came downstairs in anything other than a dress. He was wearing jeans and a gray T-shirt and a crown he'd cut out of red construction paper. It took Rosie a heartbeat to place him. It had been so long since he'd come down to breakfast looking like her little boy.

'Arrr, that's not a costume.' Roo popped up the moss-stitch eye patch Rigel had knit him to look at his baby brother.

'Yes it is.'

'You're just dressed as you.'

'Without the girl clothes,' said Ben.

'Claude as Claude instead of Claudette is not a costume,' said Roo.

'Dad said Grumwald looks like me,' said Claude.

'No one's going to give you candy without a costume,' said Rigel. Penn suspected that was not strictly true, but he did worry (number seventeen or so) Claude would feel left out at school when everyone else was dressed up.

'This isn't all of it,' said Claude.

'Where's the rest?' said Orion.

'It's a surprise.'

'Well, get it!' everyone said.

Claude grinned, clomped upstairs, clomped back down again. In his hands, a foot, maybe more, taller than he was, Claude held a cardboard cutout, crude but recognizably human: circle head atop rounded shoulders, no neck, sloping into too-long, uneven arms with tiny hands – Claude seemed to have traced his own and cut them out – a torso attached to thick legs with feet sticking out in opposite directions at right angles, the toes all stacked atop one another as if viewed from above, all of it covered head to toe in aluminum foil. A hole was cut out for the mouth with a balloon taped underneath. Glued all over the balloon were words he must have cut from catalogs, for the scraps read things like 'Available in size S, M, L, and XL', and, 'Order by Dec. 21 for guaranteed Christmas delivery!' and 'Choose from honey lavender, meadow sage, pumpkin orange, or heathered denim', and 'Now with leak guard technology!'

'What the hell is that thing?' said Roo.

'Roo!' Rosie and Penn said together, though it was not an unreasonable question.

Claude propped his cutout up against the kitchen wall and stood on his tiptoes to peer around the balloon into its mouth, and it dawned on Penn like sudden sun: Prince Grumwald peering into the armor outside his bedroom to release infinite story, words without end, the ceaseless narrative of catalog shopping. Tears came to his eyes immediately. It was the most perfect Halloween costume he had ever seen.

'That's gay,' said Roo.

'Roo!'

'It's creepy,' Rigel and Orion said together.

'It's Halloween.' Claude shrugged.

'That's true,' they agreed.

'How will you hold that thing and your candy?' Roo asked.

Claude grinned, produced a hollow plastic pumpkin also covered in aluminum foil, and hung it from a hook taped to the back of the knight's right hand.

'No one will know who you're supposed to be,' Ben warned.

'No one ever does,' said Claude.

There was a party at school in the morning, then a parade through the neighborhood so all the parents and grandparents could stand along the streets and shiver and take pictures, then a dance, the elementary-school version of which was that everyone wiggled around on the blacktop drinking hot cider and eating bat brownies and pumpkin bars and doing the Monster Mash. How that song was still in circulation, Penn could not fathom. Roo and Ben had their own Halloween dance, the alarmingly grown-up kind, at the middle school, which suddenly seemed impossibly far away. Penn had deliberated what sort of fatherly advice might be most appropriate and useful for an almost teenage dance and finally decided that the greatest assistance he could give them was not making a big deal about it. Still, he was glad he didn't have to watch. Instead, he stood and chitchatted with the other elementary school parents and watched his little ones. Rigel and Orion, stuffed together into an XXL T-shirt, looped ear to ear by a custom-knit extra-wide orange-and-black headband, were fighting about whether both of them or neither of them wanted more cider. Claude was off by himself under the basketball hoops, slow dancing with his tinfoil knight, the catalog text balloon bouncing lightly against the top of his head.

'You still here?' said a voice by Penn's shoulder. Dwight Harmon. The principal.

'Afraid so.'

'Rosie at work?'

'Halloween. Big day for emergency rooms.'

'I can imagine,' the principal said. 'How are the boys?'

'Which ones?'

'Roo and Ben. How's middle school?'

'So far . . .' Penn trailed off. He'd meant to add 'so good', but he wasn't sure. He and Dwight went back a long way – they were on their fifth boy together after all – and Penn knew better than to bullshit the principal.

'Big dance today?'

Penn nodded.

'You got out of chaperoning?'

'I had to be here, didn't I?' said Penn.

Dwight grinned. 'That why you keep having kids? So you never have to go to the middle school dance? Lucky bastard.'

'You too.' Penn smiled. The superintendent's office had wanted to promote Dwight to middle school principal, but he liked where he was.

'Speaking of dancing, isn't he sweet?' The principal nodded toward Claude and his knight errant. 'Your youngest grooving with his robot.'

'First love,' said Penn. 'Breaks your heart. Every time.'

'What's he dressed up as? An engineer? An inventor?'

'Honestly?' said Penn. 'He's not dressed up as anything.' That crisp fall afternoon – not too cold, still bright, the air sweet with cookies and cider and leaves about to die – was very nearly the last time that was true.

'Is he doing okay?' said the principal. 'Is he happy?'

Penn's first concern. He tore his eyes from Claude to look over at the principal. 'I think so?'

'I'm not so sure,' Dwight said gently.

'Is he . . . acting out? Falling behind?'

'No, no. Nothing like that. He's smart. He's bright. He's well behaved. He's a good little student.'

'But?'

'But for a five-year-old, he's awfully quiet.'

'Sensitive?'

'Yeah, maybe. But he doesn't seem to have many friends.'

'Shy?'

'Yeah, maybe. But his pictures give us pause. He does not draw himself as we would expect from such a bright child.'

'Lacks artistic talent?'

'Yeah, maybe, but he's just fashioned a larger-than-life robot out of cardboard, tinfoil, and a balloon.'

'It's a knight,' said Penn. 'And I love it, but I don't think it bespeaks artistic ability. Maybe the kid just can't draw.'

'Maybe,' said the principal, 'but I'd bet not.'

'What would you bet?'

'You'll tell me, Penn. Whenever you and Rosie figure it out. Whenever Claude figures it out. Whatever it turns out your boys need, you know you have only to let me know. And maybe everything's fine. Really. But, well, there are some warning signs. It's good to start thinking about these things early.'

As far as things that went bump in the night, this was the scariest thing that had ever happened to Penn on Halloween.

Homeworking was suspended for the holiday. Snack was deemed redundant given the number of bat brownies and pumpkin bars consumed. There was halfhearted dinner. There was full-hearted trick-or-treating. There was an even-more-protracted-than-usual-owing-to-the-amount-of-sugar-ingested bedtime. Rosie came home, finally, exhausted. Penn wiped peanut-butter-cup remnants from his lips and handed her a folder.

'What's this?'

'Claude's artwork from the last year or so.'

'They gave it to you at school?'

'Some of it. Some of it I found in his room. Some of it was just lying around the house. I'd never really looked at more than one at a time before.'

She held the folder and she held his gaze, and neither said anything. She searched his eyes for something definitive – it's really bad or we're in real trouble or it'll be okay – and finding none of the above, decided maybe it would be good news and took it. 'Can I have dinner first?'

He handed the aluminum-foiled pumpkin over to her and went to heat leftovers. She tore apart an irritatingly small bag of M&M's and opened the folder.

She smiled at what she found inside. Dozens of pictures. In crayon, in washable marker, a few all in green colored pencil. People with no noses but big eyes and big smiles. People whose hair was taller than the rest of them. Dogs with huge, toothy grins. Navy skies that took up no more than the top inch of the page. Penn came in with warmed-up pasta topped with butter and sliced hot dogs. She could think of nothing she'd rather eat.

She smiled at Penn. 'I love them.'

'The pictures?'

'I'm so relieved. When you gave them to me, I thought ... He's no great artist maybe, but he has other talents. And he's only five. I love his whimsy. I love the way he sees the world.'

'How about the way he sees himself?'

'What do you mean?'

Penn nodded at the pile of drawings. 'Look.'

She looked through and found Claude in each one. He was wearing a dress. He was wearing a ball gown and four-inch heels. He had long brown hair or long blond hair or long purple hair or long rainbow hair. Sometimes he had a tail like a mermaid. Sometimes he had a silver necklace like his mother's. That's not what worried Penn, though, who'd ordered them carefully so Rosie could see the progression. In each picture, Claude seemed to be shrinking. He had a big family, yes, so it was hard to fit everyone on the page, and he was the littlest of them, true, but Claude got smaller and smaller. He was smaller than the smiling dog. He was smaller than the stemless flowers. In one, he had wings and was flying in the sky, and he was smaller than the clouds. In another, he was lying in the garden loomed over by a snail. In some, Rosie couldn't even find him. She had to play Where's Waldo until she located tiny Claude, half a centimeter high, behind the chimney of a house or in the corner of the chimp enclosure at the zoo. Or everyone in his giant family – including Jupiter, including the butterflies, including the house itself – had giant smiles, but Claude's frown was so pronounced it dipped over the edges of his chin like a handlebar mustache. Or everyone else was in full color, and Claude had drawn himself in gray or once, worse, white on white. Or everyone was in clothes – hats, scarfs, sweaters, costumes, bathing suits, party dresses, and Claude was wearing nothing, not naked, just a stick figure, just an outline, just a sketch. And then, soon, Claude was nowhere. Rosie Where's-Waldo-ed for fifteen minutes and failed to find him at all.

Maybe

So, gender dysphoria,' Mr Tongo began. 'Congratulations to you both! Mazel tov! How exciting!' Mr Tongo was the hospital handyman Rosie called late in a shift when she was otherwise out of options for a patient. He wasn't really a handyman, of course, though he wasn't a doctor either. Technically, he was some kind of multi-degreed social-working therapist-magician. It wasn't that he made miracle diagnoses or magic cures. It wasn't that he could pull secret strings or unglue red tape. It was that he had an entirely different way of looking at things.

And a different way of looking at things was what they needed. Rosie didn't think there was anything wrong with Claude physically. She didn't think there was anything wrong with Claude emotionally or psychologically either. He was already worried his teacher and his classmates thought he was weird. The third to last thing Rosie wanted to do was make him think his parents thought so too. The second to last thing she wanted to do was make him self-conscious about what he wanted to wear and who he was. But the last thing she wanted to do was ignore her baby as he slipped away from her and disappeared.

In Mr Tongo's office, they all three sat on giant colored balls like they were in some kind of exercise class, Mr Tongo bouncing up and down on his and rubbing his hands together like a kid who'd been promised ice cream after a dinner of French fries. Penn was prepared to defend Claude against people who thought boys in dresses were sick. He was prepared to defend against people who thought his son was repulsive or deviant. He was prepared to defend Claude's right to be Claude in any of his many wonderful manifestations. But he was not prepared for congratulations. 'Uh . . . thanks?'

'Yes! Yes! You should both be very proud.'

'We should?' Penn glanced at Rosie for guidance but found her smiling unquestioningly at Mr Tongo.

'Certainly you should. What an interesting child you're raising – not that gender dysphoria, if that's what this turns out to be, is caused by parenting, good or bad. But you must be doing a fine job if he's come to you and said, "Mother, Dad, I must wear a dress," instead of hiding in shame – not that there's anything to be ashamed of, you understand. And you've said yes to the dress, as they say, the dress and the heels and the pink bikini. What fun! I'm so pleased for you all.'

Rosie put a hand on Penn's arm but did not take her eyes off the bouncing social worker. 'Thank you, Mr Tongo.' Penn could not imagine why she wasn't on a first-name basis with this man. 'We're glad too. But the drawings, the lack of friends, the worry, his changing clothes all the time, his inability to just be himself. Our first concern is his happiness, of course. But not just today.' Because it wasn't that simple, was it? Raising children was the longest of long games. It would make her kids ecstatically happy if she replaced all meals for the next month with Halloween candy consumed in front of the television and then let them skip showers until Thanksgiving, but in the long run, one imagined they'd miss school, their teeth, and not smelling like feet. 'We want him to be happy next week, next year, the years to come too. It's hard to make out this path, but it's even harder to see where it leads. We want him to be happy and comfortable of course, but we're not sure how best to make that happen.'

While Rosie talked, Penn tried to decide what to make of Mr Tongo and found nothing to hang on to. He imagined writing him into the DN and couldn't think how he'd describe him. Mr Tongo might have been sixty-five with good skin or thirty-five and prematurely gray, his smoky hair alternately patted down and sticking out in all directions. He might have had a trace of an accent Penn didn't recognize or the remnants of an old, overcome speech impediment, or it may have been simply that he spoke with an odd quizzical deliberateness at once welcoming and unsettling. Any race or nationality at all you cared to name, Penn could believe Mr Tongo was at least half a member of it. He wore scrubs, in case any of his patients had to vomit or bleed, Penn supposed, though on the wall behind him he had a drawing of a bear, also in scrubs, holding up a sign that read REMEMBER: I AM YOUR FRIEND, BUT I AM NOT A DOCTOR.

He was fiddling with a magnifying glass he picked up off his desk. 'As you may know, gender dysphoria is a condition wherein the patient's assigned sex – their anatomy, their genitalia – does not match their – some say preferred, some say affirmed, some say true – gender identity.' He closed one eye and peered through the glass at them. 'It's the Case of the Mistaken Genitalia.' Then, just when Penn was about to write Mr Tongo off as too quirky to address the gravity of their situation, he stopped bouncing and sleuthing and congratulating. 'Now, who knows? Maybe he'll grow out of this, or maybe it's here to stay. Maybe he'll be trans and maybe he'll be she, or maybe he'll be something we haven't thought of yet. There's no need to settle on a label at the moment. The important thing is this: prepubertal children suffer from gender dysphoria in direct proportion to attitudes and expectations they encounter at home, at school, and in their communities. If the parents are sending negative messages – even silent ones – that what a child does and who a child is are not okay, those are very powerful for a young person. Even though your intentions might be only to protect him from a hard, often intolerant society by helping him fit into prescribed gender molds, you may unwittingly be telling him, "Act this way, behave this way, deny yourself, or you'll lose my love."'

'But we haven't made a big deal about the dresses or the barrettes or anything,' said Penn. 'We don't make a big deal about any of the weird stuff any of our boys wear. We've barely mentioned it.'

'And that's very enlightened and generous, I'm sure.' Mr Tongo's hands waved in all directions. 'Wonderful! Brilliant! But the rest of the world won't agree, I'm afraid. It may be okay with you if he wears a dress, but it will be less okay with the kids at school. Or their parents. It may be okay with you if he wears earrings and heels, but it's not always going to be okay at camp or soccer or the park. You're not raising this child in isolation. Perhaps you've been approving, but it's been hard at school?'

'He hasn't been engaging in this behavior at school,' said Rosie.

'He hasn't been dressing up at school,' Mr Tongo corrected. 'Maybe during free choice, though, he's playing with dolls when the other boys are playing with trucks. Maybe during lunch he sits with the girls instead of the boys. Maybe when the teacher says boys line up on the right, girls on the left, he stands in the middle looking confused. Perhaps his desire to disappear or his sense that he is disappearing has to do not with you but with everyone else in his world telling him to stop acting like a girl.'

Penn was holding his head with his hands and his elbows with his knees. He did not look up. 'What does that mean – acting like a girl?'

'Oooh, good question. Well, it means any number of things, doesn't it? Cultural expectations and proscriptions touch nearly every aspect of our lives but vary, also, for each individual, not to mention the usual social determinates such as—'

'I understand that,' Penn interrupted, 'but if it's so culturally determined and individually experienced, what do you mean when you say "dysphoric"? We've never said to him that he can't play with his dolls or bake or wear a dress because only girls do those things. Absent any other influences, it's obvious to me that any five-year-old faced with the choice of toe-colored toes or rainbow-colored toes would choose the latter. That's normal. That's not dysphoric. That doesn't make him a girl. That makes him a kid.'

'Hear, hear!' The man was starting to bounce again. 'Bravo!'

'Isn't it also,' Rosie added, 'what we're all striving for? Or should be? A wider range of normal and acceptable? Kids who can wear what's comfortable and play however they like?'

'Yes, oh yes!' Mr Tongo cheered.

'Then what's going on here?' The bees behind Penn's ribs were back. 'What's making this kid feel so . . . lost?'

'He wore a pink bikini all summer long,' Rosie added, 'with great enthusiasm. But now suddenly—'

'Out in public?' Mr Tongo interrupted. 'Or just at home with his family?'

'Mostly at home,' Rosie admitted, 'but he wore it to the end-of-summer pool party. The whole neighborhood was there. People were pointing and laughing and whispering, and he didn't even seem to notice. He was so proud. What's changed?'

'What *has* changed?' Mr Tongo asked quietly.

'School,' Rosie and Penn knew together.

Mr Tongo nodded. 'Children learn many wonderful things in kindergarten. How to line up for lunch. How to use inside voices. How to not push people. Important life skills for sure. I use them every day myself. But they learn other things too: you have to conform, or people might not like you; you have to be the same because different doesn't feel good. At home, Claude's loved no matter what. At school, it sometimes feels the opposite: you are not loved no matter what.'

'So we should homeschool.' Rosie was already rearranging her work schedule in her mind. Penn could teach reading and writing. She could do biology and anatomy. Surely, those were mainstays of the kindergarten curriculum? Maybe her mother could—

'Of course not.' Mr Tongo laughed. 'These are not bad things for Claude to understand. These are things we all have to grapple with. A five-year-old has much to learn. When people are annoying, it feels good to push them but we mustn't. Even though it's often pleasant to shout, others are trying to concentrate. Though we'd always like to be first, sometimes it's someone else's turn. And when we behave in a manner other people don't expect, there will be consequences.'

'How do we teach him that?' said Penn's bees.

'You don't!' Mr Tongo clapped his hands, delighted. 'He's already learned that. You have to help him unlearn it. You have to help him see that if he's disappearing from the world, that's too high a price to pay for fitting in. He has to see how "You shouldn't push even though you want to" isn't the same as "You shouldn't wear a dress even though you want to". None of that's any different for Claude than for anybody else. It's all part of growing up.'

Rosie nodded and tried to believe this and ventured to ask, since he'd brought it up, 'What will he be? When he grows up?'

'Who knows?' Mr Tongo smiled. And though Rosie had to admit that of course that was the right answer, the only honest answer there was, the only answer there could be, the question itself was starting to take over her sleepless middle-of-the-night ruminations.

'We'll have to wait and see.' Mr Tongo shrugged but not unhappily. 'Exciting! But wherever it goes from here, the best thing about gender dysphoria is this. Ready? Claude's not sick! Isn't that wonderful?'

'Yes, but—'

'We don't have to worry yet about who he'll be when he grows up. He's only five! But since he's only five, he can't fight the entire weight of his culture alone. You know who has to do that?'

'Who?' Penn asked, though he knew.

'You must pave his way in his world. And that's very hard, I'm afraid.'

'It's not hard,' said Penn. 'It's parenting.'

'Or it is hard,' Rosie clarified. 'But so is all parenting.'

'At which you're more experienced than most' – they felt worse than when they arrived, but Mr Tongo seemed overjoyed – 'so you're perfect for the job. Let's start with journaling. Oh, this is going to be so much fun!'

Penn did not imagine it was going to be fun. But of the directives with which one left a child's doctor's appointment, journaling was more palatable – and more firmly in his skill set – than most. Every day, they were to write down Claude's boy behaviors and his girl behaviors. That's all they had to do for now, Mr Tongo promised. Step one was gather information. Step one was waiting and seeing but with an emphasis on the seeing. Since in this case, seeing looked a lot like writing and waiting looked a lot like parenting, gender journaling was something Penn felt equipped to do.

But he was wrong. When Claude came down to breakfast that Saturday in a dress made from a belted nightgown of Rosie's, Penn understood that this went in the girl column. When he spent the hour following breakfast driving trains around the track in the opposite direction Rigel and Orion were driving trains around the track so that they crashed into each other and both trains exploded off the track and all three children collapsed in giggles then did it again, he understood that this was meant for the boy column. But then they moved on to LEGOs. Then Rigel and Orion's friend – *girl* friend – Frieda came over wearing jeans and a T-shirt to help crash trains for an hour. Penn was not prepared to say that LEGOs were male or female. Penn was not prepared to say that playing with a friend was male or female. Penn was gratified to see a little girl in pants crashing trains whom no one, so far as he knew, was accusing of gender dysphoria. Penn made a third column . . .

Other
Both
Unsure
Unclear
Unfair
None of Your Fucking Business

Ways in Which This Exercise Is Asinine

. . . before he finally landed on:

Maybe.

Maybe what, he could not say. But that was the beauty of it.

After dinner, after storytime and bedtime, Rosie and Penn opened a bottle of wine and compared lists. Penn had kept his only halfheartedly. The list of maybes was long. The list of maybes was nearly everything. Rosie's list was more revealing, broken into two columns, not three, and seeing much of what Penn missed. Nearly everything fell into her girl column. While Rigel and Orion built LEGO cars and LEGO trucks and used LEGO Batman to smash LEGO police stations, Claude built LEGO vacation homes and pony ranches and populated them with LEGO mamas and babies. While Rigel and Orion set the trains back up for their recurring race toward inevitable doom, Claude tended to the victims.

'I don't understand your list,' said Penn.

'I understand yours,' said Rosie.

'What does that mean?'

'Same thing. You don't understand my list because you don't see how someone like me could have made it.'

'That's true.'

'I know.'

'You're a scientist, Rosie. Women aren't scientists. So that goes in the boy column. You're a doctor – an ER doctor, not a girly one like pediatrician or gynecology. So that goes in the boy column too. Your so-called husband is a writer, an artist, and not the kind who makes money. The other kind. He cooks dinner—'

'I cook dinner some nights.'

'Not that well. He folds laundry—'

'And puts it away.'

'And puts it away. He does homework duty. He does bedtime duty.'

'He is very girly,' Rosie agreed, kissing his neck.

'It's very boy-column to be married to such a girly fellow as this.'

'It's very girl-column to use the term "fellow".'

'It's very boy-column even to be attracted to such a girly fellow as this.'

'Who says I'm attracted to him?' Rosie asked, sucking his earlobe.

'You initiate sex' – Penn was unbuttoning her shirt – 'which is hardly ladylike.'

'Who said anything about sex?'

'Though these,' Penn admitted, undoing her bra, 'make a pretty compelling case for your feminine nature.'

'They are persuasive,' Rosie agreed.

'You're willing – nay, eager – to have sex on the sofa while your kids are upstairs sleeping. A more canonically feminine mother would never risk their walking in on us and imperil her children's emotional equilibrium in this way.'

'It's cute you think they're sleeping.' She slipped off her skirt then her underwear while she half listened to what she guessed was Rigel and Orion pounding what she guessed was modeling clay into what she guessed was the upstairs rug. 'Plus, a real woman is always available to her husband to fulfill his sexual urges.'

'But has no sexual urges of her own.' Penn slid his pants off. 'And she only does it in the bed. In the dark.'

'On the bottom,' Rosie added, climbing on top of him.

'So you see where I think this list is bullshit.' Though Penn was having some trouble concentrating on his argument, he was still pretty confident he was right. 'Even if we're willing to grant identifiably male behavior and identifiably female behavior –'

'Well, maybe in some cases—'

'– we don't embody it anyway.'

'Tell me about our embodies.'

'You are not a traditionally feminine woman—'

'I will show you how wrong you are.'

'And I'm not a traditionally masculine man.'

'Let me see.'

'He hasn't learned traditional gender roles at home. He's not failing to conform – there's nothing to conform to. He's not subverting sex-based expectations because we don't have any sex-based expectations.'

'I have a few.'

'We might not be good role models,' Penn breathed.

'We're very good role models,' said Rosie.

'We might not be the right people for this exercise.'

'We are exactly the right people for this exercise.'

'We might be thinking of different exercises,' said Penn.

'We might be speaking of different exercises,' Rosie murmured, 'but I bet we're thinking about the same one.'

At that point, Penn found he could not disagree.

The waiting part of waiting and seeing looked like it always looks: doing something else, worrying, going on with your life, raising your little boys and bigger boys and boys who might be something else or something more. Rosie and Penn could not imagine a child understanding something as complex as the thing they needed to explain to their youngest son. Wearing a dress did not make him a girl, but neither did bearing a penis indelibly make him a boy if that's not what he was or wanted to be, though if it was what he was and wanted to be, he was welcome to be it and still wear a dress if he liked. Or to put it another way: wear whatever the hell you want and who cares what anyone else thinks. Though everyone else will have thoughts. And they're unlikely to keep those thoughts to themselves or be entirely kind. Though that doesn't mean you shouldn't do whatever you want, just that you should be forewarned that if you do, there will be consequences. Not that that's not true of everything – all actions have consequences. Not that the consequences in this case suggested he should not do what he wanted to do and be who he was. None of which was to say that all decisions could be made without regard for consequences. If Roo dared him to stuff leftover Halloween candy into the Thanksgiving turkey, as he had dared Orion the year before, Claude would do well to consider the consequences of his actions. If his teacher told him it was inappropriate to talk to his neighbor during Math Trays, that was different than if his teacher told him it was inappropriate to bring his lunch to school in a purse. If his school friends didn't like his choice of clothes, then maybe they were being mean or maybe they just needed educating or maybe—

'I don't have any school friends,' Claude interrupted.

'You must,' his parents insisted. Claude was funny and bright, loving and lovable. He knew how to share. He didn't pick his nose. He was potty trained. What more would a kindergartener want in a friend?

'But I don't,' Claude said.

'How is that possible?' They meant it as if Claude had claimed gravity did not exist in his kindergarten classroom. As if he claimed the cafeteria were staffed by trained penguins. It seemed just that impossible that anyone could not like baby Claude.

'They think I'm weird.'

'Because you dress like a girl?' said Penn, and Rosie shot him a look. Of course not. He didn't dress like a girl at school. 'Because you bring a purse to lunch?' he amended.

'I don't know. They think I talk weird.'

'How?'

'It's enigmatic.' Claude shrugged. 'Or I am.' Rosie considered that his youngest-of-five vocabulary must confuse most kindergarteners. Many fifth graders. Lots of high school students.

'What would make things easier?' Penn got down on his knees so he could meet his son eye to eye.

'What would make things easier?' Rosie got down on her knees to offer something close to prayer.

'Should we talk to Miss Appleton?'

'Could you spend recess with Orion and Rigel?'

'Should we get you a different lunch tote?'

'Should we set up lots of playdates?'

'Should you join a club or a sport or a band?'

'It's okay.' Tears crawled out of Claude's eyes and nose, and besides he was only five, but he tried to comfort his parents anyway. 'I just feel a little bit sad. Sad isn't bleeding. Sad is okay.'

He was wrong about that though because his happiness was his parents' first concern. Rosie took a bottomless breath and whispered, 'Do you want to be a girl, baby?'

To which Penn, Tongo-tutored, appended, 'Do you think you are a girl?'

They waited, fathomless breath held, fathomless fear held, just barely, at bay.

Claude only cried. 'I don't know.'

And his parents had to admit the question was hard. And his parents had to admit relief that the answer wasn't yes, at least not yet. And his parents had to admit fear because if he didn't know, who did, and if the answer wasn't that, what was it?

'Do you want to be a boy who wears dresses?' Penn tried.

'Do you want to be a boy who wears dresses only on some days?' Rosie added.

'Do you want to go to school naked?' Penn offered to make him laugh.

But Claude did not laugh, so Rosie pulled him into her lap and cradled his head in the bend of one elbow and his knees in the other and rocked him like she had when he was a baby. He fit better then, but he fit pretty well still. 'What would make you happy?' She smiled down at him and shone love deep into his eyes from the depths of her own. 'You can be anyone you want.'

Claude looked love back at his parents and whispered, 'I want to be a night fairy.'

Invention

Their meeting at the school was in the melee of the end of fall term. In the absence of a (deemed sufficiently secular) tree, the ceiling in the foyer was crisscrossed with strands of construction paper garlands and Popsicle-stick ornaments. Posters reminding parents about the winter choir concert and the winter band concert and the winter drama club performance of *Winter Wonderland Wisconsin* covered the windows like an eclipse. Every flat surface seemed to have something sweet to eat piled atop it: a tin of mint green fudge, a Santa mug spilling candy canes, brownies topped with (presumably verboten) red and green Peanut M&M's.

'These seem like tough conditions in which to work,' Rosie marveled while they waited.

'You work in an emergency room,' said Penn.

'Better than trying to educate amped-up, sugar-high six-year-olds while also getting them to do decorations and rehearse a show.'

'What makes you think any education is happening here this month?'

They'd planned their speech the night before, an approximate (for that's all there was) explanation of what Claude was and what he wasn't. It involved a lot of words but boiled down to this: Claude's happiness is our first concern; what can we do to help you to help Claude? They'd been discussing and drafting at the homeworking table when Roo and Ben came downstairs in nothing but boxers and worried expressions hours after their parents had assumed they were asleep.

'We're staging an invention,' said Roo.

'Intervention, you idiot,' said Ben. 'We're staging an intervention.'

'You can't let Claude go to school as a girl,' said Roo.

'He's not going as a girl per se,' said Penn.

'And you definitely can't let him go to school as a night fairy.'

'Do you know what "fairy" means?' said Ben, very seriously. 'Do you know what that's slang for?'

Rosie did, for she was a human on the Earth. 'He's five.'

'Doesn't matter,' her eldest boys said together. And Roo added, earnestly, 'Five-year-olds are mean. Their older brothers and sisters are mean. The kids from other grades are mean.'

'They'll make fun of him,' Ben added. 'It's okay for him to wear what he wants at home, but you can't send him out in the world like that. You don't understand.'

'You're his parents,' Roo pled. 'It's your job to protect him. If we were still there it would be one thing, but now that we're in middle school, he's on his own. Rigel and Orion are not up for the job.'

'He'll get beat up. No one will pick him for their team in gym. No one will sit with him at lunch or hang with him at recess,' Ben warned. 'Why can't he just play dress-up at home? It's for his own protection.'

'Plus it's so . . .'

'What?' said Rosie when Roo trailed off.

'Gay.'

'Well, he's only five,' said Penn, 'but if he's gay, what's the problem with that?'

'There's no problem if he's gay when he's older,' said Ben. 'He just can't be gay right now. When he's older he'll know what to do if someone teases him.'

'Maybe he can learn kung fu or something,' Roo added. 'But right now, he's just not equipped to be gay. That's why kids aren't gay when they're in kindergarten.'

'I'm not sure that's why,' said Rosie.

'It's just weird,' said Roo. 'It's weird that he wants to wear girl clothes and lip gloss and heels and jewelry. It's not normal. It's freaky.'

'So are you.' Penn was met with stares of incredulity from all parties, including the one he was married to. 'You're all freaky. You're all weird. We're a weird family. Roo, how many kids in your class besides you play football and flute? Ben, how many kids in your class skipped a grade because they started making their own homework at age four? Claude's weird, but he's not just weird, he's also remarkable. It's pretty amazing that he knows what he's supposed to wear and wants to wear something else anyway, that he knows who he's supposed to be but recognizes that he's something else instead.'

'But he's so little.' Ben looked helpless.

'Little like he can't fight back,' said Roo.

'Little like you could tell him what to do and he'd do it,' said Ben. 'Tell him what to wear to school and he will. Tell him he's a boy and not a night fairy.'

'You can't tell people what to be, I'm afraid,' said Rosie. 'You can only love and support who they already are. But thank you for coming to talk to us. And thank you for trying to protect him. That's sweet and brotherly of you.'

'I am nothing if not brotherly,' said Ben.

'Not true,' said Roo. 'You're also smelly.'

'You're the one who has to leave your shoes outside at night so you don't slip into a coma in your sleep.'

'You're the one even Jupiter can't stand to smell in the morning. And she likes the smell of dog ass.'

'Don't say "ass", Roo,' said Rosie.

'Bedtime,' said Penn. 'Past bedtime. Thank you for your concern. We'll take it under advisement.'

Now Rosie and Penn were sitting in the principal's office feeling altogether less sure of themselves than they had pretended to the boys the night before. They'd made the meeting with Dwight Harmon only, but the indefatigably perky Miss Appleton was there as well, along with the district representative (representing what or whom was not made clear) Victoria Revels. Victoria Revels sounded like she'd be a lot of fun, but that was only the first of many erroneous assumptions Rosie and Penn made that day.

'Will Claude be changing his name?' Victoria Revels asked when they came to the end of their carefully prepared speech. Rosie and Penn looked at each other.

'I don't think so,' said Penn. 'Why?'

'Then we can table all name and pronoun adjustments for the moment.' She was looking at a checklist that seemed to run on to several pages. 'If that should change, please let us know right away.'

Dwight Harmon looked up from all the printed-in-quadruplicate paperwork to two blank and petrified faces. 'Relax, guys. Claude's not our first child with special needs. And Claude's not the district's first transgender child. We've got everything under control.'

Penn felt the bees in his chest turn into something hopping. Crickets, maybe, or frogs. 'He just wants to come to school in a dress for the moment,' he fumbled. 'That doesn't make him . . .'

He trailed off, and Rosie took the baton. 'He's not . . . we haven't settled on the label "transgender" per se.'

'You may not have,' said Ms Revels, 'but paperwork-wise, that's what a boy coming to school as a girl is. Transgender. That said, it is not necessary to officially change his name. Many school districts in this country require an official court order or change to the birth certificate. We are not one of those districts, so faculty and staff will be able to call your child whatever you decide, but you have to let us know, and you should be advised that change is not instantaneous.'

No. As far as Penn's frogs were concerned, it seemed quite a bit faster than that.

'Now, Claude will have to use the bathroom in the nurse's office,' she continued. 'He can't use the staff restroom due to legal considerations. He can't use the girls' restroom due to safety considerations. We can't make him use the boys' restroom if he is not comfortable doing so.'

'The nurse's office is right next to the kindergarten classrooms anyway,' Dwight assured them. 'I learned long ago that kindergarten is where you want the nurse to be able to get as quickly as possible. So it shouldn't be too isolating or inconvenient. If in the future that poses a problem – Claude transitions fully to a girl, say, and feels shut out of the social role the restroom comes to play in older girls' lives – you'll let us know, and we'll figure out a different arrangement.'

More blank stares, faces paling to a whiter shade of Wisconsin winter sky.

'Ah, that's right!' Dwight grinned. 'You guys don't know anything about the social memes of girls. Aren't you in for a treat!'

They had no idea, but they were starting to doubt it.

'Now, Miss Appleton here' – even the district representative could not call the woman by her first name – 'will talk about what this is going to look like at the classroom level.'

Miss Appleton smiled at them like five-year-olds. 'We're very excited to work with Claude. He's such a special b . . . uh, child. But I do think we should all expect that there might be some questions at first.'

'You think?' Penn was starting to see that Miss Appleton's default tense was conditional: Now, children, let's decide whether or not it's good decision making to feed crayons to the hamster. Boys and girls, should we have a cookie party this afternoon, or would we perhaps prefer to continue talking to our neighbors when I have two fingers clearly raised for quiet and have already sung the listening song?

'We don't want to discourage the other little boys and girls from asking questions,' she patiently, so patiently, explained. 'We must prepare Claude for how he will answer them. Curiosity is natural. It comes from the children's desire to help their friend. I know Claude doesn't want to hurt their feelings by refusing to answer them or by choosing to interpret their innocent questions as being unkind.'

'You should spend winter break practicing, working with him on answers.' Victoria Revels was much less patient than Miss Appleton.

'Answers to what?' said Rosie.

'You can expect elementary schoolchildren to ask questions such as' – Ms Revels was reading off her paperwork – '"Why are you wearing a dress? Boys can't wear skirts. Are you a girl? What happened to your penis? Why are you wearing earrings or other jewelry or makeup if applicable? Why is your hair long and/or in barrettes or other feminine headwear? What happened to your penis?" Hmm, they've listed that one twice.'

'Is it entirely appropriate' – Rosie directed this toward Dwight Harmon – 'for kindergarteners to be discussing penises so . . . ?'

'Willy-nilly?' Penn was nervous.

The principal just managed to suppress a smile in front of the district representative but declined to answer the question.

'Do you have answers you'd recommend?' Rosie asked Victoria Revels.

'He should tell the truth.' She was a TV lawyer giving advice to someone wrongfully accused.

'Unfortunately, he doesn't know what that is,' said Penn. 'He has no idea why he wants to wear dresses and jewelry. Do you?' Miss Appleton fingered the gold birds hanging from each ear but said nothing. 'Like all of us, he has no idea why he is who he is or why he wants what he wants.'

'I imagine the specific answers are less of an issue,' Dwight suggested, 'than the tenor of his reply. As long as he can be calm and open –'

'And remember to use the nurse's bathroom,' interrupted Victoria Revels.

'– and remember to use the nurse's bathroom, he should be fine.'

'As long as he doesn't bring peanut butter for lunch,' said Rosie.

'Or jelly you've dipped your peanut butter knife in,' Miss Appleton added. 'Like if you were eating peanut butter over the weekend or something.'

Carmelo came up for the holidays armed, grandmotherly, with gifts. She brought Roo and Ben an apparatus to turn the dining/homeworking table into a dining/homeworking/Ping-Pong table. She brought Rigel patterns to knit a bowling set – balls, pins, bowling slippers, and drink cozies. He was excited but disappointed he couldn't knit the lane as well. She brought Orion a Sherlock Holmes costume, so he spent the whole break investigating mysteries. Since there were no mysteries as such, he had to plant clues to discover himself. Soon fingerprints smeared all the mirrors, and scraps of scribbled-on paper accidentally fell behind desks, and rugs were helped to fray in suggestive and incriminating ways until Rosie put an abrupt stop to that particular line of investigation. Carmelo brought Claude a new tea-length dress because he'd outgrown the other one. She brought him a giant bag of new school clothes for a new year – skirts and casual dresses and cute cardigans with frilly tanks to go underneath and tights to keep his legs warm. She brought a pair of wings you donned simply by slipping your arms through the straps like a backpack, no more or less monumental than that. For New Year's, she brought supplies to make brownies, banana splits, and noisemakers, never mind no one celebrating anything anywhere had noisemakers louder than the children themselves.

Rosie and Penn went out, their first New Year's Eve out since the one before Roo was born, the difference now being basically everything, inclusive of the fact that they lacked the organization to have made a reservation or the energy to stay up past 9:45. They wound up at a coffee shop, where they drank tea with the grad students who had stayed in town over the holiday and made dinner out of two muffins and a chocolate-chip cookie.

Rosie didn't feel hungry anyway. Rosie wasn't sure she would feel hungry ever again. She gripped her temples and tried to decide whether, if she let go, her face would crash into the table or her head would float up through the ceiling into the sky like a balloon, smaller and smaller until it disappeared forever. 'Remind me again why we're doing this.'

Penn didn't need to ask which 'this' she meant. 'We asked him. This is what he said he wanted.'

'He doesn't know what he wants. He's only five.'

'In order to be happy,' Penn added.

'He can't possibly understand, never mind weigh, what's going to happen when he goes to school dressed as a girl.'

'A fairy.'

'A girl fairy.'

'True.'

'Next week,' Rosie added, just in case he was missing the enormity of the situation.

'Also true.'

'Why would we ask him what he wants anyway? He wants to sleep in the crate with Jupiter. He thinks high heels are comfortable. This is clearly not a human whose judgment should be used to make major life decisions.'

'You're not wrong.' Penn's face felt frozen in a pose he hoped suggested concerned optimism rather than panicked mania. He remembered their first date, all those little lifetimes ago, another evening when he could not calm his racing heart or make his face do as he wished. If this worked out just a fraction as well as that had, it would be okay. He wanted also to believe that because that evening had worked out as well as it had, perhaps they were protected, perhaps nothing could go all that wrong. But maybe it was just the opposite.

Rosie felt only fear. Rosie felt deafened by the voices howling in her head that she was mad to consent to this, that it was her judgment which was not to be trusted. And underneath that cacophony she could just make out the narrator who pointed quite peaceably to the fork in the road before them. The path on the right was paved and shady, rolling gently along a childhood filled with acceptance to an adulthood marked by requited love, grandchildren, and joy, whereas the other path was rock-strewn and windblown, uphill both directions, and led she had no idea where. Here she was at the crossroads letting her baby boy run blindly down the path on the left (in a skirt and heels) while the narrator looked on reprovingly.

'It just seems like such a hard road' – she took deep breaths until she felt herself inflated to the brink of bursting – 'such a tough life. This is not the easy way.'

'No,' Penn agreed, 'but I'm not sure easy is what I want for the kids anyway.'

She looked up at him. 'Why the hell not?'

'I mean, if we could have everything, sure. If we can have it all, yeah, I wish them easy, successful, fun-filled lives, crowned with good friends, attentive lovers, heaps of money, intellectual stimulation, and good views out the window. I wish them eternal beauty, international travel, and smart things to watch on TV. But if I can't have everything, if I only get a few, I'm not sure easy makes my wish list.'

'Really?'

'Easy is nice, but it's not as good as getting to be who you are or stand up for what you believe in,' said Penn. 'Easy is nice, but I wonder how often it leads to fulfilling work or partnership or being.'

'Easy probably rules out having children,' Rosie admitted.

'Having children, helping people, making art, inventing anything, leading the way, tackling the world's problems, overcoming your own. I don't know. Not much of what I value in our lives is easy. But there's not much of it I'd trade for easy either, I don't think.'

'But it's terrifying,' she whispered. 'If it were the right thing to do, wouldn't we know it?'

'When was the last time something was bothering one of the kids or he was acting strange or he wasn't sleeping or doing well in math or sharing nicely during free-choice time, and we knew why?'

'*Knew* why?' Rosie said.

'Knew why. Absolutely knew what was wrong and what should be done to fix it and how to make that happen.'

'As a parent?'

'As a parent.'

'Never?'

'Never,' Penn agreed. 'Not ever. Not once. You never know. You only guess. This is how it always is. You have to make these huge decisions on behalf of your kid, this tiny human whose fate and future is entirely in your hands, who trusts you to know what's good and right and then to be able to make that happen. You never have enough information. You don't get to see the future. And if you screw up, if with your incomplete, contradictory information you make the wrong call, well, nothing less than your child's entire future and happiness is at stake. It's impossible. It's heartbreaking. It's maddening. But there's no alternative.'

'Sure there is,' she said.

'What?'

'Birth control.'

'I think that ship has sailed.'

'So the comfort you can offer me about sending our son to school next week dressed as a girl fairy is that it seems like a good guess.'

Penn shrugged. 'It's worth a shot.'

'It would be nice to be a little more certain.'

'Then we should have gotten a dog.'

'We did get a dog.'

'Instead.'

'Happy New Year.' She leaned across the table to kiss him.

'It's 9:15,' he said, but he kissed her back.

Three nights later, the one before school started up again, Penn had a full set for storytime. More and more lately, it was just Claude, Rigel, and Orion, but this night, everyone was anxious – anxiety being as contagious as anything Rosie saw in the emergency room – and when Penn opened the door to Claude's room, he found five boys, ages five to thirteen, piled on the tiny single bed.

Since Grumwald had been joined by a night-fairy princess named Stephanie, Claude and the twins had been making a persuasive case against the notion of bedtime as a calm, peaceful winding down before sleep. It was more like the floor of the House of Commons. Rigel and Orion only wanted to hear about Grumwald; Claude only wanted to hear about Princess Stephanie. Fortunately, they had decided to work together and help each other out. Not Claude and the twins. Grumwald and Stephanie.

'She couldn't help him be a prince really,' Penn explained to his subdued brood. 'There was nothing she could do to lessen all the ribbon cutting and baby kissing and peasant mediation that came with the job. She couldn't ease the student government love triangle either – the secretary simply would not see reason. But Algebra II? Now that she could do something about. She didn't have much of a head for numbers herself because she was magic, and magic people have no need for math, but she thought that trick – magic – might work for Grumwald too. She had quite the toolbox, but unfortunately, the only way to see what worked for any given problem was trial and error. He got a C minus on the quiz where he kissed the frog she gave him. He got a B minus on the test where he kept the eye of newt in his pocket, and that was better, but a B minus still wasn't very princely in his father's opinion. He couldn't even answer half the problems on the homework assignment he did while rubbing a lamp Stephanie thought might be magic. Crying on the grave of a would-be fairy godmother she pointed him toward yielded a *please see me* on the imaginary numbers worksheet (Stephanie's question was if they're imaginary who really cares, but the answer to that, unfortunately, was Grum's algebra teacher). In the end, what worked was what she should have known all along: magic wands are good for practically anything. Grumwald was delighted. He could rejoin Mathletes.

'He had a harder time helping her out though. He was asleep while she was doing stars. Without wings, he couldn't reach anyway. In the end though what he could give her was better than magic wands and magic frogs and magic lamps. Better *and* more magical. What he gave her was moral support and unconditional love. He promised to be there for her always, even times when the sky proved too vast and the night was dark because she couldn't kindle all the stars. He would light her way instead, he promised. He would be her Polaris, her celestial navigator, her astral guide. And whenever she came back to Earth, Grumwald promised, he would be there, waiting.'

Roo looked his father in the eye. 'That was so cheesy, Dad.'

'See, this is why it's better when it's just a prince.' Orion rolled onto the floor. 'Princesses are so corny.'

'It wasn't Stephanie who got all emotional.' Claude stood up on the bed, hands on nightgowned hips. 'That was Grumwald. Stephanie was cool with her gadgets like James Bond.'

'James Bond has nothing in common with Princess Stephanie,' said Rigel. 'James Bond would never use a magic wand for algebra.'

'Algebra II,' said Penn.

But after everyone else left, Claude sat then scooted down the bed to hug Penn hard. 'I got it, Daddy.'

'Got what?'

'You'll always love me and support me no matter what. Even if it goes bad tomorrow, you'll be waiting for me at home.'

'Not true,' said Penn. 'I'll be waiting for you on the playground at school.'

No one slept well, and breakfast was a sleepy affair. Rosie considered whether it would be good parenting or bad to pour coffee all around. Claude came down, a little pale maybe, in a brown denim skirt, brown tights, a pink sweater, and penny loafers. He had pink barrettes in his still very short hair. His wings stood gauzy, arched and defiant on his back, and he wouldn't take them off even when it meant he had to eat breakfast standing up. He nibbled the crusts off a couple pieces of toast and handed the middles to Rigel. Rosie couldn't admonish him to eat without eating something herself, and she couldn't imagine doing so.

She wanted to go to school with him. She wanted to don a gang jacket and sit in the back of the classroom with a bat so that everyone understood what would happen to them if they messed with her kid. She wanted to go in and give a speech she'd actually rehearsed over and over in her head. The rest of you may be gender-conforming children, she'd say, but you're not nearly as smart, funny, or interesting as Claude, so you tell me which is better: awesome, dynamic boy in a skirt, or tiresome, whiny child with a runny nose who has nothing to offer but compliance. Instead – and this was probably for the best – she had to go to work.

But Penn went. That was another thing Claude wanted when asked. Yes, he wanted Penn to come to kindergarten for the day as long as he sat in the back and said nothing and left at lunchtime. So that's what Penn did. He sat on an impossibly tiny chair, knees up by his shoulders, heart up in his throat, and sweated. It was three degrees outside.

'Welcome back, boys and girls. How was everyone's break?' Miss Appleton enthused without waiting for any response. 'I'm so glad to see your smiling faces. I hope everyone had fun, and I hope you've come back to school ready to learn. We have so many wonderful tasks and treats ahead. Now, I know a lot happened to some of us while we've been away. Susan lost her first tooth. Davis went with his grandparents to New York City. Carrie got a haircut. And Claude is going to be a fairy girl! We have so much to learn from one another, boys and girls.'

Everyone looked around at Susan, Carrie, and Claude. (A week in

Manhattan seemed unlikely, even to kindergarteners, to yield anything interesting to look at.) Susan peeled back her bottom lip and stuck out her jaw like a monkey then helpfully pushed her tongue through the hole where her tooth had been. Carrie touched the back of her hair where her ponytail used to be. Claude smiled weakly at his shoes. The children wiggled.

'Does anyone have any questions they would like to ask? I would love to hear from boys and girls with their hands raised nicely who are sitting quietly on their pockets.'

Every hand in the room shot up but Claude's.

'Let's see,' said Miss Appleton. 'Marybeth is raising her hand nicely.'

'Did the fairy come?' said Marybeth, and it took Penn a moment to understand that the fairy in question pertained to Susan's tooth not Claude's wings.

'Yup.' Gap-toothed Susan grinned. 'She left me two dollars *and* a comic book.'

'Ooooh,' said the kindergarteners appreciatively.

'Next question,' said Miss Appleton. 'Jason?'

Jason turned to Claude. 'Are tights itchy? They look itchy.'

Claude flushed and shook his head.

'Very nice,' said Miss Appleton. 'Who's next? Alison?'

'Will Claude get long hair?' Alison asked her teacher.

'I don't know, honey. Let's ask him. Claude, do you plan to grow your hair out long like Alison's? Or will you have medium hair like Carrie and Josh? Or will you keep your hair short like right now?'

'I don't know,' Claude told his shoes, barely above a whisper.

'Well, we'll just have to wait and see,' said Miss Appleton. 'We have time for one more question. Elena?'

'Did you see the Statue of Liberty?' Elena asked Davis.

'No,' said Davis.

Miss Appleton clapped her hands together. 'Boys and girls, you asked good questions, and you asked them nicely and quietly, so I'm putting a cookie token in our cookie jar to help us earn our cookie party. Now, let's all find our math partners for Math Trays. Blue table, you may get up and get your math trays . . .'

And that was it. No one looked askance at Claude. No one whispered something nasty. Claude's brown jean skirt and wings were no more or less interesting than a trip to New York or a haircut or certainly an ordinary lost tooth (teeth got lost like tourists among the kindergarten set). They were, bless them, too self-involved to be invested in Claude's identity crisis. They were too much five-year-olds to give a cookie token about anyone but themselves.

As he got in line for lunch, Claude sidled by Penn's mini chair to whisper, 'You can go home now, Dad.'

'You okay, baby?'

'Yup.'

'You sure?'

'Yup.'

'I'm proud of you, Claude.'

'I'm proud of you too, Daddy.'

The next morning Claude asked at breakfast, 'How long will it take to grow hair down to my butt?'

And Rigel said, 'How long will it take to grow hair *on* my butt?'

And Orion said, *'Hairy butt, hairy butt.'*

Claude was wearing a purple corduroy jumper over rainbow-striped tights. And he had shed his wings.

Naming Rights

The kindergarteners were unfazed. Very little is unalterable as far as five-year-olds are concerned. Very little doesn't change. One day those squiggly lines in books transmute into words. One day actual pieces of your mouth start falling off. One day your beloved resolves into a kind of ratty stuffed animal, and for the first time in your life, you feel fine about leaving him home. One day, like magic, you can balance on two wheels. That one day you could be a boy and the next become a girl was not out of their dominion.

But the older kids had some questions. And they did not always ask them kindly. On the playground at recess, third-graders demanded, 'Why are you wearing a dress?' Eight-year-olds pointed at Claude in the cafeteria and sang, '*Booooy girrrrrl booooy girrrrrl,*' like police sirens. Fellow fifth-graders sneered at Rigel and Orion, 'Your gay little brother is so gay.' And when Claude tried to jump rope or use the monkey bars or the slide, there was a constant barrage of 'Are you a boy or a girl? Are you a boy or a girl? Are you a boy or a girl?' from kids older and bigger and stronger than he. Because he didn't know the answer, he said nothing. And because he said nothing, they kept asking the question.

Claude decided it was too cold to go outside at recess anyway and spent it alone in the library instead. Claude was content to eat lunch on his lap in the bathroom. But after a few times, the nurse told him her bathroom was only for going to the bathroom in, not for eating lunch in. So Claude went back to the little boys' room.

Miss Appleton kept him in from recess one day to ask, 'Where are you going to the bathroom?'

'I'm not going to the bathroom,' said Claude. 'I'm going to the library.'

She took a deep breath. 'When you go to the bathroom, where do you go to the bathroom?'

'Where I always go to the bathroom.'

'In the boys' bathroom?'

Claude nodded. He knew he'd done something wrong; he just didn't know what it was.

'Why are you using the boys' bathroom?'

'Because I'm a boy?'

She took another deep breath. 'Then why are you wearing a dress?'

Claude was confused. They'd been through this. 'I like to wear a dress.'

'Little boys do not wear dresses.' Miss Appleton tried to channel her usual patience. 'Little girls wear dresses. If you are a little boy, you can't wear a dress. If you are a little girl, you have to use the nurse's bathroom.'

'But little girls use the girls' bathroom,' said Claude.

'But you're not a little girl,' Miss Appleton said through her teeth.

At the end of the day, Victoria Revels called. 'We are happy to treat your child like a girl if that is what he believes himself to be,' she began.

'Not happy,' Penn corrected. 'Legally obligated.'

'Both,' said Ms Revels. 'But it cannot be just on a whim.'

'Meaning?'

'Meaning if he thinks he is a girl, he has gender dysphoria, and we will accommodate that. If he just wants to wear a dress, he is being disruptive and must wear normal clothes.'

'I'm not sure either Claude or I or even you understand the distinctions you're making up as you go along here,' said Penn.

'It's confusing,' the district representative acknowledged, 'for Miss Appleton and for the children and clearly also for Claude. No one knows how to treat this child. Do we say he or she? Does Claude line up with the boys or the girls? Why is his hair still short? Why hasn't he changed his name?'

'Aren't there girls in the class with short hair?' said Penn. 'Aren't there girls in the class who wear pants?'

'The point,' said Ms Revels, 'is that we can treat your child as a boy. Or we can treat your child as a girl. But we cannot treat him as . . . well, I don't even know what else there is.'

'That might be the problem.' Penn had been online. He'd read and researched. He was starting to be an expert here. 'He might be both. He might be neither. He might be a boy in a dress or a girl with a penis. He might be one for a while and then another. He might be gender variant. He might be genderqueer—'

'Not in kindergarten he is not,' she interrupted. 'He cannot be all of the above in kindergarten, and he cannot be none of the above in kindergarten. In kindergarten, a child can only be a he or a she, a boy or a girl. Kindergartens are not set up for ambiguity.'

'Maybe they should be,' said Penn. 'The world is an ambiguous place.'

'Not for a five-year-old. For a five-year-old, the world is very black and white. It's fair or it's unfair. It's fun or it's torture. There are not disgusting cookies. There are not delicious vegetables.'

'But there are,' said Penn, 'even for five-year-olds. Claude hates cookies with coconut. He loves broccoli. He does have a penis, and he does need to wear a dress. It would be simpler perhaps if these things weren't true, but they are. For all your kids. Surely some of the little girls in his class play soccer after school, and surely some of the boys play hopscotch. This is a good thing, not a bad thing.'

'It may be a good thing,' said Ms Revels, 'but good or bad, we can't accommodate it. He needs to decide one way or the other. He needs to . . . pardon me, but he needs to move his bowels or get off the pot.'

'In the nurse's office,' added Penn.

'In the nurse's office,' said Victoria Revels.

Penn wanted to call Dwight Harmon and raise hell. They had a responsibility to make sure his child wasn't bullied or picked on. And they weren't going to pressure Claude into declaring a gender-or-anything-else identity just because it made it easier for the district to refer to him in the third person. Rosie wanted to model for Claude an attitude of brushing off insults like dog hair and laughing with wry but wise amusement at hapless administrators. Rosie, like most parents, had learned this approach when she had a second child. When Roo fell down at the playground, she'd swoop in cooing, 'Are you okay? Show Mommy where it hurts. Oh my poor baby boy.' And he'd cry like the brokenhearted. By Ben, she'd learned to keep her seat and call, 'You're all right.' And so he was.

'If we don't act like it's a big deal, he won't feel like it's a big deal,' said Rosie.

'But it is a big deal,' said Penn.

As usual though, while they were trying to map the appropriate course, Claude charted his own. At dinner, he announced he was changing his name to the cocoa channel.

'The cocoa channel?' said Ben.

'Like a TV station with nothing but chocolate,' said Claude.

'You mean Coco Chanel.'

'What's Chanel?'

'Her last name. She invented perfume.'

'Chocolate perfume?' said Claude.

'Maybe.' Ben shrugged. He didn't know much about perfume. He did know his little brother couldn't go around calling himself the cocoa channel. Or Coco Chanel.

'You can just be Claude,' said Penn. 'Is Miss Appleton giving you a hard time?'

'No.'

'They can't make you change your name. You can keep your own name and still wear whatever you want.'

'I want to change it. I don't like Claude.'

'Me too. I want to change my name. Orion is the name of a star, not a boy.'

'Orion is the name of a constellation, not a star,' Ben corrected.

'Easy for you,' said Roo. 'You got the normal name.'

'Roo's a normal name,' said Ben.

'Yeah, for a kangaroo,' said Rigel.

'Let's get a kangaroo!' said Orion.

'We're not getting a kangaroo,' said Rosie.

'I'm changing my name to Kangaroo,' said Orion. 'That's what I want to be called from now on. Kangaroo Walsh-Adams.'

'At least you got a constellation,' said Rigel. 'I got a foot.'

'My foot,' Orion said proudly.

'Your foot,' Rigel agreed morosely.

'No one is changing his name,' said Rosie. 'Names aren't something you give yourself. Names are something you get from your parents. Claude, if you want a girl's name, you can be Claudia. Everyone else keeps the name I gave him.'

'Why?' Roo was using his tongue to remove the last bits of turkey from a carving knife.

'Because children are bad decision makers,' said Penn.

'You're letting Claude decide to be a girl,' said Roo, 'which is way worse than letting Orion name himself Kangaroo.'

'Roo!' said Rosie and Penn together.

'I don't want to be Claudia. Claudia's too much like Claude.'

'You could be Not Claude,' said Ben. 'The Absence of Claude. The square root of negative Claude. A Claude Hole.'

'*Claude Hole, Claude Hole, Claude Hole,*' said Orion.

'Everyone out,' said Rosie. It was easier to do all the dishes herself for the next hour and a half, which is what it would take, than to listen to her family for one more minute. She realized she was teaching them that if they were enough of a pain in her ass, she'd take over all their chores. She'd live to regret it, but at that moment, nothing she could think of sounded more luxurious than doing seven people's dinner dishes all by herself.

Penn stayed and helped and didn't say a word. She was grateful for his help. She was more grateful for his silence. Rosie was up to her elbows in soapsuds, the entire front of her soaked with dishwater, when Roo came downstairs to sulk at the now cleared dining-room table.

'He wants his name to be Coco Chanel,' he said sullenly. 'Doesn't that worry you?'

Rosie turned the water up higher, but Penn left his towel and sat down with his eldest. 'He liked the idea of a chocolate television station. It's no big deal.'

'It is a big deal,' said Roo. 'You keep pretending it isn't, but it is. What about his . . . you know.'

'Penis?'

'Yeah.'

'We aren't worried about that yet. Maybe this is a just a phase. Maybe it'll pass.'

'But if it's going to pass, why are you encouraging it?'

'How are we encouraging it?'

'You're letting him wear girl clothes and play with girl things and grow out his hair.'

'Right, we're letting him, not encouraging him.'

'Say no.'

'You'll perhaps have noticed,' said Penn, 'that that's not how it works in our household. When we can, we say yes. To all of you. When we say no, you better believe it's a serious no. We say no when you want to do something that might hurt you. Otherwise, we mostly say yes.'

'This might hurt him.'

'It might. But it seems, at the moment, to beat the alternative. At the moment, it seems to be what he thinks he needs.'

'But you said kids are bad decision makers.'

'When did I say that?'

'At dinner. You said kids can't rename themselves because they're bad decision makers. But if kids are such bad decision makers, why are you letting Claude decide to be something he's not?'

'Because what if he is?' said Penn.

That night, after teeth and stories and lights out, after the boys were asleep and the dishes washed, dried, and put away and the homework checked and the backpacks packed and the lunches assembled, after Rosie and Penn were in bed with their own lights out, their bedroom door cracked and a voice whispered into the darkness, 'I picked my new name.'

Rosie opened the blankets and scooted over toward Penn so that Claude could crawl in beside her. He put his head against her shoulder and seemed to fall right back to sleep.

'Claude?'

'Mmm?'

'Your new name?'

'Yeah.'

'What is it?'

'Poppy,' he said. 'I want my new name to be Poppy.'

'Poppy?' Rosie whispered.

'Carmy says Jews name their babies after dead people they love. I never met Poppy, but I love her anyway.'

'You do?' Rosie was full of wonder.

'Yeah. Because she liked dolls. And because she was your favorite. I like dolls. And I want to be your favorite.'

'You are my favorite.' She nuzzled into his neck.

'Do you think Poppy is a good name?'

'I think Poppy is a perfect name.'

Push

As with so many things, this needed only a name to become real. A name and more hair. Mr Tongo reported that lots of parents of kids like Claude went to court to change birth certificates and seal records, that lots of kids like Poppy switched schools so they could start over where no one knew who they really were so they could be, instead, who they really were. All that felt unnecessarily drastic to Rosie though because at this age, best she could tell, hair was all. Children with short hair were boys; children with long hair were girls. A penis-bearing child wanting to be a girl had only to name himself after his late aunt and grow his hair out for the transformation to be complete. She had, she figured, three, maybe four inches before Claude's hair grew over his ears and she lost him, possibly forever. She would have, at last, the Poppy she'd always dreamed of. She just wasn't ready yet.

They were stared at in restaurants though, at a table for seven, that had always been true. But she and Claude, running errands just the two of them, were stared at at the mall and the grocery store and the library too, and that was new. In those early days, with not-grown-out-yet hair, Claude still looked like a boy in a dress. Some fellow shoppers smiled at Rosie with admiration or maybe pity or maybe just empathy. (So they did not themselves have a little boy who wanted to be a girl; they were parents too, and it was always something.) But many frowned at her with undisguised disapproval. Some said to Poppy, 'Don't you look fancy?' or, 'What a pretty dress,' or, heartfelt to Rosie, 'What a beautiful child.' But others said loudly to each other as they passed, 'Was that a boy or a girl?' or, 'How do you let your kid do that?' or, 'That mother should be shot.'

By April though, Claude was gone, and Poppy, hair finally grown past his ears into a short but inarguable pixie cut, had taken over. His self-portraits became solo affairs: only Poppy, not his whole family, Poppy in a golden ball gown, Poppy in a purple tiara with matching purple super-hero cape, Poppy wearing flip-flops, yoga pants, and a sports bra, sitting in full lotus, grinning enlightenment off the page. He came down to breakfast every morning bubbling over, grinning before his feet hit the kitchen, laughing with his brothers, soaring really, and it was only then his parents realized just how sullen mornings had been when having to change out of the breakfast dress before school had been hanging over Claude's oatmeal. He used the nurse's bathroom. He made himself – and his brothers – sunflower-butter sandwiches, which was all it took to win the unflagging love of Miss Appleton.

Rosie and Penn were slower to adjust. They say it is what you never imagine can be lost that is hardest to live without. Rosie had always as-sumed this referred to postapocalyptic scenarios where what you had to live without was power or water or Wi-Fi, but in fact, it was deeper sown than that. It reminded Penn of the French toddlers whose family had rented the house next door the summer he was sixteen. It was *très irritant* how much better French they spoke than he did, and it was even *beaucoup plus irritant* that they remembered, without even trying, which nouns were masculine and which were feminine when he could not, even though he'd spent a thousand hours studying and they weren't even potty trained yet. Now his whole life was like that. Sometimes he called Poppy 'he' and sometimes 'she'. Sometimes he called Roo and Ben and Rigel and Orion 'he' and sometimes 'she'. Sometimes he called Roo 'Ben' (wrong kid) or 'Rufus' (wrong name) or 'Rude' (not a name at all though, increasingly, not necessarily untrue either). Sometimes he called Rosie 'he'. Once he introduced her at a party as his husband. He called the mailman 'she'. He called the guy who fixed the brakes on the van 'she'. He called the newspaper 'she'. Neither Claude nor Poppy seemed both-ered one way or the other, but Penn felt something essential in his brain had been severed. Whatever link you got for free that picked the appro-priate pronoun whenever one was called for was permanently decoupled, and suddenly Penn's mother tongue was foreign.

They all went to Phoenix for spring break. Poppy went to the mall with his grandmother, shared cinnamon pretzels in the food court, and threw pennies into the fountain to make a wish. He wished everything would always stay exactly like this because suddenly, for the first time in either of his lives, all the kids wanted to be his friend. Shy, all-alone Claude was replaced by laughing, gregarious Poppy, who saved his allowance to buy a fairy calendar on which he recorded all the requests he got for playdates.

Rosie hated that calendar. Penn adored it. To Penn, it represented a triumph, difficult things overcome and implemented. Maybe the transition from Claude had been daunting and fraught, but here was Poppy, loved, friended, present, no longer disappearing off the page. He considered the calendar a hard-won trophy. To Rosie, it bespoke people's cloying, pandering, PC bullshit and a strange Poppy cachet. Having status, she warned Penn, was not the same as having friends. Maybe parents just wanted their kids to invite Poppy over so they could gossip to their own friends or make a big show of being open-minded and tolerant. Maybe the kids wanted to play with Poppy because they were curious about him rather than because they liked him. And what would they do about invitations to sleepovers? What would they do when these kids stopped being sweet little kindergarteners and started being hormone-crazed, mean-spirited, cruel-intentioned, peer-pressuring, pill-popping, gun-toting teenagers?

'Gun-toting?' said Penn.

'Or something,' said Rosie.

'I think you're worrying prematurely.'

'If you don't worry about something until it's already a problem,' said Rosie, 'that's not worry. That's observation.'

The little girls who invited Poppy over had pink rooms and pink LEGOs and pink comforters over pink sheets on their pink beds. They had crates – actual crates! – of tutus and high heels and dress-up clothes, stuffed animals who themselves wore tutus and high heels and dress-up clothes, Barbies and clothes for the Barbies, jewelry, nail polish, fairies, and baby dolls. They liked to draw and trade stickers. They liked to put their stuffies in strollers and give them a bottle and push them around the block. They liked to have a lemonade stand. They liked to chase each other around the house but in tutus and high heels, and when they caught you at the end, they just hugged you and giggled and laughed together instead of making a big thing about who was a loser and sitting on your head and farting. Poppy could not understand why everyone in the whole world didn't want to be a girl.

Rosie was starting to have the same question. She was used to picking children up from playdates with bruised elbows and scraped shins, torn pants and reports of broken things and borderline behavior. She wasn't used to her youngest having playdates at all, never mind coming home from them all smiles, suffused with quiet, almost private, joy. The moms would beam at Rosie. 'She's such a good girl.'

'Who?' Rosie asked the first time.

'She's welcome anytime. She's so well behaved.'

Or they would lay a hand on her arm and say, 'You're so brave,' or 'You're such a good mother. You're doing so well with all this.' Rosie appreciated the support but wasn't sure parenting ever really qualified as brave – or maybe it always did – because it's not like you had a choice. But what she would have chosen, she got too. Poppy's hair was still short, but not short enough to prevent Rosie from plaiting two little braids every morning, one on each side, which Poppy tucked happily behind his ears.

Some playdates went less well. Rosie and Penn kept a no-fly list of kids with whom Poppy could not play again. One playdate ended when Poppy and the other little girl were playing princesses, and the dad made a dirty joke about drag queens. That family went on the list. One mom peppered Rosie with questions every time they ran into each other on the playground after school as to the process of physically turning Claude into Poppy, which Penn wanted to excuse on the grounds that she was showing interest but which Rosie saw for what it was: impudent nosiness. Another family went on the list when Penn went to pick Poppy up and the mom and dad tag-teamed him to explain, politely, that God did not make mistakes, and since God had given Poppy a penis, he and Rosie were interfering with God's plan. 'And that's . . . bad?' Penn guessed. He also guessed that if that family kept their own list, his name had just gone on it.

Rosie tried not to let any of it get to her. She had too much to do without worrying about her kid's friends' parents' ignorance. Her job wasn't to educate them. Her job was just to raise her kid, all her kids. And work to feed them all. As she and Penn kept telling Poppy, you don't have to like everyone. Find who's fun and smart and safe, and stick with them.

Which approach worked just fine until Nicky Calcutti. Nicky was Claude's one friend from before, and Nicky seemed a little perplexed, a little put off, by the change. He was a quiet kid, which was probably what Claude had liked about him. He was unassuming. He didn't wrestle or chase. He didn't always have to have his way loudly. Mostly, the boys played next to each other, like toddlers, and that was fine with both of them. He'd been over once, since, to play with Poppy and had murmured to Rigel, 'I never had a playdate with a girl before,' to which Rigel had replied, 'Oh it's great. Their rooms smell way better.' But Nicky did not seem mollified.

'Maybe he's taking this personally,' Penn guessed.

'Like Claude becoming Poppy is a failure of Nicky's manhood?' said Rosie.

'Something like that.'

'He's five.'

Five he may have been, but five turned out not to be too young to be offended or freaked out. Five turned out not to be too young for any number of sins. Rosie and Penn knew Nicky's mom. After Claude's announcement, she'd emailed Rosie to say she hoped the boys would still be friends. She asked if she could do anything to help. She promised peppermint ice cream – Claude's favorite and Poppy's as well – if Poppy would come over to play. Rosie dropped him off, stood in the door and chatted idly for a few minutes with Cindy Calcutti, and was in the art store buying supplies for a project Orion was doing about bats when her phone rang. Poppy was crying too hard to tell her what was wrong. Rosie was in her car and halfway to Nicky's already before he even managed a wobbly, 'Mom? Would you come get me?'

Cindy Calcutti and Nick Calcutti Sr were separated. Rosie gathered this was a no-way-in-hell-are-we-getting-back-together separation rather than the let's-take-some-space-and-work-it-out kind but, having a much better grasp than other people on what was and wasn't her business, declined to pry. She knew that Cindy was jockeying for full custody by sharing irreproachably during this trial period. If it was Nick's day with his son, Cindy did not say Nicky has a playdate. Cindy went and got a manicure and let her erstwhile husband supervise.

Rosie was close, but Penn was closer, so she called him from the car and sent him over. He was home with the boys, and though Roo and Ben were probably old enough, at twelve and thirteen, to babysit other people's brothers, babysitting their own raised an entirely different set of issues. Penn piled them all into the van and pulled up at the Calcuttis' mere moments before Rosie did. She had not, apparently, been obeying posted speed limits. Or stoplights.

Poppy opened the door before they made it up the walk and ran, sobbing and full-tilt, toward them all. He'd disappeared within a circle of brothers before Nick Sr made it to the front door. He was much larger than Penn, whose only regret was that he could not therefore meet the man quite eye to eye.

'What on earth happened?' Rosie asked Nick, his son nowhere in evidence, hers having absorbed completely the other child who could answer that question.

'Your kid's a faggot, that's what happened,' said Nick Calcutti Sr.

Rosie turned on her heels and started back down the walk. She simply did not need to have this conversation with this man. He had managed, in one short sentence, to tell her everything she needed to know. But when she got back to Poppy and took him in her arms, he whispered, 'He has a gun,' and then she could not in good conscience leave Nicky there.

'Everyone in the car,' she said, and turned to face down Nick Calcutti Sr with her husband.

Nicky peeked out from behind his father's legs. 'Daddy says I'm not allowed to play with faggots, Mrs Walsh. And I don't want to anyway.'

Nick spit between his teeth. 'What you do with your kid is your own damn business, but it's disgusting, and you better keep it far away from my son. Seems to me what you're doing is child abuse, and you should go to jail, but what do I know? Don't make no difference to me as long as you keep far away from Nicky. See, this is what I keep telling Cindy. She needs a man around the house to prevent bullshit like this from going down.'

'Why does Poppy think you have a gun?' said Penn.

''Cause I do.'

'How does he know that?'

''Cause I don't keep it hidden. Two things a man should have: this' – here, he cupped his crotch in his hand and shoved it in Rosie's general direction – 'and this' – at which he pulled back his flannel shirt to reveal a gun in a holster behind his right hip.

'Did you threaten him?' said Penn.

'Who?'

'Poppy.'

'Ain't a him, friend.'

'Did you threaten our child?' Rosie did not want to get diverted into semantics and pronoun battles. There was something more at stake here.

'I told him we don't play with faggots, we don't play with girls, we don't play with boys dressed as girls, and he was no longer welcome in our home or anywhere near my kid – not at the park, not at school, not on the playground, nowhere.'

Penn felt his brain flood with one desire only: to beat the shit out of this guy. That Penn was a lover not a fighter, a writer not a wrestler, seemed not to matter. Nor that he'd never been in a fistfight in his life. Nor that it was probably a bad idea to punch in the face a man whose face he couldn't quite reach, its being several inches over his head, a face surrounded by forty extra pounds that Penn had not, a face backed up – as he'd been pointedly shown – by an actual gun. He tried to replace the vision of Nick's bloody face with his own, Rosie looking down at it. He made himself imagine what Rosie would look like looking at him bleeding from a stomach wound in front of this asshole's house.

In contrast, Rosie had seen men with guns before. She'd cleaned up their messes in the ER. She'd treated them around the handcuffs with which they were locked to their gurneys. She'd saved their lives so they could be transferred from hospital to jail, patient to prisoner. She was afraid of men with guns. But she was not cowed by them.

She dropped to a knee and peeked behind Nick Calcutti to his son. 'Nicky, sweetie, are you okay?'

'Yeah?'

'When's your mom getting home?'

'She said eleven thirty, but she doesn't like to drive when her nails are wet.'

'Jesus Christ.' Nick Sr was on to other complaints now. Forget his son's transgender playmate, his wife's manicure habit could not be more annoying. Then he came back to Penn, who remained an uncomfortably small number of inches from his chest. 'I'll thank you to get the hell off my property.'

Penn opened his mouth to reply, but Rosie beat him to it. 'We'd like nothing more. But we'll stay with Nicky until Cindy gets home.'

'You think I can't take care of my own son?' Nick cut the few inches between his chest and Penn's in half. 'Coming from you, I take that as a compliment.'

'As you wish,' said Rosie.

'If you don't get the fuck off my lawn,' Nick replied, 'I'm calling the cops.'

'Please,' said Penn. 'Please call the cops.'

Nick reached out with both hands and shoved Penn hard enough to knock him down. Maybe not hard enough. Maybe Penn was just surprised. Maybe Penn was just incredulous to find himself in a low-budget action film all of a sudden. Nick closed the gap he'd made between them by stepping up between Penn's legs and standing over him. Rosie had taken out her phone and dialed the nine and the one in which tiny, tiny blink of time, Cindy pulled up, got out of her car, and came to understand what had transpired in an instant. It was not, unfortunately, her first time.

'Cindy, he has a gun,' said Rosie.

'I know.' Cindy's eyes were on her husband, something more than rueful but nowhere close to fear. That's when Rosie became angry. Cindy knew her husband had a gun, but she'd left Rosie's child with him anyway. Cindy knew her husband was a sexist, bigoted asshole, and yet she'd gone to get her nails done. Cindy's desire to play nicely in order to convince a judge to give her more time with her own child had put Rosie's in significant danger. Rosie briefly wondered which was stronger: Nick Sr's loyalty to the mother of his son or Nick Sr's anger toward the mother of his son and how he might feel about Rosie borrowing his gun and shooting off one of Cindy's newly lavender toes.

Penn stood and brushed himself off. Rosie could think of not a single thing more to say. She turned, taking Penn's hand as she did so, and headed back toward the van. She'd have to come back later for her car, but she could not imagine getting into it alone right now nor operating it, hard as she was shaking, nor watching her family head home without her. Cindy ushered her own family into her house.

'Why do you let our son play with faggots and assholes?' Rosie heard Nick say just before the door closed.

In the van, her phone buzzed almost instantly with an email from Cindy. The subject line said 'Sorry :('

Rosie deleted it without reading.

Shove

On the way home from the Calcuttis', they stopped for ice cream. Much as Rosie and Penn both felt as unhungry, at least for food, as they ever had in their lives, Penn's offer to get soft serve was greeted from the backseat with the relief of refugees. If Dad wants ice cream, it must not have been the big deal it looked like it was through the windows. If Mom is willing to stop for treats on the way home, what happened to Poppy can't have been that terrible. If they're hungry – and for sugar – the kids had been worrying over nothing.

The weather had turned finally. Winter had held on through the middle of May, but now, like an errant favorite uncle you forgave the moment he showed up, spring sunshine promised barbecues and fireflies and long days in the lake, and they could feel summer shimmering just in front of them. The warm wind meant a line at Señor Scoops. How this place stayed in business through the long winter Penn did not know. The boys went and begged everyone around them, 'Are you using that chair?' in order to stake out space enough for all of them in the courtyard. Cherry blossoms blew against their ice cream cones and stuck. The whole world smelled of sunshine and soil and sugar. Soft serve was as effective a numbing agent as Rosie knew.

She considered her husband. 'That was very brave back there.'

'Cowering in fear?'

'That's not what you did. You chose me. You chose us.'

'I wanted there to be blood.'

'I know.'

'His. But I'd have settled for mine.'

'I know.'

'Instead I did nothing.'

'Which was everything.' Rosie licked at the tendrils sprouting along her cone. 'Thank you.'

'Anytime,' said Penn.

A stranger from whom they'd snagged a chair winked at him. 'Beautiful family.'

'Thanks.'

'Lotta boys.'

'Oh yeah.'

'She must feel pretty outgunned.' Penn looked puzzled so the stranger nodded at Poppy.

'Her and me both,' said Penn.

On the last night of school, Rosie was at work, and Penn was doing bedtime. Grumwald's friends were over, helping him pack. Grumwald was leaving his parents' house to go make his way in the world. It seemed silly to the king and queen that he should do so. Grumwald didn't need to earn any money, for the castle was his to live in as long as he liked. He didn't need a job, for prince was job enough already. He didn't need a way in the world. He needed a way to stay out of the world, to stay home, to stay put. But Grumwald had secrets which meant he had to go. And it was time.

'How will you learn to be king if you go?' Grumwald's father and mother pled.

'How will I learn to be king if I stay? I have to go.'

'Go where?' his parents moaned.

'Away.'

'But if you don't have anywhere specific you need to be, why can't you just be here?'

'Here is the only where that's not away,' Grumwald explained. 'Away is anywhere that is not here. So that's where I must be.'

Even though they were the queen and king, his parents were confounded, as parents of young people – not too young, Penn emphasized – are meant to be. They were worried about him being anywhere but there, Away as he called it. They could not find Away on any map, though they called in their atlas maker and made him do a thorough search. Grumwald was a little worried too, truth be told, but he had to go. He also knew some things his parents did not, and these things gave him strength. He knew he had infinite stories to see him through, words without end to light his way, to tell him out of any danger, to heal all wounds and mend all hurts, to take any unsavory ending and make it not an end at all but just a way station on the way away. And he had Princess Stephanie for when a princess was called for, as they sometimes are. Between them, they had a prince and a princess, a storyteller and a fairy wrangler, a star lighter and a secret keeper, so Grumwald felt his way was, if not firmly paved, at least densely pebbled, and that was as good a start as one could wish for.

At the hospital, when the call came in, Rosie was eating a peanut butter and jelly sandwich in the break room (peanut butter being allowed in the hospital where there were, among other things, any number of ways to effectively treat anaphylactic shock). Anna Gravitz, the nurse who'd answered the phone, put her head and nothing else in the door, always a bad sign because if it weren't about to be a total shit storm, Anna would have put her whole self in, like at the end of the Hokey Pokey, and told Rosie all about the French featherweight lifting champion who had been her pen pal in fifth grade, come to visit in January, and never left. Instead she said, 'Heads up. GSW on her way in from campus. Security found her, not Madison PD. She was in the yard back behind some fraternity party. Been down more than an hour they think. Wilson says you're up.'

Rosie sighed and swallowed the rest of her sandwich. It had been a pleasant four minutes of middle-of-the-night dinner break. The ones who came in from campus were always a whole different ball game. For one, they often had complicating factors – drugs or alcohol in their systems, or they hadn't slept for a week writing a paper they'd had all semester to work on but had only just started, or they hadn't eaten for a week in order to fit into some dress for a sorority formal. For another, asking them didn't necessarily help you figure out what was going on. They lied habitually. They lied in case you were going to call their parents or tell their RA or get their adviser to put them on probation. They lied out of habit because they were so used to playing up the boring stories and down the libelous ones. But mostly they were different because they were accompanied by a circus. An injury to a field hockey player was likely to occasion all the players and coaches – from both teams – to set up camp in the emergency room. Weeping roommates and frantic phone calls from parents went without saying. Rival lovers, often only just learning of each other's existence, sometimes came a-wooing as well. Like Penn before them, no one could ever be convinced to leave, to wait at home, that there was nothing they could do here and they were very in the way. Staying equaled fidelity and faith, true friendship and true love. Leaving betrayed perfidy and doubt, wavering fear, which, to the college-aged mind, had no place in a hospital. Had they asked the adults in the room, the wounded worriers ten years their senior who waited for news of aged parents or broken kids, they'd have gotten this advice: if you get the chance to leave, take it. But the college students never asked anyone's advice.

Summer session used to be quiet but had been revving up the last few years. There were fewer minor injuries perhaps, but what came in was often a disaster. Rosie was prepared then for a circus. But nothing like the one she got.

The GSW came in unconscious and pale, intubated, blood everywhere, and swollen as hell. From the gurney as she was rushed inside, she did not look to Rosie like a gunshot victim. She looked like she'd been hit by a bus. Rosie listened hurriedly to her chest, shone a penlight in each eye, scanned her quickly to see where all the blood was coming from. It was coming from everywhere. Her clothes were sodden with it, but when they peeled them back to find the patient below, Rosie was initially relieved to find that the gunshot wound was small. The bullet had entered the left shoulder and exited cleanly. So where was all the blood coming from? Then she took in contusions, puncture wounds, visibly broken bones. And a penis.

For an instant, everything went still, and everyone took a step back from the table, hands raised, like they'd uncovered a bomb. Everyone's first thought was that it must have been the EMT's first day or that some idiot in campus security had interrupted a theme party of some sort and failed to realize this guy was in costume. But Rosie saw it right away, not only why this patient-with-a-penis had been taken to be female but also what had happened to her, why she was here. Someone opened the door and shouted out into the hallway, 'Jane Doe's a John Doe.' In that blink of a heartbeat while everyone in the room reordered what they knew and then got right back to work, Rosie saw the whole thing.

She saw Jane Doe at home getting ready for the fraternity party, her first maybe, putting on her sequined top, trying a few different skirts until she found the right one, the one tight enough to be feminine but loose enough to hide her secret, practicing in the heels (heels she loved more than it seemed like shoes should be loved, heels which, despite being a size 12 extra wide, still looked like real women's shoes), getting the hair and the makeup exactly right (not garish, just natural, but with a little extra to hide the whiskers), looking at her terrified self in the mirror, reminding herself that most students at a party would be too drunk to look closely and plus it would be dark, that no one knew her here, she could start over, she could be anyone she wanted.

Rosie saw Jane teeter into the party. It was outside on the lawn behind the fraternity house and in full swing by the time she got there. Jane stood in the doorway to the backyard and took a deep breath: beer, potato chips, watermelon, sweat, her own perfume, her own fear. Vomit, or maybe she was just imagining that. She stepped onto the lawn and turned her ankle over. Shit. She'd been a college student for fifteen minutes, and already she'd blown her cover and would have to spend the semester on crutches besides. She was an idiot to think she could go out in heels.

But then, a miracle. A hand, tender, on the soft skin under her upper arm, thumb rubbing gentle circles.

'You okay?' He was, of course he was, blond, not dirty blond like the boys back home in Pennsylvania, blond like glowing, like an angel. Or maybe just like a Wisconsinite – what did she know? And, also like a glowing Wisconsinite angel, he was beautiful.

'Um . . . yeah?'

'I told those guys they had to clean up the yard before people came over.' The angel bent to pick up what she'd tripped over. Jane was so happy it hadn't been the heels, it didn't strike her as at all weird there was a package of once frozen waffles lying in the grass. 'Breakfast.' The angel grinned sheepishly. 'Now with lawn care.'

She laughed – spontaneously and like a girl – and it felt like the first time she had ever laughed, like she was a three-month-old laughing for the very first time. And his face lit up when she did like he understood the wonder of it perfectly. He left one hand where it was on her arm but held the other out for her to – she reminded herself urgently – grasp, not shake. 'Chad,' he said.

'Jane,' said Jane Doe.

'Let me guess,' said Chad. 'You're one of those overeager, too-smart-for-your-own-good freshman girls who think they can get a head start on college by taking summer classes, like, the minute they graduate from high school.'

'I guess?'

'Good. I love girls like that.'

'You do?'

'Yeah. I like my ladies smart.'

'You do?'

'And hey, I get it. Couldn't wait to get out of your lame parents' house, away from your lame high school friends, out of your lame hometown?'

She nodded. He did get it.

'Well, welcome to college. Let's get you a beer.'

He did. He got her a slice of watermelon and a beer. Then another. And one after that. She assumed he was the gatekeeper, that he'd go back to the door or drift away to talk to people he knew or flirt with other girls he didn't, but he stuck by her side all evening. 'This is my friend Jane,' he'd say to everyone they met, and she wondered if this was what life would be like from now on. Maybe all these years it had been just this simple: put on a dress, introduce yourself as Jane, and suddenly you matched, you fit, you had fun, you felt right instead of awkward, you were the truth instead of a lie. Her real life had arrived finally, and here she was at its very start, peering over the edge. It was worth it, maybe, all the pain that came before if it brought her to this wondrous place.

Jane was happy to stand next to Chad, his hand on the small of her back protectively, while he introduced her as 'my friend Jane' all night or forever if he wanted. But eventually, she noticed the yard was almost empty. A few people lingered, laughing too loudly or kissing on a lawn chair, but mostly they were alone. She sat down on the back steps – she still loved the heels, but they were not comfortable – and he sat down next to her.

'So, you want the good news?' he asked.

There was more?

'As luck would have it' – he jerked his head over his shoulder toward the house behind him without taking his eyes off her – 'I have a bedroom right here.'

She could not do that. She knew this. Do not go inside with him, Jane told herself sternly. It will be okay as long as you do not go inside. 'It's so nice out here. The fresh air. The stars.' It was true. There weren't many stars but there were a few, and the night air was cool and smelled of summer and lake.

'Then let's stay here.' Chad smiled his perfect, glowing smile and put his arm around her shoulders and pulled her close. He kissed her on the mouth, just barely, her first kiss, and there was only one word in her head now: lucky. 'I like you, Jane Doe,' he said.

'I like you too,' she managed. He put a hand on her cheek and she flinched. Would he feel stubble?

'What's up?' He seemed genuinely concerned.

'Oh, nothing. A bug,' she said, and he laughed and kissed her again, less gentle but better, more sure, and then there was his tongue, soft and sweet, and it was true what they said: she saw fireworks; she heard symphonies; she was aware of herself and him and nothing else in the world. She let herself have this. She let go of the worry and the doubt and the lying, the strain of pretending all the time. She let go of everything and just luxuriated in this, this perfect moment, this perfect night, her life finally arrived.

And then she felt his hand on her leg, high, up under her skirt. For an instant, it was the most pleasure she'd known in her life. In the next instant, it turned to pure panic. And the next, knowledge, certain knowledge, in the moment before it happened, that she'd let it go too long, it was too late. She was Cinderella as the clock struck midnight, standing in her dirty work clothes between one life and the other, thinking, Goddammit, how could I have forgotten the only important thing there was to remember and gotten out of here five minutes ago? But when he found out, the prince didn't care about who she had been, only who she had become, so maybe Chad would—

The instant after that Chad's hand recoiled and then all of him. He stumbled up and back and away. His look in that moment wasn't anger. It was pain. He was hurt. That she'd lied? That she'd tricked him? That he'd liked someone – something – as disgusting as she was? Maybe he was hurt that he'd lost her. Maybe he didn't have to. She reached out to explain. The words on her lips were, 'I'm . . .' What? I'm sorry? I'm Jane? I'm not what you think?

But she didn't get them out. Whereas every moment leading up to this one this night stood crystalline and perfect, what happened next was a blur. He hit her across the mouth. He hit her face. He called out and lights went on in the house and guys came, guys arrived, one after another. They laughed. They yelled. They spit. They pushed her to the ground. They kicked her. She struggled. She fought back. She was strong.

She had a single moment – just one – where she thought: I'm as strong as you are. One of them, maybe, but all of them together, no. Still, they must have been scared of her because feet turned to fists, and then someone pulled the knife out of the spent watermelon.

And when she was done – stopped fighting back, stopped struggling, stopped moving even – they'd just left her. They thought, maybe, she was just hurt and would get up and limp home soon enough. They thought, maybe, she had had enough, and they were doing her a kindness by leaving her alone finally. They thought nothing at all – they were drunk and tired and ready now, after all the excitement of the evening, to go to sleep. They went inside and turned off their lights and slept like the guiltless. They did not hear the sirens. They did not hear the police banging on the front door. They did not hear their lives changing forever as well.

Sometime between midnight and dawn, a campus cop had had the worst night of his career, hearing soft moaning, soft weeping behind the overflowing garbage cans in the alley behind the fraternities and deciding to investigate.

Rosie saw all of this. She saw the whole thing. She saw it the moment she peeled back the clothes. The only thing she couldn't figure was the barely gunshot wound. If they were going to shoot her, why not in the head, the heart? If they were going to kill her, why not kill her?

Later, when the whole story came out, or as much of it as could be pieced together, it turned out it was Chad who'd gotten the gun, that having kicked off what quickly got out of control, he couldn't get his fraternity brothers off Jane Doe. He screamed and pulled at the backs of their shirts and tried to push them off her and away, but they wouldn't listen anymore, couldn't listen anymore, and so he'd gone into the house and into the room of a brother he knew kept a handgun in his nightstand. He'd meant to fire it into the air or something to get everyone's attention, but he missed. It was his first time with a gun. An inch to the left, and it would have been over instantly. He'd very nearly killed Jane Doe. He'd very nearly killed her anyway. He'd also very nearly saved her life. But not quite.

Mapping

Rosie had a map and a headache. For the latter, she had taken an aspirin she didn't have the remotest hope would work. For the former, she had three different colors of highlighters and the opposite kind of hope – the impossibly high kind, the this-will-solve-everything kind, the kind where you fix the problem you can instead of the problem you can't. It was sometime after three, maybe four. The kids would be up soon, she knew. She should go to bed, she also knew. But she had not been sleeping well. She had not been sleeping at all, and better to get up and do something – anything – than to lie there and think about why.

So she got up and spent midnights and after with her map. It was the whole of the United States, road and topographic. Fully unfolded, it took up the entire dining-room table, but she didn't need it fully unfolded. For a while, the middle five pleats had stayed closed, but that left a bumpy mass in the center that sometimes made her color coding awkward. Eventually, she got a scissor and cut them away, carefully laying tape along only the back so that she could use her pens and markers wherever she needed without interference. She was on her second map, in fact, the first having become too messy with notes and arrows and big and bigger Xs.

Penn said, 'Come to bed.' Penn said, 'Eschew the crazy,' because he thought phrasing it quirkily might make her laugh and soften – while still planting – the suggestion that she was being insane. Penn said, 'Madison is perfect. It's liberal and beautiful. It's broad-minded with smart, educated citizens and world-class medical facilities.' Penn said, 'You can't control everything. Anywhere you live, there will be some bad people. Anywhere you live, shit will occasionally happen.' But Rosie knew Penn said these things because Penn was a poet and a storyteller and a disciple of the cult of narrative theory, a grown man who still believed in fairy tales and happy endings. For her, diagnosis and treatment were much more clinical propositions. She assessed the infirmity as she always did: initial presentation, physical exam, symptom analysis. She took into account patient history and environmental factors. She developed a treatment plan.

What was clear was that they could not raise this child here. They could not raise these children here. They had to go Away. Madison was open and accepting and tolerant, yes, but tolerance was bullshit. Fuck tolerance. Madison was tolerant, except for when it wasn't. Madison was tolerant, unless you strayed so much as a mile outside in any direction or invited people from outside in – Chad Perry was from Kenosha, it turned out – and then it didn't work, did it? Poppy wasn't something to be tolerated like when you got a cold, and yes it was annoying, and no you weren't going to die, so buy some tissues and a book about zombies, and get in bed for two days. Head colds should be tolerated. Children should be celebrated. That's when she took scissors to the middle of the country and most of the south as well so that her new map of the United States looked like a foreshortened frowny face, its middle fused, its bottom, except at the very edges, excised. Her mother made an impassioned plea for Phoenix. Her mother sent articles and emails about the Phoenix gay pride festival, about a trans boy in a Phoenix high school who'd been named homecoming king by his peers, about the importance of family and especially grandmothers in kids' lives, about the weather in February (sunny every day, highs in the 70s), about the ways in which her daughter was putting the mental in judgmental when she suggested that everyone living more than one hundred miles from an ocean was a bigot. Rosie deleted them without reading.

The sky-scraping, difference-celebrating, coast-abutting megacities were tempting with all their cutting-edge medical facilities and pride parades and diversity. But Rosie wasn't so crazy, at least not yet, as to believe her multitudes could do with that little space. They needed more grass and less concrete, more meandering and less high rising, and even if they had been willing to live in one, they could not afford an apartment for seven on Manhattan's Upper West Side. The leap from tolerant to celebrated turned out to be an expensive one. So she kept looking.

When cajoling optimism didn't work, Penn switched rallying cries. 'We can't give up and slink away,' he said. 'That's letting the bastards win. We're stronger than that.'

'They beat her to death,' Rosie answered.

'You have a job you love.'

'He threatened our child with a gun,' his wife replied.

'The kids love it here.'

'In front of our whole family.'

'You can't leave because of one horrible, drunken fraternity party,' said Penn. 'You can't leave because of one terrible playdate.'

'You can't stay,' said Rosie, 'knowing what happens here.'

'You can't uproot a whole seven-person family because of the needs of just one of them,' said Penn, and it wasn't clear whether the 'just one' in question referred to Poppy, with his need to be somewhere he could be who he was, or Rosie, with her need to be Away, but that was how Penn lost the argument regardless because of course you could uproot a whole family of seven for the needs of just one of them because that's what family means.

And so it was that one predawn morning, she found it, the perfect course of treatment, the antiserum for all the Nick Calcuttis in the world and all the Chad Perrys and all the nightmare fraternity parties as well: Seattle. Seattle was so far past tolerant that heterosexual reviewers complained they felt awkward holding hands at some brunch places and were treated rudely by the waitstaff. Seattle had not just therapists and doctors touting transgender expertise but acupuncturists, nutritionists, and yoga studios as well. Would eating more grapefruit and less gluten help Poppy be a celebrated human? Rosie had no idea. Which was why she suddenly felt she needed a transgender nutritionist who did. Seattle had space – mountains and lakes and ocean and beaches, parks with paths through old-growth forests, skiing and scuba and ferries to nearby islands. And there was a job. It wasn't an ER job, but private practice might be nice for a change now that the kids were all in school and she didn't need to work nights. She could sleep instead. And she'd be able to because picking Seattle would get rid of her map and her highlighters and all her late-night searches.

Seattle also had a house that was almost if not quite big enough and that they could almost if not quite afford – if they were careful, if she got the job, if their farmhouse went for what it should, given what a perfect place it was to live if only you didn't mind threatening playdates and murderous fraternities practically in your backyard. Rosie looked at the house online night after night. The school district got high marks. There were parks and beaches nearby. Roo and Ben could share the basement. Rigel and Orion could have their own rooms for a change. They could convert the garage for her mother to come up in the summers.

The house had a turret with a pink-painted attic bedroom, and the school had a skateboarding club, so Poppy was sold. Rosie bought Rigel and Orion wetsuits, and the twins spent hours online looking at pictures of what lived underneath Puget Sound: giant octopuses who changed colors like Gobstoppers and spotted ratfish with eyes like puppies and wolf eels that looked like old men who'd forgotten to put their teeth in. Ben required no convincing at all, for he knew Seattle to be a city where someone with smarts and computer savvy who had skipped the sixth grade would be treated not like a nerdy dweeb but rather like a nerdy demigod, a hero among middle-schoolers.

Penn needed no convincing in the end either, for he had learned about leaving. He learned it from Grumwald, who went Away even though he had a castle and a kingship calling him to stay. He learned it from Nick Calcutti, who had fairly begged every fiber of Penn's being to stay and fight, but every fiber of Penn's being mustered all its strength and insisted upon leaving anyway. He learned it from Claude, who'd known leaving was only making room for someone else. He learned, finally, that when the ER doctor comes into the waiting room and tells you you can go, you can, you should, you had to go. Leaving wasn't weak, and it wasn't giving up. It was brave and hard fought, a transition like any other, difficult and scary and probably necessary in the end. Fighting it only delayed the inevitable. And as far as transitions in his family went, Wisconsin to Washington wasn't very far at all.

It was Roo who didn't want to go. Roo was first-chair flute that year. Roo was quarterback of his peewee football team and president of every activity that had one: student government, class council, band, the No Girls Aloud (Quiet Ones Welcome) Club he'd formed with three friends in fourth grade when they were studying homonyms. Roo had friends, lots of friends, friends he'd known since preschool, friends who just shrugged and then laughed about something else when he told them his baby brother was wearing dresses to kindergarten. Roo did not want to share a room or give up his rope swing or move someplace where there was no sledding because it never snowed. Roo felt that Poppy could wear a skirt or Poppy could wear pants or Poppy could wear chain mail or a tuxedo made from bacon or a cape knit out of Jupiter's fur, but that didn't mean he should have to throw out half his stuff and then pack what was left into boxes and then drive two thousand miles to someplace where he had to start all over again in every way that mattered. And Rosie agreed. He was right. He shouldn't have to do that. It was sad and unfair and very hard that he had to do that. But he did have to do it. That, she explained, was what family meant.

'I hate family,' said Roo.

'That too, I'm afraid,' said his mother.

Her new job paid to ship everything, including the furniture, including the boxes, including the cars and even the dog, so they got to fly to Seattle instead of driving. The road trip would have been romantic, cathartic maybe, to feel each mile drop behind them, to watch the landscape change and change again, to eat hamburgers in sticky diners and make picnics from sad grocery stores and take over motels so beaten they could afford to stay two to a room and everyone could have his own bed. That was, Rosie thought, what a move of this magnitude should feel like, how it should be marked, but in the end, it was already the weekend before school started up again by the time they closed on the pink turret house. On the final descent into Seattle, they flew so low over snowy, craggy Mount Rainier it looked like they could hop a few feet out of the plane onto its lid and just walk down. And that's what the whole move felt like in the end, in the beginning, epic and age-old and monumental, ice-covered and treacherous and breathtakingly beautiful.

PART
II

One Thing

School started on a Tuesday, so Poppy was allowed to have a sleep-over Sunday night. At quarter to midnight, she and Aggie and Natalie and Kim were sitting in a circle on Poppy's bedroom floor, hands held, eyes closed, the apple-passionfruit candle Poppy'd got from her Secret Santa (Kim) the year before aflame, attempting to contact Aggie's grandfather, who had died of a stroke in June. Their moms had carefully and repeatedly impressed upon them that they did not need makeovers for they were beautiful just as they were, but earlier in the evening, the girls had tried out half a million hair and outfit options anyway because you couldn't leave what you were going to wear or how you'd do your hair to the night before fifth grade actually started. The night before fifth grade actually started you would not have three friends sleeping over because it was a school night, and you couldn't expect to make decisions like these on your own. Aggie and Natalie both had older sisters who could help them if they were in the mood, which they almost never were. But Kim was an only child, and Poppy had nothing but hordes of brothers, which was actually worse, so they'd spent much of the evening weighing outfit options, doing and doing and redoing hair, painting their nails, and trying out different shades of lip gloss, lip gloss being a whole lot easier to sell than lipstick or – no way at all – mascara or eye shadow, which Poppy knew her mother would never ever agree to. Then they'd watched a movie and eaten their weight in pizza, popcorn, and ice-cream sandwiches. After the movie, Poppy got the bear (Alice) and the sheep (Miss Marple) who always came to bed with her so she could go to sleep, but Aggie said she missed her grandpa, and Kim said let's hold a séance, and Poppy had that candle so it was pretty much perfect.

They tried to contact Aggie's grandpa for a while, and then Poppy went to change into PJs, but when she got back, Aggie was asking the Ouija board if Oscar O'Mally liked someone, and the Ouija board said yes, but when they asked who, it didn't say. Then Natalie asked if Mattie Underpants liked someone – his name was Underman, which would actually prove worse for him in the years to come, but they'd called him Underpants since his family moved to Seattle like Poppy's had in first grade – and it pointed to the number seven, which who even knew what that meant. Then Natalie asked if Kim liked someone, and Kim threw a balled-up pair of socks at her, and then they had a sock fight.

Poppy thought Aggie was the lucky one because she liked Oscar all alone, and who even cared whether he liked her back because that was not the point, whereas Natalie and Kim both liked Mattie, even though neither wanted to say so, and so who he liked back did matter a lot, and whereas Poppy didn't really like anybody which probably meant she was a baby. It was weird because she'd known Oscar and Mattie since they were all, like, six which was basically forever, and she remembered when they did embarrassing things like when Mattie threw up on the floor in second grade and when Oscar was dressed as a cowboy and slipped on a Milky Way during the Halloween parade and cried and cried all the way back to school, holding his butt in both hands. So she liked them well enough, but she couldn't really like them like them. A new boy, Chester, had moved in in the middle of last year, but Chester was the name of Orion's guinea pig so she didn't like him, and Richard had come at the beginning of third grade, but he smelled like hot dogs, so she didn't like him either. There was Jake Irving, who used to be really nice, but lately he'd been hanging out with Marnie Alison, and her mean was rubbing off on him.

Not liking anyone was worse than liking the same boy one of your three best friends liked because at least Natalie and Kim had something to talk about, but when they talked about boys, Poppy had nothing to talk about. And then it got worse because Kim asked the Ouija board when will Poppy grow boobs, and everyone giggled. Poppy blushed even through the blush they'd put on when they were doing makeovers, but Aggie rolled her eyes and said, 'You're so lucky you don't have any yet.

You should hope you never get any. They're so' – she looked down at her overfull pajama top as if she'd find an appropriate adjective inside – 'floppy.'

'Aren't they supposed to be floppy?' Natalie wore one of her older sister's bras sometimes and stuffed it with underpants, which were smoother and softer than socks.

'I guess,' Aggie said. 'But it's going to be really weird in gym. Everyone will be staring at me.'

'Yeah, with envy.' Kim giggled and added, 'Or lust.' She had a tiny bra that was really more like a strappy undershirt and nothing much to fill it, but it was still more than Poppy had.

'I'll probably get my period first too,' said Aggie. 'It's not fair.'

'Maybe you won't be first,' said Natalie. 'My sister got hers in fifth grade, so maybe I'll be first.'

'I hope so,' said Aggie. 'It's going to be so gross and embarrassing.'

'Maybe they'll let us out of gym,' said Natalie.

'At least the shower part,' said Kim.

'Who will get it first?' Aggie asked the Ouija board, and they waited, genuinely worried, until it pointed to the moon, which Poppy had to admit was kind of appropriate but not really helpful, so they finally blew out the candle and worried in the dark in their own separate sleeping bags.

Sex ed in fourth grade had had nothing really to do with sex. It was about hair and breasts and blood instead. It was about how your body was going to get gross and need modification – hair needed removal, breasts needed corralling, smells had to be prevented or masked, and then all sorts of things were going to leak out. It was truly horrifying. Right after lunch for that unit of health, the boys went in one classroom and the girls went in another. Then they all came back into their regular room for the rest of the day – math and science – looking alarmed, ashen, and shy of one another. They knew from older kids and older siblings that this year, fifth grade, sex ed would truly be about sex, which horrified them even more, and there was a dance for Valentine's Day, which just seemed like a cruel confluence. And they also knew from the same older kids and older siblings that this was their last year of shower-free gym, and starting in middle school, they'd have to get actually naked and shower together after PE. And they all wanted to die.

It was nearly one when they finally went to bed, but they woke up early anyway. Poppy's dad made them the same pancakes he'd been making them since first grade: vaguely Mickey Mouse-shaped, but not really, with chocolate-chip eyes and nose and banana mouths even though they were too old for Mickey Mouse and chocolate-chip pancakes. They all but split a bottle of syrup between them, so when Orion and Rigel finally wandered down, stinky and spiky haired and sleepy-looking, even though it was practically lunchtime, they had to have their vaguely Mickey Mouse pancakes with excess syrup dribbled off the girls' plates. Orion, who was wearing a green felt fedora, held his pancake in his right hand and Poppy's plate in his left, took a bite of Mickey Mouse ear then ran his tongue over the plate like Jupiter, bite, lick, bite, lick until he was done.

'Eww,' the girls said.

'You know what they loved about me when I was your age?'

'Nothing?' Aggie guessed.

'Table manners.' Orion opened up to show Aggie a mouthful of chewed-up pancake, and Aggie laughed, and Poppy felt like she would die of embarrassment, and Penn wondered where boys learned that, that trick of attracting girls by grossing them out, which only worked for a few years, like flirting training wheels. Maybe boys had it all along, that razor's-edge balance of disgusting and charming, and for many years they didn't notice or care, and for a few years girls found it fascinating, and for the rest of the time, men fought to keep it under wraps and only let it out when they were alone.

Poppy and Aggie and Natalie and Kim had been best friends since first grade when Poppy had been the new kid, and Aggie was her new neighbor, and they'd formed the PANK Club, whose avowed pursuit changed over the years from hopscotch to bird-watching to detective agency but whose name never changed because its members never did. At first, Rosie and Penn had been silly-grateful for these girls, not just for how much they loved Poppy but for how ordinarily. Eventually, though, the girls stopped being miracles and settled into family: Poppy's friends, who were just there at the table when Rosie came home from work, ready to be asked to stay for dinner, who came out for ice cream with them after school or bowling on a rainy Sunday, Poppy's friends who came over for movie nights and said, 'Hi, Poppy's Mom,' when they met in the hall at school, Poppy's friends who disappeared into her room for hours and never sent a tray of clay models crashing into shards or came out to ask for a snack and consumed an entire jar of peanut butter and two loaves of bread as happened regularly with the boys' friends. And whereas the boys' friends came and went and even overlapped, Poppy and the PANK Club never wavered. They told each other everything.

Except for one thing.

Rival Neighbor Princess

They never planned to keep Claude a secret. It was an accident. It was an accident plus opportunity plus special circumstances. You can say that about a lot of things – Rigel and Orion said it, for instance, the time they lost their skateboard in the lake when they tried to use Jupiter as a sled dog during an ice storm – but this one was different because this one was huge. This one was different because it lasted (the twins had managed to keep their secret for less than ten minutes) and because it transformed so many lives. Usually secrets that do that are kept through foresight, scheme, and strategy, careful planning and obsessive track-covering. A lot of work. In this case though, secrets were kept by accident and then mostly forgotten. But their power was therefore no less portentous.

Four years before Poppy's *erev* fifth-grade sleepover, moving from Madison to Seattle had been like moving from Madison to the moon. They swapped the tumbled brown middle of the country for the soaring blue edge; muggy, comforting summer days for long, clear, sun-kissed ones; the much-promised rain not yet in evidence. The pink turret house had been built the same year as the farmhouse – 1906 – but the similarities ended there. Where the farmhouse was wide and white and open, the pink turret house was tall and formal with dark, newly polished floors and dark, newly installed countertops, with granite and burnished metal instead of worn wood and wainscoting. Where the farmhouse had been a car ride away from even the bus stop, the pink turret house was a mere driveway from the sidewalk, short feet from the street. You could see downtown skyscrapers from the front window. The dining room was barely large enough to fit the homeworking table, itself a worn and whitewashed relic of their other home, another life. The floors were perfectly smooth but still, the boys had been frustrated to learn, poor for roller-skating, being constantly interrupted by too many walls. The house had been edited over the years by a century's worth of owners with what were clearly widely varied visions, financial constraints, and priorities. The result was a bit hodgepodge. Orion's room was tucked into the second-floor eaves and too short to stand up in except in the middle. Rigel's was accessible the regular way but also through a trapdoor in the back of the linen closet. The steps to Poppy's turret led up from the master bedroom. Roo and Ben shared the basement, one sprawling room Ben turned into six by repurposing the moving boxes to make a labyrinth of bedrooms, workrooms, corners, and hideouts. The house was polished and functional, just a little odd on the inside when you looked close enough. 'Like me,' Poppy said.

Madison's wide, amber flat was replaced with Seattle's verdant verticality, the green hinting perhaps at the nowhere-in-evidence-yet rain but the latter a complete surprise. The pink turret house was on a hill so steep Penn thought they might need to hire Sherpas. Their main-floor living-room window looked out over their next-door neighbor's roof. And it was this that was truly the biggest change of all: someone next door. For the first time in their lives, the kids had neighbors.

Alone on their farm, Rosie and Penn had forgotten all about the way your neighbors' desire to live next to a mown lawn and weeded parking strip somehow trumped yours to not care and go to yoga instead of gardening on Saturday mornings, the way their kids lay out on towels in the backyard and played bad music loudly so there was nothing you could do to stop it entering your open windows and then your open ears, the way your own horde of children holding a science experiment to determine how loud you had to yell to shatter a wineglass meant you had to worry about more than the wineglass. And the way neighbors knocked on your door within hours of your arrival, never mind your house was a mess, your hair was a mess, your kids were a disastrous mess, and you were not in the mood to be sociable. Never mind it turned out that after all the ruminating and decision making over what to move versus what to buy new, what to keep versus what to give away, what you had but wouldn't need (sleds) versus what you needed but didn't have (something to entertain a troupe of children in the winter that wasn't a sled), what you really required didn't occur to you until it was too late.

When she heard the doorbell the first time, Rosie ignored it. The kids had never had a doorbell and spent most of the morning trying this one out until she was completely inured to its chimes. When it rang again an hour later, she was in the turret unpacking Poppy's room and assumed someone else would get it. No one did. When Rosie finally went downstairs to investigate the third ring, she found she had the house to herself, an occasion rare enough she was irritated to have it interrupted.

She pulled open the door to a perfectly pleasant-looking couple about her age. 'We don't want any.' Her father's joke when friends came to visit, though these two were strangers and she wasn't actually kidding.

'Oh. Uh,' the female half fumbled, looked at the male half who smiled gamely, first at his wife, then at Rosie, then back again, 'we wanted to welcome you to the neighborhood.'

'Ah.' Rosie squinted at them. Mystery solved. 'Thanks.'

'We brought cookies.' The male half raised and wiggled a plastic-wrap-covered plate to prove it. 'But full disclosure: they do contain peanut butter. Oh, and raisins.' Rosie thought peanut-butter-raisin cookies were an odd combination. Rosie thought it unfair that even moving across the country wasn't far enough to escape people's obsession with peanut allergies. Then the man added, 'And wine.' She thought he meant in the cookies until he produced a bottle from behind his back like a magic trick, but in the beat it took Rosie to reach for it, he put it back again. 'Although if you're allergic to raisins, you're probably allergic to wine too, right? Not that it's raisin wine, of course. Is that even a thing? Raisin wine? Or maybe you don't drink? We don't mean to presume. Maybe you aren't drinkers. Or cookie eaters. Not that we drink that much, but it is nice to have a glass of wine with dinner. If you drink. If it's good wine. Not that this is really good wine. A colleague brought it over for dinner the other night, and we never quite got there. Not that it's crappy either. Just, you know, leftover.' Then he was quiet, which was probably for the best. They both looked at Rosie. It was her turn now apparently.

'I'm not allergic to raisins,' she said.

'That's a relief.' The man nodded approvingly.

'I'm Rosie,' she added, and they lit up with relieved joy because it had never occurred to them to actually introduce themselves.

'Oh, we're Marginny and Frank Granderson,' the woman gushed, like the fact that they all three of them had names was too big a coincidence to be believed.

'Marjorie?' Rosie must have misheard.

'Marginny.' Marginny shrugged smugly, like this was a reasonable name, something to be proud of even, as if she'd had anything to do with it. (Which, who knew, she might have.) 'My dad really loved gin. And my mom.'

'Not that we're big drinkers,' Frank reminded her.

'We're so pleased to meet you finally.' Had they been waiting?

'Likewise,' Rosie said, and when no one had anything to add, sighed with relief, 'Thanks for the welcome and the treats,' and started to close the door.

Marginny and Frank leaned in together to peer behind her. 'You solo?' Frank asked. 'Awfully big van for one.'

Rosie felt spied on already. 'I don't know where they all got off to' – she waved vaguely behind her without looking – 'but they're not allergic to raisins either.'

'All?' Marginny inquired brightly.

'Penn, my husband. And five kids.'

They clasped their hands to their chests simultaneously. 'Five?' Frank grinned. 'Wow. I bet you're from the Midwest.'

Rosie hated to admit this was true, but she could not relocate Wisconsin.

'We have two ourselves,' Marginny confided. 'Girls. Cayenne's just about to start eighth grade. Aggie's going into first.'

Cayenne, Aggie, and Marginny? Did they make these names up? How was she ever going to remember them?

'And yours?' Frank prompted.

'Five boys,' Rosie said automatically, then checked herself. 'Well, four and a half.'

'You're pregnant?' Marginny guessed.

'God forbid.' Rosie tried to stuff some of her sweaty hair back into her sweaty ponytail. 'Roo and Ben are going into eighth grade too. Orion and Rigel are going into sixth. Poppy's our youngest. He'll be starting first grade.'

'You said . . .' Marginny looked confused.

Rosie blushed deeply and hoped it looked like she was just flushed from unpacking boxes. 'Poppy, uh . . .' It was at that instant, and not an instant before, that Rosie realized they'd needed a plan for this moment. In Madison, for better and for worse, everyone knew, so there was no need to tell. These people standing on her front porch had been in her life for all of six awkward minutes, and so far she wasn't terribly fond of them. Telling them about Poppy and Claude, all the heartache and confusion and sorting and decision making, all the hoping and leaping, was too intimate by half. She supposed she couldn't introduce her nascent daughter with, 'This is Poppy. She has a penis,' but clearly they needed some way in. In the moment, Rosie finally settled on, 'Poppy used to be a boy.'

'Used to be a . . .' Marginny trailed off.

'Poppy was born as Claude. Well, not born as. You know. We named her that in the hospital. Him.' She laughed nervously. Now who was babbling? 'So for a few years she was Claude. He was Claude. We thought she was Claude. When he wanted to wear dresses, well, at first I guess we thought it was just a phase.' Why was she telling them all this? 'I mean dress-up, pretend play, make believe . . . boys will be boys, you know?' They did not look as if they did know. 'But it turned out it wasn't a phase. Deep down, he feels like a girl. She feels like a girl. She is a girl. So that's what we did.'

'Did?' It was like some tiny creature inside their faces had turned the light off.

'It's a long story,' Rosie admitted.

'You, um . . . turned your son into a girl?' Frank finally managed.

'Not turned him into.' As with so many disasters, it seemed the only way forward was deeper. 'More like accepted who he – she – already was.'

They were silent for a moment, taking that in, which Rosie supposed was fair enough; she just wondered if they couldn't do it elsewhere.

'We saw this drag show once at a bar in Capitol Hill,' Frank said hopefully. 'Is it like that?'

'It is nothing like that,' said Rosie.

Then, of course, the back door opened. 'Good news, Mom,' Orion called. 'The sandwich place at the bottom of the hill gets their cheese from Wisconsin.'

'And it's at the *bottom* of the hill,' Rigel added, 'so it's an easy walk.'

'Only if you want to move in,' Ben said. And when that seemed to elucidate nothing, 'Otherwise it's uphill on the way home.'

Roo rolled his eyes. Penn piled what looked to be lunch for forty into Poppy's arms so that his could be free to greet the Grandersons.

'We live next door.' Marginny went back to the beginning. 'We came over to welcome you. *And* to invite you to an end-of-summer barbecue at our house tomorrow. The whole neighborhood will be there. You'll be able to meet everyone all at once.'

Rosie was exhausted just thinking about it and began to brainstorm ways to politely decline.

'We'd be delighted,' said Penn.

It was ten o'clock, late for company, when the doorbell rang for the fourth time. Penn and Rosie paused the movie they were collapsed in front of to open the door to an embarrassed-looking Marginny. Rosie had known the woman for all of a quarter of an hour so far, but she could already tell she didn't embarrass easily. This did not bode well.

'Settling in okay?' Marginny seemed to be holding her breath.

'Slowly,' said Penn.

Rosie winced at several loud, heavy thumps coming from somewhere upstairs. 'We have lots of hands, but it's an open question if that makes unpacking harder or easier.'

'I thought you were going to say harder or much harder.' Marginny's smile, mom to mom, was genuine all of a sudden. Rosie wondered, for the first time, if she might actually like the woman. 'Listen, I wanted to . . . not apologize for Frank this morning, but, you know, I hope he didn't offend you. Talking about the drag show and everything. He was just . . . taken aback. We both were.'

'Sorry it was so awkward,' said Rosie. 'I think I might need practice. You're the first people we've known who haven't . . . known.'

'Yeah. So about that,' and Rosie braced herself in case she might have to stop liking Marginny as soon as she'd started, 'I just wanted you to know that we decided not to tell our kids.'

'Tell them what?' said Penn.

'About Poppy.' Rosie answered without looking at him. She felt his arm go around her waist.

'It just seems like it would be unnecessarily confusing for them.' Marginny was twisting her fingers together like braids. 'Why tell them just to ask them to forget? We'd have to explain and explain just to get them to understand and then we'd have to explain and explain about how they can never mention it again. So we thought isn't it best to just let nature take its course?'

'Nature?' Rosie and Penn said together.

'As long as we don't say anything, our girls will look at yours and just naturally think of her as one of them. That's what everyone wants, right?'

'I guess so.' Rosie wasn't sure what her objection was, but it felt like there must be one.

'Anyway, I just thought I should let you know.' Marginny smiled that genuine smile again. 'May these be the most awkward conversations we ever have.'

And how could Rosie object to that?

'You told them?' Penn unwound his arm from her waist as soon as the door was closed.

'Yeah? Was I not supposed to?'

'I don't know. I haven't thought this through I guess.'

'Me neither.'

'Why'd you tell them?'

'It's the truth?' said Rosie. It came out as a question.

'It's not really.'

'It's not?'

'That she's really a boy?' said Penn. 'She's not really a boy.'

'I didn't say she was really a boy. I said she used to be a boy.'

'That's not entirely true either.'

'What would you have said?' Rosie asked.

'Nothing?'

'Nothing?'

'Nothing. I would have just said, "This is my daughter, Poppy."'

Rosie thought about Jane Doe bleeding to death in her hands. Rosie thought about Chad Perry's fingers jerking back from what they found under her skirt like he'd pricked them on a witch's spindle. If you didn't tell people to begin with, you never knew when they might find out. 'They'd realize. Eventually.'

'How?'

'That's what worries me.'

'It's been a long time since we had neighbors,' Penn allowed, 'but I don't think one generally sees them naked.'

'So we just don't tell anybody?'

'I don't know. How was the conversation?'

'Terrible,' she admitted. 'Weird. Awkward. Embarrassing for everyone.'

'Want to have it forty or fifty more times this week? With everyone we meet at the barbecue, on the playground at school, all the kids' new friends and their parents?'

'I do not.'

'Besides,' said Penn, 'on sight, how do you tell the difference between the Cindy Calcuttis and the Nick Calcuttis?'

'What do you mean?'

'How do you know before you tell them who's going to say, "Okay, cool," and who's going to be hateful and violent? Or who's going to say, "Okay, cool" and be secretly hateful and violent?' Penn pictured his imaginary gunshot wound. Penn pictured his fist slamming again and again into Nick Calcutti's face.

'You don't know,' Rosie conceded.

'I know this isn't why we moved,' Penn said, 'but it's a nice bonus. Not everyone has to know. She can be just Poppy for a while. We can always tell people later.'

'When?'

'I don't know.' Penn shrugged. 'Later. Once we've gotten to know them. When we know it's safe. When the moment is right.'

Maybe there was a moment when the moment was right, but over the years, Rosie and Penn realized the impossibility of finding it. For the first few thousand of them after they met someone, it was too soon, Poppy's story too awkward and complicated, too intimate, too risky to share with new acquaintances. But by the time those acquaintances became close friends, it was too late. Perhaps there was a perfect moment in between, when you were close enough to tell but not so close it was problematic that you hadn't done so already, but it was infinitesimal, too fleet and fleeting to pin down, visible not even in hindsight.

'You can tell anytime,' Penn said, 'but once people know, they can never unknow.'

For such a short statement, it was astonishing how much of it proved untrue.

At the barbecue, Penn remembered what else neighbors can be: entertainers of your children. The Elliotts, two doors down across the street, had twin boys a month older than Rigel and Orion – Harry and Larry – and though Penn and Rosie secretly thought rhyming twins were unnecessarily confusing and the Elliotts secretly thought twins named after stars were unnecessarily abstruse, when Rosie checked on them later, she found all four in old Rigel-knit eye patches, huddled around a neighborhood (treasure) map all but dancing with delight. Cayenne Granderson had her mother's open face and wide smile but her father's erratic garrulousness. If Frank came off at first as awkward and off-putting, his daughter read as unpredictable and dangerous. Intriguingly dangerous. She introduced Roo and Ben to some of the older kids, and when Penn went to investigate, he found seven or eight of them piled on a blanket in the corner of the yard, one boy strumming pointlessly at a guitar, Cayenne with her head in Ben's lap. Ben looked frozen, overcome with good fortune but terrified that if he moved so much as a toe she might realize what she was doing and get up and go away. (Penn, who had more experience with these things, noted that Cayenne didn't look like she had any desire to go anywhere.) Roo was scowling at the guitarist, realizing for the first time that playing the flute at a neighbor's barbecue in front of a bunch of new kids was unlikely to earn him the same cachet. (Penn, who had more experience with these things, bet that even though Roo had never touched a guitar in his life, he could still play better than this kid.)

Poppy stood shyly behind her parents' legs when they first walked in, her parents a little cowed themselves by the magnitude of living in an actual neighborhood. With actual neighbors.

'We're so glad you could come,' Marginny cooed.

'So Poppy, are you hungry?' Frank bent down to peek at her behind Penn's knees. Rosie held her breath. 'Come meet Aggie.' He offered her a hand, but Poppy shook her head mutely. 'Aggie,' he called, and a girl just Poppy's age tumbled around from the side of the house in pigtails tied up with twist ties and a cape of plastic tablecloth that had lately been on the dessert buffet. She wore one yellow rain boot, one bare foot, and was dripping wet.

'Why are you soaked?' Frank said. The girl smiled sagely as if this were one of the universe's unknowable mysteries. Frank seemed to change his mind about wanting to know. 'This is Poppy. She just moved in next door. She's going into first grade too.'

Aggie peered at her new neighbor. 'Want to see my room?' She ran off at a wobble without waiting for an answer, it being, apparently, obvious, at least to the six-year-old set. Poppy ran off after her, laughing already. It was love at first sight.

Rosie and Penn met two Melissas, two Jennys, a Suzy and a Susan, a Mary, an Anne, and a Maryanne, a Kiki and a Mimi. They met Doug, Erik, Jason, Alex, Baylor, Aiden, Isaac, Gordon, Josh, and Cal. The names went in Penn's ears and out Rosie's. There were too many to stick. 'Nice to meet you,' they said, over and over again. And 'Five,' they answered all night long, and 'Madison, Wisconsin,' and 'Yes, we like it here so far.' And, pointing, 'The turret house next door.' Rosie answered, 'The neighborhood school,' which was met with delight, and 'For work,' which was sort of true, and 'Doctor. Family practice. Right at the top of the hill.' Penn answered, 'Struggling writer,' and 'No, you probably haven't read anything I've written.' They answered, 'Fourteen, thirteen, eleven, eleven, and six.' They answered, 'Four boys and a girl.'

Over two red plastic cups of very good sangria, one of the Melissas said to Rosie, 'You must have been so glad to finally have a daughter.' She was drinking while rocking in place to keep her own pink-clad infant asleep in the sling on her chest.

Rosie sipped and nodded. 'We were thrilled. Just thrilled.' This was mostly true as well.

The older kids stayed late at the party, but Rosie and Penn said their good nights in order to take their youngest home to bed.

'Stories?' Poppy asked hopefully.

'Tomorrow,' Penn promised. 'It's way, way past your bedtime tonight.'

'Did you have fun?' Rosie tucked the sheets in all around the corners of the bed. It was too warm for a blanket.

'So much,' said Poppy, and Penn and Rosie both looked hard at their baby, so fervent was this reply. 'No one here knows. They say *she* and they say *her*, and it's like they're not even pretending, you know?'

'They're not,' Penn said.

'It's like I'm not even pretending too.' Poppy's eyes were closing, sleepy-happy.

'Well, no one here knows who we really are,' said Rosie.

'No, it's the opposite.' Her daughter shook her head happily. 'It's like they know exactly.'

Poppy would have been asleep a minute later except there was a tap-tap-tapping behind her blinds. She opened them to see Aggie leaning out her own window to poke at Poppy's with a yardstick duct taped to the end of an umbrella. Their hill was so steep that Aggie's second-floor window looked out over the roof of most of Poppy's house, but Poppy's turret put them feet from each other.

'Hi.' Aggie grinned.

'Hi.' Poppy rubbed her eyes, maybe because she was sleepy or maybe because she couldn't believe luck as magical as this.

'I'm so glad you moved here. We can be rival princesses in neighboring castles.' Aggie had been waiting a long time for someone sufficiently royal to move in next door. The previous occupants had been an elderly couple who used the turret for storage. 'We can climb up and down each other's hair.'

'We can pass notes and letters,' Poppy wonder-whispered, 'and spells.'

'Or cupcakes,' said Aggie. 'Like if you earn dessert and I don't.'

'We can trade books and dolls and cool rocks we find and pictures we draw back and forth.'

'We can tell secrets,' said Aggie. 'We can tell each other things we can't tell anyone else in the whole world. Up here, no one will ever know.'

Poppy went to bed tingling with happiness, ecstatic with impatience. She wondered how long she would have to wait before she had something secret to tell.

Everyone Who?

Mr Tongo's point was a little more on the nose: 'It doesn't smell like anyone else's business.'

Rosie had been sorry to leave her colleagues in the ER. She'd been sorry to leave her mentors and her residents, the nurses and the attendings, the place that had made her a doctor, and her home for so many years, but it was Mr Tongo, with his peculiar wisdom and quirky comfort, to whom it was somehow hardest to say goodbye. Then, at her farewell party, he'd reminded her that he wasn't officially her therapist or her social worker but in fact her friend, and this meant he could be in Seattle whenever she needed him.

'Teleportation?' Rosie put nothing past Mr Tongo.

'Telephone.' He winked. 'It's only nineteenth-century technology, but it's more effective because it's not pretend.'

Three weeks later, not even fully unpacked yet, she'd called him. Their life felt unfolded, a cardboard box they'd broken down and flattened back to a plain square then refolded into something unrecognizable. Rosie needed a voice of reason, no matter how unreasonable. And that was what he said: 'It doesn't smell like anyone else's business.'

'Smell like?'

'Well, it certainly doesn't sound like anyone else's business, does it? Don't think of Poppy as Claude under wraps. Think of Poppy as a girl with a penis, a girl with an unusual medical history. Do you usually discuss what's in children's pants with the other moms on the playground?'

'Not usually, no.'

'And it doesn't feel like anyone else's business either, right? That's your point. That it feels odd and awkward to tell.'

'Right but—'

'So I'm sniffing around, and it doesn't have that whiff of Things We Share either.' Mr Tongo made snuffling noises on the other end of the line to show that he was on the scent. 'We discuss a lot of intimate things with our friends, but our genitals, and those of our children, are private. Many of my patients and clients – kids as well as their parents, people dealing with a whole range of conditions, not just this one – find they don't want to explain themselves every time they meet someone new. They don't want to be responsible for educating everyone they meet. They don't consider what's in their pants to be any of anyone else's business.'

'I guess not but—'

'You have lots of opportunities there you never had in Wisconsin. You could go a whole winter without shoveling your walk. You could drink a cup of coffee that would occasion tears of joy. If you shed them out of doors in February, they would not freeze on your cheeks. What fun! And Poppy doesn't have to be Poppy Who Used to Be Claude. She can be Just Poppy.'

'But people need to know.'

'Who does?'

'Everyone.'

'Oh yes, I see,' said Mr Tongo. 'Everyone who?'

'Her teachers. The school nurse. The parents of her playdates. Her soccer coach. Her ballet instructor. Our friends. Their kids. The boys' friends. The parents of the boys' friends—'

'Why?' Mr Tongo wondered.

'Why?'

'Yes, why do all those people need to know? What's likely to happen at school that Poppy's penis would make a difference to her first-grade teacher or the school nurse? What kind of playdates is this six-year-old going on that her friends' parents need her whole medical history? Do you get her friends' medical histories when they come over to play?'

'No.'

'No. So why do they need hers?'

'Maybe it's not that they have a need to know but a right to know.'

'"Right to know" suggests you are being duplicitous, lying to people about something, masking certain truths. Are you duplicitous or lying?'

'No?'

'No. You're not masking a truth. This is the truth. If you told people she was really a boy, that would be untrue. There's nothing here anyone has a need or right to know. You're not keeping secrets. You're respecting your child's right to privacy, which she has both need of and right to, just like the rest of us.'

In fact, it wasn't just Poppy. Families who keep secrets don't keep just one. They all guarded like garrisons stories of who they were, who they had been.

At breakfast on the first morning of school, Rigel and Orion crafted a plan.

'Let's tell everyone we're actually pirates,' said Rigel. 'I'll say my name is Blackbeard, and you can be Captain Hook.'

'You don't have a black beard.' Ben was disappointed to find they'd moved all the way across the country and his little brothers were still idiots. 'And he doesn't have a hook.'

'I have a hook,' said Orion.

'Is that why he's called Blackbeard?' Blackbeard considered the matter. 'I'll be Stubble the Pirate.'

Ben snorted. 'You wish.'

'Hint of Whiskers the Pirate? Dad gave me his old electric razor.'

'But have you used it?'

'I see your point.' Rigel's hairless eleven-year-old face lit up. 'I'll be Nobeard the Pirate! Seattle is going to be so great.'

Ben could be the smart one all anew. The move bought him another year of revelation. By the time he'd turned seven at home, everyone already knew he was smart, which made his being smart unimpressive. His tests actually came back with sighs from his teachers: 'A+ as usual' or 'Great work as always'. Now his papers came back breathless again with 'Wow!'s and 'Amazing!'s and invitations to join Advanced Placement classes and the Debate Club.

And Poppy became Just Poppy. Not Poppy with a penis. Not Poppy who used to be Claude. Not Poppy who's really a boy. Just Poppy.

But for all of that, it was Roo's transformation that was most dramatic. He wasn't a little boy after the move any more than Poppy was. He didn't seem a man quite yet, but Rosie and Penn could see it in there, waiting, biding time in his face, making hard angles and hair where he'd been round and smooth just weeks before. He gave up football, he said, because practice was boring, but Rosie imagined it was because the team already had a quarterback and a backup quarterback and Roo worried he wasn't as good. He gave up the flute, he said, because he didn't like the band teacher, but Penn imagined it was because without football to balance it out, a woodwind section otherwise dominated by girls was asking a lot of the new guy. There already was the kid who always got elected president. He gave up football for sitting in his room sulking. He gave up leading all clubs except the Roo Is Really Pissed Off and Doesn't Want to Talk About It Club. He gave up flautist for floutist. He was not a man, not remotely, but he wasn't a little boy or even a big boy anymore either. Like Poppy, suddenly he was somewhere in between.

Rosie and Penn had to box up their old lives too. After all the unpacking, it seemed wrong for Penn to be bubble wrapping and hole spackling and slicing the flesh on the underside of his thumbnail in an effort to pry picture hangers out of walls, but that's just what he was doing. Rosie put pictures up first thing. She said it made it feel like home. She said who cares whether all the plates and books and winter clothes and old phone chargers stayed in boxes for a while; once the beds were made and the pictures hung, the place was yours. For three weeks after the move, Penn's family montaged the walls, smiling down at him through time. Baby Roo dwarfed newborn Ben the day he came home from the hospital. Carmelo held one turkey-hatted twin on each knee on their third Thanksgiving. Rosie squeezed an arm around each of her parents at med school graduation. She smiled into Penn's eyes from beneath a white veil, her top teeth sunk alluring into a lip that hadn't been painted since, while he gazed back at her with awe and wonder, a photo that surely graced the walls of many homes yet still seemed not just miraculous but unique to him, like no one else had ever felt a love quite like that, like this. There were Halloween photos through the years in one of those patchwork frames – pirates and baseball players and magicians, four pumpkins and one Prince Grumwald. There were terrible class pictures he'd fought (and lost) against framing, one for each child for each school year, mugging boys grinning gappy and gappier smiles, hair spiked in more directions than a puffer fish. And, of course, pictures of Claude: infant Claude surrounded by brothers on his one-week birthday, baby Claude being lightly chewed by a yak at a petting zoo (not his person,

just his jacket, the look of alarm on his tiny face too precious not to capture before resuming parental duties and removing bovid from child),
mortar-boarded Claude at preschool graduation, two-year-old Claude
one of eight Santas (Jupiter included) on one winter's holiday card.

The pictures collaged one soaring wall of the new house, family story,
family history, hodgepodged love and time. Penn gazed up at them, helpless. Until everyone here knew Poppy's provenance, the pictures had to
go back in boxes because otherwise who was that fifth little boy with the
serious eyes and the small smile? Because what kind of parents lovingly
archived the childhoods of the first four kids and ignored the last?
Because even though she'd know why, Penn could not bear for Poppy – or
Claude – to be lost, banned from their merry band, not just homeless but
pastless as well. Poppy's childhood did matter, and so did Claude's, but
Penn bubble wrapped them all back up anyway until he could find a way
to tell this story.

Rosie came home from work and took in the blank wall all alone. The
farmhouse had lacked discrete spaces, especially on the main floor where
the kitchen/living room/dining room sprawled into one. In this house, it
was possible to come home and start unpacking family photos in the living room while Penn made dinner in the kitchen while the kids holed up
in their own rooms and feel actually lonely.

Penn came out of the kitchen, wiping his hands on a towel. 'I didn't
hear you come in.'

'You took down all the pictures.' Not accusation. Observation.

'Had to.' He smiled sadly then added, 'You can't put them back up.'

She nodded. 'I miss them.'

'The pictures?'

'I miss . . . him,' Rosie amended.

'Who?'

'Claude.'

'She's in her room playing with Aggie.'

'That's not what I meant.'

'I know. But it should be. Claude's not gone.'

'He's changed.'

'They've all changed,' said Penn. 'They all change. Claude wouldn't
be the same kid he was in his baby pictures anyway. How is this different?'

'We can't put our family photos on the wall.'

'Not yet,' said Penn.

'When?' said Rosie.

Penn shrugged – he didn't know – and went back to the kitchen. Roo came upstairs, burrowed into the corner of the sofa, and just watched her. More and more he did this – came and watched and said nothing. She was grateful he still wanted to be near them, but she wished he would say something. And then sometimes he did and she wished that he wouldn't.

'Look what a cute baby you were.' She held out to him the gilded proof of his thirteen months of only childhood.

'All babies are cute.'

'You were cuter than most,' Rosie assured him. 'I'm a connoisseur.'

He looked for a long time at the frame in his hand. He did not raise his head when he said, 'I thought the whole point of moving was it's supposed to be so gay here.'

'Gay?'

'You know. Tolerant. Open-minded. Rainbow flaggy. Whatever.'

'Well. That was part of it, yes.'

'You wrecked our whole lives for this place.'

Rosie concentrated on her pictures, waited for whatever was coming next.

'So why are we keeping Claude this big secret?'

'We're not keeping it a secret.'

'You're hiding the family photos.'

'We haven't told anybody *yet*,' Rosie said. 'We will. We just haven't so far.'

'If we didn't need someplace gay, we could have just stayed where we were –'

'It wasn't safe there.'

'Where we were happy,' said Roo.

'We'll be happy here,' said Rosie.

'Not like this we won't.' Roo slunk back to his basement.

Rosie and Penn were still lost most of the time, never sure where was home or how to get there. Half their lives remained in boxes at that point. Plus Roo had been sulky and sullen all summer, gloomy since they announced the move, moody still now that they were here. And so she missed it, his warning, his fledgling teenage foresight that secrets are miserable things, that secrets, be they deliberate or accidental, will out, and then it won't matter where you live, for no place anywhere can protect you from the power and the fallout of a secret once exploded.

Rosie rehung the wedding photo and one of each kid. For Poppy, she chose Claude's preschool graduation. Capped and gowned, you couldn't really tell.

Strategically Naked

It didn't seem like the person in Rosie and Penn's life to whom they would be most grateful would be a six-year-old, but that's what happened anyway. Every day, they gave silent, ecstatic thanks for Aggie Granderson. For starters, she made everyone crazy. There are few children more treasured than ill-behaved ones who belong to someone else. They had five, but Aggie was louder. They all woke up one morning before dawn to Aggie, inside and next door, banging cymbals and scream-singing, '*Yankee Doodle went to town riding on a donkey/Stuck a feather in his hat and called it macaronkey*' at the top of her six-year-old lungs. Penn smiled sleepily at his wife.

'What are you so happy about?' Rosie groaned.

'Two words,' said Penn. 'Not. Ours.'

They had five, but Aggie was wilder. Somehow when she was over, bowls of popcorn defenestrated, whole boxes of cereal were accidentally fed to, then extruded by, the dog, potted plants sprouted lamp cords, crudités, and, once, the business end of a rectal thermometer.

They had four and a half boys, plus Penn, but in some ways, Aggie was maler than any of them. She was a girl who dug holes and ran hard and liked bugs and all that other tomboy shit, but it was more – or maybe less – than that. She'd dismantle toy trucks to build spaceships to fly dolls to day spas built inside killer volcanoes. You just couldn't nail the kid down.

And better than all those wonders, she lived next door. Poppy and Aggie were in and out of each other's houses all weekend long. Penn came to greet the sight of Aggie at his dinner table as no more or less surprising than any of his other kids. Rosie started to habitually buy six of anything she was only planning to buy five of. Any given load of laundry was likely to have as many of Aggie's clothes in it as Poppy's. And because Aggie lived not just nearby, but very nearby, it was eleven months before Poppy proposed an overnight her parents couldn't wriggle out of.

'Can we have a sleepover?' the girls would chorus, and Penn would answer, 'You can't bring all your stuffies to Aggie's, and if you pick and choose, some will have their feelings hurt. Wouldn't it be better just to sleep at home tonight and keep peace in the Stuffie Kingdom?'

Or Rosie would say, 'The extra sheets are in the wash. How about Aggie just comes back first thing in the morning?'

Or Marginny would show up in slippers after dark with a sleepy-looking Poppy, explaining, 'We just thought the girls would have more fun hiking tomorrow if they both got a good night's sleep in their own beds tonight.'

But a sleepover – and with her new friends Natalie and Kim too, not just Aggie – was the only thing Poppy wanted for her seventh birthday. She wanted a sleepover plus baked brie, pimento cheese sandwiches, spicy tuna rolls, Doritos, ginger ale, and, of course, cake and ice cream, plus a pass on all fruits and vegetables for a thirty-six-hour period to include the whole of her birthday plus half the next day as well. Rosie and Penn found they could not reasonably object to any of that. A girl has only one seventh birthday, after all.

They didn't want to scare her, but they wanted her to be prepared. They didn't want to make her feel unsafe, but they wanted to protect her. They didn't want to suggest to her that her body needed hiding. But unfortunately it did.

'Where will you change into PJs?' Rosie asked, lightly, while hanging streamers, as if this question were no more or less significant than what kind of frosting Poppy wanted on her cake.

'I dunno,' said Poppy. 'Can we do a craft too?'

'Sure,' said Rosie. 'How about the bathroom?'

'For the craft?'

'How about you change in the bathroom?'

'A bathroom craft would be awesome. Like those crayons you use in the tub. Or toilet decorating.'

'I just think . . . you know girls at sleepovers often . . . I think Kim and Natalie and Aggie might want to change out of their clothes and into their PJs right in your turret, so I'm just a little worried that . . .' What? What was she just a little worried that? Probably the girls would pull nightgowns or pajamas on over their underwear, right? They might even fall asleep in their clothes if she was lucky. Still, she'd seen what came from not having a plan, and she wanted to be prepared. 'You could just say you're shy.'

'I'm not shy.'

'But I mean to explain why you have to change alone in the bathroom.'

Poppy looked up from her crepe-paper bows for the first time. 'I have to be alone?'

'Well, because your friends don't know . . . you know . . . quite who you are.'

'Who I am?'

'I mean they know you, of course, but they don't know. You know?'

Poppy looked confused. 'Are you being silly, Mama?' She concluded her mother was just teasing her and broke into a huge almost-seven-year-old smile. 'Don't worry. This is going to be the best sleepover ever.'

But Rosie worried anyway. 'What are we going to do?' She was whipping green cream-cheese frosting, as instructed.

'See how it plays out?' Penn guessed.

She pointed a whisk at him. 'You're the one who wants to keep this thing a secret.'

'I don't want to keep this thing a secret. We have all, prudently, agreed to this approach for this moment. For good reasons.'

'But it's like she didn't even know what I was talking about. It's like she's forgotten she's really a boy.'

'She's not really a boy.'

'Yes, right, I know, I know. But you know what I mean. It's like she's forgotten she has a penis.'

'When you own a penis' – Penn glanced down at his authoritatively – 'you never forget.'

'She's forgotten that a penis isn't what she's supposed to have,' Rosie persisted. Maybe she couldn't quite articulate it, but she knew the point was valid. 'She's forgotten her friends have – and are expecting – something else.'

Rosie had taken to trying to walk around naked more, but it was hard.

For one thing, there was the mob of teenage boys in her house. For an-other, there were the neighbors. The problem was the kids saw each other naked all the time, changing in and out of swimsuits and sports gear and school clothes and pajamas, and Poppy therefore had the im-pression that she was totally normal. Everyone had toes. Everyone had elbows. Everyone had a penis. Maybe it lacked subtlety, but Rosie thought 'show don't tell' was the best way to disabuse Poppy of this last point. She sat in the bath until her fingers wrinkled into origami so that she could be getting out of it just when Poppy wandered in looking for glue sticks. She threw her workout clothes in the wash with the towels then changed for yoga right when Poppy was gathering supplies for the beach. It was weird – not to mention chilly – but how better, in a houseful of penises, to show Poppy that while there was nothing wrong with her body, for a girl it was pretty unusual? But it seemed not to make an im-pression. Very nearly seven-year-old Poppy's body looked no more like adult Penn's than adult Rosie's when you got right down to it. She was grateful, really, that Poppy didn't understand. But she was also panicked, really, that Poppy didn't understand.

It was a torturous evening. It was worse, in fact, than the one it com-memorated, Poppy's first sleepover, its anguished waiting escalating in intensity the longer it went on, proving altogether more painful than Ros-ie's quick final labor. The girls started with the baked brie and the Dor-itos, ignoring Penn's neat baguette slices and scooping up fancy French cheese with neon orange triangles instead. Rosie, anxious to get on with things already, tried to serve the (such that it was) main course then, but Penn pointed out it was only four thirty, and Poppy whined, 'Mom, we have so much to do.' They all four whirled up to her turret while Rosie cursed the stairs: she couldn't hear what they were doing up there by pressing her ear to the door at the bottom of them. Lots of giggling. Lots of high-pitched joy. They came down and watched *The Sound of Music*. They wanted to make clothes out of the curtains, but Penn steered them toward marshmallow monsters – Poppy's chosen craft – instead. More marshmallows turned into snacks than into monsters. Then Poppy opened presents, and then she consented to dinner: the sandwiches and sushi. Rigel and Orion did a magic show with a set they'd gotten several birthdays ago, supplemented by an actual hacksaw and a chocolate rabbit they did indeed saw in half and manage to reattach by licking the edges until they were sufficiently sticky. The girls giggled. Roo and Ben stayed in their basement and pretended none of the rest of them existed. Penn blew up a bunch of balloons for a lawless, anarchic game of balloon tag. And Rosie fretted.

They called the older boys up for singing, cake, and ice cream. It was her first all-girls birthday, and Rosie was pleasantly surprised to see them actually sit and eat, quietly if not neatly, which would have been nice except she still had her own brood to contend with. Rigel balanced a piece of cake on the top hat Orion was wearing, which slid off onto Roo's plate, which splattered ice cream onto Rigel's present: orange knit party hats that looked to Rosie like yarmulkes. The twins held each other's necks in the crooks of their elbows and rolled around on the kitchen floor for a bit, spreading dropped cake and ice cream into every corner and whipping Jupiter into a frenzy of barking and alarm. Rosie envied the dog, for whom it was socially acceptable to walk around whining ceaselessly when she was feeling anxious.

When the girls started yawning, Penn lightly suggested it might be time to start thinking about getting ready for bed. Rosie wasn't ready yet. She felt like she was breathing very quickly all of a sudden. She tried to look nonchalant while the girls trundled upstairs. Then she raced for the turret steps like an about-to-be-sawed-in-half chocolate rabbit. She climbed the stairs as quietly as she could, stopping halfway up, like Christopher Robin, trying not to pant and give herself away. She heard bags unzipping, kicked-off shoes whacking into the molding, clothes being shed, soft exclamation over Kim's Seattle Storm pajamas and Natalie's slippers shaped like bear feet. She strained but could not hear whether or not underwear was being removed. Why couldn't underpants be louder? She heard Poppy's dresser drawers open and shut, open and shut again. Suddenly, Poppy was walking back toward the stairs.

Rosie cursed and ran full-tilt into her room where she flung herself onto the bed. Penn was already there, legs crossed at the ankle, one arm behind his head, the other holding the book he was reading. He looked quite pleased with himself.

'One thousand in unmarked bills and you wear that worn-through Brewers T-shirt to bed for a week, and your secret's safe with me,' he told Rosie out of the side of his mouth as Poppy walked into the room.

'I can't find any of my nightgowns,' Poppy said.

'I think they're all in the dryer, sweetie.' Penn smiled the smile of the innocent.

Poppy wandered off to the laundry room and came back two minutes later in her flamingo nightgown. 'Thanks, Daddy.'

'Sure, baby. What'd you do with your clothes?'

'Left them in a pile on the floor,' she admitted, then brightened, 'but it's my birthday.'

'Then you get a pass.' He kissed her good night. 'Have fun up there. Don't stay up too late, or you'll be too tired for Mickey Mouse pancakes in the morning.'

Poppy raced upstairs to start year number seven.

'Thank you,' Rosie breathed. She closed her eyes. 'Thank you, thank you, thank you.'

'No problem,' said Penn. 'You get a pass too.'

And she thought: just that simple. And she thought: problem solved. But the problem was just beginning.

Rosie imagined she'd have a year – until Poppy turned eight – to recover, but Poppy and Aggie had discovered sleepovers to be even better than their chapter books purported. Having broken the parental seal, they could no longer be deterred. Rosie's reprieve lasted all of a week, and this time was worse because this time was at Aggie's house. At Aggie's house, Penn couldn't spirit all Poppy's sleepwear into the laundry, not that that was likely to work again at home either. At Aggie's house, Rosie couldn't barge in if necessary with some absurd but (alas) believable motherly bullshit like 'At our house, we change in private.'

Rosie wondered if it was too late to invoke a rule that Friday was the Sabbath and they should all go to shul rather than attend sleepovers. Penn thought it probably was. In fact, Penn had a whole different point, which was that Rigel and Orion were going to the movies with Larry and Harry, Ben was playing miniature golf with the rest of the debate team, and Roo was highly unlikely to emerge from the basement under any circumstances. If Poppy were sleeping next door, they'd essentially have the house to themselves for the night, and since Rosie was walking around strategically naked all the time, he had some thoughts as to what they might do with it.

While Penn made this case and Rosie panicked, Poppy packed. The fact that she was going just next door didn't mean packing wasn't part of the ritual. Poppy packed Alice and Miss Marple. She packed two games, a bottle of green glitter toenail polish, and a bag of Orion's costumes in case they wanted to play dress-up. To this modest assemblage, Rosie added a pair of underwear, a skirt, a T-shirt, a nightgown, and a toothbrush with the weepy foreboding of a mother sending a soldier off to war.

She sat Poppy down on her bed then kneeled at her feet. This time, she was a little better prepared. 'When you change into your nightgown tonight, baby, you need to do it somewhere private. You know?'

'Yeah?' Poppy didn't sound sure.

'Sweetheart, Aggie doesn't know you have a penis, and she would probably be really confused to see it, so you either have to tell her or just excuse yourself and go into the bathroom and change.'

'Okay,' said Poppy.

'Which?'

'Which what?'

'Which do you prefer? Should we tell Aggie? She's such a good friend, baby. You could tell her, and then she'd know, and everything would be fine. You could decide to tell other friends too, or if you told Aggie not to tell anyone else, you know she wouldn't.'

'What about Nicky?' Barely a whisper.

'Nicky?'

'Remember how Nicky used to be my best friend and then he found out about me, and he was so grossed out he tried to shoot Daddy?'

Rosie rocked back on her heels and waited for the breath to return to her lungs. How had Poppy's memory twisted that story into this? And when? How long had she been carrying this version around? 'Oh, sweetheart, no. Nicky was your friend. He was little, but he loved you in his way. It was his father who didn't understand. Nicky didn't try to shoot Daddy. Nicky's daddy didn't even try to shoot Daddy.'

'But after he found out, he didn't want to be my friend anymore.'

Rosie nodded and said nothing. This wasn't entirely untrue. And what was true was probably even harder to understand.

'What if Aggie doesn't want to be my friend when she finds out I'm really a boy?'

'Are you really a boy?' Rosie asked gently.

'No.' The first sure thing out of Poppy's mouth so far. 'I'm not, Mama.'

'No, you're not. So Aggie won't think that. We can explain it to her anytime. We can go over right now and tell Aggie together what a wonderful, brave, amazing little girl you are.'

'I don't want her to think there's anything weird about me.'

'Why?' said Rosie. 'There's plenty that's weird about her.'

'Exactly,' said Poppy. 'She's the weird one. I'm the normal one. That's the way we like it.'

Late that night, after a movie and a skit and toenail painting and LEGO building and thirty-six rounds of Hangman, Aggie took off every stitch of clothing she had on, wandered around naked looking for something she might wear to bed, and eventually donned, commando, a four-sizes-too-big swimsuit cover-up of Cayenne's. Poppy took her nightgown out of her bag, balled it up in her arms, and headed toward the bathroom.

'You can just change in here,' Aggie assured her. 'I'm not embarrassed.'

'Oh,' said Poppy. 'Thanks.'

'Are you?'

'Am I what?'

'Embarrassed?'

'No. But . . . Roverella's watching me.' Roverella was Aggie's family's six-pound Chihuahua. Penn called it a hamster. It followed Aggie everywhere.

Aggie giggled. 'Roverella is a watchdog. She watches everything. She loves to see people in their nudies, so I guess you better change in the bathroom.'

Poppy went off, relieved and pleased with herself. It was years before it struck Aggie as strange that someone would be embarrassed to change in front of a dog.

Stalls

In fact, for many years, accommodating Poppy boiled down really to the two percent of her life when she wasn't wearing underpants. Even Claude had always peed sitting down, but everything else in that department involved an El Capitan-esque learning curve. Penn joined a listserv. Penn joined an online support group. Penn followed blogs and Facebook pages, Twitter feeds and Instagram accounts, YouTube channels and podcasts. There he learned the secrets to protecting secrets. He learned where you could buy penis-masking underpants (hell, he learned there *were* penis-masking underpants) to parade around in during sleepovers with everyone else so you didn't have to blame the dog. He learned which ballet schools required bare leotards and which allowed wrap skirts overtop. He learned which day camps didn't have swimming. He learned that he could tell Poppy's principal, Mr Menendez, just in case, but still insist that Poppy be allowed to use the girls' bathroom. He learned that he could tell Mr Menendez but say no when the man recommended also disclosing to the teachers, resource specialists, substitutes, aides, school nurse, and cafeteria staff. He learned that Poppy was entitled to join girls' T-ball, girls' soccer, girls' tennis, girls' swim team. If she did join swim team, he learned she was entitled to use the girls' locker room. The best thing about girls' bathrooms, so far as Penn could tell, was that stalls were requisite. Maybe lots of girls changed in the middle of the room, but everyone peed in a stall, and if you had to pee anyway, it only made sense you'd change in and out of your suit in there as well. Penn learned the Girl Scouts would have her even if they did know, but he didn't tell them anyway.

Penn could never get to the bottom of all there was to read about kids like his online – there was no bottom – but unfortunately, he tried anyway. This ate into his writing time. In the beginning, it had seemed Seattle would be great for the DN. There were wonderful bookstores and booksellers, libraries and librarians, writing classes and critique groups by the dozens. Because Rosie worked days instead of nights, he could work when she did instead of sleeping. And the weather in Seattle lent itself to novel writing: moody with low, gray clouds layered thick and full as a down comforter. He wrote lovely dark, wet prose that matched the weather.

But unfortunately, sometimes he wore that dark, wet mood around the house as well because there just were not enough hours in the day. Elementary school didn't start until nine thirty. High school got out at two. And in between, he also had laundry, also had a house to take care of, also had doctors' appointments and grocery shopping and his writers' group and to run Poppy's cleats to school when she forgot it was a soccer day or Rigel's permission slip when he forgot it was a field-trip day or Orion's lunch when he forgot it was a lunch-eating day. Because the other thing that had changed when they moved was Rosie's job security. UW Hospital knew her well, loved her much, and owed her more. Here, like the rest of them, she was the new kid again. She had to be impressive. She couldn't take sick days or time off. She had to stay late because she couldn't go early. Working days meant she wasn't home during them to help. Penn was glad to pick up the parenting slack. But it did not leave much time to write. Especially when he couldn't stop researching penis-masking underwear and its conceits.

At work, Rosie might have told their secret but did not. There was no reason not to really. It was a small practice, and people who work in a medical office are nothing if not trained at keeping both personal data and body particulars under wraps. Yes, those wraps were made out of waxy, mortifying paper with strings no one could manage to tie, and yes, they gapped over exactly the bits patients wanted covered up. In the ER, you cut people out of their clothes or treated them over top, depending, so maybe it's just that she wasn't used to unwrapping patients like packets from the deli. But the gowns weren't the only thing about West Hill Family Medical Center that required getting used to.

The Monday after she survived Poppy's seventh birthday, Rosie's first patient of the day was three-year-old Bristol Wonks. Really it was Mrs Wonks. Never mind her move to family practice, Rosie stuck by her refusal to call patients' parents 'Mom', but she was required instead to use 'Mrs'. She wondered what kind of mother would be offended that her kid's pediatrician used her first name – it was like relocating to a nineteenth-century novel – but she settled for what she could live with. In fact, the whole job was like that. There was much that seemed pointless but was easier to consent to than fight, easier to adjust to than starvation owing to unemployment. The Wonks also fell into that category of people where Rosie couldn't understand why you wouldn't use the wife's last name instead. Tradition is one thing, but who wanted to send her kid through life with a name like Bristol Wonks? There were so many things that befell your children you could not control. Why wouldn't you do something about the one you could?

'I'm worried about Bristol's hearing.' Mrs Wonks was speaking so quietly, Rosie began to worry about her own.

'Do his ears hurt him?' Rosie asked.

'I don't know,' Mrs Wonks admitted.

'Does he complain of soreness or pain?'

'No, but he's so little. Maybe he doesn't have the words for it. Children with hearing loss often have difficulty with speech acquisition, you know.'

Rosie did know. 'Do you notice him pulling at them?'

'I don't think so.'

'Why are you covering his ears with your hands, Mrs Wonks? Does that soothe Bristol?'

'I don't want him to hear us talking about him.' Mrs Wonks tightened her earmuff vise. 'I don't want to hurt his feelings.'

'But you brought him in today because you're worried about his hearing.'

'That's correct.'

'Then why cover his ears?'

'Just in case.'

Rosie took a deep breath. 'What makes you think he's having trouble hearing?'

'When I ask him to put away his LEGOs or finish his milk at dinner or clear his place or go put his shoes on, he doesn't.'

'Ahh.' The ER had ill equipped Rosie to ask her next question gently. 'What makes you think, Mrs Wonks, that the reason he doesn't do those things is because he can't hear you?'

'He doesn't even look up.' Mrs Wonks held both hands open before her to mime such a preponderance of evidence. 'It's not like he says no or has a tantrum. He doesn't even look at me.'

'Does he hear you when you ask if he wants an hour of screen time?'

'I think he guesses what I've said because I have his device in my hand.'

'Does he hear you when you ask if he wants to go out for ice cream?'

'He does but—'

'Bristol's three, Mrs Wonks. Unfortunately, it's perfectly normal for him to refuse to do things he's disinclined to do.'

'He's not refusing.'

'He really might be.'

'Pretending not to hear me would be lying.' Mrs Wonks removed her hands from her son's ears. 'And Bristol does not lie to his mommy and daddy.'

'What?' said Bristol. 'Huh?'

Rosie gave him a hearing test. To the shock of only Mrs Wonks, Bristol's ears were in perfect working condition.

They'd been in Seattle nine months, and Rosie still wasn't convinced this counted as practicing medicine. Her mistake had been seeded during panicked Wisconsin midnights, which had demanded any job rather than the right job. She'd been surprised to have gotten it, in fact. Her ER skill set – triage, diagnosis, mild grace under extreme pressure – seemed like it wouldn't be much use to the group of three very nice family physicians – Howie, James, and Elizabeth – who welcomed her in and demanded, mostly, extreme grace under mild pressure. The practice was run by Yvonne, receptionist/organizer/miracle-worker, a woman who had more children than Rosie (six) and more grandchildren than seemed possible (fifteen) though, as she said to Rosie, 'Do the math. It'll terrify you.'

The four doctors were equal partners, kept equal hours, did equal amounts of voluminous paperwork, attended conferences and taught workshops together, and shared companionably in all the other tasks that went into maintaining a small practice. Elizabeth was quiet and pleasant, kind without being sugary, politely inquiring after one's weekend without diving into anyone's business. She came in, saw patients, exchanged small talk in the break room, and went home to a life her partners knew nothing about. Rosie adored her. She adored James even more. He was not quiet. He scuba dived in her life. But in exchange, he let her live vicariously through his: James and his husband happy-houred or fine-dined most nights after work. They went to the opera and the theatre and over to friends' houses. They slept in on weekends and ate leisurely brunches while reading newspapers and books and exchanging philosophical ideas. They generally lived the life of childless newlyweds that seemed to Rosie a fantasy on par with anything you'd see at the movies. If you ever got to go to the movies. Which she did not.

It was Howie who was the problem. Howie insisted on holding a meeting every Monday morning just in case any problems had arisen over the weekend. Howie outlawed paper down to the Post-it note so they could say their practice was green. He made everyone take home two thousand Band-Aids one weekend to marker on their URL so he could hand them out on Halloween. He guilted them into posting short, deep thoughts to a Twitter feed to show rival practices they were a force of cleverness. It was Howie who wanted them to call patients' parents 'Mom'. He wanted Rosie to be in charge of staff-appreciation breakfast and finding someone to update their website. He wanted Rosie to get Yvonne a gift from the practice to go with her holiday bonus. He wanted Rosie to go to Thailand for three months to staff a refugee clinic so he could list on their website that their doctors were sought after for volunteer work and international aid.

Howie wanted to run a practice that could claim to accommodate employees' families so he agreed, when Rosie was hired, to the flextime that was the only way she could get five children out of the house every morning. Though the office opened at nine, she didn't see patients until ten. Though the other doctors saw their last patient of the day at four thirty, she saw hers at five thirty, which, as an added bonus, meant clients with jobs could also receive medical care. Howie agreed to this arrangement so as to seem like he cared about working parents, but he scheduled Monday Morning Meeting at eight thirty anyway and was surprised when Rosie failed most Mondays to get there in time.

Howie was not her boss, but he was the one who started the practice and hired the rest of them. She didn't want to make him angry. She certainly didn't want to argue with him. She tried to be patient with the patients, to look appropriately concerned when they said they had a mosquito bite that was itchier than usual or their taste buds felt weird or that head lice was a problem one could reasonably expect a family doctor to handle. She tried to stay out of Howie's way and say yes to as much as she could, to be the doctor they had hired her to be even though she feared she was a different sort of doctor altogether. Maybe it wasn't the perfect job, but the hours were predictable and not in the middle of the night and included time to do paperwork and take a break for lunch and call home to check in between appointments, and very few patients came in screaming or gushing blood or sporting foreign objects sticking out from various regular and sometimes brand-new orifices. Maybe it wasn't the perfect job, but it paid well and insured them all. Could they fire her for saying no to hosting breakfast or hiring a website updater? Could they fire her for having a family that required a flexible schedule and a daughter who wasn't quite? She doubted it. But she didn't want to find out.

Fifty-Fifty

Eventually, Rosie realized what it had taken a six-year-old Aggie less than an hour to suss. The great beauty of living next door to the Grandersons was their houses were really close together. Thus, the adults could have dinner in one and relegate all the children to the other. It was like the paragon of kids' tables, the ultimate Platonic realization of the dream that was making everyone under eleven have Thanksgiving in the kitchen. They could have an actual adult dinner party without worrying the cheese plate would get knocked off the coffee table by someone trying, say, to jump rope in the living room. They could have a conversation and not be interrupted by shrieking from the kitchen, worrisome crashes from upstairs, soccer games near the breakfront, requests for hammers, matches, and Ping-Pong balls, or demands for additional food or different food or the removal of food from hair/rugs/underwear. They even sent Jupiter to the Grandersons' some nights because, though she was better behaved than the kids, more than one glass of red wine had been swept off the coffee table by the enthusiasm of her tail.

They gathered the last Saturday evening of every month. They alternated who cooked and who turned their house over to the children. They did it even when they were busy and work was crazy and life intervened. They did it even when Roo and Ben and Cayenne were old enough to babysit, and they could all have gone out to the movies instead. Rosie looked forward to it all month. When it was their turn to cook, she and Penn made elaborate, delicate dishes, too rich, too complicated, too expensive to waste on the everyday, to waste on the kids. They used their good china. They drank expensive wine. Someone went next door at five of every hour to check on the kids and make sure they hadn't gone Lord of the Flies.

'We should call it Dual Dinner,' said Ben.

'Yes!' Rigel and Orion chorused. 'We could get swords!'

'Not duel.' Ben rolled his eyes. 'Dual.'

'Exactly!'

And so Dueling Dinners were born. They were also the only evening all month the adults could have a conversation and not worry the kids would listen in or spy or overhear, so it was, in fairness, more or less appropriate one night, after squash soup, crepes stuffed with sole and crabmeat, chocolate soufflés, several bottles of Chardonnay, and an actual glass apiece of port even though none of them much cared for it, that Frank giggled drunkenly, 'So. What happens when Poppy hits puberty?'

Penn spilled his port all over Rosie's grandmother's tablecloth. Rosie thought this was unfortunate, less for the tablecloth, which was a bit overwrought faux-Victorian for her taste, and more because without the wine, how were they going to be drunk enough to have this conversation? Over the chaos of towels and seltzer and looking up what gets port out of lace, Frank slurred blanket apologies in all directions. 'I'm really sorry, you guys. I didn't know I shouldn't ask that question. I thought maybe we were being rude not bringing it up. We didn't want you to think we didn't care. And we've sort of worried ... well, we've sort of worried you guys wanted everyone to know and we put the kibosh on that before you even had a chance to decide.'

Penn thought but did not say: *You can ask us anything.* That should have been true, but he wasn't sure it was.

Rosie thought but did not say: *It* was *your fault.* That shouldn't have been true, but she wasn't sure it wasn't. She locked eyes with her husband. He felt like he was drawing breath from her lungs. She felt like he had lain down in the middle of the dining-room table and she'd opened his chest for surgery, that naked, that much of a look at what was supposed to stay inside and unseen. But surgery was familiar enough so once she began to explain, she wondered why it had ever seemed hard to her. It was clinical, medical, pharmacological, and she was a doctor. That was all. 'Hormone blockers,' she said simply, and Penn grinned at her like she'd made a joke.

'Hormone blockers?' Frank and Marginny sounded like they were auditioning for a bad sitcom.

'We've been using these drugs for years,' Rosie the clinician explained, 'to put a stop to what's called Precocious Puberty. Sometimes we'll see a little girl who has breast buds at six or a first-grade boy whose testes have already enlarged or who's already sprouted pubic hair. These kids go on hormone blockers. The drug puts them on hold. It buys them time for everyone else to catch up. Then, when they reach the age of nine or ten, we take them off the blockers, and they proceed through puberty normally with everybody else.'

Penn looked giddy. Frank and Marginny looked like they were waiting for the punch line, so Rosie supplied it.

'Poppy will probably go on the same drugs –'

'Probably?' Penn broke in.

' – when she's eleven or twelve or so. They would prevent her male puberty. They'd shut down the whole system so she would stay a little girl.'

Frank fake-gasped. 'You can do a sex change on a minor?'

'Hormone blockers just pause the system.' Rosie didn't like having to dip into her reserves of patience for patients on the weekend. 'The effects of these drugs are reversible. It's puberty that's not. That's why the clock is ticking. We have to stop Poppy's – well, really Claude's – puberty before it starts. If we wait until Poppy's no longer a minor, she'll be six feet tall with whiskers and a broad, hairy chest and big hands and men's size-twelve feet, and those never go away. At that point, we could load her up with all the estrogen we like, and she'd grow breasts and get rounder and her voice would soften, but she'd still be taller than every girlfriend she ever had. She'd still have to order all her heels online. She'd have to get electrolysis for the remnants left behind by every single chest hair, every mustache whisker, every bit of beard. She'd have to have surgery to shave down her Adam's apple. The blockers put a stop to what can't be undone later. Then, when she's older and ready for estrogen, it'll work better because it'll have less to overcome. Or if she changes her mind, we've done nothing that's not reversible –'

'Changes her mind?' Penn interrupted.

'– because as soon as you take them off the hormone blockers, patients' bodies proceed normally through their natal puberty.'

'But.' Marginny's brow wrinkled. It was a sentence, not a preamble to one. It was entire. Later, Rosie was struck by how Marginny understood instinctively worries she could not explain to Penn, no matter which ways she tried.

'Yes,' said Rosie. 'But. But Aggie will turn into a young woman, and Poppy will still be a little girl. But everyone else in their class will become teenagers, and Poppy won't quite. But kids with Precocious Puberty eventually mature physically and emotionally with everyone else at the normal age, but Poppy will stay prepubescent while everyone around her grows into young adults.'

'Then . . . why?' Marginny asked.

'It beats the shit out of the alternative,' said Penn. Even once he'd mastered the hows of secret keeping, he'd stayed on the listservs, the blogs and Instagram accounts and Twitter feeds, the YouTube channels with their pages and pages of comments. The kids who weren't on blockers, puberty was killing them. The affirmed boys' breasts were tumors, poisoning their bodies, growing malignantly as cancer. The affirmed girls studied their faces like maps for hints of hair, of bone spread beyond flesh. They could feel disloyal hormones blooming inside them, scattering indissoluble toxins like pollen into ill winds. They had, they harbored, such hatred, such revulsion for change as inevitable as seas, like their lives would be over if the tide came in, as it did, as it always did. The Internet was full of broken, breaking kids who spent their lives hiding beneath too many layers of too baggy clothes, beneath binders and tape and pads and straps. And those were the lucky ones because there were also the ones who tried simply to cut off the offending body parts. And there were the ones whose cuts did not stop there. There were not just a few. There were hundreds. There were thousands.

'So these kids just get to pick who they are?' Frank searched for an apt metaphor and finally settled on, 'It's like a video game.'

'No, it's like a fairy tale,' said Penn. Rosie rolled her eyes at him. 'Maybe you look like a filthy scullery maid, but inside, you're really a princess, and if you're good, you find the right grave to cry on or the right lamp to rub, and you become a princess on the outside too. You look like a frog, but kiss the right lips and you magically transform into the prince you've known yourself to be inside all along. If you're good and worthy, you always get an outside to match your inside. Virtue leads straight to transformation; transformation leads instantly to happily ever after.'

'It's a long way off,' Rosie added. 'A long, long, long way off.'

'And no one,' Penn continued, as if Rosie hadn't spoken at all, 'is more good and worthy and virtuous than Poppy.'

Next door, Poppy was torturing the dogs. Orion, dressed as a yachtsman zombie himself, had also brought over his costume stash for the occasion, and Poppy and Aggie were trying to make the dogs do a play. Poppy had Jupiter in a vest Rigel had knit years earlier for '80s day at school (so he could look like someone named Duckie from a movie called *Pretty in Pink,* though the vest looked neither pink nor ducklike to her) and Roverella girdled in six knit sweatbands, striping her middle like a zebra. She and Aggie were writing a play about neither ducks nor dogs nor zebras but rather Venus and Serena Williams teamed up to battle little green ball-shaped aliens. The dogs were doing great with the tennis balls but otherwise phoning it in.

Ben was making popcorn for the third time in three hours. They went through a lot of popcorn in the kid house. Rigel and Orion were choosing a movie for everyone to watch, a process of weight-and-measure evaluation akin to managing the debt crisis of a small nation. Roo and Cayenne were in the Grandersons' basement waiting for everyone else to come back.

'I heard you were fighting Derek McGuinness after school last week.' Cayenne was looking carefully between each of her toes, but Roo assumed she was talking to him anyway since he was the only one in the room. And since he had been fighting Derek McGuinness last week.

'Yeah?'

'Yeah you were?'

'What do you care?'

'Guys who fight are sexy.' Cayenne shrugged. 'Not like guys who fight with knives or wrestling or if they just go around beating people up. But guys who fight just sometimes.' She paused to consider. 'I bet Ben never fought anyone in his life.'

'He fights me all the time,' said Roo.

'Who wins?'

Roo snorted.

'I heard he called you gay and that's why you kicked his ass.'

Roo wouldn't look at her. 'I didn't kick his ass.'

'Did he call you gay?'

'Among other things.'

'*Are* you gay?'

'None of your business.'

'You can tell me if you are, you know. I don't care. I have an uncle who's gay. And I'm good at keeping secrets.' Roo looked up at her. 'If you're not though, you should tell me that too.'

'Why?'

She raised her eyes from her toes but not her head so that she was looking up at him through her lashes. 'It opens up some options. For both of us.'

When everyone came back downstairs, bedecked dogs included, to watch the movie Rigel and Orion had finally settled on, Cayenne wanted to play Spin the Bottle instead.

'Uh, no?' Roo and Ben said together, their voices rising at the end as if there were a question. Roo's was: Is this girl serious? Ben's was: Why does she want to kiss anyone but me? Instead of working that out, he tackled Roo so they could wrestle out the jinx. Roo won.

'Why not?' Cayenne looked incredulous that anyone would deny her anything.

'Kissing is gross,' said Poppy.

'There's four of them and three of us,' said Cayenne. 'We can sit boy girl boy girl. It's perfect.'

'If you're heterosexist,' said Ben mildly.

'Or incestuous,' said Roo, less mildly.

'You can't have everything.' Cayenne shrugged. 'Maybe you'll get lucky, and your spin will land on me.'

'I don't want to make out with you,' said Roo.

'More than you want to make out with anyone else in this room,' said Rigel.

'True,' Roo admitted, 'but not by much.'

Aggie and Poppy didn't really understand Spin the Bottle and weren't interested in anyone kissing anyone, blood-related or otherwise, so maybe it was topical or maybe it came out of nowhere when Aggie turned suddenly to Poppy and said, 'Do you think it's weird your parents only had boys?' And Poppy's heart stopped. 'I mean until you.'

'Your parents only had girls,' Poppy managed.

'Yeah, but there's only two of us. Your parents have tons. They must have thought they could only make boy babies.'

'Fifty-fifty,' Ben said quickly and loudly, so quickly and loudly every-one stopped and looked at him until he made himself explain coolly, 'Every pregnancy there's a fifty-fifty chance the baby will be a boy, no matter how many boys have been born already. Even with four older brothers, when Poppy was born, there was a fifty-fifty chance she'd be a boy, and a fifty-fifty chance she'd be a girl.'

This was true, so the Walsh-Adams clan tried to look believable.

'What if you were a boy?' Aggie moaned. 'That would be the worst.'

'Why?' said Cayenne. 'Boys are awesome.'

'If you were a boy,' Aggie said to Poppy, caught up in the horror, 'we couldn't be rival princesses, we couldn't have sleepovers, we couldn't make the dogs make a play, we couldn't paint each other's toenails.'

'Why not?' Orion wiggled his alternating green and black toes.

'Yeah but you're a zombie,' said Aggie.

'A yachting zombie,' Orion corrected.

'Boys could make dogs make a play,' said Rigel.

'We couldn't be best friends.' Aggie flung her arm across her eyes. 'If your parents didn't beat the fifty-fifty and you were a boy, it would be the worst thing ever.'

Poppy opened her mouth, and everyone waited. Roo looked at his feet. Ben looked at his feet. Rigel and Orion looked at each other's feet. Cayenne narrowed her eyes at all of them. But Poppy swallowed and agreed wholeheartedly: 'It would be the worst thing ever.'

Annus Mirabilis

Penn found himself thinking a lot about John Dryden. Dryden was one of those poets you read in graduate school but not in life. No one's email signature was a Dryden quote. Anyone whose email signature was a Dryden quote hadn't read the rest of the long, dry verse it came from. But Dryden had a poem: 'Annus Mirabilis'. The year of wonders. It was a poem about England in 1666. England in 1666 was decidedly not having a year of wonders. England in 1666 had war, plague, and a three-day fire that destroyed most of London, plus Isaac Newton invented calculus, thereby making the lives of mathematically ungifted students immeasurably worse forever. But Dryden's poem was about what a great year it was because it could have been worse. They lived to see 1667 after all. At least, everyone who read the poem did.

Penn was trying to convince himself Roo was having an Annus Mirabilis. He was trying to value it because, though it was bad, it could have been worse. So far as Penn knew, Roo hadn't set fire to anything, but otherwise, his seventeenth year had much in common with England 1666. He was at war (with his parents and siblings). He was with plague (lethargy, listlessness, an oppressive weariness with everyone and everything in the world). He wasn't doing all that great in calculus.

And the main problem Roo was having was indeed historical. His AP history teacher had tasked her students with 'making a video presentation on a current issue currently impacting America'. Had Roo argued he shouldn't have to do such a vague and poorly worded assignment, had he come to his father to allege that, by definition, current events weren't history, at least not yet, Penn might have been sympathetic. But Roo did the assignment.

Then he got an F.

Then he refused to redo it.

Then he forged his mother's signature on the notice advising her of her son's malfeasance.

When they got the report card for the quarter, Penn and Rosie could not help noticing that Roo was failing history.

Roo swore it had to be a typo. Roo admitted he had missed a quiz because he'd been at the dentist but that he'd made it up after school, and Mrs Birkus probably just hadn't graded it yet. Roo said he was doing well in everything else, except maybe calculus, so didn't he deserve the benefit of the doubt? Roo said given that he was getting As and Bs in his other subjects, what were the odds he was getting an F in history?

They turned out to be pretty high.

When Rosie and Penn went in to meet with the teacher, Mrs Birkus explained that Roo's video was about the problems with allowing LGBT soldiers to serve openly in the armed forces.

'Impossible,' Penn said confidently.

'Alas, I'm afraid not.' Mrs Birkus was used to disabusing parents of shiny impressions of their children.

'You don't understand. Roo's not antigay. He can't be because . . . Well, we know that he . . . You see at home . . .' Penn found there was no way to finish this sentence, but he was relieved anyway because clearly there had been some kind of misunderstanding here. 'Anyway, trust me, there must be a mistake.'

'Quite a few,' Mrs Birkus allowed, 'but not, apparently, the ones you imagine.'

Then she showed them the video.

It was a family affair. It starred a great many of Poppy's dolls and stuffies dressed in Orion's costumes and Rigel's knitting projects. Ben was the puppet master, wiggling each character before the camera in turn, his hand creeping occasionally (Rosie imagined, guiltily) into the shot. It began with Roo's best movie trailer impersonation: 'In a world where the US Army is the greatest fighting force on Earth, gays do not belong. The navy is navy, not rainbow-colored. There's no trans in the air force, no lesbians in the marines, no bi in the sky.' The particulars of the plot were hard to follow, but eventually a camo-clad Alice and Miss Marple spent some time rolling around in a sandbox with guns (Penn was guessing pretzel rods) and then rolling around in a bed together until an apparent superior officer (a roll of paper towels in a naval cap of Orion's decorated with a few of Ben's debate ribbons) burst in on them screaming. 'You [bleep]ing [bleep]ing [bleep]s don't belong in this man's army,' the paper-towel roll opined. 'The [bleep]ing government in its [bleep]ing wisdom may disagree, but they're not [bleep]ing running things around this [bleep]. I am. So they can suck my [bleep].' In the next scene, three Barbies dropped incendiaries (Penn was guessing raisins) from F-15s, destroying LEGO villages below, but when one of the Barbies donned men's dress blues for a party that evening, five plastic soldiers Penn had never seen before in his life (they were Aggie's) came out of nowhere, stripped the Barbie, and attacked her. Given the limitations of the medium, the precise nature of the action was not clear, but though TransBarbie eventually kicked the plastic soldiers' bleeps, it was not without more language bluer than his uniform.

'At least he bleeped himself out,' Penn offered.

Mrs Birkus was unimpressed.

In the school parking lot, Penn was incredulous. 'Roo can't be homophobic. He can't be antigay. He can't possibly be antitrans and living in our household.'

'Maybe that's why,' Rosie said softly.

'Does he need therapy?' Penn wasn't listening to her. Penn wasn't even listening to himself. 'An intervention? A stint in the military himself?'

'Maybe he didn't mean it.'

'It seemed pretty clear.' Penn was not keeping his voice down.

'Did it?' It had seemed like an embarrassing mess to Rosie.

'What is wrong with this boy?' Penn asked no one in particular. Milling-around high-schoolers stared at him disdainfully.

'Let's go home and ask him,' said his wife.

At home, they sat Roo down at the homeworking table.

'We saw your video.' Rosie dove right in. She didn't want to give him another opportunity to lie to them.

'Did you like it?' Roo sneered. It wasn't the video that was going to cause his father to end his Annus Mirabilis. It was the smirk.

'Did *you*?' Penn tried not to shriek. Roo's left shoulder more shuddered than shrugged. The rest of his body curled into itself like a comma.

'Because it seemed like a lot of work. Long way to go to make idiot points and stupid jokes.' Roo cringed, maybe at the *idiot,* maybe at the *stupid,* maybe at his father screaming like a lunatic. 'Long way to go just to humiliate people.'

'I wasn't humiliating anyone.' Barely audible. To his belly button.

'Never mind the message' – Rosie triaged the situation and began with the most straightforward, most apparent symptom – 'did you imagine you were allowed to use language like that?'

'That's how soldiers talk,' Roo moped. 'And I bleeped it out.'

'Did you imagine you could simulate sex, violence, rape, I don't even know what else, and that was going to be okay with your teacher or your parents?' Rosie continued.

'You don't get it. It's not like when you were a kid. Sex and violence are what's popular nowadays.'

Rosie closed her eyes. 'Why didn't you just redo the project when Mrs Birkus asked you to?'

'I already did it.' Roo sat up only in order to be able to cross his arms over his chest. 'If she didn't like it, that's her problem.'

'No, I think it's yours,' Penn said. And then, because he couldn't help himself, 'Do you even believe the argument you were making?'

Roo rolled his eyes. 'Would I have made it otherwise?'

'You think LGBT soldiers in the armed forces pose a problem?'

'Obviously,' said Roo.

Rosie shook her head. 'I hate too cool for school.'

'What the ass does that mean?'

'Don't say "ass", Roo,' Penn said resignedly.

'It means,' Rosie overlapped, 'that if you're going to try, try. If you're going to work hard, do it. Don't work hard to make something that only looks like you don't care and you didn't try.'

'That doesn't even make sense—'

'You're sixteen,' said Rosie. 'You're too old to think saying bad words and showing plastic dolls naked makes you cool. It's not cool to pull stupid shit just to get a rise out of everyone. It's one thing to blow off the assignment. It's so much worse to belittle everyone else's.'

'Oh, of course.' Roo's sarcasm rose to a rhapsody. 'I should have known. You're not upset about my work. You're upset about what everyone else thinks. I'm stunned.'

'You can be as snotty as you like, Roo.' Penn had talked himself down a bit and was trying for icy calm over screeching hysteria. 'We're going to finish this conversation.'

'That's all you ever care about. What other people think of you. What other people think of your kids.' Roo's face mirrored the ones who'd laughed at Penn derisively in the school parking lot. Apparently, this was what he was learning in tenth grade. 'Well, I don't care. Unlike everyone else in this family, I don't lie about who I am or what I do.'

Penn's face turned red – so much for icy calm – and his mouth opened, but Rosie beat him to it. 'You were asked why your report card listed an F in history.' She made sure to keep both the fury and the triumph out of her voice. 'You said it was a typo. Was this the truth?'

'No.' Roo pouted.

'Did you miss a quiz while you were at the dentist, which you made up after school but which had not yet been graded?'

'No.'

'Did you, in fact, deserve the benefit of the doubt?'

Roo shrugged his crossed arms.

'Did you?'

'No.'

'Then it seems to me you do lie about who you are and what you do,' said Rosie.

To which Penn added shrilly, 'And that is not acceptable in this household.'

'You guys are such hypocrites,' Roo muttered under his breath.

'I'm sorry?' Penn said. 'I couldn't hear you,' even though he could.

So Roo screamed. 'How can *you* give *me* shit about lying? You two lie all the time. You lie every second of every day. Your whole stupid-ass life is a lie. You're all "my daughter this" and "my daughter that" and, "At last! The perfect little girl I always dreamed of." You're all, "Oh just don't tell anyone about your sister, and that will be the truth." Well, it's not the truth. It's a lie. You're lying to everyone you know. You're making the rest of us lie too. You're forcing your whole family to cover up your stupid-ass lies every single day. So I don't know how you're going to stand there and scold me for lying.'

'We're not going to scold you.' Rosie made herself speak calmly even though she was shaking like a windup toy. 'We're going to punish you.'

'Living in this house is punishment enough.' Roo stormed down into his room.

'Wishful thinking,' Penn called after him.

It was a soggy, sullen weekend. On Monday morning, Rosie was hyperventilating through the rain on the way to work. The perfect thing about the pink turret house was that it was only exactly 1.1 miles from work. Unfortunately, 1 mile of the 1.1 miles was straight up. She spent the climb gasping into the phone most days anyway, however, because otherwise when would she find time to talk to her mother?

'Roo's a homophobe,' she was sorry to report.

'That doesn't sound right,' said Carmelo.

'I know,' Rosie panted. 'But apparently it's true. He did a presentation about sex, profanities, naked Barbies, and how gay and trans soldiers don't belong in the military. So he failed history.'

'School has changed a lot since you were a girl,' said Carmelo.

'He failed the project, so he failed history, so he lied about failing history. So we grounded him.'

'You didn't expect him to own up to something like that, did you?'

'I expected him not to do it in the first place.'

'Oh, well that's different. Are you mad about the sin or about the lie about the sin?'

'Neither, I'm mad because when we confronted him about the sin and the lie about the sin, he said we were hypocrites because we lie all the time.'

'About Poppy?'

'About Poppy,' Rosie admitted. 'He's so mad about Poppy he's become a bigot.'

His grandmother wasn't buying it. 'Poor Roo. I wish I were there.' Carmelo still came up every summer, but now it was nearly Thanksgiving, and it had been months since she'd seen her babies.

'He's not mad we lied.' Rosie paused for breath and corrected the tense. *'Lie.'* She caught glimpses through dripping pine tree fingers of thinning fog wisping off the water, sound and scant sunlight backed by sea cliff and old-growth forest. It was a beautiful place to live, but maybe not if it only felt like home to everyone else in your family. 'He's mad we made him move to Seattle when he liked Wisconsin. He's mad we made him live in the city when he liked his farm. We made him leave his football team and his orchestra and his friends and his presidencies.'

'He thinks you chose Poppy over him,' Carmelo said.

'We didn't.'

'I know, dear.'

'We didn't.'

'Does he?'

'It's been more than two years. It's time to get over it. We moved because it wasn't safe enough there. Not for any of them. If we'd said, "Wisconsin's too dangerous for Poppy, but you we'll risk," then he'd have reason to feel slighted. We thought here was better for everyone. We thought he was funny and friendly and outgoing so he'd be fine.'

'What happened?'

'We were wrong.'

'Not wrong,' said Carmelo. 'Just not right yet.'

'Maybe but—'

'Parents choose one kid over another all the time.'

'That's not what we—'

'You missed most of seventh grade while your sister was sick.' Her mother talked right over her protestations. 'You spent most of year twelve in a hospital room. At a time when I felt bad about everything, that was just one more layer of guilt. I had to let it go. Poppy needed extra care, and she needed her big sister with her. Daddy and I needed you there too, needed to not worry about school and homework and Girl Scouts and parent-teacher conferences. You didn't need much of anything right then. When your needs arose, afterwards, then they got addressed. It's a good thing people's needs don't all arise at the same time; otherwise we wouldn't be able to meet them all. When you left Wisconsin, it was Poppy's turn. Roo's is coming.'

It was. It was closer than anyone thought.

Preventative Madness

Ben's secret was this: he was in love with Cayenne. It was a secret for a number of reasons. One was he was embarrassed: it was such a cliché to fall in love with the girl next door. Another was he had been in love with her since the moment he met her at that barbecue in her backyard the weekend before they started eighth grade, and sometimes she loved him back and sometimes she did not. Best he could tell, her feelings toward him were unpredictable as weather and just as out of his control. He couldn't tell people she was his girlfriend because unless she was standing next to him at the time, he couldn't be sure whether it was true. Maybe that wasn't secret keeping; maybe he just didn't know. He had successfully passed off his relationship with Cayenne thus far as, variously, she was just his next door neighbor, he was just being friendly, she needed help with algebra, he had to go over there anyway to drag Poppy away from Aggie before they became conjoined twins, their parents were having dinner so they really had no choice. So another reason he didn't tell was he didn't want to tip his hand. But mostly it was this: Ben was supposed to be the smart one, and loving Cayenne was stupid. He was smart enough to see that; he just wasn't smart enough to do anything about it.

There was also this: he was used to keeping secrets.

At the barbecue the weekend before ninth grade, the one year anniversary of the day they met, not that he was counting, she ignored him and stayed in her room by herself, even though it was one of those freak Seattle summer weekends where it's ninety-five degrees and no one has air conditioning and spending a summer afternoon inside is like napping in your microwave. At the tenth-grade barbecue, she held his hand and fed him s'mores and kept pulling her sweater on and off revealing glimpses of her belly button while she let him lick melted marshmallow off her fingers. So you see how smart had really nothing to do with it.

'What do you see in her?' Roo asked that evening over six different kinds of potato salad.

'What?' Playing dumb did not work for Ben, but that's what he went with anyway. 'What do you mean?'

'I'm not asking if you like her.' Roo sighed and rolled his eyes as if he weren't the one who'd brought it up in the first place. 'I know you like her. We all know you like her. The entire world knows.' So apparently it wasn't that much of a secret after all. 'I'm saying why.'

'I mean she's nice enough –'

'No she isn't.'

'– but we're not . . .' Ben's face looked like he had dunked it in the sangria.

Roo peered at him. 'Is it convenience?'

'What?'

'Because she's right next door?'

'No,' Ben said vehemently. Whatever else it was, loving Cayenne was not convenient.

'Do you sneak out to meet her in the middle of the night?'

'We share a room.'

'*I* sleep,' Roo sniffed.

'Me too.'

'But I might not if I had a better option.'

'Like what?'

'Like getting laid next door in the middle of the night.'

'I'm not . . . we're not . . .' They weren't yet. But they would soon. And it would put an end to more than Ben's innocence.

'In that case' – Roo went back to his potato salads – 'I don't know what you see in her.'

'You don't know what anyone sees in anyone,' Ben pointed out. 'You don't like anybody.'

'That's true,' Roo agreed amiably. 'People are annoying.'

When he took Cayenne to homecoming seven weeks later, Ben commissioned Rigel to knit her a corsage. He thought she would want something different from the rosebud/baby's breath combo every other girl got, and he thought she might appreciate that whereas those mortal floral arrangements wouldn't last the night, a knit corsage lasts forever. Cayenne's knit corsage did not last forever because it embarrassed her, and she flushed it down the gym toilet after the last slow song of the night, whereupon the toilets clogged and overflowed, and the after-party was cancelled.

For the eleventh-grade barbecue, Ben decided their anniversary warranted celebration. It was three years since they met and one since she'd held his hand and fed him marshmallows, and he wasn't about to let the fact that he couldn't put an accurate label on the occasion get in the way of celebrating it. He read up on the matter and learned that the one-year anniversary gift was paper, so the night of the marshmallows he began, just in case they were together then and would still be together a year on. (Ben was a kid who planned ahead.) Every day, he folded one paper heart and one paper butterfly. By their junior-year barbecue, he had 365 paper hearts and 365 paper butterflies. He spilled them all into her room that afternoon, where they carpeted her dresser and nightstand, her bed and her desk, the piles of clothes, shoes, textbooks, notebooks, devices, and power cords buried on her floor like enemy mines. Then he dug underneath to await her arrival. She shrieked when she found him there, the first time from shock – only his face peeked out, and no one likes a disembodied head – the second with delight. Ben's heart soared. She appreciated the gesture – maybe not the gesture itself but its lavishness, the evidence it presented of a mad obsession she had herself inspired – but she still refused to nail down the occasion or let Ben call her his girlfriend. And in other ways, the whole thing was a disaster: having buried her bed utterly, they couldn't use it to celebrate.

That night was a disaster in other ways as well, ways having nothing really to do with young love, and though no one realized it at the time, its impact was vast, and not just for them. While Ben and Cayenne were trying to find her bed, in the Grandersons' yard out back, the annual barbecue had grown into a Scott-and-Zelda-level soiree. It was perfect Seattle summer weather, endless sunny afternoon cooling slowly into the need for a light sweater, dusk giving way to a crisp, clear night scented by the char of the grill, the flower of ripe peaches, the heady promise of butter and sugar. Logs in the fire pit popped and settled, cracking light and smoke into the twilight.

For the kids, there was something particular about seeing one another outside the bounds of school rules, outside the bounds of home rules, but still in sight or hearing, if they weren't careful, of their parents. They had parties, of course, when someone's folks were out of town, or they all met up summer evenings at the beach. They spent hours on screens together outside anyone's purview. So this was a different thing. Roo tried to decide whether it was more accurate or less, this version of his compatriots, Katie Ferguson without the cigarettes, Kyle Konner without the manic leaping off of anything more than four feet high, Gracey Meyer without the cursing.

But if the proximity of parents turned their progeny toward adulthood, every year without fail the party turned the adults back to kids. Drinking foamy beer out of a plastic cup was somehow completely different from sharing a bottle or two of wine when Frank and Marginny came over for dinner. Penn wasn't drunker but he felt drunker. He grabbed a water balloon out of Rigel's hands as he ran by and tossed it at Poppy, who shrieked in indignation. The parents all roared with laughter. Rosie had come over before lunch to help Marginny devil eggs and just stayed, testing and retesting the sangria to see what it might need. Along the way, she'd lost her shoes somehow, and now her feet were one part flesh, three parts dirt, the Snoopy hat she'd stolen off Orion's head lopsiding over her right eye. Partying with their kids made them less sober, less well behaved than they were with their neighbors the rest of the year. It was as if, observing their children even at half strength, they finally saw how it was done.

'This party gets better every year.' Rosie was sitting on a camping chair she was beginning to suspect she'd have trouble getting out of and trying to seamlessly reattach two egg halves.

'It's the s'mores.' Marginny poked Rosie's elbow lovingly with her toe. 'Actually, it might be the sangria.'

'Hey, I'm performing surgery here. Your feet are filthy.'

'Yours are worse.'

Rosie pigeon-posed to affirm the truth of this then high-fived Marginny's begrimed foot with her own.

The kids were mostly gathered around the fire pit, eating sugar in a variety of guises, and contriving ways to be touching one another. Penn could hear Rigel and Orion arguing with Harry and Larry. It hadn't seemed to Penn at first like that quadratic friendship would last. In the beginning, Harry and Larry had been wigged out by Orion's costumes, by Rigel's knitting, by their whole slightly odd, off family. Harry and Larry were a little normal for the Walsh-Adams clan. But it seemed instead that twindom was enough to keep them all together, that having another being in common was more common than anything else.

'Remember when that dude turned into a bug?' Larry was saying.

'That's what the whole movie was about,' said Orion.

'Yeah, but I mean the moment when he changed. He was all, "Aaaahhh, my arms, my legs, aaahhh".'

'Yeah?'

'That was epic.'

Penn winced. While he had to admit *Captain Cockroach* had turned a whole new generation of kids into Kafka fans, the resulting travesty bore so little resemblance to the original as to be a different thing altogether.

'That happened to our dog,' said Larry.

'Your dog turned into a cockroach?' Rigel sounded skeptical rather than awed, for which, from across the yard, Penn was grateful.

'Other way around,' said Larry. 'There was this huge spider in the kitchen, one of those really hairy ones, and when we tried to trap it, it crawled under the dishwasher, and the next day when we got home from school, there was a dog in the front yard, and she didn't have a collar, and we posted signs around the neighborhood, but no one claimed her, and we never saw the spider again.'

'So you think the dishwasher transformed the spider into a dog?' Rigel just wanted to make sure he was getting this.

'Duh,' said Larry.

'That's stupid,' said his brother.

'How else do you explain it?'

'That's like saying Mark used to be a bicycle,' said Harry. Mark was Harry's iguana, which their father bought him when he accidentally ran over his bike.

Then they all started laughing. 'My skateboard used to be a potato,' said Larry, 'because we stopped for French fries on the way to pick it up at the store.'

'Orion's butt used to be a tuba,' said Rigel, 'and that's why it makes those noises.'

'Rigel's feet used to be a porta-potty,' Orion countered, 'and that's why they smell like that.'

'Harry used to be a monkey' – Larry was laughing so hard he was using a marshmallow to dab tears from his eyes – 'and that's why he's so hairy.'

'We all used to be monkeys, you moron,' Harry said.

And Orion said, 'Poppy used to be a boy.'

Rosie and Penn froze. Marginny and Frank froze. Roo, Ben, Rigel, Orion, and Poppy all froze. They were spread all over the backyard – by the grill, by the keg, by the dessert table, by the fire pit, by the sprinkler. They were each in their own conversation, their own world, but like dogs who listened, perpetually and without trying, for those few words they understood in the cacophony – sit, stay, walk, good girl – their ears all pricked for what would happen next. To Penn, it seemed like the whole party held its breath. To Poppy, it seemed like not just her family but the entire world had frozen, crystalized here in the very last moment in which it would be okay, and with the next breath, the next one, the next, her entire world would thaw apart. She wondered only at her slamming heart when everything else in the universe was so still. But Rosie saw. Rosie saw that Harry and Larry were laughing like the monkeys they used to be, that Harry and Larry were continuing to compare things to other things, that no one was paying any attention to their quadsome anyway, that Rigel, bless him, had jumped onto the back wall and was acting out Captain Cockroach's transformation scene with great enthusiasm, that Orion, bless him too, face blanched white as his Snoopy hat, had leapt up alongside his brother, one of his many brothers, to play Captain Cockroach's devastated fiancée, who had yet to learn to love the beast within. The world kept turning. The secret leaked but held.

It was late when they got home. Poppy stayed at Aggie's. She had learned to protect her own secret for her own self, and maybe she felt safer there where the only person who could out her was under her control. The boys, all four of them, lingered in the living room, waiting for what would happen next. Rosie felt too tired to figure out what was appropriate here: comfort or castigate, clutch or shame. Did they dodge a bullet together? Was this something to recast as family lore, all relieved smiles, all head-shaking awe at their great escape? Or was this a moment for there-but-for-the-grace upbraiding? She remembered scolding Roo once for leaving scissors where just-walking twins could reach them. 'But Mama,' Roo had turned a tearful face to her to wonder, 'why are you mad?'

'Rigel and Orion could have gotten very hurt.'
'But they didn't. Why aren't you happy?'
'I am happy, but I'm mad for next time.'
'Mad for next time?'
'Mad so there doesn't have to be a next time.'

Preventative madness? It had seemed to Roo at the time like madness indeed, and this felt like that: preventative madness, aftermath madness, madness in relief. Rosie wanted just to go to bed.

Penn did not. 'What were you thinking?' This without preamble and directionless, toward everyone in the room and no one in particular.

Orion, tumbling over himself already: 'I wasn't thinking anything. It was an accident.'

'An accident?'

'I didn't mean to.' His voice was shaking. His hands too. 'It just popped out.'

'How do you say something accidentally?'

'Like one of those camisole thingies.'

'Camisole thingies?'

'Freudian slips,' Rigel translated. Penn often suspected Orion and Rigel of telepathy because simple twindom insufficiently explained how they understood the inanities that came out of each other's mouths.

'No,' said Penn. 'Freudian slips are when you accidentally say what you actually mean rather than what you're pretending to mean. Is that what happened here?'

Orion looked cowed and miserable but mostly lost.

Rigel put in, almost too quiet to hear, 'It was just a good opportunity. You know?'

His parents did not.

'He could say it,' Roo explained, and his mother was surprised to hear his voice, 'and it wouldn't matter. For just a minute, it was like we didn't all have to be carrying around this crazy secret.'

Rosie and Penn found themselves looking at Ben as if he were the one who could tell them whether all this was true or just boyish bullshittery. 'Secrets are heavy things,' he said, absolving neither his brothers nor his parents.

'We have to be careful.' Penn struggled to keep his voice under control. 'Now more than ever.'

'Why now more than ever?' Roo's lip curled like a caterpillar.

'Because we've come this far,' said his father.

'Yeah but if that's true,' said Ben, 'won't it always be now more than ever? Won't every day be more than the day before?'

'Enough excuses.' Rosie was done with this conversation. 'Orion, you were messing around with your friends, showing off, and you said something you shouldn't have. It's only luck this wasn't much, much worse. It's not your business; it's Poppy's. It's not your life; it's hers. Let's not make this out to be gallantry. This was a warning shot, so heed it. Everyone else can keep their mouth shut. Everyone else has managed not to tell. You can too.'

These were perfectly reasonable points. But in the end – somewhat before the end actually – a large percentage of them proved untrue.

Transformation

P arent time is like fairy time but real. It is magic without pixie dust and spells. It defies physics without bending the laws of time and space. It is that truism everyone offers but no one believes until after they have children: that time will actually speed, fleet enough to leave you jet-lagged and whiplashed and racing all at once. Your tiny, perfect baby nestles in your arms his first afternoon home, and then ten months later, he's off to his senior year of high school. You give birth to twins so small and alike, they lie mirrored, each with a head in the palm of one hand while their toes reach only to the crooks of your elbows, but it's only a year before they start looking at colleges. It is so impossible yet so universally experienced that magic is the only explanation. Except then there are also the excruciating rainy Sundays when the kids are whiny, bored, and beastly, and it takes a hundred hours to get from breakfast to bedtime, the long weekends when you wonder whose demonic idea it was to trap you in your home with your bevy of abominable children for a decade without school.

They were all of them, even Poppy, still little boys in Rosie's eyes, never mind four-fifths of them were now eight-plus inches taller than she was with voices deep as wells. That was something she would explain to people about Poppy if she ever actually decided to explain to people about Poppy instead of keeping her a secret: your babies are always your babies. Roo and Ben were nearly six feet tall with limbs like giraffe legs and wingspans that augured flight. Fourteen-year-old Rigel appeared no more like baby Rigel, fourteen-year-old Orion like toddler Orion, than

Poppy did like little Claude. But those tiny boys, those tiny bundles of baby, were right there before her every morning over breakfast and every evening over dinner and every time they woke up sick in the middle of the night or came home with some school miracle accomplished or ranged into moments of stumbling maturity. Poppy's transformation, she would have told people, *if* she told people, was no more miraculous or astonishing or, frankly, absurd, than any of the others, nor any more apparent to her rainbow mama eyes. Parent time is magic: downtempo and supersonic all at once, witch's time, sorcerer hours. Suddenly, while you aren't paying attention, everything's changed.

Poppy was about to start fourth grade, the twins ninth, Roo and Ben their junior years of high school. On the way to work, Rosie considered that she had only two more years with her whole tribe, and then she'd be down to three. She had only two more years – after a dozen of them – with a child in elementary school. Only two more Halloween parades. Only two more turkeys shaped like hands. She could scarcely imagine a holiday season without 'Up on the Rooftop' stuck in her head, but she looked forward to trying it out. The weather was all turquoise sky, sunshine spread wide and warm like butter on new rolls, dappling shadows that somehow made clear it was the end of summer not the beginning, back to school not semester's end.

They had a pediatrician of course. And a dentist. Jupiter had a vet, especially as her muzzle grayed and her hearing went and it took a full minute to get up from her bed for a walk. The twins had an orthodontist. Ben had an optometrist and an allergist. Roo had an orthopedist from the time he broke his wrist skiing the first winter after they moved, over-confident that his Wisconsin snow experience trumped his classmates' rain, forgetting their Washington mountain experience trumped his Midwestern flat. Poppy, in the years to come, would have a whole host of ists and ologists. But Rosie and Penn stuck with Mr Tongo.

They met with him online, rather than over the phone, so he could see their faces and they his and anything else he wanted to show them: to no one's surprise, Mr Tongo was a fan of the visual aid. He still favored his giant exercise balls over actual office chairs, and it gave Rosie and Penn the impression he was talking to them from a train, bouncing lightly up and down, rolling occasionally side to side. Then suddenly he would break off and rush about the room, in and out of the shot, on and off the screen, pulling books off shelves or models out of drawers or standing on the desk to make a point, even though that meant they could only see his shoes and the bottoms of his trousers.

This day, Rosie and Penn at first thought they'd clicked the wrong contact, for when they connected, the window opened onto what seemed to be a preschool classroom, pastel wooden alphabet blocks stacked into high-rises and skyscrapers, a city of wobbly block towers.

'Mr Tongo?' Penn ventured.

No answer.

'Mr Tongo,' Rosie called. All these years later, they still did not call him by his first name.

Still no answer.

'Is the Wi-Fi wonky?' Penn wondered. 'Or maybe it's a glitch on his end?'

'Disconnect and try again,' said Rosie.

Suddenly, they heard a roar. Godzilla lumbered into view. He lurched into one precarious building and another, turning all to ruin, before mounting one of the rubbled piles and facing the camera triumphantly. Around his neck hung a sign in Mr Tongo's neat block handwriting. It read: PUBERTY.

Godzilla was menacing enough until Mr Tongo's face loomed three times larger at his side looking ready to accept his Oscar nomination.

'Hi, Mr Tongo,' Penn and Rosie chorused from somewhere between bemused and wary.

'It was me all along!' Mr Tongo wiggled his plastic Godzilla as if they might need proof. 'A monstrous welcome to us all.'

They smiled at him weakly. 'How are you, Mr Tongo?'

'Me? I'm wonderful. Delighted to be with you. Thrilled to see you both. So! Back to school. Such an exciting time. *Quelles felicitations!* Mazel tov!'

Penn found it remarkable that a dozen or so years of school was sufficient to keep everyone on an academic calendar for life so that even people like Mr Tongo, who had no children, wished him a happy new year every September. It was as if those school years bred a nostalgia so deep into the cells that the body woke to it each fall as naturally as the squirrels in the park began their frenzied harvest, never mind the weather was still fine, the sun still gracing them all. 'It's very exciting,' he acknowledged, then added awkwardly, 'thank you.'

'Most welcome, most welcome. So my friends, in honor of the new year, today I think it's time we do a little after-school special: "Puberty Versus Blockers. A Love Story."'

Rosie watched her eyebrows rise in the miniature window in the corner of her screen. 'Oh, Mr Tongo. Poppy's only nine.' Had he lost count? 'We're years away yet. Years away.'

'Time flies like a banana, my dear.' His eyes actually twinkled. 'When was the last time you two talked seriously about hormone blockers?'

Rosie recalled the Dueling Dinner with Marginny and Frank. They'd had squash soup to start, which meant it had been fall which meant it had been a year already. 'It's been a while,' Rosie admitted.

'Well, let's do it!' Mr Tongo clapped his hands together. 'This is going to be fun!' Over the years, Penn's brain had come to play, under Mr Tongo's promise of fun, the theme music from *Jaws*.

Rosie shook her head. 'Puberty is later for natal males than natal females. It's not time yet. It's too early to be thinking about hormone blockers.'

'It's too early to be *taking* them,' Mr Tongo corrected gently. He was methodically bricking Puberty Godzilla into a prison of hormone blocks. 'It's exactly the right time to be thinking about them. You all have some tough decisions just ahead. Blockers, and for how long? Cross-sex hormones, and when? Surgeries, and which ones? All/some/none of the above? Hard stuff. Is Poppy worried about all this, do you think?'

'Not at all,' Rosie assured him.

But Mr Tongo was not assured. 'That's what worries me. You know, it used to be there were no transgender kids. Your son would come to you in a dress, and you'd say, "No son of mine!" or "Boys don't wear dresses!" and that would be the end of it. That kid would grow up, and if he made it through childhood and if he made it through puberty and if he made it through young adulthood, maybe, if he were lucky, he'd eventually find his way to a community of people who understood what no one ever had, and he would slowly change his clothes and hair, and he would slowly change his name and pronouns, and he would slowly test the waters of being female, and over years and decades, he might become a she. Or he might kill himself long before he got there. The rate of suicide for these kids is over forty percent, you know.'

Penn closed his eyes. He did know.

'Now, it's so much better in so many ways. Claude was lucky. He came to you and said he wanted to wear a dress and said he wanted to be a girl, and you said okay, and you said you'd help, and you said it didn't matter to you because you'd love him no matter what. So you grew out his hair and bought him a dress and moved across the country to a city on a sound: add water, instant girl. And that's so wonderful for all of you. Except puberty is going to blindside Poppy. She doesn't think of herself as a boy. You don't think of her as a boy. Because she didn't grow up hating it, because it's never stood in the way of her being who she felt and you accepted she was, she's totally normalized her penis. It doesn't connote maleness for her. It doesn't mean anything. It's just how she pees. But that's about to change. And soon, long hair and a dress aren't going to be enough to keep her a girl. You have to prepare her for that.'

'You're saying we've done too good a job?' Rosie laughed, half joking.

But Mr Tongo nodded. 'That's exactly what I'm saying. Rude, I know. It's irritating when people tell you that you're such good parents you're failing your kid.'

Penn and Rosie looked at themselves looking overwhelmed and guilty, but Godzilla broke into a little dance.

'Cheer up, you two! Poppy's not going to turn into a man overnight. Just start planting the seeds. Think about how you'll talk to her about the changes – the beautiful, miraculous, to-be-celebrated changes – that come for all boys and girls as they get just a little older than she is now. You'd have to help your little girl turn into a woman under any circumstances. These are just a little more fun!'

At nine, fourteen, fourteen, sixteen, and seventeen, Penn's brood wasn't finished growing up, but they were finished with childhood – finishing anyway. They were getting ready to go off into the world, but it wasn't therefore true that they didn't listen to stories before bed anymore. They did. Some nights. Especially if they were camping or on vacation. Especially in the summer, when they were all likely to be out in the backyard around the fire pit after dark. But Poppy's bedtime was earlier than the boys', who had their own stories to tell to which their parents and their sister were not privy. So Penn and Poppy were often on their own for storytime.

Grumwald didn't have a lot of friends anymore. He'd had to leave the ones he grew up with behind when he went Away, and he hadn't made new ones. Princess Stephanie, on the other hand, had lots of girlfriends, but only Grumwald knew her secrets. For instance, her girlfriends didn't know she became a fairy every night. They didn't know she could fly and light stars. They thought her hair was neon green only because she was just that cool. She felt bad about lying to them, but she didn't want to risk losing them by telling the truth. And it was easy. If she wore a T-shirt when they went swimming, if she always changed in the bathroom, they never saw her without a top on so her wings were hidden. If they went out for brunch instead of dinner and had book club during the day, no one thought it was strange she could never do anything in the evenings.

'She was in a book club?' said Poppy.

'Everyone's in a book club.'

'Like with wine?' Poppy was intrigued.

'It's not a book club if there isn't wine.'

But then a scary thing started happening. Princess Stephanie started transforming into a night fairy without warning. She was at the mall shopping for shorts when one of her wings popped out suddenly, right in the middle of the day. She was in the dressing room at the time, luckily, but it made her nervous. Then, just when she'd convinced herself it was a weird one-time thing, she was at the coffee shop getting breakfast one morning when she realized the barista was staring at her in amazement, and no wonder – she was levitating. Not only had her wings unfolded at not yet eight thirty in the morning, she hadn't even noticed. She spilled her latte, found her footing, and ran home crying. She was so scared she went to see the witch.

'Which witch?' Poppy giggled. 'The one who was making Grumwald capture the night fairies?'

'The very same, which is why Grumwald was wary of her, but Princess Stephanie could tell that the witch wasn't always friendly maybe (she was a witch after all) but she was smart. Stephanie could see that the witch had a lot to be cranky about – she was very old and had trouble getting around and most of her teeth were rotten, which must have made it hard to eat – but that didn't mean she was unkind. Stephanie knew people didn't usually ask witches for help, but she couldn't think who better to turn to.'

'But the witch hated the night fairies,' said Poppy. 'That's why she was making Grumwald capture them.'

'Who better then,' Penn wondered, 'to help her corral the night fairy within?'

And indeed, when she went to her, the witch was unfazed. 'It happens to everyone,' she assured Princess Stephanie.

'It does?' Stephanie doubted it.

'Sure. Everyone's someone else sometimes. Everyone transforms. Maybe not in quite the same way as you, but that's sort of the point, the curse if you will. It happens to everyone but not to any two people in the same way, and no one likes it, no matter who's waiting inside. The good news is I have beans.'

'I don't cook,' said Stephanie.

'Not soup beans.' The witch thought damsels in distress should be quicker on the uptake. 'Magic beans. I've got beans that will keep you from turning into a night fairy ever again.'

'Who will light the stars?'

'Who cares?' The witch shrugged. 'Someone else's problem.'

'What will I be at night then?'

'Just Princess Stephanie.' The witch grinned her awful brown witch teeth.

'But if I'm not a night fairy, who am I the princess of?'

'"Of whom am I the princess?"' The witch was a bitch about grammar, but then she considered. 'Huh. I guess if you're not a night fairy, you can't be a princess either. You'll be Just Stephanie.'

Stephanie thought about this. She wasn't sure she wanted to be Just Stephanie. On the one hand, it would certainly be simpler. On the other, what would the stars do without her? And besides, it was nice to be a princess. 'Do you have beans that will control my wings just in the daytime? I'll still be a night fairy and do the stars as long as I can keep my secret from my friends during the day.'

The witch sighed and rolled her eyes. Princesses were so demanding. But yes, she had those beans. And she felt for Princess Stephanie – it *was* different for her – so she handed them over. Stephanie went home, soaked them overnight, then turned them into hummus and ate it with carrot sticks for lunch the next day.

'Did it work?' said Poppy.

'It worked like a charm,' said Penn.

As soon as her parents' lights went off, Aggie deployed her yardstick umbrella. Despite great advances in technology over the course of their childhoods, it would remain their communication device of choice. 'Your brother's in love with my sister.' She was talking before Poppy even had her window all the way open. 'It's gross.'

'Which one?'

'Do I have another sister? Cayenne. Duh.'

'Which brother?'

'Who knows? One of them. All of them. Her phone pings every five seconds, and she's in there laughing her head off. Which one of your brothers is still up?'

'All of them probably. No one showed up for storytime but me.'

'What happened tonight?' Aggie followed the adventures of Grumwald and Princess Stephanie like a soap opera.

'Steph's wings were popping out all over, but she didn't want anyone to know, so she went to the witch and got some magic beans. She made hummus, ate it, and felt better.'

'Weird,' said Aggie. 'What do you think it means?'

'I dunno.' Poppy shrugged. 'Something. There's always some kind of secret message.'

Aggie considered the matter. 'I think your dad wants us to know it's okay to do drugs. And not tell anyone about it.' Improbable though it seemed, Agatha Granderson grew up and eventually became a professor of literary studies at the University of California at Berkeley. She had a gift for textual metaphor. 'Fourth grade is going to be so great!'

Red Roo Rising

That January, as his grandmother had predicted they would, Roo's needs arose. Roo needed understanding. Roo needed comforting. Roo needed his parents to realize what he was fighting and why, to see his hurt and confusion, to sort his legitimate anger from the other kind, or, if you prefer, his ordinary teenage angst from his more particular teenage angst. He needed them to take deep breaths and look at the big picture, but all Rosie and Penn could look at was the gash weeping blood from his forehead. Mostly what Roo needed was stitches.

It was a cold, wet Monday morning, and Rosie was running Howie-late as usual. She preferred Seattle January's rainy forty degrees to Madison's snowy four, but she also thought her toes might be growing mold from walking through the constant damp. Yvonne didn't even look up from her computer when she arrived, red-nosed and sodden. 'Fourteen minutes late.'

'I had to stop at the top of the hill to catch my breath.'

'For fourteen minutes?'

'Getting out of the house is hard.'

'Maybe you should drive.'

'Think of the environment. Did they wait for me?'

'Nope.'

'Shit.'

'Yup.'

Howie ostentatiously stopped Monday Morning Meeting mid-sentence when she opened the door to the break room. 'Ah, Rosie, thank you so much for joining us.' His opening move was the same every week as if passive-aggression were his own invention. 'We can't tell you how honored we are you could make it.'

Rosie didn't even look at him. 'What'd I miss?' she said to James.

'Nada.'

'Quite a bit actually.' Howie glared back and forth between them. Elizabeth pretended to look at her (blank) notebook. 'We're almost done. Since you weren't here, we decided in your absence to put you in charge of the staff-appreciation breakfast again this year.'

'It shouldn't be me,' said Rosie.

'Why not?'

'It won't get started until lunchtime.' She grinned at James.

'The rest of us have families too, you know,' said Howie.

'I was kidding.'

'The rest of us manage to balance work and family.' He wasn't yelling; he was scolding, which was worse. 'It's not fair that we should suffer because you are incapable of doing so.'

Rosie rolled her eyes. 'How are you suffering, Howie?'

'I have to recap Monday Morning Meeting before I've even gotten through it. And I have to take shit if you're asked to do one thing outside seeing patients.'

'I'm pretty sure I'm the one taking shit, but I'll be in charge of breakfast again.'

'Attagirl.'

'I'm not a girl.'

'Come on time.'

'By which you mean early.'

After her first patient of the morning, she found James in the break room.

'Why do we persist in pretending we work for Howie when we're all equal partners and he's basically a grass stain?'

'Grass stain?'

'Annoying, probably permanent, essentially harmless. Kind of ugly.'

'You've been doing too much laundry, Ro.'

'Penn's in charge of laundry.'

'He's equal, but he's senior. He hired you.' James stirred more sugar into his coffee than it seemed like it could absorb and still remain in liquid form. 'Myself, I was skeptical after your interview.'

'You were?'

'Five is a lot of children. I thought you were probably some kind of fanatic or in a cult or something.'

'James! You can't make hiring decisions based on how many kids an applicant has.'

'The whole time you were talking I was humming, *"There was an old woman who lived in a shoe. . . ."* Point is, Howie fought for you. You owe him your job.'

'Maybe, but he's not my mother. He doesn't get to scold me for being late. I'm an adult. And not his employee.'

'No, but it's worth keeping him happy, or at least not pissing him off, especially when it's easy.'

'Taking his condescending shit is easy? Taking on the jobs no one else wants because I was fifteen minutes late to a meeting I said I'd be fifteen minutes late to? That's not easy.'

'Sure it is. Pick your battles. Don't you do this all the time at home?' James and his husband no longer went to the opera. Instead they had one-year-old twins. 'I feel like that should be the subtitle. Parenting: Pick Your Battles.'

'That's why I shouldn't have to do it here.'

'Think of it as a power grab. Pick your battles rather than having them thrust upon you. He's antsy. You know he gets this way every few years, so he's overdue. He wants to start an office blog. He wants to chart a fifteen-year plan. He wants to put together a humanitarian mission to Thailand.'

'I can't go to Thailand. I have a job and a life.'

'You're preaching to the choir, kid. Buy some doughnuts for the staff and come even earlier for Monday Meeting, and you won't have to.'

The door opened. Howie poked his head in and heaved a huge sigh in Rosie's direction though clearly he had been looking for her and clearly he had found her. 'Rosie. We need to talk.'

'Sure,' she said lightly. 'But I've got a patient in ten minutes.'

'It won't take long,' said Howie, 'but we have to—'

Rosie's cell phone rang. The high school. 'Mrs Adams?'

'Dr Walsh. Yes, this is she.'

'Roo's mother?'

'Yes.'

'This is Franny Plumber up at school. I'm afraid Roo's been suspended. You'll have to come get him.'

Christ. 'Kid emergency,' Rosie half-apologized to Howie. 'I have to
go pick up Roo, but I'll be back this afternoon. Tell Yvonne to reschedule my appointments until after lunch.'

If it weren't for the gash in his head, he'd have kept getting away with it.
In fact, Roo and Derek McGuiness had been fighting during recess on
and off for years. It felt more like an ancient feud than a tussle at this
point. Ben knew this and left Roo to it. Ben saw where his strengths lay,
and it wasn't hand-to-hand combat. If Roo had asked for his help, he'd
have provided it (strategically if not muscularly), but Roo did not ask,
and Ben knew to respect that too. Rigel and Orion knew it but couldn't
do anything about it. For one thing, they were only fourteen. For another, ninth grade was on a different schedule. They had English every
day while Roo was getting his ass kicked. Even Cayenne knew it, and
maybe she even found it sexy, and that might even have played a part in
why Roo was still doing it. But, well trained in the art of secret keeping,
Roo had managed to keep it from his parents for a year and a half and
counting.

Rosie and Penn were angry he was fighting. They were angry the
school hadn't noticed he was fighting until there was a gushing head
wound. They were angry he'd implicated all his brothers in his cover-up.
They were angry that when they'd asked about the various scratches and
bruises and red marks, he'd made up stories about gym class or joining
fencing club or wrestling with Ben (this last may not have been a lie).

Even though he'd gone to lengths to hide it, Roo was angry anyway
that they hadn't noticed he'd been getting his ass kicked. He was angry
they hadn't noticed that sometimes he was the one doing the ass kicking.
But mostly, he was angry they didn't care what he was fighting for.

Angry all around, they went straight to West Hill Family Medical
Center. Roo wanted his own doctor. Roo did not want to be treated by
his mother. But Rosie was more confident in her own ability to stitch up
her son's forehead than her son's GP or whomever happened to be staff-
ing whatever emergency room. And though Penn worried that she was so
upset her hands were shaking, that was only so until she had Roo on the

table in the treatment room. Then her hands steadied and her eyes focused, and she laid a line of stitches at which even Howie, when he came to check on all of them, whistled in appreciation.

In some ways, it did not seem fair to have this conversation while she had both Roo's bleeding head and a needle in her hands. In some, it was the only way.

'Hold still.'

'Mom, wait, I—'

'I said hold still. I know you have trouble with authority Roo, but even you must see this is a time to listen to your mother.'

'I don't have trouble with authority.'

'Have you been fighting?'

Roo paused to consider whether it was too late to convincingly lie about this and concluded it probably was. 'Obviously.'

'I don't mean today.' Rosie irrigated her eldest son's gaping head wound. 'I mean was today the first time?' She looked at his eyes. 'And don't lie.'

'Yeah. I've been getting in fights. Some.'

'For how long?' She sterilized Roo's head.

'I dunno. A few weeks?' The question mark at the end was for whether he was going to get away with the timeline.

'A few . . . weeks?' Penn shrieked, and Roo was glad he lied.

The first time had been the second week of school – the year before. Derek McGuinness was an asshat. Derek McGuinness called him – and a couple dozen other kids – gay and faggot and fucking fairy. Derek McGuinness called him these things precisely because he thought Roo wouldn't fight back. It was the fact of Roo's unlikeliness to fight back that made him those things and that made it safe for Derek McGuinness to call him them. Which meant kicking his ass killed two birds with one stone. How to explain to his parents that there were some things worth defending, some things worth standing up for?

'Why?' said Rosie.

'Why what?'

'Why were you fighting?'

'You don't understand, Mom. It's different for guys.'

'Please.' She rolled her eyes.

'You have to be a man.'

'You're seventeen.'

'You can't be, like, a wuss.'

'Roo, in this family of all families, you'd think you'd have a better handle on the absurdity of gender stereotyping.' Her needle went in and out, in and out at the slow, steady pace of a heartbeat much calmer than anyone's in the room. 'Remember when your father walked away from Nick Calcutti? That was the bravest, manliest thing I've ever seen.'

'Yeah.' Roo shrugged, winced. 'But Nick Calcutti had a gun. Derek McGuinness isn't even fast.'

'Don't move. Who started it?'

Roo was still. He couldn't quite answer that question. He had thrown the first punch, it was true. But it was more complicated than that.

'Roo.' His mother moved her gaze from his forehead to his eyes.

'He begged me to do it, Mom.'

'He's hitting kids,' she said to Penn, as if Penn weren't right there and hadn't heard himself, as if Roo weren't lying beneath her busy hands. 'He's seeking out and beating people up now.'

'He called me . . . something bad.'

'What?' said Penn. 'What could he possibly have called you that warranted violence?'

'He said. He said I was gay.' Roo went with the serenest epithet. He didn't want to say 'fucking fairy' to his mother while she had a needle in his forehead, even if it was a quote.

She went white above his eyes. 'That's why you beat him? That's the horrible, tragic insult you simply could not abide? Gay?'

Roo's head and mouth held still. His eyes nodded.

'Roo,' his father breathed, 'that's not even . . .'

'True?' said Roo. 'I know it's not true.'

'Mean,' Penn finished. 'It's not even an insult. All you have to say is, "None of your business," or "No, I'm not actually," or "What's it to you?"'

And suddenly Roo was laughing. He tried to look at his parents to see if they were serious, but his mother was clenching his jaw almost as tightly as her own.

'You think I beat him up because I'm homophobic.' Not a question. An accusation.

'Isn't that what you're telling us?'

'No. I beat him up because *he's* homophobic. He's out there calling anyone he doesn't like faggot and pussy, like being gay is the worst thing he can think of. Some kids actually are gay. Or they have gay parents.

How do you think they feel? I beat him up so he'd stop being an ass-hole.'

'Don't say "ass", Roo.' Penn was trying – and failing – to keep relief out of his voice.

'But your history project.' Rosie finished her stitches, tying off the thread but not the issue.

'What history project?'

'The one last year. The one you failed.'

'That was so long ago, Mom.'

'It was antigay.'

'No it wasn't.'

'It was about the problems with letting LGBT soldiers serve openly.'

'Yeah. Problems the military should address. Responsibilities they're, you know, shirting.'

'Shirting?' said Penn.

'Redshirting. Benching until they're ready to deal with them.'

'Shirking, I think,' said Penn.

'But that stupid voiceover.' Rosie mimicked Roo mimicking a movie trailer: 'The navy is navy. Gay soldiers don't belong.'

'Exactly,' said Roo. 'The navy should be rainbow-colored, but it's to-tally not. Gays should feel like they belong, but they don't. The army can't just change the rules and think their job is done, problem solved. That's what the video showed. That's why there's violence and abuse. They have to change the rules, but then they also have to help everyone make them work.'

Penn was so relieved, he was light-headed. Roo wasn't a bigot. Roo had a smart, nuanced, important point. Absent the gushing head wound, it was good news all around.

'Roo!'

'What?' Why was she still mad?

'Roo, that project was terrible,' Rosie shrilled. 'We watched it. Mrs Birkus watched it. We all concluded you were some kind of ho-mophobic zealot. It would be one thing if you had nothing to say. But you have a message to spread, an important one, one you are uniquely posi-tioned to impart in an environment where it's crucial that you do so, and it's buried under all this stupidity – fighting and cursing and shit videos. If for no other reason – and there are many, many other reasons – you must do better work.'

'*You're* going to lecture *me* about speaking out about gay rights?' said Roo. They were back to this again. 'You're the one who's ashamed Poppy's trans. We all think it's fine. No one else cares.'

'We all?' said Penn.

'Ashamed?' said Rosie.

'All of us,' said Roo. 'Ben, Rigel, Orion, and me all think—'

'And I,' said Penn.

'Ashamed?' said Rosie.

'You seem ashamed of her.' Roo pressed tentatively at the bandage Rosie had affixed atop the stitches. 'Otherwise you wouldn't be so afraid to tell people. I'm not homophobic. I'm not antitrans. Are you though?'

'We're not ashamed.' Penn stood so his supine son could see his face. 'We're proud as hell of her. All things being equal, we'd shout it from the rooftops. But all things are not equal. First and foremost, we have to protect her. There are lots of Derek McGuinnesses in the world. You can't beat up all of them.'

'Any of them,' Rosie corrected. 'You can't beat up any of them. What about college?'

'What about it?'

'How will you get into college with suspensions on your record and Fs in history?'

'I'm not the smart one,' said Roo. 'Ben's the smart one.'

'Roosevelt Walsh-Adams. You are smart. And you have important things to say. And for damn sure you need help learning how to say them clearly and appropriately. You need to learn something about responsible decision making, cause and effect.'

'Why?' said Roo.

'You are bleeding from your head,' said his father.

'You need to go to college,' said Rosie. 'So you also need to knock this shit off.'

Maybe it was the strain of the day, the sympathetic blood loss that came from watching it seep out of your child. Rosie felt punished because he was punished. Penn felt relief that he wasn't their worst nightmare, hateful and intolerant and prejudiced. Rosie was alarmed that he was in pain, alarmed that he had inflicted it too. Penn was worried Poppy somehow felt like Roo did, that they were keeping her secret from shame rather than shelter. Maybe it was that they were still angry, still had much to be angry about. Maybe it was the layer-upon-layering of all of the above. Whatever the reason, they missed it again, Roo's warning, Roo's wisdom, Roo's mysterious ability, myopic though he was, to see far down the tracks to what was steaming inexorably ahead.

Fire

I t was June before anything else broke. When it did, it wasn't as obvious as a gushing head wound, but it was less easily repaired.

Ben and Cayenne were at the beach celebrating the end of school, becoming seniors at last. They were rushing the season. Right on the water, Alki was often cold even on an August afternoon. On an early June evening, it was freezing. But that was part of Ben's plan. If it were cold, they'd have to build a fire, which would be romantic. If it were cold, they'd have to get under a blanket and press their bodies together for warmth.

Ben had only thought to bring one blanket, so they had to lie in the sand, the quilt tented above them on a piece of driftwood and tucked in at the sides. They had their phones in the way of mood lighting. Ben was anxious that the bonfire not alight the blanket. Cayenne drew circles in the sand with her toes and said, 'How much do you love me?'

Ben stopped thinking about the blanket. 'Tons.'

'Prove it.'

'How?' He tried to ask this nonchalantly, but it seemed to Ben that knowing this one answer would unlock all the others the universe held.

'Tell me a secret.'

'What will that prove?'

'It'll prove you trust me. Here: I'll start. My dad wears tighty-whities. It's, like, totally gross.'

The former wasn't much of a revelation. The latter was self-evident.

If this were the kind of secret that would prove his love, Ben imagined it would be easy. 'So does mine?' he tried.

'Eww.' Cayenne seemed pleased with this confession. 'What else?'

'Roo and I wear boxers. Rigel and Orion wear boxer briefs.'

'That's not what I meant. Tell me another secret.'

'It's your turn,' Ben pointed out.

'My sister wore diapers to bed until, like, last year.'

'Aggie?'

'Do I have another sister?'

'No but . . . Poppy never said anything.'

'Why would she?' said Cayenne. 'Anyway, Aggie's sneaky. When she has sleepovers, she makes a big show of walking around naked, and then she puts on pajamas, and then she sneaks out of bed later to get a pull-up in the bathroom.' Ben let that one sink in until she prompted, 'Your turn.'

'Um. Once, in Wisconsin, before we moved, my parents almost got shot.'

'Really?'

No. 'Really.'

'What happened?'

'Poppy was at a playdate, and the dad pulled a gun so she called my mom, and when my parents showed up, he threatened them.'

'Why?'

'Oh.' Ben found it was difficult suddenly to breathe. 'Well. I don't know. He was just mad I guess.'

'But what did he say? Why was he mad?'

'He . . . didn't say anything.' Was the blanket too tight? Could enough air get in? 'He wasn't mad like angry. He was mad like crazy.'

Cayenne propped herself up on her elbow in the sand. She shone her phone on his face. 'You're lying.'

'No, I'm not.'

'You are,' she pronounced. 'You have another secret. A good one. I can tell.'

'I don't,' Ben said. 'I swear.'

'If you loved me,' Cayenne lay back down in the sand and pulled Ben's hand onto her stomach underneath her shirt, 'you would tell me.'

'I can't tell you,' Ben said, 'but I do love you.'

'Aha!' said Cayenne. 'I knew it.' They made out for a while in the sand under the blanket. Her stomach was warm and yielding and held much promise for what lay above and below it. Then she said, 'Tell me.'

'Really, I can't.' Ben tried to catch his breath. 'Doesn't it show you what a good guy I am that I have something I'm not supposed to tell so I'm not telling?'

'I guess so,' Cayenne admitted, 'but then, I don't really care if you're a good guy.'

They made out some more, and every time he put his hand slowly, tentatively higher under her shirt, she'd let it go a little farther. She let him touch the edge of her bra and then put her hand on his to stop him there. Then she guided his hand to its clasp before she hit the pause button. Then she let him finger the top of her skirt. That time, she put her hand on his but moved it down instead of up. 'There,' she said, and smiled at him and he smiled back and then, hand still over his, then she said, 'I promise, whatever it is, I'll never ever tell anyone ever no matter what cross my heart and hope to die.'

Ben was a smart guy, yes, with an off-the-charts IQ and a double-stacked bookcase, but he was still sixteen. And he'd been patient for a very long time. That and he saw something his parents did not, which was that when something was this significant, this consequential, you didn't keep it from someone you loved, even if that someone was Cayenne Granderson.

Hedge Enemies

Fall was good for the DN. Penn found it hard to stay inside and write during Seattle's sunny days because there just were not enough of them. Though Carmelo had yet to find a rundown lake house to rent, Seattle summers were worth sleeping over her daughter's garage for, so she still came up every year. In contrast to Phoenix, it was pleasantly warm and sunny every day rather than sole-meltingly hot (she'd lost a pair of flip-flops to the asphalt in a grocery-store parking lot one May and taken it as a sign to come north a month earlier), and she could sit in the backyard with a gin and tonic and smoke and read a book until after ten in the evenings and still have light enough to read by. She came to see her daughter, and she came to see her boys, but mostly, she loved to be with Poppy.

Penn wondered whether Carmelo was mentally subbing one Poppy for another, her granddaughter now at ten the age of the Poppy she lost, but he didn't wonder much – Poppy had always been close with Carmelo, even when she was Claude. In the early Poppy years, there'd been a lot of shopping together and manicure dates and trips to the salon, girly indulgences they'd been desperately missing (Rosie refusing them both), but now Poppy mostly sat out back barefoot and read books with her grandmother or told stories or listened to hers. Still, never mind the addition of two adult hands, there was the subtraction of school, which, combined with the sunshine, made it hard for Penn to get enough done in the summer. Now Carmelo was back in Phoenix, the kids were back at school, the sun was generally wayward, and Penn promised himself this was the year: this was the year he'd finish the DN, get it done, get it good, get it off. It was time. It was past time. It was time.

Every day, he wrote. At the homeworking table, Roo and Ben applied to college, and Rigel and Orion worried over their namesakes and labeled star charts, and Penn decided to start part two all over again in the first person and see if that helped, and Poppy said, 'Who's the hedge enemy?'

'Badgers,' Rigel said promptly.

'You're such a Wisconsin kid,' said Ben.

'Badgers eat hedges. They love hedges.'

'That's hedgehogs, you idiot,' said Orion.

'Hedgehogs don't eat hedges,' said Ben.

'Then why are they called hedgehogs?'

'They eat *in* hedges – bugs and snails and stuff – and they have a snout. Like a hog.' It sometimes seemed to all of them that Ben knew basically everything.

'Sweet, are you studying hedges or hedgehogs?' Penn tried to get back to the point.

'We're studying what we want to be when we grow up,' said Poppy.

'You want to be a gardener?' said Roo.

'You want to be a hedgehog?' said Orion.

'I said I want to be a baseball announcer, but Jake Irving said I couldn't because I'm a girl. He was all like, "Girls aren't allowed in baseball because they take forever to get ready and they have too much hair," but Mr Mohan said women could be baseball announcers, it's just that they usually aren't, and I said why not, and Mr Mohan said it was because of the hedge enemy.'

'Ahh.' Poppy's vocabulary no longer towered over her age. 'Hegemony. Hegemony means when one group has control or authority or dominance over another.'

'Like baseball players are dominant over baseball announcers?' said Poppy. 'That seems kind of fair because they're doing the actual playing.'

'No, like men have power over women,' said Roo.

'Men throughout history,' Penn amended, 'have often wielded more power than women, in many ways, if not all, and generally speaking.'

'They have?' Poppy: awed, openmouthed, incredulous.

'Afraid so.'

'Because there's so many more of them?'

'Of who?'

'Males?'

Penn laughed. 'Only in this household.'

'Then how are the men more powerful?'

'Well, in this case what Mr Mohan meant is that men have most of the jobs in sports, especially the ones that pay well, and that's not fair, nor is it the rules, but that's the case anyway, and it's self-perpetuating. Do you know what that means?'

Poppy shook her head.

'It means the fact that that's the way it is means that keeps being the way it is. It means when a little girl says she wants to be a baseball announcer when she grows up, someone tells her she can't because there are no female baseball announcers, which means no one grows up to be one. And so on.'

'What will I be when I grow up?' Poppy was still young enough – if maybe just barely – to think Penn had all the answers, so thoroughly had all the answers that he could see even the future.

'Anything you want,' he said.

'Will I be a boy job or a girl job?'

'You should be a boy job,' said Roo. 'They pay better.'

'Why?' said Poppy.

'The hedge enemy.' Ben didn't even look up.

'Most jobs aren't boy jobs or girl jobs,' said Penn. 'Most jobs are open to either.'

'But the boys get paid better for them?'

'There's a lot that breaks down about how the world . . . breaks down.' Penn was astonished, at once pleased and alarmed to find that gender in-equality was news to this child. As usual, they had apparently done too good a job sheltering her from her world. 'It's true that men are often paid more than women, even for the same jobs. It's true that jobs traditionally dominated by men pay more than jobs traditionally dominated by women. It's also true that you can be whatever you work hard to be.'

'No.' Poppy shook her head. They weren't getting it. 'When I get my job, whatever it is, will I get paid more, like a boy, or less, like a girl?'

'It doesn't really work at the individual level,' said Penn, 'and it's a bit more complicated than that, but—'

'But if you went back to wearing pants,' said Roo, 'you could retire ten years earlier.'

Poppy stuck her tongue out at Roo and went back to her homework, but the conversation lingered for all of them.

She knocked on her parents' door that night.

'What's up, sweetie?' Rosie and Penn were in bed reading. 'Can't sleep?'

'No.'

'How come?'

'I'm worried about what to be when I grow up.'

'I don't think you have to worry about that tonight,' said Rosie.

'It's for school.'

'Pick something. They won't hold you to it.'

Poppy shook her head unhappily. 'And I'm worried about *who* I'll be when I grow up. A boy or a girl.'

Rosie closed her book. 'You can be whichever one you want,' she said carefully.

'It's expensive to be a girl.'

'It is?'

'Because of the hegemony. Boys make more money than girls.'

Rosie's expression split the difference between impressed and concerned. 'I make more money than Daddy.'

'You do?'

Her parents both nodded.

'But it's because you do a boy job.'

'Doctor's not a boy job.' Rosie thought about the lopsided politics of her practice. No one was asking James to make breakfast.

'And you have to spend a lot of money on makeup if you're a girl and buy lots of shoes and hair stuff.'

'None of that's a requirement.' Rosie owned four pairs of shoes: winter, summer, exercise, and fancy. 'Remember when we said you could bake cakes and play with dolls and have pink things, and that did not make you a girl?'

She remembered.

'Neither does makeup and lots of shoes.'

'Are you . . .' Penn wasn't sure how to put it. 'You can't determine your gender identity or your career identity or your anything identity based on what's going to make you the most money. You shouldn't not be a girl because you could make more money as a boy.'

'And you shouldn't stay a girl,' Rosie said, 'if you think you are or want to be,' she hesitated, 'or could be a boy.'

'And if you want to be a baseball announcer,' Penn added quickly, 'then that's what you'll be.'

Poppy dug her toes into the carpet. 'I said I wanted to be a baseball announcer, but really I want to be a scientist.'

'What kind of scientist?' Rosie tried to sound nonchalant instead of overjoyed.

'I think I want to study fish,' Poppy said shyly, 'but a fish scientist is called an ichthyologist. And when we were researching our jobs in the library, I was looking up ichthyologist, and Marnie Alison said "icky-ologist" and everyone laughed, so when we had to tell about our job to the whole class, I said baseball announcer instead, but then Jake was a jerk about it, so now I don't know what to be.'

Rosie couldn't decide where to focus first: her daughter's apparent interest in science, which was thrilling, her familiarity with the word 'ichthyology,' which was news, her concern with the hegemony, which warranted further discussion for sure but, it being already past her bedtime, perhaps another night, or the fact that her classmates were bullying her about her career choices and who knew what else. She settled on, 'Ichthyologist? Is that like marine biology?'

'Sort of, but better. Marine biologists have to do everyone who lives in the ocean. Ichthyologists get to focus on just fish. Did you know,' here her voice dropped to a conspiratorial whisper even though it was just the three of them, 'lots of fish switch genders?'

Her parents had no idea.

'They switch or they're both. Both at once, or first one then the other. Clown fish all start as boys, but some of them become girls later. Parrot fish are all girls, so then one of them has to become a boy – she changes color and everything – but then if another boy comes along, she might go back to being a girl again. Cuttlefish can split themselves down the middle so all the girls on one side can flirt with his boy half, and all the guys on the other side see his girl half so they don't feel threatened.'

Her parents' eyes were wide, their mouths half open and almost, but not quite, smiling, a look she felt she occasioned from them too often. But she was too excited to stop.

'But the best ones are the Hamlet fish. They're called simultaneous hermaphrodites. That means Hamlet fish are both at once. When two of them get together to . . . you know . . . the first one lays eggs like a girl and the second one fertilizes them like a boy, but then, the second one lays eggs like a girl and the first one fertilizes them like a boy. Everyone's both. They take turns. Isn't that amazing?'

It was. Rosie knew this moment from raising four other children to this point already, the one where suddenly your kids know more than you do about something they've discovered all on their own, something real and important not just cartoons or video games. Amazing was exactly what it was.

'Ichthyologist sounds like a wonderful job,' Rosie said. 'Why wouldn't you write about all of this?'

'I can't write about any of this. Obviously.' It wasn't just ichthyology, apparently, about which Poppy knew more than her mother. 'Marnie Alison's already making fun of me, and she doesn't even know about the transgender fish.'

Penn waited until he heard Poppy's turret door close. 'Could be?'

'Could be what?'

'She shouldn't stay a girl if she could be a boy?'

'That's not what I meant.'

'What did you mean?'

'Okay,' said Rosie. 'That's what I meant.'

'You think she should change back?'

'She hasn't changed forward. She hasn't changed at all.'

'She's changed completely.'

'Okay. She's changed some. But some she hasn't. She's done nothing yet that can't be undone. She needs to know she can reverse course if she wants to.'

'Reverse course?' He said it like she'd recommended burying Poppy in sand up to her ears and leaving her in the desert for three days. He said it like she'd offered their youngest heroin as a midnight snack. 'You think it would be easier if she'd just be Claude?'

'I don't think it,' Rosie said gently. 'It would be. It would be easier. Maybe we put to bed long ago the idea that easier was the goal. Maybe when easier is a matter of degrees like these, it doesn't even count. But no question, by anyone's definition, it would be easier.' She considered their last New Year's Eve in Madison when they'd decided 'easy' wasn't on their wish list. She considered how much harder 'hard' had gotten in the years since then.

'How can you think Claude would be easier?'

'Well, for starters, she's right: she'd probably make a lot more money.'

'Is that what you're—'

'Jesus, Penn, of course that's not what I'm worried about. It's. Her. Penis. Are you daft? It's her penis!'

'But puberty blockers—'

'Are not the perfect miracle you imagine them to be.'

'They are though.' Penn got out of bed to kneel on the floor in front of her like he was going to propose. 'They are. These kids on blockers? You should read their stories.'

'No, you should stop reading their stories.'

He'd known that was what she would say, so he kept going. She was the doctor, but he was the reader, and he knew things too. 'The blockers are effective. They're safe—'

'How do you know they're safe?'

'Mr Tongo said—'

'Mr Tongo is not a doctor. Mr Tongo has not read all the studies.' She closed her eyes. 'And even if he had, the research isn't reliable. It's incomplete. They've only been doing this treatment for a few years in this country, so there are no long-term studies. It's biased and unrigorous—'

'How can it be—'

'Because when a little girl wants to wear jeans and play soccer, her parents are thrilled, but when a little boy wants to wear a dress and play dolls, his parents send him to therapy and enroll him in a study. We just don't know yet the long-term effects on these kids of puberty suppression.'

'But they know the effect on those other kids, right? The precocious ones? And they're fine.'

Rosie's fingers squeezed and unclenched, squeezed and unclenched under the covers. 'The drug itself seems safe, but that's only some of the picture. Those kids restart puberty in the normal way at the normal time. Here, you're stopping the body's natural inclination—'

'But Poppy's body is wrong. It's always been wrong.'

'It's not that simple, Penn. This is the problem. You're oversimplify-ing.'

She understood his point because it was not logical. She understood because once she'd decided they had to leave Wisconsin, no amount of reason from her husband or misery from her eldest child or evidence from her mother or history at her hospital or love for her life just the way it was made any difference. On the way home from the ER after those unspeakable hours with Jane Doe, she had watched the sun come up and understood already that the only way forward was deeper. She saw this with her patients all the time. Through weeks of symptoms and months of tests, they didn't want to believe it was what it was. But once they ac-cepted, deeper was their only way forward too. They stayed up all night doing advanced medical research they couldn't begin to understand. They joined support groups and read books and bought T-shirts and ran 5Ks. They rededicated their lives to what they'd rejected utterly only days before. And then when their story strayed from that path – the cure didn't work, the cure worked too well, the indicators indicated some-thing else instead – they found themselves more lost than ever. The wood was dark indeed, perilous and terrifying, but Penn could see a way through. She didn't want to bar that path to him. But she wasn't sure that around the bend up ahead, it didn't plunge into the sea.

Rosie took a deep breath and tried again. 'You're stopping everything, not just her turning into a teenage boy. I understand why you don't want her to grow chest hair, but it's more than that. It's slowing her growth – right now she's supposed to be getting taller, her bones denser, longer, stronger, and if you stop the hormones, that won't happen. It could im-pinge on her maturation, mental and emotional as well as physical. Hor-mones contribute to intelligence and creativity, critical thinking, abstract analysis. We might be taking that away from her. Aggie and Na-talie and Kim are going to start to turn into young women, Penn. They'll start to look older and more mature, but they'll also start to act older and more mature. It's not just that they'll have breasts and she'll stay flat. They'll have crushes on classmates and anger at authority figures and moodiness at home—'

'Yeah, it'd be a real bummer to miss that.'

'You want to halt her puberty so you don't have to deal with her foul moods?'

'Of course not. I was kidding.'

She knew he was. She just didn't think he was funny. Or she knew he thought he was funny, but she also knew he wasn't entirely kidding. Or somewhere in between those things. Just because she couldn't pinpoint his objection didn't mean she couldn't disagree with it. Poppy or Claude, Poppy *and* Claude, needed to go through the part where they hated their family and no one understood them. They had to go through the part where they questioned who they were and where they came from and all they'd ever been told and taken for granted. They had to fall in love for a week and then get their heart broken over the weekend and then fall in love again on Monday. Whichever one, Poppy or Claude, he or she couldn't stay a little girl forever.

Penn raised himself from his knees to sit next to her on the bed and hold both her hands in his. They were switching roles here, she could see. It was like the Changing of the Guard. For no other reason than it was time, she was going to be the crazy one for a while and he got to be the calm one. 'Puberty is one thing' – his voice was irritatingly reasonable – 'but she shouldn't have to hate her body.'

'She's going to be a woman,' said Rosie. 'She should get used to it.'

'Yes, ha-ha, but seriously—'

'No, seriously.' Rosie could hear herself shrieking but could think of nothing to do about it. 'You think Poppy will be the only kid to feel betrayed by her body when it goes through puberty? All teenagers feel betrayed by their bodies when they go through puberty. You think Poppy would be the only woman to hate the way she looks? All women hate the way they look. Her body may not be immutable, but it's not like changing the water filter. The drugs, other drugs, yet more drugs, a lifetime of drugs, the surgeries, the stuff that can't be made whole regardless of surgery, these things are huge. These things are scary. These things are mysteries, unpredictable, uncertain. There are strange effects, side effects, unintended effects. There are hard decisions that can never be unmade. There are hard decisions she's not old enough to make. There are decisions that just shouldn't be made for you by your parents. If she is a girl, if deep inside this is her truth, if she needs this, if she wants this, if she must, if she's sure, then yes, of course yes, thank God yes, we will support her and help her and do all we can and much we can't yet but will have to figure out, as we have already, as we do for all our children. But easier? It would be easier for her to be a boy. So if she's questioning, if she's on the fence, this is information she should have.'

It wasn't that Penn didn't understand these things. It was that he didn't care. The blockers were like magic, like a child's answer to a child's prayer: just make it stop, just turn it off. Blocked kids did not turn into people they were not, did not hide, did not despair, did not stand in the sand pleading with the sea, endeavoring to stop the tides. They did not poison or mangle their bodies. They did not choose death instead. Claude had been a boy, had had a penis, would grow into a man, but Poppy did not have to. Blockers meant Poppy's time of being Claude was all behind her, never to resurface. She could stay child-Poppy until she could become adult-Poppy, Poppy-entire. Penn understood all of Rosie's careful doctor points. But they were nothing compared to the capacity of magic.

'Has she shown any signs at all' – Penn made sure not to sound condescending – 'that she might want to go back?'

'I don't know how she'd know.' Rosie answered a different question. 'She can't even remember Claude. Poppy is what's normal. And not just Poppy, Poppy with a penis. That penis is as unremarkable to her as her elbow. For something that's the focus of all that's coming and the zenith of the trouble here, she doesn't give it a second thought. It doesn't signify maleness to her. And you know what else?'

'What?'

'Soon it's going to be something north of unremarkable. It's going to start feeling better and better. It's going to be fun to play with. And that's hers too. I don't want her to feel bad about it. And I don't want to take it away.'

'She's a girl, Rosie. She is. Look at her. Listen to her. She's not a fish. She can't be both. She doesn't have to take turns. Or maybe she's that other kind of fish she told us about. At first she was male, but then she transformed – her colors changed, her patterns, her biology, her roles and relationships, everything. Whatever she used to be, now she's female. Fully female.'

'Prepubescent female.'

'Yeah?'

'So sometimes it's testosterone that makes people seem male, feel male, be male,' said Rosie-the-physician. 'And you, you want to block it.'

'That's not what I want.'

'It is, Penn. It's what it means when you object to my telling her she can still change her mind.'

'I don't want anything. I want . . . I only want to do whatever's best for her.'

'Me too. Of course me too. If we knew what that was. But unfortunately, that exceeds my skill set. That's not prognosis. That's prognostication. We need a seer, not a doctor.'

'Then that's *my* skill set,' said Penn.

'You can see the future?'

'It's the stuff of fairy tales, not hospitals.'

'That's a nicer place to be,' Rosie admitted, 'but it's not real.'

'Sure it is,' said Penn. But Rosie rolled over and went to sleep.

Who Knows?

When the phone call came, Rosie was in with a sixty-two-year-old patient who was complaining of knee pain. She had been complaining of knee pain since Rosie met her four years earlier. The patient was a runner. She ran fifty, sixty, seventy miles a week. She ran every day. Some days, she ran twice. Run less, said Rosie. Every other day, swim instead or do yoga or lift weights. Run half as far and make up the rest with walking or a bike ride or, hell, sitting and reading a book. But the patient only ran more. And her knees hurt worse. Rosie had the conversation down by heart and was in the middle of the part that began, 'As we get older, the lining in our joints begins to break down,' when Yvonne knocked on the door.

'I'm with a patient,' Rosie said.

'It's Poppy,' said Yvonne.

'On the phone?'

'Yeah.'

'Is it an emergency?'

'She says no' – all those children and grandchildren, not to mention thirty-four years in a doctor's office, had precision-tuned Yvonne's urgency barometer – 'but I'm not buying it.'

When Rosie picked up the line, Poppy was silent. She could hear her breathing but that was it.

'Poppy?'

No answer.

'Poppy? Are you there?'

No answer.

'Honey, are you okay?'

Nothing.

'Sweetheart? You're scaring me.'

And then, on the other end of Rosie's phone, in the barest barely whisper of a breath, from a darkness that was very far away indeed, Poppy said, 'Mom. They know.'

Rosie did not ask what – she knew. She did not ask how – it did not matter yet. What she asked was who. Who knows?

'Everyone,' Poppy only just managed. 'Everyone knows.'

'I'll be right there,' said Rosie.

Parenting in the Dark

At school, Poppy had just finished hanging up her jacket and her backpack that morning when she turned around and found Marnie Alison and Jake Irving pretending to be trying not to let her see them laughing at her while actually making sure she – and everyone else around – saw them laughing at her. If she ignored them, she'd look like an idiot. If she asked them what they were laughing at, she'd look like an idiot. If she battered them both with her backpack until their noses spouted blood like whales, she'd get suspended. So she said as little as she could manage, barely a syllable, but it contained all the surrender of the Treaty of Versailles, which they were learning about in social studies. 'What?'

'We heard you're a guy.' Marnie snickered.

Poppy felt the blood leave her face, her head, her chest and legs, and gush away from her heart like an eruption. 'What?' That syllable again, the one that said: *Kick me*.

'We heard,' Jake fake whispered, 'you have a giant dick.'

'Actually, it's probably a little one,' Marnie said to him.

'Probably,' Jake agreed.

'Care to comment?' Marnie wore mascara and purple eye shadow every day. Poppy wondered whether her parents allowed this or she put it on after she got to school. Small beads of black globbed the tips of her lashes, which made them look like tiny licorice lollipops.

'I don't have a . . . um . . .' Poppy could not bring herself to finish that sentence.

Marnie and Jake looked at each other. 'She says she doesn't have an um,' Jake said to Marnie.

'Then I guess she doesn't have an um,' Marnie said back.

'Unless she's trying to hide her um. Or is embarrassed by her um. Or she knows her um is disgusting.'

'All ums are disgusting.' Marnie pushed Jake, who pushed her back playfully like what they were doing here was a game rather than ruining Poppy's careful, perfect life. Poppy followed them to their classroom and found her desk and tried to concentrate.

At lunch, Aggie threw herself into her usual seat with her usual lunch tray with its usual offerings: rectangle of pizza, pile of French fries, Granny Smith apple, chocolate milk. 'You are not even going to believe what they're saying about you,' she reported as if what they were saying to other kids weren't what they were also saying to Poppy. 'Marnie Alison and Jake Irving are telling everyone you're a guy.'

Natalie snorted juice box through her nose, not because she was laughing but to show as clearly as she could how ludicrous she found this suggestion. Poppy saw this for the kindness it was. 'As if. You're the most popular girl in our grade. Marnie's just jealous.'

'And mean.' As she did every lunch, Kim was deconstructing her sandwich so she could eat in pieces – the meat then the cheese then the bread. 'Marnie and Jake are jerks. No one cares what they say.'

'But everyone's talking about it,' Aggie reported soberly. 'Cara Greenburg even asked me if I'd ever seen your thing when you slept over.'

'Did you say, "Duh, of course not"?' Kim asked.

'I said, "None of your business",' said Aggie.

'Which is true,' said Natalie, 'but maybe if you told them they'd leave us alone.' PANK realized they were all in this together. If Poppy went down, they all would. That's how being ten worked.

'Told them what? I've never seen Poppy's . . . thing.'

'She doesn't have a thing,' said Kim.

'Maybe you could say, "We don't stare at each other naked when we have sleepovers. What kind of sleepovers do you have?"' Natalie suggested. 'Then they'd be embarrassed and just drop it.'

'They aren't going to drop it,' said Aggie.

Then Keith Rice piped up from between Poppy's legs under the table. 'I see it! I see her thingy!'

Poppy kicked him and then, when he scrambled away, they all four kicked him, and he crawled out, transparent shredded lettuce sticking to his knees, a French fry flat as fruit leather mashed into his shin, hands raised, and protesting, 'I'm just doing research for an article. My readers have a right to know.' Keith kept an elementary school blog the rough equivalent of Page Six and used it as cover for all sorts of sins.

Poppy was pretty sure he could not see her anything. She was wearing thick tights, and her legs had been crossed. But she was not completely sure.

'Dirty perv,' said Kim. And then to Poppy, 'Aren't you eating?'

Poppy's whole self folded in half. She held her lunch bag in her lap, over her, well, thing, but she could not bring herself to open it. She shook her head.

'Come on,' said Aggie. 'Let's go outside.'

On the playground, PANK gathered around Poppy. 'You're so pretty,' they said. And 'Of course you're a girl,' they said. And 'Marnie Alison is such a stupid jerk,' they said. And 'People make up the weirdest things,' they said. What they did not say was, 'Who cares what's in your pants?' And they did not say, 'It wouldn't matter if you did have a penis. We would still love you.' And they also did not say, 'We know you, and we know who you really are.' Poppy knew they didn't say these things because they didn't know to say these things. But because they did not, she got scareder and scareder, and because she got scareder and scareder, her classmates started to believe that Marnie Alison, though a jerk, might be on to something. Otherwise, wouldn't Poppy laugh about it, or say it was just stupid and funny, or go ahead and prove she was who they'd always thought she was?

In gym, someone said, 'Poppy, shouldn't you be on the other side with the boys?' and everyone laughed.

In health, when they broke up for sex ed, someone raised her hand and said, 'Ms Norton? I don't feel comfortable with Poppy being here,' and everyone laughed.

In math, Josh Edison complained the homework took forever, and Mr Mohan said, 'That's why it's called long division – it's long.' No one laughed. Then someone said, 'That's what Poppy said,' and everyone laughed.

That's when Poppy packed up all her books right there in the middle of math and walked straight out of the classroom and down the fifth-grade hallway and out the front door of the school and called her mom.

Rosie expected tears and yelling and cascades of snot, but what she got on the way home was a silence she did not press. When they walked in together – when Rosie should have been at work still, when Poppy should have been in math still – Penn took one look at his wife and daughter and knew what had happened, the form anyway if not the substance. They both looked sick, ashen, but he could see that this was not the flu, for Poppy would not meet his eyes, and Rosie's, in the blink of their crossing, confirmed everything. They let Poppy go off alone to her room and quietly, heartrendingly shut her door.

'How?' said Penn.

'Don't know,' said Rosie.

'How is she?'

'Don't know that either.'

'What do we do?'

'Or that.'

It did not matter how, really, but they still wanted to know. Had someone peeped into a bathroom stall at school? Had the principal hinted to a teacher who'd figured it out and told another teacher who was overheard in the staff room? Were the ten-year-olds who populated Poppy's world somehow more perceptive than anyone gave them credit for?

Or had someone told?

They had a family meeting. There was no use pretending to Poppy this was not a big deal. She was living in the eye of it and knew better. There was no use acting as if this outing did not change all their lives because those lives were here, already changed. There was no use spreading blame, but that did not mean it was not worth asking the question. Did anyone want to confess to confessing, disclose their disclosure, transgress their transgression? No one did. 'I'll tutor you from home,' Ben offered, 'until you're ready for college. Then you can start over again. Again.' Roo rolled his eyes. Penn made pancakes for dinner, which no one much ate, but that was okay because he knew what was called for here wasn't food but fairy tale. There was nothing like some other hapless kid getting boiled or eaten or turned into a tree to make your own life seem less terrible. There was nothing like the promise of magic to make okay even that which seemed like it would never be okay again.

Penn had never tried to disguise the ways Grumwald's adventures mirrored his kids'. Fairy tales aren't about subtlety, after all, and teenagers will ignore a moral if you let them. Grumwald had been practicing a lot of safe sex lately (sex which was all the more gratifying because he'd waited until he found true love). He had gotten into his first-choice college by triple proofreading his application and not going to the movies with Cayenne the night before the SATs. If only Penn knew the moral of Poppy's horrible day at school, he felt certain Grumwald and Stephanie could effectively impart it, but because he did not, he started at the end and worked backwards. Sometimes your secrets get out; sometimes the world seems like it's ending; somehow it will all be okay.

'Princess Stephanie was out with Grumwald's study partner, Lloyd,' Penn began.

'Lloyd?' Roo interrupted. 'No one's named Lloyd, Dad.'

'Lloyd you object to,' Ben didn't even look up from his phone, 'but Grumwald you're fine with?'

Penn ignored them. The story wasn't for them tonight; it was for Poppy. 'Princess Stephanie and Lloyd were having a lovely dinner. But after the appetizers, the restaurant door slammed open, and a cold wind blew in, colder than Stephanie had ever felt, colder than real wind ever got, so she knew something was up. In walked a figure in a veil and dark cloak. All the lights went off. All the candles blew out. The air in the room turned to sludge, and Princess Stephanie found herself gasping for breath, panicked, so she didn't even notice that no one else in the restaurant seemed to be having trouble breathing or seeing or keeping their candles lit. The cloaked figure came closer and closer, and it was the witch. The one who'd commanded Grumwald to harvest night fairy hair all those years ago. The one who'd given Steph magic beans when she needed them. The witch leaned right into her and said, "I know who you are," and Stephanie was afraid and said, "I'm Princess Stephanie," but the witch said, "I know your secrets, and I'll tell everyone," and Princess Stephanie—'

'No!' Poppy yelled.

Rigel put down his history textbook to look at his sister. 'It's just a story.'

'I don't want this story,' said Poppy. 'I want to go to bed.'

'It has a happy ending,' Penn promised desperately. Princess Stephanie told Lloyd her secrets. Lloyd knew all about her but liked her anyway. There were cream puffs for dessert.

But Poppy said, 'I hate happy endings.'

'No one hates happy endings,' said her father.

'They're so fake.'

'It's a fairy tale.'

'So?' She looked as tired as Penn had ever seen her.

'So it's supposed to be magical and wonderful. It's supposed to be made up.'

'Yeah, but if it's not real, then what's even the point?' She wiped tears out of already swollen eyes.

'Oh baby,' he whispered, 'it's real.'

'You just said it was made up.'

'Just because it's made up, doesn't mean it isn't real,' said Penn. 'Made up is the most powerful real there is.'

'It was me. Mom? Dad? Are you awake? It was me.'

They were awake. They could not sleep. They were lying together in the dark, turned toward each other, unseeing, unsleeping.

'It was me.' Ben was whispering, in part because it was the middle of the night and in part because it was too awful to say out loud. 'I told Cayenne. Over the summer. I told her she could never, ever tell anyone no matter what. She swore she never would. She was really . . . convincing. I can't believe she told. I should never have trusted her.' However things turned out, Ben was right about that last part. He confessed he told, but he did not confess he did it so she would love him back (he didn't think of it like that). He did not confess he didn't truly love her after all (he didn't know that yet). He left out the part about the sex. But he told them the rest of it.

Parenting in the dark was something Rosie remembered from when they were babies. It was all so much harder in the middle of the night. In the dark, you couldn't see them clearly, the pallor of their skin, the brightness of their eyes. When they cried during the day, she could tell from another room if the hurt was physical or emotional, to be attended or ignored. But after midnight, all cries were cries of terror, all augured alarm. Were they warm from fever or from sleep? Confused by nightmare or premonition? Might there actually be someone hiding in the closet? You couldn't treat patients in the dark of course, but Rosie had always imagined ERs were so well lit because during the day, fear stayed at bay and sensible perspective reigned. In the dark, only the horror stories rang true.

Rosie tried to triage this situation. She wasn't used to Ben being in

trouble. She thought he probably deserved clemency as a first-time of-
fender. But on the other hand, Ben was smart enough to know better, so
perhaps it was more just to hold him to a higher standard of accountabil-
ity. Did she admonish Ben for telling Cayenne (of all people) even though
he clearly realized it was stupid? Did she impress upon him the enormity
of his sin, the great harm he'd done his sister, his family, even though he
plainly knew? Or the opposite – should she comfort him that it wasn't his
fault really, that all secrets out eventually, that he hadn't completely ruined Poppy's life? That when they'd chosen the path of secrecy they'd
known its terminus to begin with?

Penn opened his mouth to ask Ben how hard it was to keep his closed,
how hard it could possibly be to not tell this one thing, when he realized
the answer to his question. It was very hard. It had not occurred to him,
until Ben told his story, that Poppy's secret could not be kept alone. Not
telling about Poppy, he understood for the first time, meant not telling
about Nick Calcutti, not telling about Jane Doe, not telling about Madison and how they'd loved it there and why they left, not telling about
baby Claude and the joy of his childhood and the way he completed their
family. For the first time, Penn understood that all that not-telling was
hard as diamonds and just as surely flawed.

But before either Penn or Rosie could sort the shadows and decide
what to do about Ben and Cayenne, it got more complicated. Ben was
not the only one. They came in the middle of the night, in the dark, one
after another, like dreams.

'I said it to Derek McGuinness one time while I was kicking his ass.'
Roo was distraught enough not to notice Ben in the dark already in
his parents' bedroom. 'I didn't think he was paying attention, but I guess
he was. I didn't think he'd know what I was talking about, but I guess he
did. While I was punching him in the head I was also saying, "That's. My.
Sister. You're. Talking. About. Asshole."'

'Don't say "ass", Roo.' There were so many things to object to here,
Penn defaulted back to the one that was familiar.

'"That's my sister you're talking about, Hole",' Roo amended, and
then added miserably, 'It was a crime of passion.'

'Mine too,' Ben nodded, also miserably.

And which was worse, Penn thought. Out of hatred or love? Loyalty
to one's sister or loyalty to one's beloved? In the heat of battle or the heat
of bonfire? But before he could decide, the door opened again.

'We did it.' Rigel and Orion sounded like creepy twins in a horror movie. They sounded like little boys. They sounded like they might cry, and Rosie tried to recall the last time they had.

'Remember when we accidentally told everyone at the Grandersons' barbecue?' said Rigel, and Penn did. In fact, he remembered that it wasn't Rigel who'd said it but Orion, and he was touched at Rigel's instinct to shoulder some of his twin's blame. Maybe in the dark, it wasn't clear even to them which one was which.

'The next week at school, this kid we sort of know came up to us at recess and asked why we said that about Poppy,' Orion explained.

'We started saying how we were just joking and about *Captain Cock-roach* and Harry and Larry's dog,' Rigel continued.

'But then he interrupted and said he thought he might be . . . like that too. Like Poppy. And maybe we knew what he should do or who he should talk to or whatever.' Rosie noticed how steady Orion's voice had become.

'And we did,' Rigel said simply. 'So we told him.'

'He was really sad and scared,' Orion added, 'so it seemed like the right thing to do. We thought of all people, he wouldn't tell, but maybe he had to so someone would help, you know? Maybe he had to so someone would listen.'

And maybe it was because it was becoming less clear by the moment who was responsible, and maybe it was because it was becoming more clear by the moment the size of the hole in the hull of this secret, and maybe it was because the good reasons there were to tell were finally unfurling – or maybe it was just that it was nearly morning and no one had yet slept – but Rosie and Penn found their predominant emotion wasn't anger but pride. At least for a predawn hour or so.

The only one they never heard from that night was Poppy.

I'm Nobody! Who Are You?

The next morning, two hours later, everyone was generally groggy and cranky and still a little shell-shocked. Their world had changed again; they were just waiting to see how. In the meantime, there was school to go to. There were patients to see and words to write. And they were all of them grateful for those traces of normalcy, all except Poppy, who, as everyone else was rinsing out cereal bowls and getting dressed, still hadn't emerged from her room. Penn imagined she'd had trouble falling asleep and didn't want to wake her if she'd finally managed to do so. Rosie imagined she'd committed ritual suicide any of twenty or thirty ways just off the top of her head and had to be bodily restrained from barging in to check. When at last she could stand it no more, she and Penn opened Poppy's door without knocking, one creaky millimeter per breath, slow enough to bore slugs. When they finally had it wide enough to look inside, what they found was not as alarming as suicide, but not all that far off either. What they found in Poppy's room, there on her unslept-in bed, was Claude.

They recognized him at once though he was, in fact, a stranger. They had not seen Claude since he was five, so here at ten, he was an apparition. Poppy, their creative, confident, shining daughter, was nowhere to be seen. This child though, this ghost of a child, was dark and sullen with puffy red eyes he would not raise from the floor and arms that would not unwrap themselves from their stranglehold on his ribs. He was wearing Poppy's most masculine pants – a plain pair of gray sweats – and a much-too-big Mariners fleece of Orion's. In a large box next to the bed were piled all Poppy's dolls and stuffed animals, her dream catcher, her ballet shoes, and all her framed photos – one of PANK on the last day of fourth grade, one of Poppy and Aggie both dressed as ponies one Halloween, one of Poppy in a lavender sundress smiling out from among her brothers at Rigel and Orion's middle school graduation. And all around Claude – on the pillow and the sheets, in the box, on the desk, on the floor – spread Poppy's long, thick hair, streaked around the room like threads of dark blood. Rigel's electric shaver, put to use at last, lay on the floor next to the bed like a murder weapon, and tears coursed down Claude's cheeks under an uneven, stubbly scalp that broke his parents' hearts.

'I am not going to school,' Claude wept, his first words to his parents in five years, 'ever again.'

Rosie went to call Yvonne to cancel all her appointments for the day. Penn held his sobbing child against his chest and wondered at this moment come at last, come anew, come again.

When Penn called school to explain why Poppy would be absent, Mr Menendez was not surprised. 'Everyone's talking about it.'

'It'll die down.' Penn, after all, had done this once before.

'How did people find out?' the principal asked. 'Who told?'

'Don't know.' This was true. There were, apparently, a whole host of candidates. But Penn wasn't prepared to say that the answer to this question, even if he had known it, was any of the principal's business. He wasn't sure that his other kids didn't need protecting in this moment too. 'Doesn't matter,' he told Mr Menendez. This was less true.

It took the principal three days to figure it out, and when he did, the answer was none of the above. None of the middle-of-the-night confessors had been the culprit. It was all Marnie Alison's fault as Poppy, for one, had known all along.

Roo's English class was writing practice college admissions essays. The mock-prompt was *Write about a moment of great change in your life.* Roo's essay was not about Claude or about Poppy, but it was about how his own life had changed when his brother became his sister – what could be counted on, what was unalterable, what was rooted in the physical and what eluded it. The past should be immutable, Roo wrote, but it wasn't. The future hadn't happened yet, so it shouldn't be so strange when what you imagined could no longer come to be, but it was. The essay was

THIS IS HOW IT ALWAYS IS   221

heartfelt, well written, and insightful, and a few months later, an only slightly revised version would gain Roo offers from several institutions of higher learning despite his failing a quarter of history in tenth grade and having a suspension for fighting on his permanent record.

Roo's English teacher graded papers at her dining-room table. One morning, her husband grabbed her folder instead of his on the way to work. When he realized his error in the middle of a meeting, he called in his assistant to swap it out. The assistant looked inside and recognized Roo's last name and read his essay and relayed that remarkable piece of gossip to her own husband in bed that night. The assistant was Marnie Alison's mother. She had a very loud voice. Or a daughter with very good ears.

This is the way the world ends.

In the three days it took the principal to put this together, Poppy – Claude – refused to take phone calls from Natalie or Kim. He refused to notice that Aggie did not call or text or come over. He refused to reply to his teacher who emailed to say that Poppy or any version of Poppy was welcome back at school at any time, where she would be loved and accepted for who she was, and anyone who didn't like it could consider that fact from detention. He deleted without rereading a message from Jake who texted to say he was sorry and Marnie was a bitch and he'd only been teasing, and if he'd known it was true, he'd never have gone along with it. Claude did take a call from Carmelo, whose grandmotherly advice was, 'Fuck the bastards', and though those were in fact the most comforting words he received all week, they weren't enough to convince him to leave his room. He ate only cereal. He did not answer the door when his parents knocked and called gently from the other side, 'Sweetie? Are you okay? Can we bring you anything? Would you like to talk?' He was not okay, obviously. There was nothing they could bring him, also obviously. A time machine? A new body? A different life? Those were what he needed, and they were things his parents could not bring. He did not want to talk. He would rather die than talk. There was nothing to discuss about a life that was over except where to bury the body, and his life *was* over but there was nothing to bury. As usual, his body betrayed him in every way.

On the third night, the knocker was Ben instead of his parents.

'Go away.' Not angry. Desperate. A plea.

'Dude. It's me,' said Ben. 'Let me in.'

Claude peeked his bald head through the door. 'Why are you calling me dude?'

'That's what guys call each other.'

'It is?'

'Let me in.'

He did. 'All guys?'

'Yeah. So. How's it hangin'?'

'How's . . . what hanging?'

'It's an expression,' Ben explained. 'It's how guys ask each other how they are.'

'Why don't they just say "How are you?"'

'They don't want to get beat up.'

Claude's eyes were wide. 'Guys get beat up for asking how you are?'

'Guys get beat up for everything. Asking how you are. Caring how you are. Using big words. Pronouncing them correctly. Wearing colorful things.'

'Really?'

'Oh yeah. And that's just the beginning. If you're too smart, too dumb, too cool, too worried about being cool, too nicely dressed, too hiply dressed, not hiply enough dressed, listening to the wrong music, listening to the right music on the wrong device, asking stupid questions in class, asking smart questions in class, asking questions in class that lead to more work in class, slow in gym, nice to a little kid, nice to a teacher, nice to your mom on school grounds, too good with computers, too often reading, or discovered during a field trip to Washington, DC, to be in your hotel room watching a movie with subtitles, if you're a guy, someone's going to beat you up.'

Eyes wider still. 'Who?'

'Someone.' Ben shrugged. 'So it doesn't really matter who. You also have to walk the right way, which you don't. You're too bouncy. You're too sure about where you're going and too excited to go there. Low. Slouchy. Don't give a crap where you're going or whether or not you get there. These are your goals.'

'I walk like normal.' But it came out more like a question.

'Not for a guy you don't. And no more giggling. In fact, laughing at all is bad unless you're laughing *at* someone. No speaking in French anymore, *ever,* not even in French class if you can help it. No words over three syllables. I mean it. And you're going to have to change your name – again – because Claude is seriously European and borderline gay.'

Claude narrowed his eyes. This story, like all the stories told in his household, was starting to smell suspiciously like there was going to be a moral to it. 'Why are you telling me this?'

'I'm helping. You want to be a boy now, you're going to need help. A tutorial. Regular boys learn this stuff along the way. You were all playing with dolls and being accepted for who you were. But don't worry – I can catch you up. I got your back.'

This was not his point, and Claude knew it. 'This is not your point.'

'Obliquely.'

'What is your point nonobliquely?'

'I have two. One is that fitting in and being normal doesn't exist. Not for a few years in the middle. Your thing is you're a girl with a penis. My thing was I walked wrong and talked wrong and wore the wrong clothes and read books and knew a lot about computers and knew a lot about a lot of things but not enough about when to keep my mouth shut and feign ignorance or disregard. You can have matching genitalia and still not fit in. You can have matching genitalia, and still kids will be mean and make fun of you.'

'So what do you do?' Claude kept trying to tuck his hair behind his ears. Except he had no hair anymore.

'Come home. Have a cry with your family. Let them tell you you're awesome. Wig out. Shave your head. Go back the next day and try again.'

'Does it stop? Does it get better?' He was crying again, which didn't seem possible. At some point, shouldn't your face run out of water?

'Some,' Ben promised. 'If anybody overheard it though, I could still get beat up for having this conversation.'

'And the other one?' Claude said miserably.

'Other one what?'

'You said you had two points.'

'The other one is you're not a guy.'

'I am a guy.' Claude held his arms out from his sides like he would fly right out his window if he could. 'Look at me.' He touched his head. 'Look at me.' He peeked down the neck of his sweatshirt. 'Look at me.' He pulled his sweatpants open at the waist and gazed down. 'Look at me. Look at me. *Look.*'

'I am looking,' said Ben. 'You look sad. You look like someone who's going to regret very rash hair decision making. You look like someone who's just realized ten-year-olds can be horrible human beings. But you don't look like a guy.'

'I don't because it's worse than that.' His voice was breaking, and every other part of him felt like it was breaking too. 'I don't look like a guy, but I am one anyway. I can't pretend I'm not. I have to learn to be one. I should have been learning all along. Now I'm behind and I'll never catch up. All I needed was help. I live with like a thousand guys, and no one would help me.'

'We did help you.' Ben could hear his voice rising. 'Are you kidding? We did nothing but help you. We said okay when you switched to dresses. We said okay when you changed your name and grew out your hair. We moved across the country for you. We kept your secret for you.'

'That's not the help I needed.' Claude's hands tried to grab fistfuls of hair at his temples but came up empty. 'I needed help being a boy. I didn't need help being different – I *am* different – I needed help being the same. I needed help being like you, and no one helped me, and now my life – both my lives – are over. I can't be Poppy and I can't be Claude. I can't be anyone.'

'Everyone's someone,' said Ben.

'I'm nobody.' Claude was studying Emily Dickinson in school. Back when he used to be enrolled in school. 'Who are you?'

'I'm nobody too.' Ben's voice was shaking. 'There's a pair of us.'

'No there isn't.' Claude was crying again. Ben looked like he might too, which made Claude feel a little bit better. But only a little bit. 'There isn't. I'm the only only one.'

Claude ignored the tapping on his window, which commenced at 11:24 and continued until five minutes past midnight when he just couldn't take it anymore. He pulled open his blinds and then his window and leaned into the dark rain. Could a rival princess be a prince? Could a princess have a penis if it weren't a secret? Or was Aggie just one more thing Poppy had to lose? The night wind chilled Claude's hairless skull. It was raining hard enough to soak them both but not enough to mask the tears he'd have given anything to hide from Aggie but could not keep from rivering out of his swollen eyes.

'Nice hair.' Aggie sounded mad.

'Yeah. Thanks.' So Claude sounded mad back. Mad was better than gnawing grief, than agonizing mortification and terror, so it felt something like relief.

'So. You're a guy?' There was something under Aggie's mad, but even Claude – even Poppy – could not tell what it was.

'No. I'm nothing.'

'But you have a . . . thing?'

He nodded. The only way to keep the crying from turning to sobbing was to clamp his mouth tight as a tourniquet.

'My mom said that doesn't make you a guy,' Aggie shook her head hard, 'but I don't understand.'

Claude shrugged miserably. 'Me neither.'

'Is that why you always change in the bathroom? It's not because of Roverella?'

'I guess,' Claude said.

'You lied to me.'

'Not really. I didn't want Roverella to see me either. I didn't want anyone to see me. I'm gross.'

Aggie nodded. That made sense to her, which made Claude feel even worse, which he hadn't realized was actually possible.

'Well' – Aggie made her eyes widen and her head shake and her shoulders shrug in the most adult way she knew to express befuddlement – 'have a nice life I guess. Though I don't really see how that's possible.'

She pulled her head inside and started to shut her window.

'You hate me because I'm a boy?' Claude sobbed. He was going to just go back inside too, but when he accidentally opened his mouth, that was what popped out. When he imagined life without Aggie, he imagined tipping himself over the lip of the turret window and crashing into the pavement three stories below.

'You said you aren't a boy,' Aggie sneered. 'You said you're nothing.'

'You hate me because I have a penis?' Claude whispered the last word.

'I hate you' – Aggie was being too loud; their parents were sleeping – 'because you didn't tell me.'

'I was afraid you wouldn't like me anymore if I told you.' Claude was whispering all his words now because it felt like any force behind his voice might come out as howling.

'That's even worse,' said Aggie.

Claude raised his gaze from the ground finally. 'Why?'

'Because you don't trust me. I'd have loved you no matter what except you don't trust me and you lied to me. You think I care what's under your underpants? I don't. You could tell me anything. But you didn't.'

'Your mom told my mom not to.'

'We ignore practically everything my mom says.' Aggie just looked at him. 'Why'd you listen this time?'

'I don't know,' Claude admitted.

Aggie's head went back into her room and then slipped out again. 'I couldn't hold it at night until like a year ago. I got up after we got in sleeping bags and put on a diaper every time we had a sleepover. Does that change how you feel about me?'

'No,' Claude said.

'See? *I* told *you*. *I* had faith in *you*. You should have had faith in me.'

She pulled her head back in and shut her window before Claude could consider that she'd never told Poppy until now.

Vagina Shopping

There was no real reason for it since Poppy – Claude – was self-sequestered, but Rosie stayed home those three days too. Rain thrummed the windows as if the whole house were weeping. Quilted clouds the color of dead mice sunk low enough to cap the hill. Claude cried and cried in his bedroom. How could Rosie go to work and treat other people's children when her own was shut up in his room, refusing food or any other kind of comfort? She knew the suicide statistics, and she knew what unhappy almost-teenagers did to their bodies, and she knew that she could not protect her child if she was not there. Poppy and Claude had both chosen isolation from the world. How could their mother rejoin it?

On the morning of the third day, James called. 'You have to come in tomorrow.'

'Things are still shaky here,' Rosie hedged.

'Trust me,' said James. 'You have to come in tomorrow.'

'Howie?'

'Howie. What the hell is going on over there anyway?'

'James, I have something to . . .' Now everyone at Poppy's school knew, was there any reason she couldn't tell this close friend, fellow physician, colleague, and confidant? 'Never mind. I'll be in tomorrow. Tell Yvonne she can offer my cancellations Saturday hours this weekend.'

'Good start. You okay, Ro? What's going on?'

'Nothing. I'll . . . nothing. I'll see you tomorrow.'

On the morning of the fourth day then, she trudged up the hill. Howie met her at the door. 'Let's take a walk.'

'Oh God. Do we have to?'

'This is not a conversation we can have in reception.'

'Let me catch my breath.'

'You're not going to be talking anyway,' said Howie. 'Listen Rosie, I know you've got some shit going on at home. I don't want to bust your balls. But you're just not pulling your weight around here.'

'Howie, how am I not pulling my weight around here? I keep thirty-five appointment hours every week, same as you. I maintain emergency appointment slots and on-call hours, same as you. My patient load is full, same as yours.'

'How can you say you're keeping thirty-five patient hours every week? You've cancelled all your appointments since Monday.'

'Once. One week. This week I've had to cancel appointments – all of which have been rescheduled, and for each of which I will carve out time. In the four years I've been working here, this is the first time I've had to reschedule more than a day's worth of appointments. People get sick, Howie, people's families get sick, even doctors'. That's why we have sick leave and personal leave and family leave.'

'Is that what's happened this week? Sick kid?'

Rosie nodded but failed to elaborate.

'Penn can't take care of this? He doesn't even work.'

'Howie, how my husband and I manage our family and household responsibilities is none of your business.'

'No, my business is running this practice, which I cannot do if its members don't honor their commitments.'

'Three days in four years is hardly failing to honor my commitments.'

'Except that meeting patients is only part of your job requirements.'

'I'm a doctor, Howie. Seeing patients *is* my job.'

'In a hospital setting, in a large organization, maybe that's all there is to it. But as was made clear to you when you were hired, more is expected, more is required of you in a small practice. The rest of us are meeting our patient load and taking on extra responsibilities. You're showing up for your patients and then going home. This means the rest of us are picking up your slack. You need to contribute to the whole of this enterprise. The rest of us have families and personal lives and patients we care about too. We need team players who can share our burden.'

'What have I been asked to do that I haven't done?'

'Everything you've been asked to do you haven't done,' he shouted. 'You haven't helped market the practice. You haven't helped bring in new patients. You haven't gone to conferences to represent us. You haven't attended seminars to expand your skill set and thus our offerings. We needed someone to take on social media and the website, and you refused. We'd like someone to look into aid work and other volunteer opportunities. I actually did the work to liaise with a clinic in Thailand, but you won't go there, even for a brief stint. Do you know how great something like that looks for a small practice? *Seattle Met* might do a profile on us. Maybe even NPR. We'd get recognized by the AMA. This is how people choose doctors, Rosie. There's a thousand big and small things that go into running a business like this, and all you're doing is meeting with patients. Except when you can't.'

'Howie, I can't go to Thailand – I have patients here, not to mention a family and a life. I can't do weekly volunteer hours – I already have a full-time job. I also already have all the skills you wanted me to go to seminars to learn. We can't attract new patients because we're full with the ones we already have. I can't do social media because I'm not eighteen, and I can't do marketing because I'm a physician, not an ad exec. However, because I'm a physician, I can treat our patients, which I do, very nearly without fail, and I'm getting no complaints. The key to a successful practice isn't volunteer work in Thailand or a Twitter feed or a staff-appreciation breakfast which I have just taken on for the fourth year in a row; it's happy patients, and mine are happy because I am a good doctor.'

'And I'm telling you it's not enough. If you want it to be enough, go be a doctor elsewhere.'

'Jesus, Howie. It was three days.'

'Three days plus four years. Enough is enough. Think about it.'

At lunch, she called Mr Tongo. 'Everyone knows.'

'Oh shit.' It was so unlike Mr Tongo to curse, Rosie almost laughed. Almost. 'Everyone?'

'Everyone. Well, no, nearly no one. But everyone at Poppy's school.'

'Oh my. How did that happen?'

'Who cares?'

'I suppose. How is she taking it?'

'Bad. Very bad. She shaved her head. She's wearing sweatpants. She put away all her stuff. She won't talk to us. She won't come out of her room. It's bad.'

'Oh good.' Mr Tongo's voice rang with relief. 'Sounds perfect.'

'Really?'

'Perfecto. Great timing. Strong work. I'm so proud of her and all of you.'

Rosie was not sure she had the patience for Mr Tongo's idiosyncrasies today. 'What are you talking about?'

'Coming out. It's a queer right of passage. She had to do it, and the sooner the better – the closet's no good for anyone. She's young now, not yet in the throes of adolescence. Shaved head. Locked door. Not speaking to her parents. It's perfect! She's doing great!'

'She's not . . . she's not queer,' said Rosie.

'She's not,' Mr Tongo agreed. 'And that's the problem. You've so thoroughly accepted this child from the beginning. You accepted Claude as Claude. You accepted Claude as Poppy. You made this child feel so completely, entirely, unquestionably, comfortably female. You've deprived her of her queer.'

'You're saying we've been too loving and understanding.'

'Yes.'

'Yes?'

'Yes. She's queer. She's a girl with a penis. That's wonderful, but it's not usual. It's weird. It's odd. It's queer. There's a whole community, a whole world, a whole worldview worth of queer support that makes being a girl with a penis and any number of other less than usual things not just okay but also celebrated. And we want her to be part of that world.'

'But you said don't tell anybody.' Rosie tried and failed to keep herself from shrieking. 'You said it was nobody's business.'

'And that worked beautifully for a little while. You didn't think that was the plan for forever, did you?' Mr Tongo asked, maddeningly, as if his weren't the advice they'd been following in the first place. 'Six-year-old Poppy was too young to have to educate her peers, to have to stand up for herself all the time, to have to explain about sex versus sexuality or gender identity versus gender expression. In first grade, we're still trying to teach little boys and little girls that nothing in their pants is appropriate conversation for school. But now she's ten. She's almost off to middle school, almost a teenager, about to start becoming a grown-up, so it's time for her to explore and decide and be strong, to talk about who she is, to stand up for herself, and to deal with what sets her apart.'

'How does she do that?'

'Same way everyone else does,' he crowed. 'Suffering! Your small town can't accept you so you leave. Your family can't accept you so you find a new one. Your little life of shame and wishful thinking becomes too confining, so you strike out for something larger.'

'So you're saying she hasn't suffered enough.'

'Yes! Bravo!' he cheered. 'That is exactly what I'm saying. You haven't let her suffer enough. You've protected her too thoroughly. You've treated as normal something that isn't so she hasn't learned to live the abnormal life she actually has. You may not care, but other people will. Of course they will! For you, Poppy with a penis isn't any more or less variant than any of your other kids' wonderful quirks, and you love them all no matter what, and you just wake every day and raise them up. But that doesn't help Poppy live anywhere in the world besides your house. No wonder she won't leave her bedroom.'

'So what do I do?' She felt like she had talking to Howie, like what was being asked of her was both impossible and absurd.

'You? Nothing. You've done too much already. She has to do. And she's already done. Step one is come out.'

'Done,' she conceded. 'However unwillingly. What's step two?'

'Step two is get rejected by lots of people and feel just terrible about it.'

'Also done. What's step three?'

'Step three is where it gets fun. Step three is moving on.'

'How long does that take?' she sulked.

'It takes a whole lifetime' – Mr Tongo sounded overjoyed as usual – 'so it's a good thing she's starting early.'

Yvonne rescheduled Rosie's patients well past regular office hours. Her last patient of the day finally left at 9:45. She was hungry, and she was tired, and she was eager to be home and see what lay in wait there, and she was terrified of getting home and seeing what lay in wait there, and her head was abuzz with patient complaints and treatment plans and drug regimens, and her head was also abuzz with Howie's threats, and her head was also abuzz with Mr Tongo's admonishments, and it was a dark, wet, steep walk home. She had gotten used to the rain over the years. She had gotten used to the gray clouds that covered the city like a radiation apron nine months a year. But by 9:45, it had been dark already for more than five hours, and twilight at four in the afternoon was not something she'd ever gotten used to. It seemed like the middle of the night, and when she let herself in the front door, she felt nothing so much as jet-lagged.

The house was unusually quiet. No one homeworking. Everyone shut up in his or her room. His room. No one peeked out from a shut bedroom door to say hi or how was your day or you must be exhausted let me heat some leftovers for you. She knocked on Roo and Ben's basement.

'Guys?'
'Yeah?'
'You okay?'
'Yeah.'
'How was school?'
'Fine.'
'Anything new?'
'No.'
'Did you guys eat?'
'Yeah.'
'Okay. Love you.'
'You too.'

She had a similar conversation with Rigel's door. Orion was hanging upside down off the arm of the sofa wearing vampire teeth and a cape and playing a video game. 'Before you vonder, no I don't vant anything to eat, no I don't vant anything to drink, yes I finished all my homevork. I am gaming upside down only because I vant to be a vampire bat, so there's no need for you to vorry.'

She knocked on Poppy's door.
'Poppy?'
Nothing.
'Claude?'
Nothing.
'You okay?'
'No.'
'Wanna talk?'
'No.'

'I chatted with Mr Tongo today, and he had some thoughts. Can I share them with you?'

'No thanks.'

'Okay, baby. Whenever you're ready. Did you eat something?'

'Yeah.'

'What?'

'Cheerios.'

'Want something a little more substantial? I haven't eaten yet either. We could heat up a pizza or something.'

'No thanks.'

'Okay, love. Anything I can do to help?' Please? *Please please please please please.*

'You could stop asking me that question and go away.'

In her bedroom, she found all the lights off and Penn's glowing laptop open on the bed, but Penn himself was absent.

'Penn?'

'Bathroom,' he called. 'Sorry, I didn't hear you come in. Long day?'

'Very. What's new here?'

'Not much. Quiet night. Leftover pasta in the fridge if you want.'

'Thanks. What are you doing in here?'

He hesitated. 'Uh . . . work. I just wanted a little privacy so I'm doing it in here.'

She looked at his laptop. Vaginas. A plethora of vaginas. Insides and outsides. Close-ups, glamour shots, selfies. Films of vaginas in action. Please God, Rosie prayed, let him be looking at porn.

He came out of the bathroom, looked at her looking and looked sheepish.

'Feeling randy?' she asked hopefully. 'Just wanted a little alone time?'

'Vagina shopping,' he admitted.

'Oh, Penn.'

'Just . . . looking.'

'She's ten. No surgeon in the world is going to cut off her penis.'

'They don't cut it off. They more like . . . turn it inside out.'

'No surgeon in the world is going to turn a ten-year-old's penis inside out.'

'Not yet, obviously. I'm just starting the research. There are some really remarkable doctors who—'

'You're getting way, way ahead of yourself here.'

'I'm just starting the process.'

'Why?'

'Why?'

'Yes, Penn, why? She's got another year, maybe more, she can be free of medical intervention at all. She'd have years, who knows how many, on hormone blockers if that's the direction she and we decide to go. There are a zillion possibilities between here and vaginoplasty. What you're doing right now makes about as much sense as shopping for a suit for Roo's wedding.'

'It's just . . . well, it's pretty exciting, Rosie. Do you know a lot about sex-reassignment surgeries? They can make her a working vagina. It can do everything yours can. Her lovers won't be able to tell the difference. Her gynecologist won't even be able to tell the difference. They're doing it on minors in other countries. We could get this done before she went to college. Talk about a fresh start. It's some kind of miracle. You should see these sites. They—'

'You didn't answer the question, Penn.'

'What question?'

'She's ten. Why are you doing this now?'

'I don't know if you've noticed, Rosie, but push has crossed right over to shove here. In between, half-assed, secretly, just socially, it's not cutting it anymore. We have to commit. We have to go all the way. Otherwise, she's just a guy in a dress.'

'I don't know if *you've* noticed, Penn, but *he* cut off all his hair, put away all his girl clothes and toys, and is, as we speak, reverting to Claude with Cheerios.'

'And she hasn't come out of her room in a week. That's how depressed she is about it.'

'Or scared. Or confused. Or worried about disappointing us. Or worried about changing her mind. Or maybe she is depressed, but it's not clear to me why. It could be that she's depressed about not being all-girl. Or it could be that she's depressed about everyone finding out, which is not the same thing. Or it could be she's depressed because she doesn't know who she is or who she wants to be, and she can't stand thinking about it anymore.'

'No, I think that's you.' Penn closed his laptop.

'But instead of trying to figure out all that might be going on, you just want to do surgery.'

'I don't just want to do surgery. I want to look into the option of surgery. And I want to do it long before we think we need it because it's not a minor undertaking, and that's how seriously I'm taking this.'

Without the laptop glow, it was suddenly very dark in the room. 'I get that, Penn. I do. But even thinking about this right now is part of the problem.'

'How can that be? How can doing research and having more information and thinking through complicated issues with time to spare possibly be a problem?'

'Because she's having doubts' – Rosie held her arms out from her sides like her daughter did when she was upset – 'so we have to live in the doubt place with her. She's undecided, so we have to be undecided too. If she doesn't know, we can't tell her, can't even have something in mind. These are her decisions to make.'

'How can she make this decision, Rosie?' Penn's voice was shaking. 'She's ten. She doesn't know what genitalia is for beyond peeing with. She can't make decisions about sex, about the importance of sensitivity, lubrication, dilation, reproduction. She can't consider what a sexual partner will make of what's under her pants. We don't even know if she's going to be gay or straight. She can't possibly make these decisions. As you keep saying, she's ten. So we're going to have to do it for her.'

'We can't. Penn, we can't. These aren't our decisions to make. If she can't make these decisions for herself, she's going to have to wait until she can.'

'She can't wait.' Penn was surprised to find his hands clasped in front of his chest, not quite pleading but not so far off either. 'The younger you do it, the less of the wrong puberty she goes through, the better it works, right? If we wait until she can decide for herself, we've taken the choice away from her because we waited too long.'

'Penn, there are reasons they don't do surgeries like this on minors, and only some of them are physical.' It felt like playing dirty to pull doctor rank, but this was important. 'She cannot consent right now. She has to consent before procedures like these. So she has to wait. And so do you.'

'This is our job as parents, Rosie. You didn't say we couldn't pull Roo's wisdom teeth because he was a minor. You didn't say Ben couldn't get his ear pierced because he was only fifteen. As parents, we make a thousand decisions a year with life-altering impact whose implications our kids couldn't possibly get their heads around. That's our job. That's what parenting is. We decided to move across the country via some insane calculus that concluded Poppy being safer outweighed Roo being crankier because Ben might be happier and Orion and Rigel were a wash. We had no idea if it would work. We had no idea if it was the best thing. We researched. We thought about it. We discussed. And we made the best guess we could with the information we had on behalf of our children whose lives we thus changed indelibly forever.'

'Penn, tell me you see how vaginoplasty is different from ear piercing. Tell me you see how removing a penis is different from removing wisdom teeth. Tell me you see that equating gender reassignment with address reassignment is an absurd comparison.'

'Of course. Clearly. I'm just saying we make decisions for our kids all the time. We do this because we know they aren't as smart or experienced or informed as we are, so they can't make these decisions for themselves. That's what we're supposed to do.'

'You're scaring the shit out of me, Penn.'

'Why?'

'You're going too fast. She's just decided to re-become Claude, and your response is to turn her into Linda Lovelace. Maybe she doesn't mean it. Maybe she's not really changing her mind. But we have to slow down and figure it out, let her figure it out. You're ticking off boxes here because it's something you can do, and I get that, believe me, but she's got to be lost for a bit, and she can't be lost if we're leading her out of the woods.'

'She isn't lost, Rosie.' Penn took her hands and, though she tried, would not let her pull away. 'We made this decision long ago. We made it when Claude was in kindergarten, and Poppy's never regretted it, not for a day, and neither have I.'

'Then why'd she shave her head?'

'I don't know.' His face looked worn, wan.

'Penn, in so many ways, we're so lucky. In so many ways, I'm grateful this is what our kid got, gender dysphoria instead of cancer or diabetes or heart disease or any of the other shit kids get. The treatment for those isn't necessarily clearer. The drugs are harsher and the prognosis scarier and the options life-and-death but never black-and-white, and my heart breaks every time for those kids and those parents. But those are more or less medical issues. This is a medical issue, but mostly it's a cultural issue. It's a social issue and an emotional issue and a family dynamic issue and a community issue. Maybe we need to medically intervene so Poppy doesn't grow a beard. Or maybe the world needs to learn to love a person with a beard who goes by "she" and wears a skirt.'

'But that's not going to happen.' Penn spoke so softly she wouldn't have heard him if she didn't already know what he was going to say.

'In which case maybe she – and you and I – need to learn to live in a world that refuses to accept a person with a beard who goes by "she" and wears a skirt and be happy anyway. Maybe our response to that world should not necessarily be to drug and operate on our daughter.'

'How?' He looked up at her. It felt like a long time since their eyes had met.

'How what?'

'How do we learn to live in that world and be happy anyway?'

Rosie woke from fitful sleep sometime well predawn to send Howie a text: WILL GO TO THAILAND. IF I CAN BRING POPPY.

PART
III

Exit Rows

They would have needed a new wardrobe anyway. The clinic did not allow skirts. The clinic did not have air conditioning. The clinic, the whole jungle really, was plagued by mosquitos. These few, small facts they managed to glean combined with the one that was readily available – that highs would hover in the mid to high 90s every day – meant they both needed all new clothes, and those clothes proved fortuitously androgynous: long cotton pants, breathable shirts with long sleeves, walking sandals, sunhats. The night before they left, Rosie packed for both of them, then knocked on the turret door.

'So. Are you ready? Are you excited?' Rosie felt neither but tried to sound both, and when she got no response turned instead toward the practical. 'I packed for you.'

'Okay.'

'Is there anything special you want to bring with us?'

'No.'

'I mean, I have all the essentials, but maybe you want to bring Alice and Miss Marple?'

'I'm not a baby.'

'Or a picture of your friends.'

'I have no friends.'

Rosie winced but plowed on. 'I think I have all we need but one thing.'

'What?'

Rosie sat on the edge of the bed and took her baby's hands and said as gently, gently, gently as she knew how, 'I don't know what to call you, my love.' Her love looked slapped but spellbound by something just over Rosie's head. 'Should I call you Claude or Poppy? Should you be my daughter or my son? You can be either one, and you know we'll all support you. You know we'll love you no matter what, no matter who. You have only to tell me: who do you want to be?'

'It doesn't matter who I want to be.'

'Nothing matters but,' Rosie insisted.

'It only matters who I am.'

'And who is that?'

'Claude.' He spat the name. 'I have to be Claude.'

'You don't, sweetheart—'

'I do. Claude is my punishment.'

This child is only ten, Rosie's breaking heart implored the universe. 'What are you being punished for, my love?'

'For lying to everyone. For pretending to be something I'm not.'

'You aren't lying. You aren't pretending—'

'Not anymore,' said Claude.

In the thirteen days that had passed since Rosie's midnight text, Claude's stubbly bald head had sprouted weak downy shoots, but he still looked like a cancer patient, and that's what everyone assumed he was. Rosie had learned during Poppy-her-sister's first round of chemo, and a thousand times since, that once one of your identities is sick, that's the only one that matters. She knew the sympathetic looks she was getting were only because everyone assumed her child had cancer, but she didn't care. She felt deserving of the kindness of strangers, in fragile need of a little extra space and succor, so she was grateful for their blessings, however misguided. Whether Claude could see everyone around him assuming he was dying, Rosie wasn't sure, but that didn't matter either. Claude felt like he was dying, so he'd have appreciated the conjectures, had he raised his eyes from the ground long enough to take them in. He did not.

Rosie thought eighteen hours on an airplane was the perfect occasion for heartbreak anyway. Into every life, a certain amount of misery must fall, and if you could get some of it to coincide with the eighteen cramped, queasy hours you had to spend in coach, so much the better. Claude stared out the window with swollen red eyes, waved away all proffered food, chain-sipped ginger ale, and garnered sympathy for his mother.

Rosie had sold the trip to Penn and Claude together. It'll be an incredible opportunity, she'd said, to travel somewhere new, to see the world, to help those less fortunate.

'No one is less fortunate than me,' said Claude.

'Than I.' Penn did not care for 'than' as a preposition.

'You are healthy and strong and able' – Rosie felt there was more at stake here than grammar – 'with food enough and clean water, a safe neighborhood, a secure home, indoor plumbing, medicine when you need it, family and friends who love you, a world-class education, and a very cute dog. You are more fortunate than many, many people.'

Claude rolled red-rimmed eyes. 'If it means I don't have to go back to school, I'll go anywhere.'

'That's true too.' Rosie tried not to seem too eager. 'This trip would allow you to take some time and perspective, to take a break from here.'

'From here or from me?' Penn said.

Claude looked up, alarmed. His parents didn't fight often enough for it to be no big deal when they did. On the one hand, Rosie was gratified to see him notice something, anything, that wasn't happening inside his own head. But this wasn't a conversation to have in front of him, and they both dropped it. Later though, Penn said, 'Thailand is a long way to go just to get out of an argument.'

'That's not why I'm going.'

'Sure it is.'

'I need to do something to mollify Howie.'

'You never have before.'

'That's why. We can't afford for me to lose this job.'

'It's never going to come to that, and you know it.'

'It's a good cause, Penn. The clinic serves Burmese refugees, undocumented residents, people from the hill tribes. It's important work—'

'In which you've shown no interest until this moment.'

'It's not that I wasn't interested. It's that it was never possible before with the kids and school and—'

'What part of that has ceased to be true now?'

'It'll be good for her – him – whomever to see a little bit of the world,' Rosie stumbled. 'Thailand is friendly, safe—'

'Not as safe as here.'

'We need to slow down. We all need to slow down. You need a break from researching vaginas. This child needs a break from school, from secret keeping, from Aggie, from this whole situation. This family needs a break from all the weight and drama—'

'And you need a break from me,' said Penn.

Rosie closed her eyes. 'And I need a break from you.'

He watched her behind her closed lids and said nothing for moments that stretched on like Wyoming highways. Then he walked away. So she was able to coincide heartache with international air travel as well.

She didn't call Carmelo until she was actually at the airport. She didn't want to be talked out of it. Predictably, her mother was full of being a mother.

'What about malaria?' she led off.

'We took drugs.'

'What about typhoid?'

'More drugs.'

'What about that tropical fever?'

'Dengue?'

'Yeah, dengue.'

'We'll use DEET.'

'Isn't DEET bad for you?'

'Not in small quantities.'

'Are small quantities enough to prevent mosquito bites?'

'We brought long sleeves.'

'Won't it be hot?'

'You live in Phoenix, Mother.'

'What about the boys?'

'They'll be fine.'

'How long are you going for?'

'I don't know.'

'What about Penn?'

Ah. There was the rub. 'He'll be fine without me.'

'But will you without him, dear?'

A perfectly reasonable question. 'He's just . . . he's writing a story instead of living our life.'

'Maybe he's doing both.'

'He can't do both, Mom. Both isn't an option. They're irreconcilable. Our kid is an actual person and therefore can't be a character in a story. Penn thinks everything that's wrong is just prelude to the magic, and one day soon, we'll all get to forget what's past and live happily ever after.'

'Sounds good to me.'

'Fantasies always do.'

'Penn's never been a realist, sweetie.'

'Not being a realist doesn't make reality go away,' Rosie shrilled. 'The transformation on offer here isn't magic. It isn't instantaneous, and it isn't painless. It's years and years of frog kissing. It's frog kissing for the rest of your life. It's frog kissing with nasty side effects and unpredictable outcomes you can't undo if you change your mind that results maybe in your being more princess and less scullery maid than before, but not quite in your being all princess and no scullery maid.'

'What does Poppy say?'

'Nothing.' The name was growing strange again to Rosie's ears already. 'Poppy's gone, Mom. He wants to be Claude again.'

'Wants to be?' Carmelo asked.

'Wants to be. Has to be. Thinks he is. Thinks he should. Thinks he must. I don't know.'

'Have you asked her?'

'Him,' Rosie corrected.

'Have you asked?'

'I've tried, Mom. He can't tell me. Maybe he doesn't know. He's very sad.'

'Isn't that your answer then?' Carmelo wondered.

'I don't know either,' Rosie said, and then, softly, because she was trying to be an adult and not cry on the phone to her mother in the airport, 'I'm very sad too.'

Carmelo said nothing for a moment. Then she said, 'What about elephant attacks?'

'Elephant attacks?'

'They have elephants in Thailand, dear, and they're not repelled by DEET.'

It seemed telling to Rosie that getting trampled by a five-ton animal came last on her mother's list of concerns.

But if she shared (some of) Carmelo's worries, she was still finally going to Thailand, fulfilling a promise she'd made to her sister most of a lifetime ago. If she was unhappy about how she'd left things with Penn, about wanting, for the first time since they'd met, to be apart from him, she was still flying to far-off Asia with her youngest child. If she was worried about leaving the boys in their own precarious state, about choosing Claude over them again, about abandoning them to negotiate their daily lives without her for a little while, she was still road tripping with her baby. And if it wasn't a road trip so much as transnavigated international journeying via hope, imagination, panic, and plane, that was also good, and she had learned over the years to take what she could get. She'd been dreaming of the trips she'd take with her daughter since her sister died, and if it wasn't quite Poppy anymore and she came home with Claude instead, a prodigal son, well, it wouldn't be the first time.

Away

The plane was cramped, freezing, and boring, the flight longer than long division, and nearly the moment he landed in Bangkok, Claude longed to be back aboard like the time he (well, Poppy) had fallen out of a whale-watching kayak into Puget Sound. On the plane he had personal space, cold soda of which his mother was apparently allowing him an unlimited amount, and a bathroom with toilet paper. And though the plane bathroom smelled like a bathroom, the rest of the plane did not smell like a bathroom. All of Bangkok smelled like a bathroom, none of it had toilet paper, and the temperature had been nice for about sixty seconds while the icicles from the airplane thawed off, and then he became as hot as he had ever been in his life, not hot like when he visited Carmy in Phoenix, hot like wet, like in a bathtub, like one minute he was dry and the next he had sweat shooting out of him in all directions like a spastic sprinkler.

Claude was not remotely ready to rejoin the real world, but fortunately, Bangkok bore little resemblance to it. He tried to keep not caring about anything, but it was hard. The sidewalks were invisible, so full of people he could only guess there were sidewalks underneath them. The cars were all hot pink and gloss turquoise and neon green. The buses were multistory, like squat apartment buildings on wheels. Squadrons of scooters weaved in and out and between and around everyone like a plague of insects. The scooters had whole families piled on board, the dad wearing a helmet, the mom and the kids and the babies bareheaded and sandwiched in and looking unfazed by the heat or the smell or the fact that their dad didn't care about their heads as much as his. When Claude stared at these sweaty families as they squeezed by his air-conditioned van, the kids would wave and smile at him, the moms and dads too. In fact, it seemed like everyone in Thailand wanted to look right into his eyes and smile at him. They wanted to ask if he was okay and if he was happy and if he needed anything. Yes, he needed extra strength air-conditioning, toilet paper, and some personal space. And helmets maybe for the little kids on the scooters.

There were stray dogs everywhere who looked sweet but who his mother absolutely forbade him to touch, and since this was unlike his mother, he listened. There were malls that took up all four corners of the intersections, connected by hamster habitrails over the streets. There were whole restaurants right in the middle of the sidewalk that looked like hot-dog stands except they sold complicated noodle soups or fried bananas wrapped in puffy dough or a whole giant deep-fried fish sprinkled with millions of colorful toppings like a sundae. And there were little tables and seats right there in the middle of the sidewalk too, which made sense since you could eat a hot dog on the way to catch your bus but you couldn't walk while eating soup or a fish sundae, but it meant you had to somehow weave your way around all the people and all the dogs and all the tables and chairs too.

They spent the night on the nineteenth floor of a fancy hotel Claude was too tired to enjoy. (Like some kind of strange enchantment, two days had passed since they left home, but he hadn't been to bed yet.) Then first thing the next morning they went with Ling, their guide, to a market to get supplies for the clinic. His mother seemed tired and overwhelmed and trying too hard. She kept fake laughing and making comments like, 'Sweetie, look at those tubs of fish,' as if Poppy-the-ichthyologist would be cheered to see them twisting over and around one another, fighting to get under too little water, or 'Mmm, smell those spices,' as if Claude-the-child-baker would be cheered by the rounded piles of curry big as basketballs, or 'Oh wow! Giant bins of bugs!' as if anyone would be cheered by bins of bugs. As if they were on vacation having the time of their lives instead of running away from home. He let his mother hold his hand though because the market in Bangkok made the sidewalks in Bangkok seem deserted and because beneath his new sandals it was wet and slippery, a surface somewhere between ground and floor. Claude smelled dry blood and wet blood. He smelled sweating people and rotting fruit and mothballs. He smelled diesel because, impossibly, the scooters were allowed to drive right down the middle of aisles narrow as straws. There were pastel strands of sugar like night-fairy hair. There were small plastic bags filled with syrup, ice, and fruit, which people dangled by their handles and sipped through a straw. There were greens of every shade, shape, and size, including one that Ling explained was used to cure heartbreak. Claude wondered what it was about him that suggested he needed it. His mother smiled sadly at him and squeezed his hand but managed not to say anything out loud.

All of that turned out to be prelude though. The bugs and the spun sugar and the weird vegetables were the easy part, which he should have guessed because bugs, spun sugar, and weird vegetables do not smell like dry or wet blood. In the next part of the market, all Claude wanted to do was sit down and cry because cages the size of Jupiter's kennel held piles and piles of shiny black chickens, chickens on top and underneath, chickens squawking at one another for stepping on their heads. At first Claude wondered vaguely if he could hold or at least pet one, but then, woozily, he saw his error because on top of the cage was a giant tray of dead chickens, their skin naked and pale and puckered, their yellow feet reaching out for rescue, but, headless, they were way too late for that. Next door was another even smaller cage with geese inside, fairy-tale geese, snow-white bodies with Halloween-orange feet and beaks. There were far too many for the small space, and they were as wedged in as he was, but at least they all had both feet on the floor. The geese had taken a vow of silence because their cage was also topped with a tray of bodies swaddled in plastic wrap with their price scrawled on in red marker. And next to them the ducks. They couldn't see their grisly future, but probably they could smell it. Then there were pig faces – not the head, just the empty, saggy face: snout and curling ears and horrible hollows where the eyes had been. At the end of the row, an ancient wrinkle of a woman hunched on a stool scooping tiny jumping shrimps into plastic bags. She squeezed lime over them and sprinkled them with salt, kind of like when Aggie's cousin was baptized, and the businessman who bought them popped them into his mouth, still jumping, like he was eating popcorn at a movie. Claude understood suddenly what it meant to say the walls were closing in on you. He tried to take deep breaths, but the smell of terrified birds burned his nose and throat and chest.

There were dead animals everywhere. There was weird food every-where. It was loud everywhere, like a turned-up-too-high soundtrack of selling and buying and negotiation and sweat. But the other thing Claude saw everywhere in Bangkok, which was the miracle of Bangkok, were people – women – like him. Like Poppy.

They were beautiful. Their hair was long and black as bad-luck cats and curved just where their necks did, tucking perfectly behind their ears with flowers that had to be fake but weren't – gorgeous, perfect, amazing hair. They had gorgeous, perfect, amazing ways of moving that hair too, touching it just lightly with their hands, laughing so it lay prettily over their faces or shaking so it danced down their backs like a shampoo commercial. They moved everything just right, in fact. Their hips went back and forth, back and forth when they walked, but con-cisely, not like sexy women in movies who moved like windshield wipers, more like willow trees in wind. And their clothes – Claude loved every-thing these women wore: Long embroidered skirts. Tops that hugged their figures, modest but hinting, like a wink but not on purpose. Jeans and T-shirts that looked just like regular jeans and T-shirts except some-how completely feminine. Scarves that seemed to float against their necks like leaves on autumn ponds, and though Claude thought he would liquefy if he wore a scarf in this heat, and though Claude remembered he was being punished and had to be Claude, the scarves enchanted him anyway.

One was running a fruit stand. One was making marigold garlands on a plastic table outside a 7-Eleven. One was a waitress in the noodle restau-rant where they stopped for lunch. Claude saw them on the sky train going to work in an office or somewhere it was important to wear a suit and heels. Did his mother even notice? He couldn't tell. But if you looked at them closely, and Claude did – Claude could not keep his eyes off them – you could see that that swallowy bit of their throat was bigger than usual. You could see their hands and feet were bigger too. When they spoke to you, it was with lovely, husky voices, or they wore their makeup a little more thickly than the other women around them, or their eyebrows were more assertive, more certain, more there. They were beautiful, and they were everywhere, and everyone seemed to know their secret, and no one seemed to care, which, Claude guessed, meant it wasn't really a secret at all.

But just as he was spying, improbably, kindred spirits halfway around the world, Ling announced, with a brave smile neither Claude nor his mother were buying, that it was time to drive the five hundred kilometers north to the clinic, a figure she may as well have expressed in quarks for as much as Claude knew how far five hundred kilometers was. What he did understand were quavering adult smiles: it was going to take all day, and it was going to be excruciating. Their new van had little pieces of paper-thin gold stuck all over the ceiling above the rearview mirror to show it had been blessed by a monk. Unfortunately, it had apparently not been blessed by a mechanic because whatever those springy things are that prevent you from bouncing all around and hitting your head on the ceiling and wanting to puke every time you went over a bump were missing.

'Shocks,' his mother said grimly the millionth time it happened.

'What about them?'

'We could use some.'

'I'm having lots,' said Claude.

His mother got up and moved to the row of seats behind him, lay down across it, and closed her eyes without another word. But tempting though his mother made it look and miserable as he felt, Claude could not sleep. There was too much to see. Outside of Bangkok, Thailand looked like something his father would make up. There was a hospital for elephants. There were hundreds of schoolchildren picking up brush in the trees to prevent forest fires. There were roadside stands selling giant, papery wasp nests to eat with sugar and chili. When they stopped at lights, old women covered head to toe with masks and hats and scarves in the hundred-degree heat would try to sell them sticky rice or salted banana chips. Even the familiar was unfamiliar. Even the things he seemed to know he could not name.

Along the road, he saw tiny miniature houses everywhere, sometimes on the ground, sometimes on posts like elaborate mailboxes. He'd seen them in Bangkok, outside his hotel and the market stalls and the 7-Elevens and the noodle shops. Now, on the road north, he saw them outside of every house, large or small, temple or shack, outside every run-down strip mall and gas station. He could see them in the jungle through the trees and on the tops of mountains. He could see them in the corners of the rice fields and the coconut plantations and where they were reforesting teak. Water buffalo and cows grazed around them under the banana trees. Dogs ignored them all over the country.

'What are those?' It was the first anyone had spoken for miles, and Ling seemed startled to hear from him.

'Spirit house. We put them outside our home and business place, temple, restaurant, everywhere. We have lot of spirits in Thailand. Spirits is mischievous. You know? Naughty. We want them not making trouble in our house or job, so we give them place to make funny business outside. Then we offer treat to keep them happy there. They get what they seek outside so they not come inside.'

'Treats?'

'Offering: Flower. Fruit. Incense. Maybe beer. Maybe cigarette.' She shrugged. 'Depend what they like.'

When the road started to climb in earnest, they left the houses, people and spirit, behind. It was a jungle. A real one. What was the difference between forest and jungle? Both had lots of trees. Both hid much you could (worrisomely) hear but not see. This one even had, to Claude's surprise, long-needle pines, just like at home. But this was jungle for sure. For one thing, it was a million degrees and humider than an indoor pool. For another, there were vines like the trees were being eaten, and in between every two trees, a palm was pushing its way through at odd angles like it had meant to grow someplace else altogether and ended up here only by accident. The whole jungle was wall-to-wall-carpeted with moss and fern and leaf and yet more vine, and there was ceiling between the trees that was green and tangled and, alarmingly, moving as well. Instead of soft rain and low buzzing and birdsong like at home, here the insects and frogs and probably monkeys and possibly tigers screamed and shrieked and hollered, staking their claims for space between the palms, yodeling at the stars. But mostly the difference was this: fairy tales were set in forests, never jungles. The van slogged through enough miles of this wilderness for Claude's brain to arrive at the reason why: it was because you could get lost in the forest and come out the other side. If you got lost in this jungle, you got lost forever.

Aid Ambiguous

They heard it before they saw it, their first impression of the clinic, as they biked in the next morning just after sunrise, no overnight cool for the dawn to burn away, the air sodden already. There was the sound of metal on metal, a whine like a train whistle, woesome thunks, and shouts Rosie could not identify as Thai or Burmese but knew for sure were curse words. She guessed someone yelling at cats in battle or maybe heat, though they'd seen only dogs and dogs and more dogs so far, and never in her life had she heard a dog make a sound like that, a high-pitched keening, more screech than scream. Some kind of insect maybe? It would have to be bigger than she was willing to think about so early in the morning. A monkey? An army of frogs? Animal attack? And indeed, when she and Claude arrived at the mouth of the chewed-up dirt drive leading into the clinic, they found soot-caked, mud-stained feet and scratched-up shins kicking desperately at the end of a body otherwise entirely consumed by a voracious, growling maw.

When it revealed itself, the battle proved age-old but not animal: motion versus stasis, senescence versus youthful tenacity, the maw in question neither beast nor human but mineral: an ancient, heretofore pickup truck. It had a mechanic swearing under its open hood and two small children giggling in its cab, one on the floor using two hands to depress and release (usually all at once) the clutch, one shifting and turning the key (with more tenacity than would have been ideal) as directed.

'Truck' was a generous term. It was more rust than engine, more dirt than vehicle, and not the kind of dirt you could just wash off with a good scrub either because Rosie had a feeling this dirt was load bearing. The body had once been green and probably lovely. It was one of those pick-ups from the 1950s with the bubbled hoods and rounded wheel wells that someone at home would have dressed up with whitewall tires, a chrome grill, a thousand hours with a Q-tip and a cloth diaper, and then paraded for the Fourth of July. This one didn't look like that. Apparently, it didn't run like that either.

The filthy truck spit out a filthier mechanic. 'You new doctor?'

'I am. Rosie Walsh. This is my dau . . . um, son,' she stammered. 'Claude.' She glanced at him to see if she could apologize with her eyes, but he was staring at the ground and wouldn't meet them.

'You drive?'

'No, we biked.' She turned back to the mechanic, distracted. 'The guesthouse where we're staying lent us bicycles.'

'Sorry, my English.' The mechanic tried again. 'You *can* drive? Manual shift car?'

'Oh. Yes!' Rosie's own English comprehension was apparently jet-lagged.

The mechanic shooed the two children out of the cab, performed final ministrations under the hood, and gave Rosie the international sign for 'Pray to your gods and hit it again.' The motor turned over like a well-trained seal. There was much rejoicing. Rosie's first procedure at the clinic was a success. The patient – improbably, it seemed to her – lived.

The mechanic was slick with grease from the elbows down, but fortunately, greetings in Thailand involved not shaking hands but pressing your own together in front of your chest and bowing toward one another. 'Very glad to meet you. I am K. Do not ask what K stand for. It stand for so much. We happy you here. I show you around. First, meet Sorry Ralph.'

'The truck is named Ralph?'

'Sorry Ralph,' K corrected.

'Why?'

'He very sorry.'

'I can see that.'

'Sorry Ralph is ambulance. Also fetch medicine and supply if there is medicine and supply. Also hearse. Usually sorry though so hope you do not need.'

Rosie nodded. She was surprised to see that the mechanic was both female and the apparent welcoming committee. K turned and headed off at what appeared to be a saunter, but Rosie and Claude found themselves practically running to keep up. At each turn, their entourage grew, everyone eager to welcome them with pressed hands and a bow and to trot alongside, everyone happy to let the mechanic lead. Claude was whisked away, and Rosie reached for him as if the wreckage they clung to had suddenly split in stormy seas, but he was already too far off, waves of people between them. Rosie felt at once swept along and struggling to keep up. A chorus of voices in a variety of languages informed her what was where and offered helpful hints that were probably important. A shoe tree of fingers pointed in all directions at once.

There was a building that was clearly obstetrics. At least you could tell obstetrics by looking. There was a workshop from which disembodied limbs hung – legs and feet mostly in various states of doneness, some still being assembled, a band saw, a drill press. There were patients sitting in chairs or wheelchairs whose legs ended before their pants did, so she could see where they belonged too. There was an open-air portico – really just a swept dirt floor under a roof of flattened cardboard boxes tied to the underside of a tarp – littered with plastic lawn chairs, sleeping bags, and blankets in piles where whole families seemed contentedly camped out. Whether they were awaiting treatment or news about someone else receiving treatment or something else altogether, Rosie could see only that they were not bleeding or moaning in pain or about to give birth. There were half-formed, halfhearted lines everywhere. There was an eye chart taped to a cement wall at the end of a rock-strewn dirt path. There were stray dogs wandering lazily in and out of all the buildings, including the one labeled Surgical Department, a building with holes for doors and windows but with no doors or windows filling them. There was a large patch of dirt with lounge-style lawn chairs and then the regular sitting-up kind behind them, and though patients were reclining, openmouthed, on the former, and though there was a medic, lab-coated and rubber-gloved, on the latter, Rosie could not quite believe this was a dentist's office, but she was wrong.

The buildings were cinder block with barred windows or patched plaster with grated cutouts like lace. Corrugated metal roofs covered in debris gapped several inches over the tops of the walls. Curling linoleum floors, their patterns worn nearly away, spilled onto dirt or cement spaces out front. Empty, open drains lined all the walkways, auguring a rainy season that must turn all the dirt floors to sopping, sticky, insect-harboring mud. All of it un-air-conditioned, unsterile, unsealed, and undifferentiable. But the entrances, the doorways, the open spaces where doorways should have been, were all heaped with flip-flops and plastic clogs and sandals, a broom made of straw always propped nearby, and so, though the walls and ceilings were grimy with decades of dirt, the floors were miraculously, significantly, clean.

Her seeming entourage led Rosie to the largest building and ushered her in. It was unlike anything she'd seen before in her life – it was beyond imagining – but she recognized it immediately as home. The rush of the few doctors and nurses at hand, the focus of the medic doing eye-of-the-storm triage amid the rest of the room's hurricane, the tang of blood and panic, the antiseptic smell augmenting rather than assuaging all the other ones, equivocal spills best avoided, patients unable to ask, afraid to know: an emergency room.

There were no gurneys, no beds, no curtains, no monitors, no machines. Patients lay on plain wooden platforms covered in scraps of sheets or old, felt-lined tablecloths falling into tatters. Patients lay spooning other patients in a tangle of IVs. They shivered against the walls, trailing blood or vomit or bandages into the corners. They sat on the floor between the wooden platform beds so the staff darted around them like swallows. It was impossible to tell who was waiting for treatment and who was waiting for a loved one, whose mangled and missing limbs were emergent and whose had been that way for decades, whose drawn and pallid faces, damp brows, hollow, shining eyes bespoke fever and whose fear and whose had merely frozen that way after too many years in that sorry state. There was a small folding snack table just inside the door with a foot-tall stack of papers weighted down by a rock: single-sheet intake forms.

It was not yet seven a.m.

Having deposited her where she was clearly meant to be, Rosie's entourage faded away, back to whatever posts they had temporarily abandoned in order to welcome her. Who had taken Claude, and where? There was no one even to ask.

'Ready?' A teenager at the folding table nodded encouragingly toward the pile.

Rosie wasn't sure what she'd been expecting. A jungle orientation of some sort? An HR tutorial on tax and benefit forms? A lecture from Legal on sexual harassment? Somehow, she'd expected calm assurances regarding her child and what he would do while she worked. Somehow, she'd imagined something between truck repair and meeting patients. But there was nothing.

The paper on the top of the stack directed her to bed 8. There, Rosie was surprised, having identified obstetrics some buildings ago, to find a patient in labor, healthy labor from the look of it. When she investigated further, she was even more surprised at what she found between the patient's spread knees.

'You're the mechanic,' she could not quite stop herself from saying.

K grinned. 'Also midwife.'

Improbable though this seemed, K the mechanic seemed to have everything under control, but she asked Rosie to stay anyway.

'Early,' K explained. 'She schedule C-section in hospital next month but she not make it.'

A scheduled hospital caesarian delivery somewhere this rural and remote struck Rosie as nearly as improbable as an auto mechanic delivering a premature baby. 'Why did she have a C-section scheduled?'

'She have scarlet fever when she was child.' K delivered from the patient's clenched fist a damp, crumpled envelope from which Rosie extracted a letter, faded and ancient and, besides all that, in a script she could not name, never mind decipher. The patient paused between contractions to look very proud.

'She have scarlet fever and then two-week walk to city to see doctor. Probably her family have some little money. Doctor took picture, looked her heart, wrote down some note for if she pregnant. She lucky. But then she labor early.'

Was Rosie here to treat mother or baby? 'How early?'

'Maybe thirty-two week.'

Rosie looked around. It wasn't just that she saw no NICU incubators, no mechanical ventilators, no bili lights. It's that asking about them seemed absurd. Surely if they had a neonatal cardiopulmonary monitor, they'd also have sheets and actual beds? 'And the letter? What does it say?'

K shrugged and made soothing sounds at the patient as the baby crowned. 'Cannot read all. And very short. But damage. Lesions. You know?'

Rosie at once did and did not know. She'd never seen heart disease caused by rheumatic fever – they were so careful with strep these days, and it was so easily treated – but patients with the sort of damage it caused were generally advised against pregnancy, the stress of not just labor but the pregnancy itself too great on compromised heart valves. That ship having clearly sailed, the only tack left was to wait and see who needed help afterward: mother with a too-weak heart or baby with too-weak lungs. Rosie stood and held her hand while the patient pushed and cried and waited, panted, pushed, and cried, while K eased out the head, turning gently, then the shoulders, no hesitation, the rest of the baby rushing out wet and slick as an otter, the baby crying, the new mama crying, even Rosie tearing up a little. It had been a long time since she'd been on this end – either end really – of labor and delivery, and she was jet-lagged and overwhelmed. And relieved. The baby was very small, too small, but pink, crying – if not loudly, if not lots, at least a bit. K swaddled him in a scrap of heretofore T-shirt that read EAST LAKE HIGH BEACH WEEK 2009: SURF THIS! and laid him in his mama's arms, right up against her scarred heart. The patient was euphoric, weepy-grateful. K and Rosie too and the other waiting, watchful patients on their wooden platforms all around them. All was miracle and celebration. Through the haze of this wonder, Rosie gazed over the throngs of people still waiting and decided to leave the coda of this case in the car mechanic's apparently multitalented hands.

Then, in a language Rosie had never heard before in her life but under-stood as if it were her mother tongue, the patient wheezed that she could not breathe. Her inhalations became short then gasping all in a seeming moment. Her face went gray, her eyes then her head rolled back, and it was K who had the presence of mind to grab the baby as he tumbled from her slackened arm.

Rosie listened to her lungs and heard wet, like a conch shell, though in this case she heard not water, not waves, but crackles like a campfire of wet wood: rales. Pulmonary edema. The patient was drowning. Was there a ventilator? She supposed a mask would do for the moment.

'Oxygen,' she said to K.

But K shook her head. 'Have mask,' and she looked proud at that but, 'and one tank oxygen but empty. Request more three month ago but not arrive yet.'

Rosie took that in. The rest of the patient's skin was going gray. Spu-tum, pink with foreboding, frothed at her mouth and nose. Rosie would have to treat the heart and hope that allowed the lungs to do their job as well. She knew but nonetheless asked, hoped, prayed, Hail Mary'd: 'Echocardiogram?'

K shook her head again.

'Her chart at least?'

K waved the crumpled letter. Rosie closed her eyes to practice proceeding without senses, without sense. No patient history, no way to ask about her symptoms, no information as to what might once have been tried and worked, tried and failed. No way back to those moments, moments ago, when all was shiny and suffused with joy. No picture of the heart in question, the heart in failure. Were her damaged valves leaking or scarred nearly shut? Was her heart straining with too much blood or too little? Should they speed her heartbeat or slow it down? There were answers to these dichotomies; they were not ambiguous. And with answers, there were clear treatment plans, effective and straightforward. But Rosie had been blindfolded, numbed, handcuffed, and tied to a pipe halfway across the room. Absent an echocardiogram or X-ray vision – and the former seemed as fantastic as the latter in this place – there was nothing she could do.

There was one thing she could do. Even with her hands tied and her fingers numbed and her eyes blinded, she could listen. It was possible, she knew, to hear which valves leaked and which stuck, which ventricles filled and which backed up, where blood flowed and where it flooded. She bent. She listened. The heart sped and sped. Was that making things better or worse? She couldn't tell. She closed her eyes again. She shut it all out. She broke it all down. She listened for aortic versus pulmonary valve closure; she listened separately. She listened for increased venous return and negative intrathoracic pressure. She listened for the right ventricle to empty and for mid-systolic clicks. She listened to see, to peer with her ears, to force them into servitude as organs of imagination, precognition, and miracle. She tried to hear in the too-fast, too-loud, panicked pulse a story, tale and detail, what it meant and what it foreshadowed, its history and backstory. But she couldn't make it out. Doctors used to do this, she knew, before echocardiograms and EKGs and chest X-rays. But that was well before her time. She had done it once, maybe, in school, as an exercise. At 130 frantic BPM in the melee of this limping clinic shoved wall to corner to wall with the frantic and the feverish, it was beyond her. She could only guess.

'Esmolol?' she asked K. K shook her head. Rosie wasn't happy, but she also was not surprised.

'Labetolol?' Esmolol would have been better. It was rapid onset but short duration so they could see. If it helped, great. If it made it worse, that yielded enough useful information to make it worth the risk, and when it wore off five minutes later, they'd know how to proceed. But Labetolol would do. Slowing the heart rate was a good guess, and Labetolol was much more common and inexpensive; she should have known it was the drug they'd have on hand.

But K shook her head at that too.

Rosie felt the adrenaline come on like a reckless but not unwelcome old friend, one you were glad to see but would regret in the morning. She would have to make do with morphine. It would calm the patient at least. It would ease her pain. It would slow her heart and dilate her blood vessels and buy her – buy them all – a deep breath.

But K shook her head at even cheap, easy, ubiquitous morphine. 'So sorry,' said K. 'We are have not.'

Rosie backed away from the patient, one step, two, and sat heavily into a plastic blue picnic chair. 'I'm sorry,' she apologized to the patient, to K, to the large percentage of the world that did not have what the other large percentage of the world took for granted. They had blue-ribbon hospitals a forty-minute flight away in Bangkok. They had blue-ribbon hospitals for elephants. How could this place be so near and so far?

'I also,' said K.

Rosie thought back to the time, three minutes earlier, when she'd have traded a son for an echocardiogram. It wouldn't have mattered. Knowing what the problem was didn't help if none of the solutions were available in any case. 'What do you do?' she said to K.

'Next case,' K said.

'We just let her die?'

'Not let,' said K. 'We watch, help ease, be witness. Next time be better.'

'The next patient?'

K shook her head. 'Next life.'

'Can't we put her in your truck and drive her to a hospital? A real one?'

'Cannot spare,' K said sadly, and whether what could not be spared was the truck, herself, the medicine, or a favor from an underfunded hospital for a patient not likely to make it at this point anyway, Rosie neither knew nor supposed it really mattered. She did the only thing left to do. She went back to the pile of intake forms and picked up the next one.

Bed 15's patient was leaning up against it rather than lying atop. It was a woman with infant twins, one in each arm, and a tree branch stuck inside her vagina, an (obviously) desperate and (so far) failed attempt to terminate a pregnancy. After her, there was a boy younger than Poppy – than Claude – with a snakebite that looked poisonous, had to be poisonous, came from one of eight venomous snakes he'd seen near his home and casually but proudly ticked off on his fingers like he was naming cartoon characters, but then, miraculously, the swelling went down and it wasn't poisonous. There was a baby with infantile beriberi, which Rosie had only a vague recollection of ever having studied. There was a man who claimed to be fifty but looked eighty with colonic tuberculosis, a diagnosis that seemed jaw-droppingly rare to Rosie and jaw-yawningly common to the nurse helping her translate. A case of Ludwig's angina had gone so long without the simple antibiotics needed to stop the infection that the patient needed a tracheotomy.

But mostly that first day, as every day before, as every day to come, there was diarrhea, diarrhea and fevers and patients who were dehydrated and emaciated and exhausted. It wasn't that Rosie didn't see such symptoms in family practice. It was that here they were worse enough to seem something else altogether, and they were. Here, they were a portrait of what happened when avoidable things occurred instead and then festered, when the treatable went untreated, when the affordable could not be afforded, when the ambiguous got misread, mislabeled, misdiagnosed, misaligned. Here, fever wasn't caused by that flu that was going around, nor exhaustion by the SATs coming up and college applications coming due and a field hockey coach with unreasonable demands. Here, they were caused by dim, insomniac mosquitos. Here, they were caused by water that was dirty or food that was infested or not having shoes. They were caused by lack of aid or aid diverted or aid misspent or aid ambiguous. Here, they were causing each other. Malnutrition left the body too weak to fight off bacteria. Diarrhea stripped muscle and flesh and reserves. Fever rendered patients unable to eat. So what made any given patient so thin and sick and tired? Who could say?

In the first week, she saw twenty-one different presentations of malaria. She saw what land mines did to tiny hands that picked up something shiny in the grass and what those hands looked like after walking three days through jungle to reach the clinic. She saw more upper-respiratory infections than she had in her entire career thus far. And she saw what she always saw, what she had always seen – what sick children did to their parents, what aged parents did to their kids, how worry and fear and lack of options finished off what mosquitos and land mines and bacteria began. She did not have a facility and a staff she knew like her own kitchen. She did not have an ER with all the comforts of home – CT scanners and MRI machines and a blessed echocardiogram. But she possessed those most important of skills: reflex without panic, action without alarm, cool head and cool hands, mild grace under extreme pressure.

Bed 26 on day one slept a family of seven, the youngest of whom had run through the ashes of the apparently but not actually dead fire that burned every night in front of her home. The ashes looked like the snow she'd seen in a picture book that had come as part of a first-aid and family-support package. The child had second- and third-degree burns and an infection, a lot of pain, a long recovery ahead, but it wasn't her Rosie was worried about.

The father spoke a surprising amount of English, the most of any patient she saw all day. Rosie explained carefully how to keep the burns clean, apply the salves, change the bandages. She asked if he had any questions. 'Yes,' he said. 'Where I make mistake?'

'What do you mean?'

'If I do not light fire every night, mosquitos come, bring malaria. If I do not go to fields every morning, first light, I cannot feed family. If I bring daughter to fields with me, she do not learn, run, play. If I do not let her have book, she never get better life. But book make her see ashes is snow. Fire to keep away mosquito and disease no matter if she burn. I make mistake. Where?'

Rosie went back over his story, but she couldn't see it either. 'No mistake,' she told him, which in fact was more horrifying than what had happened to his daughter as a result.

'Must,' he said.

At the end of this first day, Rosie was spinning herself, trying to reckon, to accept what this father had to balance and account for. 'Par-

THIS IS HOW IT ALWAYS IS   263

enthood is like that.' She tried to be doctorly. 'The harder the choice, the less likely any of the options are good ones.'

'Here, so many bad thing. You can protect from some but never all.'

'Here and everywhere.' This was true. But here it was truer. 'And always. You've done well by your family. Her burns will heal, and someday she will see real snow. You've saved that for her. And you've saved her for that. You've done very well.'

When she emerged at the end of that first shift to find the morning gone and the afternoon gone and the night come on, she also found the crowds of people – the waiting-patiently patients, the waiting-patiently families, the people waiting patiently for nothing in particular – gone. Admitted by other doctors? Absorbed into other departments? Healed and sent home? Just sent home? She did not know. It was hard to imagine where they'd all gone. It was even harder to imagine they'd all be taken care of. But Rosie was too tired to puzzle it out. She needed to find Claude and know all about his first day. Had it been as foreign and familiar as hers? As known and unknown and whirling? Was he okay?

But as she took her first steps toward the tree where she'd left her bicycle, what she found she lacked more than the machines and a lab and a pharmacy and sterile bedding was Penn. There was no waiting room as such, but had there been, he would not have been in it, waiting to tell her stories and listen to hers, waiting to take her home at the end of a long day of patients and prose so they could talk together and be together and make love and family together. Instead, there was a wall of humidity and an infinity of screaming insects and a daughter – son – nowhere in evidence. And this was a poor trade indeed.

Novice

Claude's first day at the clinic began with breakfast, which was actually, literally called 'joke' and probably was one since it looked like watered-down kindergarten paste sprinkled with grass clippings and had a raw egg cracked right into the middle of it. The sight of it made Claude woozy. Or maybe it was the smell of it. Or maybe it was just the fact of it. He had not been hungry since what had happened, happened. He thought it was possible he might never be hungry again. But he managed to eat at least a little bit of it. He didn't want to hurt anyone's feelings. And now that he knew they ate still-jumping shrimp in Thailand, he thought it prudent to force eggs when they were on offer, even raw and in jest.

There were infinity people who wanted to meet and thank and say nice things to and about his mother and then take her away. 'Do not worry,' a woman with white smears painted on her cheeks and nose called after his mother. 'We take good care your child,' but his mother evidently was already not worried because she didn't even turn around. 'So' – the woman squinted at Claude from under a ratty straw hat – 'what we do with you all day?'

Claude couldn't even guess.

'Your mama is big helping us. Maybe you big help us too.'

It took Claude a little while to understand that the building he'd been brought to was a school. Schools had classrooms, desks, whiteboards, computers, art projects, homework trays, and playground equipment. This place had a dirt yard out front with a bunch of old tires sinking into dust and one big, open room with a falling-apart bookcase piled with papers spilling out of folders and small heaps of ancient-looking books and a stack of dog-eared, water-stained flash cards in English. The students were mostly younger than he was, and there were a lot of them, spread over the thin, tatty linoleum, its bluebells and buttercups faded to rumor, chatting in small groups or napping curled up against the wall or just sitting and staring into nothing. If Claude sat on the floor at school staring into nothing, he'd get in trouble for being off task, but he could see that there were not many more productive alternatives available here.

'You teach?' the painted woman asked.

What did this mean? She could not possibly think he was a teacher. Even people who imagined this worn, wounded room a school would not imagine a ten-year-old a teacher. Would they? 'No?' Claude guessed. 'I don't teach?'

But apparently that was the wrong answer because the woman grinned and shook her head. 'You sit here. I bring student over. You teach English.' She left and came back moments later with three smiling pigtailed girls and a stack of picture books. She said something to the girls about Claude in some language that didn't sound like Thai but was just as incomprehensible, and the girls looked at him and giggled. Even in Thailand, everyone laughed at him. He understood why they did though because he knew he looked completely absurd. His lumpy head was ugly. His lumpy clothes were even uglier. And every time he walked or sat down or crossed his legs or stood back up, he had to think about how to do it because whatever natural movements he used to just have seemed to have gotten lost in transit. He would laugh at him too. At least they had that in common.

'Okay?' The painted-cheeks woman smiled at him. It was a question that seemed to encompass many things. Did he have everything he needed? Did he understand what he was supposed to do? Did he need water? Supplies of some kind? A snack? A lesson plan? An anything plan?

'Okay' did not seem like the truthful response to any of these questions – like hungry, okay was something Claude didn't think he'd ever be again – but it was what he answered anyway.

'You fine.' The woman winked. 'Begin read. You know what do next.'

But Claude did not know what to do next.

'Where your robe?' one of the little pigtailed girls demanded before

Claude could even sort out the books on his lap. Her name was Mya, and Claude was relieved because apparently she spoke English already. Not that he knew what she was talking about.

'My robe?'

'You monk, right?'

'A monk?'

'*Nen?* You call, I think, "novice"?'

'I'm not a monk. I'm a gi . . . kid.' He felt himself flush. If Marnie Alison and Jake Irving ruining his life weren't reminder enough of who he was now, what had to happen to make Claude remember? The little girls seemed not to notice though.

'But your head is' – Dao, whose pigtails were tied with red ribbons, searched for the right word – 'naked,' and Claude wondered who had come before him, who had taught these girls some English and how and why 'naked' was part of their vocabulary. He didn't think it was probably from the picture books.

'I used to have long, dark hair just like you.' He spoke slowly so they would understand him. 'But I shaved it before I came here.'

'To become monk?'

'No . . .'

'To be not hot?'

'Not that either.'

'You want hide?' said the third little girl, Zeya.

And that was it exactly. 'Yes. I wanted to hide.'

'But why? You so pretty.'

At home, you did not call boys pretty. Pretty meant girl. But probably it was a foreign-language problem because there was no way these little girls thought he was one. Was there?

'I was . . . angry,' Claude half explained, but the girls' faces lit with comprehension.

'Oh angry,' they agreed all around with huge smiles and much clasping of Claude's and one another's hands. 'Angry very good reason.'

Interrogating him was probably a pretty good way to learn English, and Claude didn't have a better idea, but he put a stop to it anyway. They couldn't ask very many questions before they were ones Claude wouldn't answer, answers they wouldn't understand even if he were willing to give them, even if he knew the answers, which he did not. He didn't want to think about those answers, or even those questions, anyway.

Then he remembered the origami fortune-tellers PANK had been obsessed with in third grade. Aggie's uncle had shown them how to make them one rainy Saturday afternoon, and soon every worksheet, homework assignment, and notice home got folded into a square that got smaller and smaller until each plane revealed a color or letter or secret symbol to choose from and each corner untucked a final question. With the paper folded into bird beaks over your first fingers and thumbs, you opened the bird's mouth, closed, and spread, closed, opened, closed, and spread, as many times as the fortune-teller directed, and at the end, you had to answer the question thus revealed by the origami gods.

Claude got a precious sheet of paper – the school seemed to have so little of anything to spare – and wrote four questions in the heart of the heart of it. He let Zeya be the first fortune-teller. He was going to do it, but they were all bouncing-while-trying-to-sit-still excited, and Claude remembered being an eight-year-old girl.

The first question went to Mya: 'What do you want to be when you grow up?'

'Next life?' said Mya.

It took Claude a minute to understand what she was asking. 'This life,' he assured her, then tried again: 'What job do you want to have when you become an adult? If you could have any job in the world?'

Mya looked like she had never considered this question before. 'What my choice?'

'Anything.' Claude opened his hands wide to hold all the options. 'Whatever you want.'

Mya trawled for ideas. 'What *you* want when *you* grow up?'

Poppy. This answer burst into Claude's brain uninvited. He wanted to be Poppy when he grew up. He knew if Jake Irving heard this answer, baseball announcer would sound much more plausible by comparison. If Claude wouldn't grow up to be Poppy, he couldn't imagine growing up at all. This was another thing he and the pigtailed little girls had in common: none of them could imagine growing up.

Since no one – not the pupils, not the teacher – could think of any answers, the second question went to Dao. 'What is your favorite subject in school?' That had been the kind of question PANK had asked one another even though they all knew each other's favorite subject in school as well as they knew their own.

'What is subject?'

'You know, like math or reading or art or whatever.'

They all looked at him blankly, so he tried a different way. 'What is your favorite part about school?'

Dao brightened. 'Oh, we love school.' She seemed to speak for all of them. 'First time.'

'This is your first time in school?' They were eight. How could that be?

'My father sick so we come long way to clinic. Then he die and I am sad. But then I live here, go school, am happy.' She had taken the fortune-teller from Mya and was tapping her fingers together within its tiny walls.

Claude thought he felt wind on the damp back of his neck, but the air was still as stone. He had always heard adults say something took your breath away because it was beautiful or surprising in a good way or precious like a baby. But this really did take his breath away, and it was the opposite. This was loss that ruined your life leading straight to gain that saved it. It wasn't silver lining; it was a whole silver sky. Claude was totally over fifth grade, but even he could see that school was a miracle for Dao except she couldn't have it without first becoming an orphan. It was the least fair thing he had ever heard in his life, which, considering the state of his life, was saying something. But Dao, Mya, and Zeya were all nodding and smiling as if Dao's were as good an answer to 'What's your favorite subject in school?' as science or social studies would have been.

When he origamied that first paper fortune-teller that long ago rainy afternoon, Aggie's uncle had wiggled his fingers over it and sung a bunch of nonsense words which, he promised, turned it actually magic so that now it would tell real fortunes, reveal real secrets. Poppy's hands were shaking so hard on her first turn she could barely operate the bird beaks. She was terrified she'd count out her number and color and letter and symbol and untuck a panel that read: SECRET PENIS!! Of course, Aggie's uncle was just teasing, and of course, even at eight, she had been pretty sure that was the case all along. But as awful as that would have been, it was still less upsetting than the answers untucked here.

Claude had nowhere else to go, so he stayed late at the school. The woman with the painted cheeks put him to work cleaning brooms, which seemed like a waste of time to him though he supposed you couldn't get clean floors with dirty brooms. When he finally got back to their room at the guesthouse, it was empty. It felt late – it felt like tomorrow – but his mother was nowhere. As soon as he opened the computer though, it rang. Claude hoped his father wouldn't be too disappointed to find yet another son instead of his wife.

From fifteen time zones away, Penn held his breath as electrons danced across oceans and connected and a window opened in Thailand to reveal his daughter. Her stubbled bare head, her baggy clothes, her swollen red eyes burned through his computer screen and made her look like a small, sad, tired version of his little girl, but his little girl nonetheless. She could go halfway around the world and transform herself utterly, but she was still right there before him. He remembered back when she first became Poppy, how his brain could not use pronouns anymore, and this felt the same. This strange new boy who called himself Claude was only pretend. Penn could still see Poppy right there, unmissable as Christmas.

'How was your first day at the clinic?' Penn could hear the inanity of this as if he were asking how was school or had she done all her homework. But he didn't want to scare her or, worse, plant as yet seedless ideas, so he refrained from asking what he really wanted to know.

'Stupid,' Claude sulked.

Penn kept his voice upbeat. 'What did you do?'

'They made me teach.'

His father's face lit up. 'Teach what?'

'English. To little kids.'

'How wonderful!' Penn launched brain waves of ecstatic thanks toward Southeast Asia. 'Pop . . . Claude, what a gift to you and to these children. What a fine teacher you must be.'

'They think I'm a monk,' Claude said.

'They do? Why?'

'Because I'm bald.' Claude ran a miserable hand over his miserable hair. His miserable nonhair.

'They're little,' said his father. 'They're just confused.'

'Can girls be monks?' Claude did not raise his eyes from the keyboard. 'Or does that mean they can tell I'm a boy?'

'I don't know,' Penn admitted. 'I don't know much about Buddhist monks.'

'I thought maybe . . .' Claude trailed off.

'What?'

'Nothing. It's stupid.'

'I bet it's not.'

'I thought maybe it would be like when you do an experiment in science and you make it so the results are fair.'

Penn's eyebrows reached for each other. 'Blind?'

'I thought since they were little kids and they never met me before if they could tell I was a boy I must be a boy, but if they thought I was a girl, then maybe . . .'

Claude trailed off again. Halfway around the world, his father chose his words very carefully. 'You know, for you, this has been a big question all your life. Boy or girl. But not just for you – in this country, it's one of the first things we notice about everybody. When someone has a baby, that's our first question. When we meet new people, we like to be able to tell right away. Here, even people who've never asked the question about themselves still think about gender all the time. There, your little students probably see other things first.'

'What things?'

'Well, it's probably unusual for them to meet a white person. You might be the first American they've ever met. You probably have a lot more money than most of the people they know, a lot of privileges they never dreamed of. They must have so many questions about who you are; boy or girl just isn't what's most pressing to them.' Penn imagined Claude's identities reordering themselves like a split-flap display announcing train departures and arrivals. It made sense that these students saw foreign, white, American, healthy, rich, and whole before they ever saw male or female. Penn watched the flaps spin over and over themselves until they displayed forlorn, lonesome, and lost. 'What do *you* see, sweetheart?' This was one of the things Penn really wanted to know but was worried to ask.

Claude thought about his day of children without futures or at least with futures unforetold. 'I see nothing,' he told his father. 'I am unforeseeable.'

Bonesetters

hings unforeseen were plaguing Rosie as well. Everyone reported that Claude was great for the school, patient and gentle, an extra set of much-needed hands for the understaffed staff, for the understaffed students who had never imagined anything as exotic and far-flung as her baby. But Rosie was working when Claude was at school, so this poise and grace went unseen. She knew that the clinic's students must be teaching Claude as much as he was teaching them, for the protected world of even a transgender ten-year-old is awfully small compared to what these kids had seen, foreseen. But Claude was usually asleep by the time she got home from the clinic, so how he was learning or growing or becoming went unwitnessed as well. Instead she got tears over breakfast or, worse, worry that precluded talking about it, that drew his eyebrows together and his mouth toward his shoulders.

She expected heartache and sadness of course. She expected shock: culture shock from being a stranger in a very strange land and gender shock from being a boy again for the first time in five years and general shock from finding oneself, suddenly, a bald English tutor in Thailand. But she had also expected all that would have started to fade, at least a little, now that they'd been here a few weeks. It was so beautiful in Thailand. There was so much wonder. But if Claude was still miserable, maybe it was time to leave already. Maybe bringing him had been a mistake. 'Do you hate it here, my love?'

'Here and everywhere,' Claude said without looking up. For some reason, he felt worse with his mom than he did in his classroom. He knew she was just trying to help him, but maybe he had more in common with his little students. He knew she loved him more than anything for seven thousand miles in any direction, but somehow that just made him cry harder.

She softened her tone. 'Should we go home?'

He looked up at her at once, the worry turned sharply to panic. 'No. Mom, no. We can't go home.' Like their ancestral land was set upon by marauding hordes. Like their intergalactic space pod had crashed on landing.

This was unforeseen.

But accounting for the unforeseen was one of Rosie's particular talents. At home this manifested as never having to go to the grocery store. She would look at a pantry that contained only the dregs of boxes of four different kinds of pasta, half a bag of brown rice, four cans of kidney beans, three of tuna fish, and a bag of expired sun-dried tomatoes and concoct dinner. She would be missing two-thirds of the ingredients in a recipe, and by subbing skim milk for cream and olive oil for butter and lentils for beef and frozen broccoli for fresh spinach and red pepper flakes for mushrooms and nothing for fresh sage leaves (because really, what dish actually hinged on fresh sage leaves?), she could achieve lasagna béchamel without leaving the house.

And it turned out it was this skill – not her years of ER experience, not her advanced training, not the decade and a half she'd spent in a teaching hospital – that made her so valuable at the clinic. What the recipe called for, they did not have on hand. What a Google search, not to mention said years of experience and her not-inconsiderable medical intuition, suggested as a viable substitution was not available either. But what Rosie could do was look at a yawning supply closet with its paltry stock, at moldy equipment and unreliable drug supplies, and figure out something that would work.

Sometimes.

She made a wound sequestration area out of palm fronds and coconut husk. She made an inhaler out of a plastic soda bottle. She prescribed drugs in all sorts of ways the FDA never allowed themselves to imagine.

It had been week two before someone came in with a broken bone, odd because fractures were so common, there and everywhere, and at first Rosie had been relieved. The woman was very pregnant and in a wheelbarrow, both she and her husband, who was pushing, flushed and out of breath, and Rosie had at first thought it would be something much worse. Whereas labor and delivery had tended, in her previous medical experience, to be the most triumphant rotation, here most people gave birth at home, and only came in when there was a complication, often only after it was too late or became too late during the journey. Rosie came to greet the sight of mounded belly with sinking dread. This patient grasped her domed front, shook her head, and assured K, who assured Rosie, 'Baby stay. Ankle go.' It was then Rosie noticed her propped leg, purple and blue, her ankle swollen to the size of her thigh. 'Fall off water buffalo,' K explained. 'Hard to balance with such big . . .' The woman grinned then grimaced then grasped her belly again.

Rosie checked her pupils and her pulses, listened to her heart and the baby's, had the woman endeavor to wiggle toes on both feet. 'Let's get you up to X-ray.' It was out of her mouth before she realized that at least the 'up' was entirely erroneous. The X-ray too? Surely they had some kind of antiquated-but-better-than-nothing X-ray machine. How could they run the place without one? That said, she'd been there every day for two weeks and never seen one, heard one mentioned, located a building where one might have been. Maybe it had just never come up.

'K? I'm afraid to ask but . . . X-ray?'

K's particular talents had proven to stretch further even than from auto repair to midwifery. K was her medic. That's how the clinic director had introduced her on day two: 'This is your medic, K,' as if Rosie had not already saved a truck, lost a patient, and delivered a baby with the woman. Rosie had not been aware she got or needed a medic or what a medic in a clinic like this one even was per se. It turned out the medic was everything except for what Rosie was. And sometimes she was what Rosie was too. K did injections. She did the vomit and the blood and the feces, which was saying something because there was a lot of all of the above. She did wound-care work and handholding work and being patient with patients work. She did the translating work of explaining prognoses and which drugs to take when and how to clean abrasions and stanch blood and how to rehydrate babies and when to let fevers run their course versus when to seek medical care. She translated English into Thai and Northern Thai and a variety of Thai dialects and Burmese and Karen, and she translated Rosie's stern and complicated Doctor into kind and reassuring Nurse, instructions clear enough to follow precisely, gentle enough to inspire confidence and calm. Rosie assumed K had gone to nursing school at least, but K could not get into nursing school because K had never finished high school.

K was also her physical therapist and her social worker and her security detail. When a child came into the clinic with her father but then her father died, K knew how to comfort the little girl and find her someplace to stay and something to wear and enroll her in school. When a teacher came in to complain that his leg fit incorrectly so that he could walk, yes, but he could not stand for long periods of time in front of his classroom, K worked with the prosthetics department to fashion him a leg that stood as well as perambulated and with the patient to think about exerting discipline on small children from a seated position. When the injuries one woman claimed came from falling off a water cistern proved instead to have come from a husband incensed to find her pregnant again, K had him removed and found beds for all seven of his children. But K had never been to physical-therapy school or social-work school. K had never even taken a martial-arts class. What K knew, and it was a stunning, encyclopedic amount, she had learned from the doctors who'd come before Rosie, from the doctors who came and stayed for weeks or months or years, from watching, from experience, and from necessity. Rosie found herself asking K's advice more often than the other way around. Rosie had more formal training, but it wasn't training for this environment. K knew quite a bit more about worms and snakebites and what, based on your symptoms, probably laid eggs in you than had been covered by the University of Wisconsin's medical school program. And of course she maintained Sorry Ralph, never mind the fact that her functional, sensitive, callus-free hands were precious as palladium. It took a while, longer than it should have maybe, but Rosie gradually realized the many versions of K layered atop one another like sediment. And like that striated earth, what remained of K after the buffeting of wind and wear and time was solid as rock.

'No X-ray,' K answered cheerfully. After two weeks of working together, K had grown amused by all Rosie requested as if she were asking if the clinic stocked mind readers.

Rosie eased the patient from wheelbarrow to bed. She remembered the night she'd accidentally X-rayed Poppy – well, Claude, almost-Claude, Claude-in-utero – all those years ago in the ER in Wisconsin. Here, she often found that absent being able to see entirely, insides included, it was better to see not at all. Until Thailand, closing her eyes was not a di-

agnostic technique she'd reverted to much, but it beat going to the grocery store. Especially since there was no grocery store. She held her hand
above the patient's leg to feel how hot it was. She pressed gently with
her fingers, feeling for the break, feeling where it was twisted and misaligned. She pictured the X-ray sketched for her by her gently tracing
fingers, the ghostly bones reaching for one another as if through time. It
was remarkable, really, how well she could see without seeing. Later, she
would detect fractures with the far more advanced technologies of a
tuning fork and a stethoscope, but she was a couple weeks away from
that trick yet. This first one, fortunately and unfortunately, was broken
enough she could feel it easily, displaced enough, maybe from the wheelbarrow ride into the clinic rather than the break itself, that the patient
was going to need something more than just a cast.

The art of bone setting is not a modern one. Rosie knew this. She
knew that once upon a time, broken bones were treated by barbers and
blacksmiths, that physicians felt fractures were beneath them. But she
also knew why. You sought a blacksmith because you needed someone
strong to realign the bone, to overcome the complete freakout the mus-
cles around it were going to have when you started pulling. You sought a
barber because you lived in the Middle Ages and were totally screwed.

K was tending to a patient who'd been carried in on a ladder, so Rosie
was on her own. Her patient's husband spoke no English at all. Rosie
steered him by the shoulders and positioned him behind his wife's head,
his arms looped around her shoulders up to his own. Rosie went back to
the other end of the wooden pallet and took the woman's ankle gently
into both hands. The patient gasped. This boded ill. She made the
patient take five deep, slow breaths. She made the husband take five
deep, slow breaths. She took five deep, slow breaths. Then she pulled
like hell. The patient screamed. The husband screamed. But the bone
realigned. And the baby stayed put. Lacking an intramedullary nail – she
knew enough not to even ask for that one, not that she could have placed
it without an X-ray anyway – she stabilized the leg with fabric wrap, a
section of branch, and plates made of coconut shells. As long as the rem-
edy required was something that grew on a palm tree, you were all set.

The patients in Thailand also knew what to do without what they
never knew they were doing without. Absent antibiotic ointment, honey
would stop a burn from getting infected. Dried papaya seeds crushed
into powder would get rid of intestinal worms. Tea made from corn silk

would reduce swelling. It was the way here. It was the only way. So it was this skill Rosie started employing, a few weeks into Thailand, a few weeks into Claude 2.0, not so much looking for remedies on palm trees as looking for them where she hadn't been looking before.

She wasn't so naïve as to imagine there was something she could crush up or stir in or scavenge from a plant to help her child live in the world. But if she could doctor without drugs, medical equipment, or sterilized bedding, surely there was another option besides the ones she and Penn had been considering so far. Surgeries, side effects, appropriated choices, and life interrupted on the one hand versus misery, failure to fit, and life disallowed on the other was not a choice any more than dying from dehydration or dying from an enema used to treat dehydration. The trick was neither to make peace with medical intervention nor to eschew it altogether. The trick was to doctor a palm frond to help Poppy and Claude find their way in the world. Rosie didn't know what that trick was yet, but she was getting a crash course in looking for it.

Oral Tradition

After three weeks at the school, Claude's hair was two and a half centimeters of pathetic brown fuzz, and his class had grown from three to seven to ten to twenty-five children. The woman in charge with the painted cheeks (principal? teacher? secretary? mayor?) who'd assured him on the first day, 'You fine,' had evidently not believed it herself. It became gradually clear to Claude that Mya, Dao, and Zeya were sent over first because they were the easy ones. They were well behaved, and their English was strong, and they weren't really in need of the dubious skills of a ten-year-old American tagalong. This meant they were the ones Claude most wanted to spend time teaching. It also meant, Naw Ga, the principal/teacher/secretary/mayor explained, they were the ones who needed it least. She'd sent them over in the first place so as not to overly traumatize the new teacher – who in addition to being not even a teenager yet had no training whatsoever – but she got over that quickly.

'I don't know how to teach English.' Claude was mildly panicked as his class doubled in size then doubled again and again.

'You speak.' Naw Ga gave him international so-what's-the-problem eyes.

'I speak it, yeah, but I don't know how to, you know, teach it to someone else.'

'No one know.' Naw Ga waved her hand, already turning off toward other students, other lessons. 'How *you* learn?'

'To teach?'

'To talk.'

'Oh. I don't remember. I was a baby.'

'So be they mama,' Naw Ga advised. 'You learn from listen, talk, read. They same.'

Whereas the original three had sat quietly and respectfully and listened, the twenty-some wiggled and giggled in a language Claude didn't know while he tried to be serious with them in a language they were supposed to be learning but weren't. Whereas the original three had been happy to have old books read to them, the new ones complained (at least that's what he thought they were doing) that they'd read these books already many times before. As far as learning English went, Claude suspected they'd already expanded their vocabulary as much as it could be expanded from their dusting-into-dry-leaves copy of *Mother Goose*. He did not think terms like 'tuffet', 'curds', 'cockleshells', and 'pease porridge' were likely to come up in everyday English language conversation anyway. At least they had yet to do so for him. And whereas the original three were little girls like he was, like he had been at any rate, at least half of the new kids were boys, and though once upon a time he'd been one of those too, it seemed like something his father had made up: long ago and far away and pretend. The little boys were scary because he didn't know how to talk to them. And because what if they looked at him and realized he was one?

'You tell us new story,' one of the alarming little boys demanded.

'A story about what?'

'About new.'

'I don't know any stories about new,' said Claude.

'Tell story about old,' suggested Zeya, who at this point felt like an old friend. 'New story about old.'

'I don't know any new stories about old.' Did telling them stories instead of reading them stories even count? Was that learning English?

'Tell us favorite story,' someone said, and even as Claude was about to say he didn't know any stories, he realized that of course he did.

'Well, I do know one story. One long, big, long story about a prince named Grumwald and a night fairy named Princess Stephanie.'

'Oooh,' the kids all said, an apparently universal sound meaning 'Do, please, continue.'

So he told them the beginnings of the adventures of Grumwald, beginnings he himself had gotten only by deduction, osmosis, the plot filling in slowly like holes in the sand when the tide is out. The beginning of the Grumwald story way predated him. He knew his father invented

Grumwald so his mother would go out with him. That was as much a part of the fairy tale as the fairy tale itself. Grumwald was a decade older than Claude, so he had to make some parts up, fill in what he could, guess at what he couldn't. It was tiring to make stuff up. He had no idea all these years how hard his father was working when he wished he would just read them a book like everyone else's dad.

The clinic children had questions. What 'Grumwald' mean? What Grumwald was last life to come back as prince? Why he never look inside armor before? Why he no wanna be prince since he earn prince? Claude had no idea. He would have to ask his father and get back to them.

'In the meantime, you tell me a story,' he said to them. Storytelling was hard. He needed a break. Telling him a story was a good way to practice speaking English anyway, he thought.

'A new story?' said Dao.

'An old story,' said Claude. 'A classic story. A fairy tale.'

That was how they started trading stories. Every day, Claude would tell his students an American fairy tale, and every day, his students would tell him a Thai or Burmese fairy tale. He told them about Beauty and the Beast, and they told him about two birds who were reincarnated as a princess and a farmer. He told them about the Little Mermaid, and they told him about a rabbit whose squirrel tail got bitten off by a crocodile with a long tongue. He told them Cinderella, and they had that one too, which he could not even believe, except in theirs the dead mom sent a fish instead of a fairy godmother, and the prince fell in love with her because of her trees instead of her shoes.

'Why he love her shoes?' they wondered.

'It's not that he loved her shoes. He loved her whole outfit, and that's why she really didn't want him to see her in her dirty old clothes.'

'Why she forget her shoe?'

'She didn't forget. It fell off, and she didn't have time to go back and get it.'

'How long it take to stop and pick up drop shoe?'

This seemed a fair point to Claude. It made about as much sense, as far as he could figure, as their explanation, which involved a talking fish who got eaten then reincarnated as an eggplant and then as a matchmaking tree.

His father called early in the mornings, but sometimes his mother had already left for the clinic anyway. It wasn't just that it was night in Seattle when it was day in Thailand, it's that it was still yesterday in Seattle when it was today in Thailand. Sometimes they had cell service and sometimes they did not, so mostly they kept in touch over Wi-Fi. Claude could chat with his brothers easily enough because they were up all night, but his parents were having trouble connecting. He was glad, though, to have his father all to himself sometimes, an occurrence rare enough in his life it wasn't surprising he had to go halfway around the world to find it.

Penn was sorry those mornings to have missed Rosie but also happy to have some time alone with his youngest. 'How are you, baby?'

'Fine, Dad.'

'Really?'

'Really.' This was only sometimes true. Sometimes Claude considered that probably they were not going to stay in Thailand forever, and probably his parents were not going to think a fourth-and-a-half-grade education was sufficient, and probably he was going to have to go back to his old life except his old life was gone. Poppy had friends, but Claude had none. Poppy had talents, but Claude sucked at everything. Poppy was normal, but Claude would never, ever, ever, ever stop being a freak. He had been able to picture Poppy's life next year in middle school and then high school after that and how Poppy and Aggie would go off to college together and how someday Poppy would have a job and be a mom and eventually an old lady like Carmy, smoking and swimming in lakes and drinking gin and tonics and making her grandchildren laugh. Poppy had futures, but Claude had nothing. He couldn't even picture Claude's life *now,* even while he was looking at it in the tiny picture in the corner of his computer screen.

But sometimes he really was fine because none of it was possible, and this was a comfort. Claude was impossible but so was Poppy, so was Aggie, so was fifth grade, so was Seattle, so was last month when her biggest worry was those stupid, embarrassing movies they showed in health class. Sometimes all there was in the world was the jungle and a school that was barely a building and little kids whose parents had been killed by bugs and the small, scant, desperate possibility that somehow maybe he could help them a little bit, and in that case, who he was didn't matter, not even to him. 'Really,' he told his father. 'I'm okay.'

'I miss you, baby,' said Penn. 'I wish I were there.'

'You do,' Claude agreed, 'because you can't even believe it, Dad.

They have Cinderella in Thailand. It's like the exact same story only completely different.'

'Of course.' Penn played nonchalance, but even over grainy, laggy Wi-Fi, he saw his child spark. His daughter spark. For the first time since what had happened, there was a glimmering there. Seeing it was like a benediction. Seeing it was like a laceration. There were too many miles in between them to reach across and cup his hands around this precious flame, his arms around this precious child. This precious girl.

So he settled for chalk talk. 'That's how fairy tales work.'

'It is?'

'They're renewed and retold and reimagined everywhere forever. The oral tradition. That's what makes them endless.'

'I thought it was magic that made them endless. I thought it was the magic armor.'

'Well, sure, that too.'

'I was telling them about Grumwald—'

'You were?'

'Yeah?'

'Oh. Poppy. Claude. Sweetheart. I'm so . . .' But then his voice broke, and he didn't finish saying whatever it was he was saying.

'There's a lot I don't know about because I never heard the beginning of the story or I don't remember.'

'It's your story, sweetheart. Not just your story to pass on. Your story to make up as well. Over time, stories change; they shift; they become something new but with elements of the original and elements of what's to come.'

'Oh.' Claude was suddenly sullen again. 'Like me.'

'Exactly.' Penn panicked for the precious flame. 'Exactly like you. What a wonderful thing. Why would change make you sad?'

'Because it doesn't mean different,' said Claude. 'It means ruined. Why can't one thing just stay the same?'

'Some things do stay the same. Like how we love you no matter what.' Penn thought how much easier it was to say things from halfway around the world sometimes. It wasn't because it was on a computer instead of in person. It was because remote love hurt but gave you clarity. Sending your child to a jungle seven thousand miles away was oddly elucidating. 'And some things change because it's good and natural that they do. Because it's time. And you wouldn't want to stop them.'

'I would.' Claude started crying, and then he was embarrassed because if he was a boy now he couldn't cry anymore.

'And some things change exactly because we try to prevent their doing so.' Penn dropped his voice and then his eyes.

'What do you mean?'

'Oh baby, I think what happened was maybe my fault.' He'd been thinking about this since they left. He'd gone over it and over it. Marnie Alison was a nicer scapegoat and probably a more deserving one, but Penn recognized all that was at stake here. 'I think maybe we waited too long to tell everyone how special you are. We tried to keep you a secret, but why would we keep anything as wonderful and remarkable as you a secret?'

'So everyone at school isn't thinking about what's in my pants.'

Penn had to admit this was a good reason. He remembered sitting in wet paint at recess once when he was in fifth grade and thinking he would die of embarrassment before the end of the school day, and then kids were just thinking about what was *on* his pants. And they probably weren't even thinking about that. But Penn had realized something new. Something new about something old. Something important. 'It's funny you were telling stories with your students. I've been thinking about the same thing. You know what I like about fairy tales?'

'Everything?'

'No. Well, yes. But one of the things I like best is the magic is so simple. It's painless. It doesn't hurt Cinderella when she turns into a princess. It's easy. It's fast. A wand is waved, some pixie dust is strewn, and presto – perfect princess. The transformation is immediate and complete, and no one looks back. It erases all the pain of her past, and it guarantees her happily ever after going forward.'

'Sounds nice.' Claude wiped his eyes.

'It does.' Penn tried to keep his voice steady as his own eyes filled because this was important. 'And it makes for great stories. But it's not real. It's not possible. I think it's not even desirable.'

'I desire it.'

'I don't.' Penn shook his head. 'I don't want to erase your past. You were a perfect baby. You were the smartest three-year-old I ever knew. I don't want to erase your transformation either. You're so special, and you're so brave. You proclaiming who you are and being who you want to be in a world that makes that hard is awe inspiring. I'm so proud of you,

Poppy. I don't want to pretend you're ordinary. I want to climb your turret and shout your extraordinary to the entire city.'

Claude pictured his father clinging like Godzilla to the turret roof, roaring Poppy's slow but inspiring transformation to the sky. He was glad he was in Thailand.

The next day at school, Claude started back in with the fairy tale. But not his father's fairy tale. Having introduced all these other characters, it seemed a shame to him not to use them.

'Princess Stephanie had tons of friends. They all knew she was a princess, but none of them knew she was also a night fairy, and she didn't want them to find out.'

'Why?' Claude's students could not imagine being something as cool as a night fairy and not wanting anyone to know.

'She was embarrassed,' Claude explained.

'Why?'

'Because none of her friends were night fairies. She was the only one.'

'Why that does not make her feel special?'

'Because it was weird,' said Claude. 'And disgusting. Her friends would be grossed out if they knew she was really a night fairy, so she hid it from them. But one day they were all hanging around after school, and suddenly, without warning, her wings popped out, right before their eyes. Princess Stephanie was so upset she ran away crying. But her friends ran after her. They totally understood.'

'It's no big deal, Steph,' Cinderella assured her. 'The same thing happens to me all the time. If I'm running late, my shoes, my clothes, my car – POOF – suddenly it's like they're someone else's. I don't even recognize myself.'

'Me too,' said Ariel. 'I swear to you I used to be a fish.'

'You did?' Stephanie was so grateful to her friends she started crying again.

'Well, half.'

'And you should have seen me before I got eaten by a wolf,' said Little Red Riding Hood. 'You would have hated me. I was such a weak little thing I got in trouble picking flowers. Lame.'

'What happened?' Stephanie sniffed.

'I got eaten, that's what happened. I grew up. I figured out I needed to be smart and strong, and I took control.'

'How?'

'I worked out.' Little Red smiled and flexed her biceps. Claude demonstrated. The class giggled. 'I got a personal trainer. I'll give you her number.'

Claude's students nodded along, pleased so far.

'So all of Princess Stephanie's friends finally knew who she really was, and they all loved her anyway, all except one. Her rival neighbor princess was angry.'

'But not her fault,' Claude's students objected en masse.

'It wasn't her fault she turned into a night fairy,' Claude acknowledged, 'but it was her fault she lied about it.'

'She *have* to keep secret,' the students insisted.

Claude shook his head. 'The rival neighbor princess told Stephanie everything, so she didn't think they had any secrets.'

'Every princess and person have secret,' Dao said.

'That's true.' Claude tried to think if he'd ever seen a teacher cry in front of the class. 'But some secrets are secrets, whereas some secrets are lies.'

'Every person have another person inside,' Mya insisted. As in: the rival neighbor princess shouldn't have needed to be told. As in: it doesn't count because Stephanie's secret was actually the human condition.

'Princess Stephanie couldn't convince her not to be mad,' Claude continued. 'She tried to explain and she tried to say sorry, but the neighbor princess didn't care. So Stephanie had to use magic on her.'

'Turn her into frog?' one little boy guessed.

'Turn her into big giant big gross monster who stink?' guessed another.

'Turn her into night fairy also?' said Zeya.

'No, no, no,' though Claude thought these were not half-bad ideas. 'Stephanie waved her magic wand and turned the angry neighbor princess into an understanding neighbor princess, one who didn't mind and wasn't mad and still loved Stephanie and always would.'

Claude took a deep breath. That seemed like a good place to stop, so he did. But his students looked unconvinced.

'Not magic,' complained Zeya. As in: spells are for enchanted transmutation, not changing someone's mind.

'Not enough,' complained Dao. As in: bitchy neighbor princesses deserve some kind of actual punishment.

'Not possible,' complained the boy who'd suggested turning her into a frog. As in: homo-amphibian metamorphosis might not be real, but it's still more credible than Aggie getting over Poppy's secret.

But Claude felt better. He realized this was what his father had been up to all these years, not entertaining his children but perfecting his world. If you wrote your own characters, they didn't disappoint you like real people did. If you told your own story, you got to pick your ending. Just being yourself never worked, but if you made yourself up, you got to be exactly who you knew yourself to be.

Under Pants

At the ends of their long days, Rosie and K retired together to the cafeteria and a quiet plastic table and chairs – backyard furniture purchased by college students at a grocery store in another world – and ate and talked. Rosie was always anxious to get to a cellphone signal or a computer and try Penn. She was anxious to get back to the child she had brought to the jungle with her, a child who was, by all accounts, working wonders in the classroom, wonders about which she longed for details like raindrops long for the sea. K had daughters as well as sons as well as a husband to get home to too, not to mention that the food at home was probably better than in the clinic cafeteria, which had to feed five hundred patients and their families every day, but Rosie and K sat together quietly every evening anyway, sometimes talking, sometimes breathing pungent steam off of hot tea and saying nothing at all.

Rosie told K all about Seattle and her own hill tribe, about private-practice family medicine, then about Wisconsin and the ER at UW, the farmhouse, the burgeoning family, the love affair, the storytelling, her sister, working her way backward through everything that mattered. K told Rosie her story backward as well. Medic at the border clinic, rewarding work in hard conditions over long days, two boys and two girls at home too young yet to leave for so many hours, a Burmese husband-soldier who'd lost too much in the war to heal, a three-week trek through the jungle to a whispered-about clinic which might be able to help, which turned out in fact to be able to help, not to cure the husband but to em-ploy and empower the wife, and that was something, all the way back through the months of war in Burma that preceded his injuries that preceded their flight, all the way back to her childhood in northern Thailand before she crossed the border with an uncle for unspecified rea-sons, a childhood that sounded poor and lacking to Rosie but which K described as full of color and soil and possibility.

At the beginning, as they got to know each other, it was all surface details, rough sketching rather than precise portraiture, autobiography instead of memoir. They had not had long enough together to become close friends yet – though in fact, after Rosie left, they kept in touch for the rest of their lives – but they were both mothers, so they shared that instantaneous connection Rosie knew so well from years of being exactly that. You could sit down with another mom, even one halfway around the world whose life was very different from your own, and find easy con-versation, shared spirit, someone who understood why you might bring your ten-year-old into a malarial jungle rather than leave him behind, someone who understood what unspeakable things sometimes befell children and to what lengths you might go to fend them off, someone who saw the horrors and the threats and the carving up and the carving out and also how hard they were to schedule around and how little they cared about your job and how much they wanted just to be touching you all the time and what they looked like when they first woke up in the morning and how they learned to talk and walk and read and how quickly they outgrew their clothes and how it was to live every moment of every day in that world – even the moments when someone else's kid was shit-ting thousands of tiny larva into a bucket, even the moments when some-one else's kid was shaking with a fever whose cause you could not discern, even the moments when someone else's kid had her own baby stuck against her pelvis, draining her life in its efforts to be born.

So Rosie's question, though it seemed both rude and random, was nei-ther out of line nor a subject change. 'Can I ask about your kids?' She slurped unadorned noodles from a plain broth which somehow, via who knew what crossed wires, tasted like her mother's matzo ball soup.

K's tired face lit up.

'How?' asked Rosie.

'How?' K grinned. 'You mean, how I get them?'

Rosie blushed and nodded, concentrated on her noodles, reconsidered those sedimentary layers she'd realized K harbored all those weeks ago.

'Because you have noticed . . . I am like Claude.'

Rosie's glasses were fogged from the steaming soup when her head shot up, so she couldn't see K clearly. 'No. I mean yes. I mean yes I noticed you are . . . like Claude. But I didn't notice you'd noticed Claude was . . . like Claude. How did you know?'

'I cannot know how I know,' K smiled smugly. 'He seem not comfortable in body. He seem more than what he seem.'

'He is,' Rosie said. 'She is.'

'What is name at home?'

'Poppy.'

'Poppy,' K echoed. 'Pretty name.'

'And yours?' Rosie prompted.

'We adopt them. We did not mean to. Choochai and I marry but not official marry, you know? We think we will be childless, and this is okay. There is fighting. There is war we are not part of and not apart of. We are very poor, country very broken. So we okay just to be two. Then in first month here, man bring in wife in labor three days, lost so much blood. The mama die. The father leave. The baby live and come home with me and Choochai. Every of our babies was a baby here who need home. But we cannot home all the babies here who need.'

Rosie put down her spoon to breathe, to count the ways this was barely imaginable, never mind sitting right across from her. 'You are a wonder.'

'I am?'

'You are.'

'Why you say?'

'You left your home, your family. You work here, in these conditions, year in and out, without sufficient training or equipment or supplies. You've taken in these children who needed a family and made them your own. All while suffering the stigma of being . . .' She trailed off.

'*Kathoey.*' K supplied the word. It sounded like *cat toy*. 'One of the thing K stand for. Translate as *ladyboy*. What you say?'

'Transgender.' Rosie sounded defeated to her own ears and wondered why.

'But not really suffer stigma,' K added.

'Oh, no, I didn't mean—' Rosie began, but K went right on.

'Not like for Poppyclaude I think. In Thailand, lots *kathoey*. Not so big deal. We all Buddhist. Is karma. Is life. Is just another way to be.'

'Really?' It was the most astonishing thing Rosie had encountered in her travels thus far, including the woman who had arrived in labor and literally gotten down off an elephant.

'Buddhist way.' K shrugged. 'Last life one thing, this one another, next another. Whatever happen last life to make me like this not my fault. Everyone know that. Me, my soul, will be lot of bodies before done, some male, some female, some both. So okay. No one care what is under my pants.'

'What is . . .' Rosie-the-clinician battled Rosie-the-courteous and won because so much was on its head here. 'What is under your pants, if you don't mind my asking?'

'Like Sorry Ralph, I have all original parts.' K smiled. Rosie was impressed with a language facility that extended to puns. 'Lot of clinics in Bangkok do surgery but mostly for foreigner. Many *kathoey* here let be. Which parts not what matter. Is soul, how move, how dress, how love, how be. Just like Poppy, I am female soul so do not matter to me or Choochai or sons or daughters or anyone what is under pants. Makes sense?'

Rosie nodded, speechless. It was hard to talk about these things in one's own language, never mind someone else's. 'So you just . . .' Just what? She wasn't sure herself what she was asking.

But K nodded. 'I grow up north Chiang Mai. Not really even town. Rural. Farm. But my cousin *kathoey* so I know it is okay. Then at school, older students *kathoey*. Show me how. Hair. Clothes. Hormone easy to get if you want but lots do not. Just me is enough. Is not same for Poppy I do not think?'

'No.' Rosie shook her head and told herself sternly that it would be inappropriate to cry in front of this woman with whom she had spent the afternoon removing shrapnel from the side of a six-year-old. 'It's not the same. Everyone cares what's under Claude's pants. Poppy's pants. And many of them mind. First everyone knew, and it wasn't safe. Then no one knew, and then they found out, and that was worse.'

'Why you keep secret?'

'Because I didn't learn. I saw. I saw what horrors come from keeping it a secret. I saw what storms unleash when it's uncovered. But somehow, somehow, I made the same mistake.'

'Mistake good because you learn, you fix.'

'I don't know how,' said Rosie.

'Middle way.'

'At home, there is no middle way. You're male or you're female. There's no in between. You conform or you hide. You conform or you're wrong. If you dress like a girl, then you have to be a girl, all girl, and if any part of you's not, that's not okay.'

'Not just middle way between male and female. Middle way of being. Middle way of living with what is hard and who do not accept you.'

'How do you do that?'

'You keep remember: all is change.'

'All what?'

'All life. You are never finish, never done. Never become, always becoming. You know? Life is change so is always okay you are not there yet. Is like this for you and Poppy and everyone. The people who do not understand are change. The people who afraid are change. There is no before and no after because change is what is life. You live in change, in in between.'

'And how do you do *that*?'

'You learn over lifetimes. You keep try. You will find middle way to be. This life. Next. You find your way.'

Rosie did not know if she could wait that long.

K smiled. 'You know story of the Buddha?'

Rosie shook her head.

'Just like you and Claude. Poppy. Just like everyone. Story of change, of not-knowing to knowing, ignorance to enlightenment. But enlightenment is long, take a long, hard time. If it does not, it does not result enlightenment. Buddha was many lives before last one. In last life, Buddha was prince. You know?'

Rosie did. Rosie knew all about stories about a prince.

'Very shelter life in palace so ignorant of poverty, sickness, old age, death. Then he go out into world and learn. Then he help. That is important part. Once he learn, he listen and tell, he help. He leave family, leave palace, leave being a prince.' Rosie nodded along. This part sounded familiar. 'He learn about the world and the people. He meditate to learn to be. He give up all food and water and house, but then his body too loud to achieve peace so he learn again: too little as bad as too much. He teach, tell his story, help people see truth. He say be kind and forgive, honest and share. He say everything will change so okay. He say middle way. He enlighten. That is the story. Learn mistake and fix and tell. Not-knowing to knowing. Even the Buddha. You see?'

'But I'm not knowing,' said Rosie.

'Not yet,' said K.

The Color of Monday

The Buddha was everywhere. Not Everywhere everywhere, though maybe that too for all Claude knew. His ubiquity was worrisome because you weren't supposed to point your feet at him, but you could never tell where he might pop up – there was a Buddha statue in the cafeteria, two in the schoolroom, three in the intake center, one in the waiting area. Claude had counted five so far in the guesthouse. On the bike ride to the clinic, they passed seven of them. When they went into town for an afternoon, he counted fifteen. The Buddha hid round a bend or on the crest of a hill or among the trees. Claude's little students had tried to explain all about the Buddha who was Lord but not God, a prince, a teacher, a reminder, and a path, but what Claude liked about him was he looked like a girl.

He didn't realize this until their trip to Chiang Mai, where they went to get supplies for the clinic and then stayed a couple extra days because his mother decided they had earned some time off. K told them Chiang Mai was Thailand's second city, so Claude steeled himself for Bangkok again, but Chiang Mai was nothing like Bangkok. There were gardens and parks and mountains in Chiang Mai. There was a quiet treetop restaurant and a hotel with the giant cushy beds the guesthouse so completely lacked and a market where you could buy supplies without live animals looking at you tragically from buckets or cages. There were flowers everywhere and fruit stands and bike paths. There was a fish spa, where you sat on benches over an aquarium, and hundreds of garra rufa fish came and nibbled at your calves and feet.

But mostly in Chiang Mai there were *wats,* which meant temples. There were more than three hundred wats in the city, and Claude was pretty sure they saw every single one of them. They were right in the middle of everything, plopped next to a restaurant or a bank or a grocery store, right where you were going anyway so that they served, their guide Nok explained, as a reminder. What the temples wanted to remind you about was the Buddha. Maybe he wasn't God, but then why were there so many statues of him? Each temple had legions of Buddhas. Oodles of Buddhas. Buddhas galore. There were paintings and drawings and murals of Buddhas. Stories of the Buddha. Statues of Buddhas with flames blooming from their heads toward the sky. Buddhas walking or meditating or sitting on a snake or talking to animals. Buddhas who looked like they were taking a nap. Buddhas with their eyes all cast down (because it is important to see oneself before others, Nok explained) and their ears stretched long (to listen, to observe, and also because long ears mean long life; Claude fingered his own but could not judge their relative length).

But what drew Claude to the Buddha first was not his eyes nor his ears but his fingers. Actually, his fingernails. They were long and shapely. They were elegantly filed. Often, they were painted gold. His hands lay quietly in his lap, easy and neat and turned gently open, like he was asking, and genuinely caring, how you were, like he was getting ready to offer to make you a snack or some tea. Like a girl. The Buddhas wore jewelry and snailed their hair. They had full lips and secret smiles and shy eyes, high cheekbones and delicate noses, eyebrows that swept like swallows. Some had soft little bellies. Some had two squiggles that formed a triangle between their legs, and maybe that was the bottom of his jacket, but maybe it was something better. Sometimes the Buddhas lay on their sides, heads propped on hands, looking like if they could speak they would say, 'So! Tell me everything!' just like Poppy's friends did during sleepovers. One was wearing a floor-length beaded gold gown, the sparkling diamond weave of which snugged the Buddha's gentle curves, and a black updo framing eyes that gazed modestly down at the dress and said, 'Damn, I look good.' The Buddha had long, rounded thighs, smooth shoulders, flared hips, and a narrow waist. He had delicate feet, hands poised at his sides like patient birds. Sometimes up top, he was flat as the stone he was carved from. Sometimes robes or dresses or sashes seemed to hide something more up there because no matter the material, posture, expression, or outfit, the Buddha looked like a girl.

Claude wasn't sure it was polite to ask why – the Buddha may not have been a god, but in all the stories, he definitely was a he – but he did anyway. It was unlike him, but he had to know.

Nok said, 'Buddha peaceful, gentle, nonaggressive. So look female.'

He said, 'Buddha many lives and bodies before enlightenment.'

He said, 'Nothing belong to you. Not even the body of you.'

None of which really answered the question. What was clear, however, was that the Buddha was born male, then cut off all his hair one day and got enlightened, then ended up looking like a girl. And as if that weren't enough, the Buddha also seemed to feel that even things as unalterable as bodies were temporary, and what mattered was if you were good and honest, and forgiveness solved everything. That was how, whatever else they were, Claude and Poppy became Buddhists for life.

Their last day in Chiang Mai was the king's birthday, and the whole city, the whole country, was having a party. People were giving out free food in the markets, shoving oranges into Claude's hands and fish balls on a stick and a bowl of sweet, creamy pumpkin soup. And everywhere he looked, everyone was wearing yellow: yellow shirts and dresses, yellow hats and shawls, yellow shoes and yellow scarves.

'Why is everyone wearing yellow?' Claude had to yell so Nok could hear him over the chanting.

Nok smiled that smile that meant he must have made a mistake with his poor English comprehension skills because no one could possibly be as ignorant as Claude was. 'It is color of Monday.'

'What?'

'Yellow.'

'What's yellow?'

'The color of Monday.'

'Monday has a color?'

'Every day have a color.'

'It does?'

'Of course.'

'But it's Wednesday.'

'Today is Wednesday, but king is born on Monday, so his color yellow. What day you born?'

'June seventh.'

'What day of week?'

'Oh,' said Claude. 'I have no idea.'

This news was greeted with incredulity. 'Then how you know your color?'

Claude did not know his color.

'What day he born?' Nok asked Rosie.

'June seventh.'

'What day of week?' Nok repeated patiently.

'No idea.'

'Find out,' Nok advised. 'Is important. Your day tell what your color and also what your Buddha position.'

'Buddha position?' Claude and his mother said together.

'King's Buddha position – Monday – is Dispelling Fear. Standing with one hands up or two hands up.' Claude had been thinking of these as talk-to-the-hand Buddhas. He looked like he was about to do one of those moves where you do three snaps in a Z and add, 'Whatever it is, girl, I do *not* want to hear about it.' But apparently (and not, Claude reflected, surprisingly) it was more loving and generous than that. He was dispelling fear. Sometimes the position was meant to suggest holding back storms or an angry sea. Sometimes it was calling for peace, keeping fighting and fear at bay, reminding people to choose calm, choose love. Let be.

That night after dinner, they went back to the fish spa. Armed with a cell-phone connection, Claude discovered that, like the king of Thailand, he had been born on a Monday as well.

'Makes sense.' His mother wiggled her toes to give the fish a ride.

'What does?'

'Your color being yellow.'

'Why?'

'Yellow's what you paint the nursery if you don't know whether the baby will be a boy or a girl.' Claude did not look up from the fish, so Rosie couldn't tell whether this was helping or hurting, but she pressed on anyway. It was as good an opening as she was likely to get. 'You were in the yellow baby room longer than anyone.'

'The yellow baby room?'

'The nursery in Madison. You were so little you probably don't remember it. We kept that room yellow, just in case you were a girl.'

'When?' Claude wondered but his mother seemed not to hear.

'I also like the idea of dispelling fear.' Rosie swished fish and tried to pass this off as idle musing. In all the wonder and whirling of the day, the golden wats and teeming Buddhas, the joyous celebrants, the ravenous fish she was feeding with her own flesh, this was what stilled for her, smooth and clear as glass. Dispelling fear. Taming what was scary not by hiding it, not by blocking it or burying it, not by keeping it secret, but by reminding themselves, and everyone else, to choose love, choose openness, to think and be calm. That there were more ways than just two, wider possibilities than hidden or betrayed, stalled or brokenhearted, male or female, right or wrong. Middle ways. Ways beyond.

They had, she could finally see, been choosing out of fear. Penn's rushing fevered drive for magical transformation was fear, but so was Rosie's insistence that they wait and see and make their child choose. They needed their fear dispelled, she and Penn and Claude and Poppy, because they could not live in fear anymore. But everyone else needed their fear dispelled too because that's where all the trouble was. Nasty fifth-graders and violent college students and ignorant playdates and people who gave you rude looks in the grocery store and missing-the-point school administrators and proponents of the hedge enemy and a wide world of not-yet-enlightened people were nothing more or less than scared. They needed their fear dispelled, their seas calmed, their storms allayed. And the person to dispel the fear was Rosie. She couldn't cower anymore; she couldn't wait; she had to leap. Ten-year-olds were not so scary, after all, and this one before her was coming clear and clearer. It didn't do to make lost children find their own way out of the woods. This child, this tender child, was young yet and new in the world. The way was hard, and help was called for. Penn could not choose the route and pave the way. But neither could Rosie sit back and wait for what would come. There were other ways. They were not easy to see, and they were not easy to execute, but easy had been taken off the wish list long ago.

'It's the middle way, my love,' she said.

'I don't get the middle way.' Claude made his legs make figure eights through the warm water and tried to match his mother's certain tone. 'How come?'

'Because there is no middle way.' It came out between a groan and a whimper. 'There are only two choices, and they aren't even choices, at least not ones you get to choose. If you only tell some of the truth, that's a lie. If only one tiny stupid part of you is a boy, you can never be a girl.'

'All of that seems true. It does.' His mother reached across the water and took his hands. 'But it's not. I think the middle way is hard for the same reason the middle way is right.'

'Why?'

'Because it's invisible.'

'Like in a fairy tale?'

'No,' his mother said to the fish, then looked up at him. 'Actually, yes, sort of like a fairy tale. There's a fork in the road. It seems like there are only two choices. It seems like the task is to figure out which way to go, left or right, forward or back, deeper or safer, but in fact any of those choices is easy compared to the real trick. The real trick is you have to forge your way straight ahead through the trees where there is no path.'

'Why doesn't that sound peaceful?' Claude, the budding Buddhist.

Rosie didn't know. 'Maybe it is in the long run? Maybe it takes time. Maybe peaceful and easy turn out to be opposites.' She thought of the whole lifetime it takes to grow up and become an entire person. She thought of the day she and Penn – a family of two at the time – painted the nursery yellow, the color of either way, of dispelling fear, of not-knowing. The color of Monday. 'Can I tell you a secret?'

Claude looked up from the fish.

'I miss Poppy.' Rosie smiled.

Claude didn't say anything. Then he said, 'But didn't you miss Claude when you had Poppy?'

'That's not quite what I mean,' Rosie said carefully. 'You know, I've called you Claude here because you asked me to. But it doesn't really matter to me what your name is or what your hair looks like or if you're my daughter or my son because no matter what, I only, I always, see *you*. You are always the same child to me, my brilliant beautiful shining child, my baby. You became Poppy, but you never stopped being Claude. You became Claude again, but you never stopped being Poppy. Boy or girl, Poppy or Claude, they seem so different to you, to the world. Not to me. Used to be, I couldn't even tell them apart.'

'Used to be?'

'Now I see how different Poppy and Claude are, but not how you think. I miss Poppy not because I miss my happy, strong, laughing little girl but because I miss my happy, strong, laughing child. Claude is a lost, sad child out of joint. That's what I've realized since we've been here. It's not that Poppy's the girl and Claude's the boy. There's boy and girl in both of them. They both have what they parade and what they hide. It's that Poppy's the happy child, and Claude is the sad one. Poppy's the one who fits and feels comfortable, and Claude is the one who chafes in ill-shaped holes. And that makes it so much easier to choose between them.'

'But you said it's hard, and you have to plow through the trees anyway. You said invisible middle way.'

'Because Poppy is the happy child, but Poppy is also the way through the trees I think. You have to be – you get to be – Poppy, even though it's hard. What was wrong at home wasn't being Poppy. What was wrong was trying to make it easy to be Poppy. Being Poppy isn't easy. What we have to do is help you be Poppy even though it's hard.'

'I never said being Poppy was too hard.' Claude crossed his arms over his chest, whether defiant or hugging himself his mother could not say. 'I'm not afraid of that.'

'Maybe it's not being Poppy that's hard,' Rosie acknowledged. 'Maybe it's staying Poppy. Staying Poppy is going to get complicated for a while here. You have some tough decisions to make, but we'll help. You have some tough reentry to go back to, but it won't be as bad as you think. Being Poppy will never be featherweight, but I think it's lighter than being Claude. And fortunately, Poppy is strong as seas.'

Claude – Poppy – shook garra rufa fish off dripping legs and went to find the restroom. Right there in the hallway, exactly where you'd expect the bathrooms to be, there were three of them. One sign had a blue person in pants. And one sign had a red person with a cute flip hairstyle in a skirt. And one sign was half of each, a person whose left, blue leg was in pants and whose right, red leg came out from under a skirt. Claude – and Poppy – stood for a long time looking at it, making sure it wasn't a trick, making sure they understood. It seemed impossible, but here it was. For the first time in their whole, whole lives, there was a right door.

Inside, there was a bathroom. Sinks, toilets, toilet paper even. Ordinary. Nothing special. A miracle.

An Ending

Rosie's first day back at the clinic was a long one. She and Poppy – they were making an effort to reclaim the name, a statement of hope, a declaration of intent – had gotten back late the night before, and then Rosie had come in even earlier than usual. A woman pregnant with twins delivered the first baby quick and easy but the second baby slow and hard. It was after one in the morning when Rosie got on her bike and checked her phone. Fifteen missed calls from Penn. Fifteen. And seven texts, two words apiece, all exactly the same: CALL HOME. She did so instantly. Call failed. She raised her arm and waved her phone in all directions. No cell service. Though she doubted it could bear her weight, she tried standing on the bright-blue plastic table that passed for the clinic intake desk. It wobbled, held, but did not result in bars on her phone. Was it true or some kind of desperate urban legend that getting higher up led to cell service? She made it as far as the first branch of the (she thought acacia?) tree next to the Ambulatory Care Center before the threat of whatever might be living there and the insanity she was displaying outweighed the remote possibility of some kind of altitudinous arboreal connectivity.

She thought: There's Wi-Fi at the guesthouse.

She thought: He'll have called Claude – Poppy – and she'll know what's going on.

But when she arrived at the guesthouse seven breathless minutes later, knees bloodied from falling when she jumped out of the tree, thighs screaming from pedaling twice as hard as her thighs were inclined to left to their own devices, the Wi-Fi was down and Poppy was sound asleep.

At first she was relieved. If it were bad, Poppy would have waited up to tell her. If it were bad, Poppy wouldn't be able to sleep. Then she became unrelieved because if it were not bad, but *really* bad, Penn wouldn't call Poppy. Penn would wait to talk to Rosie.

It was going to be a long night.

Rosie's first thought, after she cleaned up her knees, checked the Wi-Fi a few hundred more times, and finally, resignedly, climbed into bed, was of Carmelo, who, after sixty-some years with her pack a day habit, probably had it coming to her, but her daughter was still not ready. *Please,* she pled to the Buddha, to the darkness, to the jungle, to any powers that be'd, *I am not ready. I cannot lose my mother. She is all the family I have left.*

Then she thought of all the family she had left. There was no reason to assume it wasn't one of the boys. Youth did not protect from everything, not even in the United States of America. A menacing cough that came on so quickly and sounded so ominous it could only portend something ill starred. A pestilent lump uncovered somewhere hideous. A catastrophic allergy no one had foreseen, retribution for all those cavalier PB&Js she'd sent to school in Wisconsin. Or an accident – car, bike, skateboard, stair, fist – there were endless permutations, none of which strained the imagination. Or they were into something they shouldn't have been. Her fault for being halfway around the world. Drugs, drink, guns, gambling. They were teenage boys and therefore morons. She knew this in her heart.

Or the other boy in her life. She could not live without Penn. It was as simple and awful as that.

She spent a sleepless night with her dead mother, her diseased/bleeding/foolhardy/allergic sons, the love of her life doomed to malignant monsters. She thought, she could not help but think, of Jane Doe, who was still a child when she died in her hands, bloodied, beaten, and broken, shot and shamed and snatched untimely. You could not avoid being who you were, could you? You could not avoid being who you were, and sometimes it destroyed you. She thought, she could not help but think, of Nick Calcutti and the fallible infallible fact that, no matter how fast and far and fleet you go, you cannot always outrun violence. Sometimes you got to turn away, but sometimes you did not. She tried to think of Nick as proof that often, usually, you trialed and triumphed, but he was a near miss, and in her up-all-night, petrified heart she knew it. She tried to think of Jane Doe as a relic of a time and place and fear long past, but Jane was there-but-for instead, and she knew that too. When the sun rose finally and she left sleeping Poppy, blissfully ignorant, and made K drive her to town and a working telephone, she could draw only thimble-fuls of breath, shallow as dust, nothing as substantial as a whisper.

It was afternoon in Seattle. Penn, in the middle of his workday, trying to squeeze a few more paragraphs out before everyone got home from school, answered the phone quite a bit more languorous and distracted than Rosie felt the occasion required.

'Penn!' Torn, broken, desperate.

'Rosie!' Delighted to hear from her.

'What's wrong?'

'Wrong?'

'Is everything okay?'

'Everything's fine. Better than fine. I have news.'

'Jesus, Penn. You scared the shit out of me.'

'How?'

'You called fifteen times. You sent seven texts. Seven texts and no information. I thought something happened to you. I thought something was wrong with Mom or the boys. I thought terrible, horrible things.'

'I only sent one text.'

'I got seven.'

'Sometimes when service is intermittent, it just resends until—'

'I can't breathe.'

'Take deep breaths.'

'How can I take deep breaths if I can't breathe?'

'Call a doctor.'

'I am a doctor.'

'Call another doctor.'

'I'm not at the clinic. I had to come into town. It's six a.m. I'm at a pay phone outside a 7-Eleven. There might be someone inside with gum-selling expertise, but that's as close as I'm likely to come.'

'Rosie. I have news.'

She paused to take the deep breaths instructed and to savor the moment before she knew whatever it was, because whatever it was it was
going to be okay. Her mother was okay, and her boys were okay, and
Penn was okay, and Claude – Poppy – sleeping back at the guesthouse,
was okay, so nothing could be all that wrong. Poppy was going to require
some repair, some mending and figuring. Life always required mending
and figuring. But mending and figuring – unlike forbidding cancer, banning car accidents, convincing teenage boys they were not immortal, or
going back in time to prevent stupid shit from happening – was something she could do. They had to see the invisible paths and forge their
way through the jungles. They had to find, to demand, to create the
other bathrooms, the other boxes, the middle ways to be. It was not
going to be easy. But easy and peaceful turned out to be opposites. And
the choice between them was a simple one.

'I sold the book.' Penn felt it come out of his mouth like a bubble.

Just as she was catching her breath finally, she lost it again. 'Oh. Penn.
My love.'

'Can you believe it?'

'No. I mean yes. I mean how?'

'How do you mean how?' She could see him. Penn in jeans and a T-shirt
and bare feet, a notebook in one hand, a pencil in the other, floating
around in space, over the moon. She was sorrier than Sorry Ralph she was
not there to witness, to share in, this joy. 'I'm a genius author is how. I'm
a prose rock star. I'm a soon-to-be-published novelist.'

'I should go away more often. You get so much accomplished. I had
no idea the DN was even close to done.'

'Not the DN. The fairy tale. *The Adventures of Grumwald and Princess
Stephanie*. Next fall, Rosie. At a bookstore near you.'

'*The Adventures of Grumwald and Princess Stephanie*? Is it a children's
book?'

'No. I mean yes. I mean sort of. They'll cross-market it. They think
parents will read it to kids. They think parents will read it themselves.
They like its nuances and metaphor. They think it appeals and applies to
everyone.'

'But it doesn't have an ending.'

'It does now.'

'It does?' She was surprised to find herself, at once, heartbroken. She
had been there at Grumwald's inception. She had followed him through

years of saga and setback, trial and triumph, palace and seashore, home and Away. She had seen him through transformations great and small. She had seen all his selves and loved him more than anyone. 'I missed the end?'

'How could you miss the end?' Penn wondered. 'Grum couldn't end without you. It has *an* ending, not the end, a stopping point, no more than a pause really. You know how much of Grumwald's story made the book? One percent. One percent of one percent. Most of Grumwald is only yours. Only a tiny, tiny bit is anyone else's. Grumwald and Stephanie got an ending for the moment, an ending for everybody else. That's all.'

'What is it?'

'What is what?'

'How does it for-the-moment end?'

'You'll have to buy the book.'

'I live with the author.'

'Not at the moment you don't. Come home. I'll tell you the whole story.'

A few hours later, the five-year-old girl who'd presented with diarrhea, weight loss, and terrible stomach cramping was throwing up a foot-long worm into a bucket and looking very pleased with herself. She spoke not a word of English but kept pointing to herself then the worm then herself and grinning. Her mother, who also spoke not a word of English, was doing the same, gesticulating wildly back and forth between daughter and worm, but her face wore the opposite expression. She was not screaming in a language Rosie knew, but she understood clear as lagoons anyway the mother's horror of this worm that had lately come out of her little girl. If they'd spoken the same language, Rosie would have laid her hand on the woman's shoulder to commiserate: Oh the things that hide secretly in our children, lying in wait, doing untold damage, yearning to be free. Alarming us beyond all measure.

Rosie listened to K mediate an argument between the mother, who longed to put this incident behind her, and the girl, who apparently wanted to take the worm home as a pet, and then watched as K mimed, with great dignity, the need to wear shoes while defecating in bushes designated for doing so and to wash hands as well as food that came from the same patch of ground. Rosie's eyes welled. How could she give all this up?

The woman who had given birth to twins the night before was meeting with the monk. Apparently, monks in the hills were something like pubs in small towns in the English countryside – there was one main one which served everyone and in all capacities. Because the second baby had taken so long being born, the twins actually had different birthdays, one born late Friday night, the other early Saturday morning. The mother was weepy and weak, and Rosie was standing by to reassure her – and the monk – that both babies were healthy and that their mother, though she had lost a lot of blood, would be back on her feet after a few days of spinach and red meat. From what she could gather, however, via K's UN-style simultaneous translation, this was not the woman's concern.

'I will keep the baby born on Friday,' the mom wept to the monk, 'but I am giving the Saturday one to you. Saturday babies are stubborn. They don't listen. I have three more children at home. I can only take one more. I can only have ones who are well behaved.'

'I understand.' The monk nodded kindly then added, to Rosie's shock, 'This baby is mine now.'

'Thank you,' the mom wept, clasping his hand to her forehead. 'Thank you, thank you.'

The monk dipped a bundle of twigs in a pan of water and sprayed it over both babies and their mother. He said a great many things Rosie did not understand, which caused the mother to cry even harder and to which K merely nodded along. Then the monk told the mother, 'I have blessed this baby and spoken with him. He will be a good baby and well behaved always. I wonder if you would take care of him for me? I promise he will be a good boy.'

'Yes, oh yes,' the mother sobbed. 'Thank you, thank you. I would be honored to take care of him for you. We will take him into our family as our own.'

Dispelling fear, Rosie thought. Choosing peace and calm instead of battle.

'I have to go home,' she told K after the monk left.

'Bad news this morning?' K worried.

'No, good.'

'Ahh, better reason.'

'I have to go home, but I'll be back soon.'

'You move to jungle?' K grinned, the question so absurd as to present as a joke.

But Rosie had been considering it more than idly. She knew the reasons she could not sleep could not always be solved by uprooting and fleeing, that Madison to Seattle felt a mammoth move but was nothing compared to Seattle to remote northern Thailand, that the jungle may have been a fine place to doctor and was probably even a fine place to write books but it was a hard place to raise children or send them to college or keep them safe from and embraced by the world. She knew that what came out of kids was often terrifying, but its coming out, rather than staying inside, was the happy ending. There was much unfinished business at home, and hiding out, burrowing deeper away, was not the answer.

But she also knew this: they needed her here. And this: she needed them too.

Here, they needed more doctors, more teachers, more skilled hands, more creative ideas, more instincts that stood in for CT scanners and echocardiograms. They needed more of other kinds of teachers too, and Claude – Poppy – was proving a natural in the classroom. Rosie could not say who was learning more, the students or her child, but she gave thanks for the apparent answer, which was both, together. She imagined what the boys could do here, the technology and ideas Ben could impart, the patients Roo could keep company and comfort with his modest Rooness, the tunnels and trenches, roofs and rain barrels, potties and porticos Rigel and Orion could help dig, build, move, and repair, not to mention the sick kids who would adore the Rigel and Orion Show.

And she needed them too, first of all because knowing they were here meant she could never completely leave, and second of all because they reminded her, with the stark clarity that seemed to pervade everything they did here, that she belonged in an emergency room. She couldn't move here, she knew, and she couldn't stay, but she could come back. She couldn't work here year-round, but there were clinics and patients closer to home who needed her too.

And Poppy could not be Claude, and she could not hide, and if they could not entirely plan for who she might be two and ten and twenty years from now, they didn't need to. They could make hard decisions, together, when it was time to decide, and in the meantime, they could embrace what was now and what was good. They could be mindful of what was hard for everyone, not just what was hard for Poppy, the trouble all humans in the whole world had knowing who they were and what they needed and what would help the mysterious, unknowable, miraculous beings in their care. Their lives would be a different kind of fairy tale, less magic and more ambiguity, less once-upon-a-time and happily-ever-after and more in between. A middle way. In the meantime, they had to live with not knowing, *got* to live with not knowing, got to help other people with what they had to live with too. Tell their stories, dispel fear, let be. Amend as necessary.

Rosie went to check on the worm girl so she could finish her shift so she could go home and start packing and go home.

PART
IV

Ever

Grumwald stood in front of the mirror in Princess Stephanie's clothes and wondered what it would be like when someone knew and then, shortly thereafter, everyone knew the secret he'd been keeping for so many years. He remembered the time the witch gave him magic beans. He remembered the time she came to the restaurant when he was having dinner with Lloyd. He remembered all the way back to before he met the witch the first time, back when he was still Grumwald only, Grumwald alone. He could picture it, cloudily, in that way that you do when you know it was true but you just can't believe it anymore.

He remembered that night with the fairies, the night his life had begun in a way, Princess Stephanie's birth day. The witch, impatient for the makings of one spell, had cast another: he would be Grumwald by day, Princess Stephanie by night. At first it had been an odious curse. The way between his forked selves was through the trees, root-tangled and muddy and overgrown, and the hike back and forth each day was crushing.

So he forged a path. He realized he knew how to be a princess because he knew how to be a prince. The particulars diverged, but they were more alike than different. Helping his charges feel loved and respected, their talents honored, their loads lightened was his job in either guise, and he was good at it, from long practice, which of course didn't change based on what he was wearing or what name he was called.

Except then, slowly, day by night by day, it got harder and harder to find the path. Grumwald thought he'd have to start repaving, rehacking the roots and branches, refilling the potholes to reclaim his way, but no, it turned out his two worlds had moved closer together, had very nearly merged. Like magic. He still didn't think there was anyone he could tell, but he and Princess Stephanie felt home.

When he thought back to the dinner with Lloyd though, he decided it was time to talk to the witch. Making peace was better than living in fear. So he snipped off a piece of Princess Stephanie's green hair one night – Why had this been such a big deal? He couldn't remember – and took it to the witch's cottage the next morning.

'Thank you, Grumwald.' She looked relieved enough to cry. 'Night-fairy hair so helps my arthritis. I can't catch the night fairies because my hands are too stiff, and my hands are too stiff because I can't catch the night fairies. Some contradictions are too stupid even for magic.'

'Anytime.' Grumwald hadn't realized she was in pain. 'Really. I have unlimited supply.'

'Night fairies are impossible. They don't listen. At first I thought they were hard of hearing, but no, they're just, well, flighty. Have you ever tried to reason with a night fairy?'

Grumwald grinned. She was preaching to the choir.

'Ahh, that's right.' She looked chastened. 'I'm sorry about that. It hurts so much sometimes I lose my good sense.'

'It's okay,' Grumwald assured her.

'Let me get my wand.' It took her a minute and a half to get up from her chair. Her bones creaked like bare branches in the wind. 'I should have lifted your curse years ago. There's no excuse for leaving it. Sloppy witchery, that's what that is. I'm losing it in my old age.'

She shuffled slow, slow, slowly across her worn floors, away from the heat and flickering light of the fire, over to the kitchen where from a pot rack hung dozens of wands in shapes and sizes Grumwald had never seen before, some topped, traditionally, with white caps or stars, others curled up into snail shells or coiled like snakes or fraying out at the ends like tangled hair. 'Now, which one did I use in the first place? I can't remember. Well, this one will do.' She gave a few tentative waves to a bright-yellow wand no bigger than his longest finger. 'Now, remind me again which way we go.'

'Which way?' said Grumwald.

'Do we lose Grumwald or Princess Stephanie? I forget who you were to begin with.'

Grumwald had never thought of it like that. Losing one. Revealing which he'd been to begin with would mean conceding that once upon a time he was someone other than both, and that was what he could no longer imagine. He knew the answer – probably the witch did too – but he found he didn't believe it anymore. And mostly, he was loath to give it up, to give *them* up. The idea of life without Grumwald was devastating. The idea of life without Princess Stephanie was devastating. But the idea of life being just one or the other had become, simply, unimaginable.

'I want both,' he was surprised to hear himself stammer. 'Both. Grumwald and Princess Stephanie.'

'Ah.' The witch was less surprised. 'That happens sometimes. Can't give up the perks of either one. Each incarnation has its rewards. Easy then. I'll just leave the spell, and you can keep going back and forth.'

'Not each.' Grumwald shook his head. 'Both. I want to be both.'

'Both at once?' Even the witch was shocked.

'Each is good, but the back-and-forth is so tiring.'

'I can imagine. But I don't . . . I don't know how to make you both at once. I'm not even sure I know what that means.' They spent the afternoon together in her cottage discussing, looking through books of spells and potions, trying one oddly shaped wand after another. At last, her soft, gray face lit with revelation. 'What if we looked betwixt?'

'Betwixt?' Grumwald was skeptical. 'Isn't betwixt just a witchy way of saying in between?'

'Betwixt is more complex, more twisted threads, more layers than in between.' She smiled at him through rheumy eyes. 'Betwixt a prince and a night fairy is neither-nor as much as both-and. You see? Something new. Something more. Something better.'

'Something betwixt.'

'Exactly,' she agreed. 'Betwixt I can do. Well, I can do my part.'

'What else is there?'

'Your part.' Of course.

'Is it hard?'

'It is very hard.'

He closed his eyes and steeled himself. 'Tell me.'

'Exactly,' she said again. 'You have to tell. It can't be a secret. Secrets make everyone alone. Secrets lead to panic like that night at the restaurant. When you keep it a secret, you get hysterical. You get to thinking you're the only one there is who's like you, who's both and neither and betwixt, who forges a path every day between selves, but that's not so. When you're alone keeping secrets, you get fear. When you tell, you get magic. Twice.'

'Twice?'

'You find out you're not alone. And so does everyone else. That's how everything gets better. You share your secret, and I'll do the rest. You share your secret, and you change the world.'

'It's not that easy.' Grumwald felt his lungs scritching to become one in his chest. 'I can't just share my secret. It's hard to explain. It's hard to understand. It's complicated.'

'Of course it is. It's life.'

'So how do I do it then? How do I share my secret? What do I tell?'

'Your story.' The witch didn't even hesitate. 'You tell your story. That is what we all must do.'

'That's not magic,' said Grumwald.

'Of course it is,' said the witch. 'Story is the best magic there is.'

After

Poppy could not believe that the gym could look so completely different and smell so exactly the same. It's not that the garlands and lace hearts and glitter and confetti didn't make the place look nice. It was more like why bother if it still smelled like socks.

At first she had rejected utterly the suggestion that she do her big coming back at the Valentine's dance. It was stupid to have a dance in fifth grade. They weren't even middle-schoolers yet. Plus, no one had seen her for months. They might not even let her in. Her hair was growing back, but it was still short and strange-looking. If she showed up in a dress with a bow in her too-cropped hair, it was going to look like she was trying, and failing, too hard.

But the low lighting was too tempting to turn down. The low lighting plus Ben's point that nothing – not a guy in a dress, not a girl with a penis, not a shorn, world-traveling, jungle-dwelling weirdo – was more awkward than a fifth-grade Valentine's dance. Especially one where everyone (not just the guy in the dress, the girl with the penis, or the shorn, world-traveling, jungle-dwelling weirdo) had been made to dress up. At first she wasn't compelled by his argument that the entire evening was sure to be uncomfortable, embarrassing, humiliating, and tense. Who would be compelled by that? Then she saw his point: her reentry was going to be uncomfortable, embarrassing, humiliating, and tense anyway; the question was only if she wanted to be the only one.

Aggie was apparently not talking to her. Poppy had tapped on her window her first night home, and every night since, but Aggie's curtains had not so much as quivered. Now that they knew to though, Natalie and Kim said all the things they hadn't in the cafeteria that terrible day those terrible months before. They knew who she really was. They saw her and loved her anyway, loved her more even. They had stuff that was weird about them too. They sometimes didn't know who they were either. They did not care what was under her pants or her skirt, whichever it was. They told each other everything. Even the one thing.

She huddled in a tight knot against a wall with the two of them. Everyone was huddled in a tight knot against a wall – it was hard to imagine there'd be very much dancing – but at least she had her own knot. The gym overheads were not just low but off. Poppy supposed they had only one setting: basketball blazing. But there was some kind of spastic bulb-and-mirror apparatus strung from the ceiling so that dim flashes lit here and there unpredictably as bats, illuminating a pack of students like lightning then plunging them back to blessed darkness. Poppy occasionally made out faces she knew, their eyes often already staring at her when they flared, but much more often, her sleepy recognition lit but not her memory. I know that kid from . . . somewhere, as if she'd been gone years, not months, as if she'd become an old woman while everyone else froze in place like people in photographs, as if she'd become an adult, or at least less like a child, while everyone around her was just a fifth-grader allowed to wear eye shadow for the night.

Kids broke from their knots and wandered by hers occasionally. 'Hey, Poppy.' Neither nasty nor apologetic, cruel nor welcoming. Not even curious or appalled. 'Hey,' she said back, careful in case it was a trick, their 'Hey, Poppy' a prelude to taunting or worse.

Then she saw Jake Irving. She saw him because he was walking right toward her. He got up from where he was slouched against the opposite wall and walked right across the gym and right up to her. Everyone saw. Every single eye in the gym, every single eye in the school, maybe every single eye in the world was on him, but he either did not notice or did not care or did a really good job of pretending not to care.

'Hey, Poppy.'

'Hey.'

'You're back?'

Was she supposed to answer that? Obviously she was back. If she weren't back, how could he ask if she were back? 'Yeah.'

'I heard you went to Taiwan.'

'Thailand.'

'Oh. Did you get my text?'

The one he sent a million years ago? The one he sent before time had stopped for him and sped for her? The one she deleted practically without reading? 'Yeah.'

'Oh. Good.'

The questions were weird, but at least they gave her something to say –

'Sorry again,' Jake added.

– whereas she had no idea what she was supposed to say to him now. *It's okay?* It wasn't okay. *I understand you think I'm a disgusting freak, and you're probably right, but my parents are making me go to school anyway, so please be nice to me?* That was true, but she wasn't going to say it. If only he would go back to the inane questions, at least she would know what to say.

'So. Wanna dance?'

She had no idea what to say.

She looked at the completely empty middle of the gym where no-body – nobody – was dancing. The music was so loud she could feel it through her shoes, but no one was so much as wiggling to it. He looked up from his toes for the first time all night (month, year, lifetime, eon) to follow her gaze to the uninhabited, masquerading-as-a-dance-floor bas-ketball court. He grinned – like the Jake Irving she'd sat next to in third grade who brought his grandma in for show-and-tell – and said, 'We'll be the best ones out there.'

How could she say no to that?

The song that was playing as Poppy followed Jake Irving onto the dance floor started to end, and she closed her eyes and willed Mr Me-nendez not to play a slow song. She was a woman of the world now and saw that this was exactly the sort of move adults liked to make. Here were two lonesome souls, braving a wilderness together – what could be cuter than to put on some sappy slow song and do a little experiment in sociological torture? *Don't. You. Dare,* her brain told Mr Menendez's brain at the telepathic volume of a howler monkey. And she was in luck, not because Mr Menendez did not indeed think it would be lovely to put on a slow song for this fine young couple, but because his kid had prepro-grammed the playlist, and the principal had no idea how to do anything with his phone but make phone calls.

So she regular-danced with Jake Irving. It was hard because everyone in the entire world was watching them, but it wasn't that hard otherwise.

You moved your feet one way and your hips the other and kept your arms mostly at your sides and your eyes mostly on the floor.

Jake said, 'So.'

'Yeah?'

'How was Thailand?'

'Kind of amazing,' said Poppy. 'I got to teach little kids.'

'Really? What?'

'English.'

Jake looked impressed. 'I mean, I speak English, but I wouldn't know how to teach it.'

'You figure it out.'

'I guess. I bet you were a good teacher.'

'I guess. What makes you say that?'

Jake shrugged and looked back to his toes. 'You're nice. You're smart. I remember when you helped me with that report on dolphins in second grade.'

'You're nice and smart too.' Poppy said it mostly only because she didn't know what else to say, and when someone says something nice to you, you're supposed to say something nice back.

'I'm smart' – Jake frowned at his toes – 'but not very nice.'

She remembered in fourth grade when he let Owen Gregg win the fifty-yard dash at Field Day because Owen's parents were getting a divorce. She remembered in third when Aggie dropped her brownie at the Halloween party, and Jake just handed her his without even waiting to see if there were any extras. 'You're nice,' Poppy told her own toes.

'Not to you.'

She shrugged. 'Not once. But other times.'

'I'm really sorry, Poppy. I really, really am.'

'I know,' she said.

'You do?'

'Yeah.'

'How?'

She made herself look up at him. 'You asked me to dance.'

Then a slow song came on. He looked up at her too. 'Wanna get some juice?'

———

Rosie and Penn had replied to the email asking for volunteer dance chaperones at the speed of sound. Then they spent forty-eight hours vowing to their youngest child that they would not talk to her, look at her, take pictures of her, intimate knowledge of her, stand near her, offer her food or beverage, or address her in any way. Should the building catch on fire, they would not approach her but would allow her to find her own emergency exit and then seek one – a different one – on their own.

They had not, however, promised not to dance. In fairness, this was because Poppy, in her wildest nightmare scenario, had not conceived that she would dance herself and certainly had never considered the horrifying possibility that her parents might. But that's just because she was still a little jet-lagged. Presented with a cheesy slow song in an elementary school gym decorated for Valentine's Day, her parents were obviously going to dance to it.

As she took her husband in her arms, Rosie also took a moment to savor the smell of him, the feel of his hand in her hand, the way in which he was hers, for sure and forever. She remembered the high school years when she didn't have a boyfriend and the college years when she had one but he was mean to her and the first years of med school when she was sure she'd never be in love again, and she remembered the feel of the wall on her back at the middle school dances when her friends got asked and she didn't and the boy she liked chose someone else, and she felt how it was all worth it if it earned her, if it won her, if it resulted, karmically, narratively, miraculously, in Penn at last, Penn forever, Penn who was always and only and always hers, certain as sky.

As he took his wife in his arms, Penn also took a moment to remind himself he was in the presence of ten-year-olds. *Don't touch her ass, don't touch her ass, don't touch her ass.*

'Thank you for coming home,' he whispered into her hair.

'I'm so proud of you, Penn.' She drew back from his shoulder to meet his eyes. 'Author-Husband. I never doubted this day, not since the first time you took me to bed.'

'I am very persuasive in bed.'

'But your getting published is not why I came home.'

'I know.'

'Was there ever any doubt in your mind?'

'Never. But that doesn't mean I am not grateful.'

'After all these years,' she said, 'what made you finally write it down?'

'It wasn't finally.' He pulled her closer. 'But it was time.'

'Why?'

'We've always been living a fairy tale, Rosie. From the moment we met. From the moments before we met. We have this perfect love story. We have this love story that feels like a fairy tale and must be because how else to explain something so magical? But the problem with fairy tales is that they end, and quickly too. The lead-up is everything. Then you get transformation, love, and happily-ever-after all in one breath. That story's nice, but it's not big enough to hold us. There's no room for the hard parts. There's no room for the transformations and the loves that come next and next and next. In a story, nothing is unalterable, but nothing is alterable either. After the magic, there's no more change.

'That's no way to live, but I was trying to anyway. Make sure Poppy stays a little girl. Make sure Poppy stays a secret. Change her so she'll never change. Metamorphosis to ward off transmutation. It makes no sense; that's what I realized when you went away. So instead I tried the opposite: write it down, carve it in stone. Or, if you like, paper's just as permanent once you send it out into the world. It seems like it closes the story, settles on one ending eliminating infinite possibilities, fixes it in place, in voice, but no, it does the opposite. You write it down so others can read it, and then it can grow. You nail it to a moment so it can pass through time. A book is just a foundation. Like us. You write it down to build upon. Our love, our magic fairy-tale love, is what supports the rest of it. It doesn't mean the kids can't grow – of course it doesn't – but it lays down a place for them to do it from. That's what story's for.'

'That's very pretty, Author-Husband.'

'Thank you . . . uh . . . Doctor-Wife.'

'But it doesn't answer the question.'

'What question?'

'All the questions,' said Rosie. 'Closet or rooftop? Blockers or puberty? Surgery or hormones? Both or neither? Girl or boy or in between? Today or tomorrow? Next month or next year? Fifth-grade meanies or home-schooling in her turret by the sea? DN or fairy tale?'

'It's true.'

'What's true?'

'It doesn't answer the question. But it opens possibilities, and that's even better, possibilities we never saw before, possibilities no one ever saw before. And it promises that when the time comes to decide, we've built someplace solid as ramparts from which to do it.'

Rosie was quiet for a while. Then she buried her face in Penn's shoulder again so Poppy wouldn't see her jubilation. 'Can you believe she danced?'

'Of course I can.' Penn held her closer still. 'Because you know what's even better than happy endings?'

'What?'

'Happy middles.'

'You think?'

'All the happy with none of the finality. All the happy with room enough to grow. What could be better than that?'

'For a while,' said Rosie.

'A while's a long time,' said Penn.

Poppy could not actually stand there and watch her parents dance, so she finished her juice and told Jake she'd be right back. She remembered the bathroom of her own at the fish spa in Chiang Mai, the nurse's bathroom they'd made her use in Wisconsin, all the stalls she'd changed in over the years when she took swim lessons or went to the beach with PANK or it was pool day at summer camp. Sometimes being her was difficult and complicated. Sometimes only the bathroom was.

When she emerged from the stall, Aggie was leaning against the sinks, her hands tucked into her armpits and squeezed into fists. Poppy's stomach did the same. She was so happy to see her, she thought she might start crying. She was so nervous to see her, she thought she might start crying. There was some chance she was also angry, but Aggie was her best friend in the entire universe so probably not. There was some chance that traveling halfway around the world to work with poor, often sick, sometimes orphaned children had given her a mature perspective on humanity that was going to help her handle this situation. But Aggie was her best friend in the entire universe. So probably not.

'Hi,' said Aggie.

'Hi.' Poppy remembered the first time Aggie had ever tapped on her window, the night they met, the night they became rival neighbor princesses. That conversation had started the same way – 'Hi,' 'Hi' – shy but full of promise, a million good things to come. Poppy had to admit that 'Hi,' 'Hi' wasn't that uncommon a way to start a conversation and therefore probably didn't reveal some fated belonging, but for one grace-filled moment, it felt like that anyway.

But then the spell was broken because Aggie's mouth said, 'How was Thailand?' but Aggie's tone said, *I could not even care less about anything you have to say ever again.* Aggie had followed her in here though, so maybe she meant something else altogether.

'Hot. Crazy. Kind of amazing. How was here?'

'Sucky. Stupid. Totally boring.' Then, with a sneer, 'Did you make a new best friend?'

'No.' Poppy thought of the friends she made in Thailand – her little students who showed her all about the Buddha and how school changes your life and how to tell stories and how to love your family, K who showed her how to be in between and live in the middle. 'Did you?'

Aggie snorted in answer to this question. 'Are you even allowed to be here?'

'School?'

'The girls' bathroom.'

Oh. 'I guess,' Poppy said to her toes. 'My parents told Mr Menendez at the beginning of first grade. He said I was allowed.'

'You told Mr Menendez but not me?'

'I didn't,' Poppy said lamely. 'My parents did.'

'Maybe you aren't allowed anymore.'

'Nothing's changed.'

'Everything's changed,' Aggie said but not mean. Sad.

'Why?' Not just sad. Heartbroken.

'We can't be friends anymore.' Was that why everything had changed? Or how?

'Why not?'

'How can we?' Aggie was almost yelling. 'What are we going to do together? We can't have sleepovers anymore. We can't talk about all the things we talk about anymore. We can't be rival princesses. We can't do plays.'

'Because you don't like me anymore?'

'Because I don't know you anymore.'

'I'm the same,' Poppy cried. 'I'm exactly the same as ever. We can still have plays and princesses. We can still have sleepovers.'

'I don't even . . .' Aggie's face looked like she was trying to do long division in her head. 'Poppy, if I ask you a question, will you tell me the truth?'

'Yes.'

'Promise?'

'Promise.'

'Are you a boy or a girl?' said Aggie.

'No.' Poppy made herself look up at her best friend in the entire universe. She thought of the fairy tale she'd told her students in Thailand, how much easier this would be if she had magic and a wand. 'I'm not.'

'That's not what I meant.' Aggie made a face. Then she softened it. Then she asked, 'What are you then?'

'I don't know. Something else instead.'

'What else is there?' And for the first time all night, Aggie sounded like the question she was asking was actually the question she was asking.

'I'm all of the above.' Poppy couldn't help smiling, which was kind of like magic because then Aggie couldn't help smiling back. 'And I'm also more to come.'

'What does that mean?'

'It's complicated.' Now that Aggie had smiled at her, she felt almost giddy. She realized she was dying to talk to her about all this. 'I guess *I'm* complicated. I'm hard to explain. I'm kind of a weirdo.'

'You're not the weirdo,' Aggie said. 'I'm the weirdo.'

'True,' Poppy admitted. 'Very true. Then I guess we're both weird. Maybe that's why we like each other so much.'

'We're too old for princesses anyway.' Aggie was full-on grinning now. 'We can be rival neighbor weirdos from now on.'

Everyone was still up when they got home.

'Did Mom and Dad dance?' Ben's face was pure commiseration.

'Yup.'

'Eww.' A chorus.

'Slow dance?' said Rigel.

'Yup.'

'Eww.'

'Did he touch her ass?' said Roo.

'Don't say "ass", Roo.' Penn was looking for ice cream.

'Eww, Roo, gross,' said Orion.

'But he did, right?'

Poppy squeezed her eyes shut and tried to think of something else.

'Your mother has a great ass,' Penn conceded from the freezer.

The ewws rose to a cacophony. Which was just where he liked them. He found ice cream as well as fudge to heat and cherries pinked by some brine that could probably provide fuel in the event of an apocalypse.

'What did you guys do all night?' Rosie started slicing bananas. No reason not to impart at least a few vitamins.

'Kept our hands to ourselves.' Ben got out bowls and spoons.

'Worse luck for you,' said his father.

'If Dad touching Mom's ass is the most embarrassing thing that happened to you at your first school dance, you're doing pretty good,' Roo congratulated his sister. 'Ben went to the eighth-grade Halloween dance as a robot with those fake arms coming out of the front of his robot body, and when he asked Cayenne to dance, they totally groped her. First time he got to second base, and he missed it because they weren't his real hands.'

'What about the time Alexie Gawersky asked you to retie her sash-thingy at the Spring Fling?' Ben could play this game all night and never run out of embarrassing Roo stories. 'You tied it to the balloon rainbow as a joke, and she pulled over the entire thing plus the sound system when Andy Kennedy asked her to dance.'

'For our eighth-grade Christmas concert' – Orion didn't even look up from the sprinkles he was sprinkling – 'everyone had to wear a white top and black pants, but Rigel showed up in this yellow shirt.'

'What does this story have to do with school dances?' Rigel took off his socks and threw them at Orion's sundae.

'It has to do with a time you embarrassed yourself.'

'That shirt was off-white.'

'It was the color of a banana.'

'It was beige.'

'So Rigel had to borrow a shirt, but the only person who had an extra was Mandy O'Lackey, and it was all gathered and padded and girly at the front so it looked like Rigel had boobs.'

'Where'd she get it?' said Poppy.

'And his solo in "The Twelve Days of Christmas" was, "Two turtledoves", and he had to sing it twelve times, and every time he sang it, everyone cracked up.'

'Eleven times,' said Ben.

'Duh. It's the twelve days of Christmas,' said Orion.

'Duh. The first day she gets a partridge in a pear tree and nothing else.'

'How do you know it's a she?' said Poppy.

'Guys don't want a partridge in a pear tree for Christmas,' said Roo.

'No one wants a partridge in a pear tree for Christmas,' said Poppy.

'That's where these gifts fall apart for you?' said Ben. 'You think this person – regardless of gender – had ten lords a-leaping on his or her wish list?'

Rosie smiled at Penn. She felt that truly she could be perfectly content sitting at her kitchen table eating ice cream with her family and listening to this conversation go on forever. These kids, her multitudes, they could grow up. They could move Away. They could – they would – become new, become changed, become actual adult people in progress, people she wouldn't recognize, people she could not imagine. People remade. They would undergo miracles. They would transform. They would make magic. But they were her story, hers and Penn's, so however wide they wandered, they would always be right here.

'I don't believe it,' she said to her husband while their progeny debated the relative merits of maids a-milking versus swans a-swimming.

'What?'

'It's your happy ending.'

'I told you.'

'You did.'

'But this isn't it.'

'It's not?' She smiled at him. She couldn't stop smiling at him.

'Not even close.' He couldn't stop smiling back.

Author's Note

The question writers of fiction get asked most often, ironically, is this: 'Is it true?'

I hate to make you wait, so let's get this out of the way. Yes, it's true. Also, no, I made it all up.

Sorry, did that not answer the question?

It's true that my child used to be a little boy and is now a little girl. But this isn't her story. I can't tell her story; I can only tell my own story and those of the people I make up. I didn't make my kid up. She's a real person, so she's the only one who can tell her story. This story is fiction, pretend. It's not about my kid. It's not about her experiences. It's not even about my experiences. Writing a novel is like making soup. The base is a broth we make up wholesale – for instance, I have one child, not five, and am not only not a doctor but, in fact, am made woozy by paper cuts. Then, to that entirely made-up broth, we add a sprinkling of research, some chunks of childhood memories, a handful of sautéed morsels overheard at the playground, a few diced bits we weren't planning on but turned out to need for depth of flavor, and some finely chopped pieces of our own lives. Simmer until all the disparate parts mellow and blend but still enhance and augment one another. This is how you cook a novel. Some made up, some real life, all true.

Sometimes people ask that same question like this: 'What inspired this book?' by which they mean, 'Is this really your own life with the names changed, or what on earth gave you this idea?' which in this case might be an easier question to answer.

The novelist in me was inspired in the first place by the debate about treating trans kids with puberty blockers, by the way loving, open-minded, well-intentioned people could reasonably come down on what seem to be opposing sides of this issue. Hormone suppressors are miracles for kids who simply cannot live in the body into which they were born. I would not suggest otherwise. Trans and gender nonconforming kids and adults suffer a suicide-attempt rate of more than 40 percent. Drugs which avert that qualify as miraculous indeed. But that doesn't make them the only miracle on offer. Wider ranges of normal make the world a better place for everyone. To me, both those positions seem self-evidently true. Other people frame them as opposites. That's the kind of stuff that makes you want to write a book.

The novelist in me was inspired by the metaphor too, how no matter the issue, parenting always involves this balance between what you know, what you guess, what you fear, and what you imagine. You're never certain, even (maybe especially) about the big deals, the huge, important ones with all the ramifications and repercussions. But alas, no one can make these decisions, or deal with their consequences, but you. High stakes plus unknowability equals great writing fodder.

The novelist in me is inspired by how much raising children is like writing books: You don't know where they're going until they get there. You may think you do, but you're probably wrong. Corralling and forcing them against their will to go where you first imagined they would isn't going to work for anyone involved. Never mind you're the one writing and raising them, they are headed in their own direction, independent of you. And scary though that is, it's also how it should be.

So at the beginning of this project, the novelist in me felt pretty great. But the mama in me was panicked. The mama in me was watching her little boy transform into her little girl before her very eyes. In some ways, that wasn't any weirder or scarier or more unbelievable than watching kids grow up ever is. In other ways, it was a little weirder and scarier and unbelievable-er. I'd written many, many words before I figured out exactly what it was that was so much scarier about this transformation than any of her other ones. The answer had nothing to do with her. It had to do with everybody else.

I am so proud of my kid, but I am terrified about how others will respond to her – today and next year and down the very windy road ahead. I am every day amazed by how bright and wise and strong and sure she is but petrified by the fear and ignorance she's likely to encounter along her way. I fret about her every moment she's out of my sight (and many of the ones when she's in it), so in some ways, all this does is make a little longer an already very long list of worries. One of the differences between your novel and your life, at least as regards parenting, is you want the former to be perilous, unpredictable, full of near misses and heartbreak and disasters narrowly averted. The latter? The latter you want to be as plot-free as possible.

So here's what's true: This book is fiction. My child is neither Poppy nor Claude. I am not Rosie. Do we share some things in common with them? Yes. But this book is an act of imagination, an exercise in wish fulfillment, because that is the other thing novelists do. We imagine the world we hope for and endeavor, with the greatest power we have, to bring that world into being. I wish for my child, for all our children, a world where they can be who they are and become their most loved, blessed, appreciated selves. I've rewritten that sentence a dozen times, and it never gets less cheesy, I suppose because that's the answer to the question. That's what's true. For my child, for all our children, I want more options, more paths through the woods, wider ranges of normal, and unconditional love. Who *doesn't* want that?

I know this book will be controversial, but honestly? I keep forgetting why.

Acknowledgments

It is my blessing, my joy, and my honor to call Molly Friedrich and Amy Einhorn mine. Thank you, thank you to you both from the top, middle, and bottom of my heart.

Thank you too to Lucy Carson, Alix Kaye, Kent Wolf, and Nichole LeFebvre; to Bob Miller, Caroline Bleeke, Marlena Bittner, Amelia Possanza, Liz Keenan, Ben Tomek, Molly Fonseca, Karen Horton, Emily Mahon, Steven Seighman, Kerry Nordling, Marta Fleming, David Lott, Lisa Davis, Rachelle Mandik, Stacy Shirk, Martin Quinn, and all the amazing people at Flatiron Books I am only just getting to know and am thrilled to be working with; to Marion Donaldson, Vicky Palmer, Caitlin Raynor, Hannah Wann, and everyone at Headline Books, and to all the wonderful teams working on editions around the world; to Jennie Shortridge, Katherine Malmo, Julianna Baggott, Karen Hogue, Preecha 'Ping' Jokdee, Songsri 'Ling' Jiwarattanawong, Barbara Catlin, Clare Meeker, Kevin O'Brien, Andrea Dunlop, Jeff Umbro, Garth Stein, Maria Semple, Elizabeth George, Ruth Ozeki, Hedgebrook, and extra piles of thanks to Carol Cassella, novelist and physician extraordinaire, who is the only reason I am at all able to write about doctors.

Thank you to my parents, Sue and Dave Frankel, who have so totally supported this, me, and mine always. Thank you to Dani who is, in so many ways, an inspiration: I am so proud of you. Thank you (the under-est of understatements) to Paul (the greatest of humans) for more wonderful things than I can name (or even have names for).